NO REST
FOR THE
SLEEPING

KERRY MORRIS

ISBN-13: 978-1-7335491-0-3

CONTENTS

ACKNOWLEDGEMENTS

To God, for giving me the grace and ability to live, to sleep, and to dream.

To my family and friends for their support, encouragement, and patience.

To fellow writers Mark Pifer, Hubert Kang, Marie Dias for always being willing to share ideas and provide feedback.

To the many unnamed individuals sitting next to me on so many long flights, for surrendering that extra inch of elbow room that made typing so much easier.

THANK YOU!

INTRODUCTION

Even a complete moron has a brain with more processing capacity than a multimillion-dollar supercomputer. Yet, when a person is asleep, all that power just goes to waste. Such a shame.

Zach Tanner was blissfully enjoying his narcolepsy at a booth in a crappy airport bar. For Zach, waking hours were a blur of compulsive observation, constant analysis, and generally exhausting contemplation. But, given a few moments of stillness, he was whisked away to a world of quiet and repose, where his hyperactive brain could grow quiet. It wasn't that he hated his brilliance. It had made him successful. But it had also made him alone. And, more than that, it made him tired. As his chin rested on his chest, his eyelids once again lost their battle with gravity, and Zach was embraced by the only anesthetic that made it possible to live with his own mind.

Meanwhile, Patient 23 was drifting off into a much different kind of sleep. His mind was bombarded with questions, puzzles, calculations. A relentless mining expedition designed to extract every iota of mental capacity. He wanted desperately to wake up, but his mind was not free to disengage. His brain was an engine running too hot, a machine hell bent on doing work without regard for the consequences of tomorrow; because for him, there would be no tomorrow. In a few moments the machine had surrendered its last bit of valuable output, and there really was no point in waking up at all. And little did Patient 23 know that at that moment, his best hope for survival was miles away, gently nodding off in an airport bar.

ONE

THE WHEEL OF THE CLEANING CART squeaked and wobbled just a little as it followed its evening path between the empty offices and cubicles. Jeff Wallace heard the squeaking grow quieter as it rolled away, until the thud of a closing closet door told him he was finally alone.

Jeff picked up the remote control, and a wall of LCD monitors sprang to life. Results from Project 33 streamed in front of him. He had been forced to keep it a secret for now. His superiors were luddites of the highest order, and this project had been co-developed with a competitor of sorts. But, once they saw the results, their minds would change. He was going to be rich and powerful and help change the world all at once. It was useless to try and prioritize between those objectives. There was no reason he couldn't simply have all three.

As he studied the results of the test, Jeff's face darkened. This was not what he expected. There appeared to be side effects, serious side effects. He would never be rich and famous if too many people got hurt. Then he thought about her and quickly pulled the results of a little sub-project of a personal nature. He winced. She wasn't doing well at all. She would never forgive him if she knew. He would never forgive himself.

At that moment, he heard another sound in the hallway. This time it was the muffled sound of nice shoes on thick carpet. No one should be here this late. Unless...shit.

Jeff turned off the monitors and dropped the remote to an uncertain fate on the hardwood floor. He reached into his pants pocket for his cell phone. Not there. Shit. He grabbed for his blazer, knocking over a chair as he pulled it to him and frantically searched the pockets. Footsteps were right outside his door now. Shit.

His eye caught sight of the phone on the floor by his desk. He dove for it, picking it up as he scrambled to hide beneath his desk, fairly certain he had torn the knee of a very nice pair of trousers. Trembling, he frantically typed a text message to her. Then another, misspelled in haste but hopefully still readable. By now the footsteps were inside his office. He typed a third message, the one he should have sent first, but never got the chance to hit send. The "chirp" of an outgoing message would alert the intruders to his location and remove any chance of escape. He quickly grabbed chewing gum from his mouth and used it to stick the cell phone to the underside of the desk, just as two sets of hands reached in to drag him from his hiding place.

Only at that moment did Jeff Wallace comprehend the true cost of his experiment.

A few hundred miles away, a sixty-something man in a brown tweed blazer cleaned his glasses using a small cloth he kept in his vest pocket for that purpose. Reginald could have worn contact lenses, of course. But those require maintenance in the form of removal and cleaning; unjustifiable inefficiency for no real incremental benefit. No, he would stick with glasses. Simple metal frames holding round lenses in front of grey eyes.

His style was more stainless steel than burled walnut, and the room reflected his starkly polished sensibilities. This room could have been pulled from the set of a Hollywood science fiction movie, and not a cheap one. Twenty-three computer workstations faced a wall three stories high and at least as wide. He had designed the chairs and workstations himself, right down to the charcoal matte paint on the desks; to minimize glare, of course. He was a man of few passions, but was deeply passionate about efficiency. A fan of minimalist aesthetic might have found the room beautiful, but for Reginald, beauty was an irrelevant byproduct. For him, this space just worked. And work was his greatest passion of all.

Work shaped culture, built fortunes that created power. Mankind's ability to work towards a goal is one of the defining characteristics of the species. Work created the Pyramids of Egypt, the Great Wall of China. The Roman Empire was more about roads and aqueducts as soldiers and spears. World War II played out on battlefields, but was really a war between mighty industrial workforces. The Soviet Union fell, not because they did not have a strong military, but because, as a society, they had lost the ability to get things done.

Of course, nowadays, the really important work is not performed by people, burdened as they are by the frailties of body and soul. The real work is performed by machines, by computers. Computers control money, communications, governments, armies. States and businesses invest billions to ensure their systems are stronger, smarter, resistant to hacking and attacks.

The arms race of the future would play out with processors and technology. Power would go to those who break codes and prevent theirs from being broken. In a world where everything is managed by computers, the one with the most powerful computer wins. And Reginald was building the atom bomb of computing.

The human body is a crude machine that requires time away from work to eat. To sleep. Elegantly beautiful, but outdated tech. The human mind, however, is a computational engine completely without equal.

Reginald walked to a workstation and tapped one of his associates on the shoulder. "Are we ready?"

"Yes, sir. We are ready to bring the first cluster online and run diagnostics."

"Excellent. Proceed."

On the giant screen appeared a map of an area perhaps a hundred miles square. Clusters of blue dots were scattered around the map, with higher densities in some areas.

"Execute Diagnostics – Cluster Alpha?"

The analyst in the chair typed "Y," as he had been instructed.

Immediately the blue dots began to change to green; soon, a few of them turned to yellow. At the bottom of the screen were three numbers:

"Capacity: 90%

Impaired: 10%

Attrition: 0%"

No one spoke as the test continued. After a few minutes several of the yellow dots began to blink red. The message at the bottom of the screen changed.

"Attrition: 7%"

"Manageable," Reginald said matter-of-factly. "Ok, that's enough for today." With the press of a button, the dots returned to blue except for a few that now glowed solid red. "Manageable," he said again.

Reginald let out a long, slow breath as his thin lips bent into a smile. It had taken years to get to this point, test after test. There had been attrition, of course. The bigger the rule you break, the higher the cost. But Reginald had decided long ago that the benefit was worth this minor sacrifice.

At that moment, Reginald's phone flashed with a message. "In custody. Awaiting instructions."

Sometimes when you build something really big, you need scaffolding: A temporary structure whose only purpose is to provide support during construction. Once the great ship meets the water, the scaffolding is no longer needed. Reginald smiled. Time for the scaffolding to go.

A moment later a needle found its way into a vein. Jeff Wallace barely resisted. He knew there was no hope. He closed his eyes and drifted into the deepest sleep of his life. And just when he thought the warm arms of death would wrap painlessly around him, his mind was bombarded. Streams of chaos too loud to ignore. Questions, challenges, anxieties. Numbers, formulas, languages, riddles, paradoxes. Like taking a thousand exams at once, facing a thousand questions you could not answer if your life depended on it.

And his life did depend on it.

Jeff wanted desperately to wake up, to turn off. But his subconscious could not disengage. He could not stop trying to answer the questions that flooded his mind. He was drowning in mental chaos, awash in a tidal wave of stimulation going directly to his brain. His brain told his body the situation was dire, his body dutifully redirected resources to muscles so he could flee the danger. Only, he could not flee. He could not move. His sleep was too deep. In a doom loop of fear and adrenaline and paralysis, his heart accelerated until it could pump no harder.

And then it stopped pumping at all. Only then did rest come.

Reginald's phone lit up with another message. "Done."

Reginald smiled. Time to get to work.

It would be an overstatement to say that Jill Bates was in love.

But, at the very least, she was having fun. She had become so accustomed to being accountable to no one, dependent on no one, vulnerable to no one. Spending a decade carving up the globe and waiting tables on four different continents adds a certain kind of patina to one's psyche. As she studied her face closely in the mirror, she noted that decade had imparted the slightest hint of wrinkles around her eyes.

She wore those tiny wrinkles without apology or self-consciousness. They were trophies of a decade well-lived. She was the vagabond scion of a wealthy but soul-crushingly boring family. Jill had never been ungrateful or entitled, she was just perpetually bored. She had two speeds—run and sleep—and had little patience for those who lived their lives in the purgatory between.

Jill was stunning, in her own estimation and that of others; raven black hair, perfect complexion, eyes the color of the Caribbean in the moonlight. But that wouldn't always be the case. A pretty globe-trotting twenty-something wild child is charming, a lonely forty-something with no family or friends is a little sad. But that was a problem for another year.

Right now, her attention was focused on the heavy black circles under her eyes. She felt like shit. Two weeks without real sleep will do that to you. The guy she had been seeing hadn't seemed to notice, but he probably still saw her through the eyes of the love-sick teenager he used to be. He had given her one of those fitness tracker bracelets that tracks sleep, and its little LED screen taunted her with a reminder of just how miserable her nights had become.

Jill didn't understand the dreams that had been ruining her sleep, but she desperately wanted them to stop. It wasn't that she couldn't sleep. But, when she did, there was no rest. Doctors had given her sleeping medication. But, the more she slept, the more tired she became. She hovered in a kind of pseudo consciousness for hours while her mind raced. The slightest ambient sound would invade her dreams, a ceiling fan made her dream of a hurricane. And, even when all was quiet, her dreams were a barrage of questions and challenges and hazy riddles.

The damage was deeper than just puffy eyes. At first, she was just a little groggy during the day. But then she started noticing she was having difficulty remembering things, solving simple problems like how to execute a recipe for fish tacos, or remembering where she put her purse. Within a few days, her physical reflexes started to slow significantly.

She was clumsy, dropping things, stumbling. The doctor said all these were normal symptoms of sleep deprivation, and that, if left unchecked, more serious symptoms would occur. One of those symptoms was intense migraines, and they started about ten days in. These headaches were almost disabling. Two weeks of sleeplessness causes its own special kind of madness, and she was starting to wonder if she was going to lose her mind. She was used to being smart, coordinated, clever, happy. But as the weeks without sleep dragged on, she was becoming less and less the person she had always been.

Jill took a deep breath. At least she could do something about the dark circles. She reached for her eye cream and whether Clinique made an "Anti Tired Old Hag Serum." But then her cell phone chirped to tell her a new text message had arrived from Jeff. Puffy eye triage would have to wait.

She picked up her phone and read the message.

"I am so sorry. Didn't mean to hurt you. Envelope behind TV. Find Zach my office. You are not safe. I"

Jill quickly texted a reply. "What the hell?"

But there was no reply. Jill dropped her phone into her purse and rushed to the door, her mind racing. Jeff hadn't mentioned working with their old friend Zach, which seemed like a pretty big omission. "Zach, I sure as hell hope you know what's going on."

It occurred to Zach Tanner suddenly, a non sequitur from his subconscious. There was no dirt here. Why was there no dirt? Five hundred thousand square feet of space, thousands of people, thirteen Cinnabon locations, fifty-five newsstands, ninety-seven restrooms. A living, breathing, air-conditioned mini city dedicated to man's mockery of gravitational law, but no dirt except for what happened to be sticking to the shoes of the visitors as they entered. He was pretty sure he had seen a potted plant by the desk in the Delta Sky Club. And there were ten such lounges in the place. Probably a three-gallon pot, two by each desk, ten desks. So, that would mean 13,860 cubic inches of dirt for the thirty thousand people in the airport. Less than a thimble full per person. Not nearly enough to grow grain sufficient for a dozen pastries at the aforementioned Cinnabon. If some cataclysmic event were to render the world uninhabitable, and the human race needed to survive based solely on the resources of this airport terminal, they would definitely need more dirt.

Cataclysms are good fodder for daydreams and nightmares, but not worth the mental effort he was expending. Still, Zach enjoyed, perhaps had even become mildly addicted to, the recognition and quantification of such minutiae. This analytical mini-obsession made him something of an oddity back in Oakdale, TN. These mental exercises began as a way to sharpen the mind, stave off boredom, maybe a way to make small talk with particularly geeky women. But things had progressed to the point that he found it hard to watch an episode of Andy Griffith without mentally trying to figure out what Floyd's pretax income might be or estimate the GDP of Mayberry.

This penchant for observation and analysis had helped him carve out a very lucrative, if somewhat lonely, career. Zach was a consultant, or more accurately put, a fixer. When a business was struggling to grow, or fighting to survive, Zach was the one to call. He looked at a business the way an ER doctor looked at a mangled patient on a gurney. To the business owner, it was their heart and soul, the distillation of a lifetime of dreams and years of hard work. Zach, unburdened by such emotional filters and imbued with a remarkable intellect, could recommend a treatment plan with a cold, clinical brilliance that left both wounded egos and remarkable success in his wake.

Many clients, impressed by his work, had offered Zach full-time jobs. He could have been a CEO a dozen times over, but Zach did not work for titles or power or even money. He worked for stimulation, for the thrill of wrestling a big, complex problem that left others befuddled. But lately, that challenge had been difficult to come by. After a while, even the most dire challenge could fit into a pattern of something he had faced before. No matter how horrific the stab wound, after a decade, the ER doctor knows the treatment is still the same. Stabilize and clean and suture, just like a thousand times before. So Zach spent most days on autopilot, an isle of boredom in a sea of variety and chaos, with mental energy left over to contemplate airport dirt.

To Zach Tanner, dirt was more than just the subject of another random mental exercise. Dirt, specifically the bright red dirt of the rural south, held special significance to him. His entire childhood seemed hued with a pervasive layer of red dirt—the dirt of little league baseball fields, the dirt stirred up while mowing a lawn that was more soil than flora, the brick hard dirt that burned away a swatch of skin during an ill-fated attempt to prove his bike could fly, the dirt his sweet grandmother cursed and tilled to produce her annual crop of butterbeans and tomatoes. City dirt was black, an amalgamation of tire rubber, car exhaust, and the finely grated soles of wingtips and sensible pumps. Zach's kind of dirt was red, hot, gritty, and really, really far away.

In this world without dirt, Zach was a man without roots. His childhood friends Jill and Jeff seemed like characters in a movie he watched too long ago. His mother died while giving birth to him. His father died of a seizure while Zach was still in grammar school. His grandparents were his only family, clinging to their last few years huddled around television reruns and homemade biscuits. He did still talk to his grandparents, his grandmother mostly, usually at times like this while he had a few unexpected minutes free. He pulled out his phone and started to dial. Then he realized they were likely asleep now, the song of crickets and bullfrogs penetrating the single-paned windows of their Hoover-era white A-frame house. They had been having trouble sleeping lately, and a call from him at this hour would probably elicit the kind of shock that leaves folks their age scrambling for pills and taking deep breaths.

Putting his phone away, he slid into the sticky vinyl seat of the booth at the airport bar. His plane was delayed by storms leaving St. Louis, and he would be here for at least a few hours longer. So, Zach found himself once again replaying a standard business traveler cliché. Exhausted, wearing the same clothes he first donned 16 hours earlier, badly in need of a shower, and tired of making small talk with strangers, he sought out a faux wood-paneled corner of an airport bar with a generic name and tried not to think about how long it would be before he stumbled up his front porch steps and into his bedroom.

The TV in the bar was playing the same sports highlights he had already seen at least six times that day, so he turned his attention to the rumpled newspaper he had only read twice. Yesterday's sports scores, a preview of new fall TV shows, a short vague article about some new data processing outsourcer that was making a ton of money, a story about a sitcom actor running his Porsche into a telephone pole. In a world with virtually unlimited media options, Zach turned to the label on a condiment bottle to stave off boredom.

His eyes settled on a jar of "Mother's Best" brand jelly. He was fairly certain no one's mother had a direct role in producing the jelly, but it was a nice aspirational connotation. Fatigue eventually overcame the compelling content on the jelly jar label, his chin sank to sternum, and he dozed off.

Zach had always had the ability to doze off quickly, even involun-tarily. It was kind of his thing. Anytime, anyplace, any circumstance. It was as if sleep was his default setting, a brief lapse of vigilance would cause his consciousness to dissolve in the warm embrace of repose. This ruined dates with more than a few talkative but boring women. With a few deep breaths and a comfortable chair, he could go from "such a good listener" to "that loser who fell asleep during dinner." As talents go, it wasn't much. But it had served him well on long flights and unscheduled sojourns in airport terminals.

The clink of stainless-steel utensils on a cheap glass plate eventu-ally awakened him. As his eyes opened, he was startled to see he now had a companion across the table.

"I see you are enjoying our product," the visitor said with just a hint of a smile.

"Excuse me?"

"I'm sorry. I didn't mean to startle you."

He was an older gentleman, smartly dressed in a navy blue suit, with a crisp white pocket square and a thick stand of pomade-infused silver hair. He looked like a snapshot from the cover of any *BusinessWeek* 1967-1976, or a high-level official from the Nixon administration, or maybe Ward Cleaver's boss. He was probably the only man in the airport at this hour whose tie was still knotted firmly across his top button. An open folio with maps and charts was open on the table beside him.

Zach's boothmate introduced himself as Mr. Hightower. They exchanged pleasantries, made small talk. Hightower was clearly very well-traveled and intelligent, but with a degree of formality and an almost complete lack of knowledge of the colloquial. As they con-tinued, it was apparent Hightower was preoccupied, worried about something. When Zach asked about work, the older man looked away for a moment, took a sip from his coffee cup, savored it perhaps a moment longer than normal, and said, "My firm has faced some difficulties of late. Our performance is not what it once was."

"Well, the economy has been pretty bad. And customers can be fickle. You'll turn it around," Zach offered. Of course, Zach knew this was just meaningless faux encouragement, a band-aid for the man with the hole in his chest.

"I'm afraid it is much more than that." Again, he looked away. There was an air of foreboding that seemed out of scale with a simple business problem.

They continued in this vein for a while. Zach asked questions, offered what advice and encouragement came to mind. Hightower provided cryptic responses drenched in worry. The older man seemed hesitant to disclose the company name or product. Zach assumed he was trying to be discrete.

During one particularly long pause, Zach let his eyes wander to the papers peeking out of the portfolio beside him. The page on top was a color-coded map. Different areas bore shades that ranged from a soothing blue to a dark, angry red. He was pretty sure he recognized one of the areas bathed in angry red.

"Hey, that looks like a map of Oakdale! That's my hometown!" Zach said, hoping to have found segue to a less depressing line of discussion.

Mr. Hightower seemed oddly rattled by his comment. "Oh no, that must just be a coincidence. That is a town in Iowa."

"How do you know I'm not from Iowa?"

At that moment, the forcefully cheery voice of a gate announced the departure of Mr. Hightower's flight. The older man said goodbye, slid a business card across the table, wished Zach luck, and strode quickly out of the bar.

Zach glanced at the card, basic gray with black lettering. There were only two lines, a single cryptic word, "Sopros," and a phone number. There was no name, no email address, no street address. He looked at it for a moment, flipped it over to see if the other side provided additional insights. It did not.

Back at his home office, Zach slid the card into a box with a few hundred others. Random encounters and random opportunities. Conversations and paydays and months of work, none of which were interesting enough to remember, all of which would seem even more insignificant very soon.

TWO

JILL DUG THROUGH THE CLUTTERED CONSOLE of her Corrola while she waited for the light to turn green. "Shit. It has to be in here somewhere."

She grabbed fistfuls of random detritus from the console and tossed it into the pile of random detritus in the floorboard. The cornucopia of gum wrappers and business cards and single earrings and tampons and Snapple lids was hampering her search. But her frantic excavation yielded fruit just as the light turned green.

"Yes!" She grabbed the key and floored the accelerator in unison. Somehow the little car managed to muster a chirp of tires on pavement. She was in the parking deck of Jeff's condo tower just a few minutes later. Jill remembered the night Jeff had given her a key. Sitting in his kitchen, they were talking about dreams and sleep. He was obsessed with the topic. But then conversation drifted to hotels and airports and a decade as a vagabond, and Jill said sometimes she just wanted to be home. Jeff took the key from his kitchen drawer and put it in her hand. "You will always have a home here."

It was gallant and dramatic and a little awkward. But she took it as a kind gesture from an old friend who had a little too much merlot. She could never love Jeff the way he loved her, but he never asked her to. He was just happy to have her around, and his persistent but unrequited infatuation with her provided Jill with a strange sense of continuity in her otherwise chaotic life.

The elevator doors opened on the twenty-seventh floor, and Jill made her way quickly to Jeff's apartment. The key turned, and she walked into a sleek, modern, impeccably clean space. One wall was glass, providing a panoramic view of the city below, and one wall was punctuated by the largest TV Jill had ever seen. She chuckled at the sight of it. Jeff had been thrilled with the amazing screen, but when he installed it, he forgot to make allowance for the massive strain it put on his apartment's electrical wiring. The first time he plugged it in, he nearly shorted out every other appliance in his place. Jill reached behind the screen, and her fingers felt the edges of a large envelope taped to the wall. She ripped the envelope from the wall.

Jeff was dogmatically digital, proudly bragging about how he only used a few dozen sheets of paper a year, so Jill was shocked to find, not a memory card, but a small stack of paper. She was even more surprised to find the sheets were handwritten. The first sheet contained only a very brief handwritten note:

"30.1254, 28.1324. Volunteer"

Maybe GPS coordinates? Perplexed, Jill flipped to the second sheet. It was labeled simply, "J Dream." Below that heading was a hand-drawn table with columns labeled "Dosage, Urine %, Blood %, Sleep Hours, Sleep Quality, Dream Induced."

Several handwritten rows were filled out in the dosage, sleep hours, sleep quality column. The urine and dream columns were sparsley populated.

"What the hell, Jeff? What have you done to me?" Jill knew Jeff would never intentionally hurt her. His was not a vengeful or vindictive love. But unrequited love can destroy with good intent as easily as it can with bad.

As she opened the door to leave, Jill looked back at the ridiculously giant TV screen. "Jeff, what the hell have you done?"

When the elevator doors opened to take Jill downstairs, four expressionless men in black suits exited carrying duffle bags. They walked briskly to Jeff's door and began working on the lock. One of the men glanced and saw Jill staring dumbfounded down the hall. "Wait!" he said, holding up a hand as he started walking quickly towards her.

Jill ducked inside the elevator, her heart pounding, and pressed the "Lobby" button about thirty-seven times in rapid succession. Black Suit Guy quickened his pace and reached the elevator just as the doors closed. She could see her reflection in his sunglasses. She looked terrified.

Zach didn't think much more about his conversation with Mr. Hightower until his phone rang promptly at 9:00 a.m. the following Monday. A female voice with remarkable diction and no discernible accent greeted him.

"Good morning. Mr. Zachary Tanner, please."

"I am Zach." There was a brief pause.

"Is this Mr. Tanner's assistant?" she said with just a hint of confusion. Zach wasn't sure if she was surprised that he answered his own phone, or that an assistant might have a voice so deep.

"No, this is Zach. How can I help you?"

"Mr. Hightower would like to know if you would be willing to take a meeting with him later this week." She spoke as if there was only one Mr. Hightower on the planet, and everyone must, as a matter of course, know who he is. Fortunately, Zach recalled the nice gent from the airport.

"Absolutely, can I ask what he would like to discuss?"

"I'm sorry, I am not at liberty to say."

Despite the ambiguous nature of the invite, curiosity compelled Zach to see what the strange older gentleman had to say. Zach had always been drawn to things that were different, unknown, maybe a little scary. Growing up, he justified this by saying that "different" and "unknown" comprised 99.85% of all matter and information outside of Oakdale, TN. That being the case, to ignore the unknown would be to ignore the bulk of all human knowledge and experience. Nothing the mayor would ever put on the "Welcome" sign at the city limits, but true nonetheless.

A few days later, Zach was walking into a Starbucks to meet Mr. Hightower. Zach always preferred a neutral location for first-time meetings. Everyone is more at ease, and, if the conversation turns out to be a waste of time, at least everyone gets a scone and a mocha-whatever. So it's never a total waste of time.

Zach found a stool at a table near the door. At 7:59, he pulled his phone for a few minutes of email while he waited. But before the phone was free of his pocket, the clock struck 8:00 a.m., and Hightower was standing in front of him with a hand extended. At an hour when most people were just beginning to stumble into the day, Hightower looked remarkably crisp and engaged. They shared a handshake and, having secured both coffee and pastry, took a seat by the window.

Hightower spoke first. "You have a very impressive set of skills, Mr. Tanner. I have heard about several of your turnaround projects over the past few years. Remarkable. But I never attempted to contact you before because, well, only the sick need a doctor, correct?"

"Yes, that sounds right. I suppose I am a physician of sorts."

"And a fine one at that. Now, as you probably gathered from our little chat at the airport, my organization is quite sick. I am afraid the issue I described with our product has only gotten worse. A friend of yours actually worked with us for a time, a Mr. Wallace. Smart fellow. But he is away on long-term leave. He spoke highly of you, suggested we may want to engage with you at some point."

"Jeff Wallace? I haven't seen him in years. We were very close friends. How is he? Where did he go?"

"I am afraid that is confidential information. You understand. Now, as I was saying, we are in a dire situation, and I believe you are exactly the person we need to extricate us."

Zach had more questions about Jeff, but those would apparently go unsatisfied. So his mind shifted into consultant mode and launched into his standard list of diagnostic questions.

"So, what exactly is your product?"

"Well, that is the delicate part. The organization is named SOPROS, just like on my card. But our business is not like most others. In fact, it is not like any other. And while I cannot disclose the exact nature of our product, I can assure you it is nothing you have ever encountered before."

Frustrated but intrigued, Zach asked his next question. "So, who are your primary competitors?"

"The thing about having an unusual product is that you have unusual competitors. Our marketplace is crowded, and we compete with an almost unlimited number of other alternatives."

This was going nowhere slowly. "Would you say the nature of your problem lies internally, with competition, with customers, or some other source?"

"We have concerns in each area, but potentially others as well," Hightower said with some hesitation, apparently aware of the enigmatic nature of his responses. "Mr. Tanner, I understand you have developed a pattern of analysis that has served you well in other engagements."

He took a sip of coffee. "But I can assure you this situation is one for which you do not have a pattern."

"Well, I am not sure how you can expect me to help you if you cannot answer my questions."

Hightower slid a manila folder across the table. "Inside this folder is a six-month exclusive contract, paying two times your normal rate, as well as a privacy agreement that is absolutely non-negotiable. Our offices are near your home in Atlanta, so this assignment will provide a bit of a respite from the discomforts of business travel. Bring these signed documents to the address inside, and I will answer whatever questions you have."

This was unconventional, but reasonable. "Ok, I will consider it."

"Please take 48 hours, but no more. I'm afraid our situation is very time senstive." Hightower stood and extended his hand. Zach shook his hand and followed him outside. They went in separate directions to their cars. As Zach reached for his keys, he heard Hightower's voice from across the parking lot.

"Mr. Tanner?"

"Yes?"

"The map you saw on the table in the airport. That was Oakdale, Tennessee."

Zach began to ask a question, but Mr. Hightower was already in his car. Zach tossed the folder into the passenger seat and slid into the car. He had 48 hours, but his decision was made before he ever even opened the folder.

THREE

ZACH WALKED TO THE ADDRESS PRINTED on his employment
contract and found a large, non-descript building. He must have
passed it a hundred times, but never noticed it. Unremarkable in every
way, it blended into the cityscape as if clothed in concrete and marble
camouflage. Opening the door into the spacious, well-lit lobby, he
walked quickly across the marble floors to the security guard station.
He handed the security guard a card as he had been instructed and
was directed to the farthest of a bank of elevators. The door opened,
and he stepped inside, but found no buttons to press. Before he could
ask the guard for help, the door closed. A few seconds later, the
elevator opened, and Zach was greeted by the starched elegance of
Mr. Hightower.

"Welcome to Sopros," Hightower offered with a broad smile and
an outstretched hand.

A few moments later, they were sitting in a large conference
room that was all wood paneling, leather, and complete absence of
modernity. They made themselves comfortable on opposite sides of
the conference room table.

"Tell me, Zach. How do you spend your time?"

Zach spent most of his time either working or sleeping, but this
was not something he was willing to share. "Just like everyone else,
I suppose. Go to the office, eat, sleep, play a little golf sometimes."

Hightower leaned forward, holding up three well-manicured fingers. "There are three ways a man can spend his time. All of human

history can be divided into one of three categories." He paused for effect. "Work, Pleasure, and Sleep. Every minute of your life will be spent on one of these three. We are Sopros—The Society for the Promotion of Sleep."

"That's it? You encourage people to sleep? That's the big secret?" Zach was incredulously underwhelmed.

"Zachary," Hightower closed his eyes for a moment, as if scanning a mental library for exactly the right passage, "You have heard it said that time is money?"

"Yes."

"Well, time is much more than that. Time is life. What is the most valuable asset any person has?"

"Their house." That was stupid. That's what a decade of reading the *Wall Street Journal* will do to you. Zach offered again, "Health? Children?" Hightower opened his eyes and stared at Zach but didn't speak. He seemed intent on waiting for the answer he wanted. Zach thought for a moment. "Life."

"Yes, Zach. The most valuable possession—gift, really—that any person has is their life. And what are the units of life?"

Zach thought for a moment. "Time." The picture was coming into focus.

"Human life is the most valuable commodity in the universe, the purest manifestation of the touch of God. It is almost pure power. And life on Earth is measured in time. Zach, you can only spend your time on one of three things."

"Work, pleasure, sleep."

"Yes. Human life is the purest form of energy, the closest anyone can get to the divine. Humans hold such extraordinary power in the way they spend their time—their life. And, of all the ways people can spend their time, sleep in particular has special significance." Hightower took a deep breath and continued, "Zach, who do you work for?"

"Sopros."

"And when you are putting away dishes or tending the azaleas in your little lawn?"

Zach wondered how Hightower knew his lawn was tiny and populated with azaleas. "I'm working for myself."

"Is that all?"

"I suppose I'm also doing it for the neighbors who have to see my 'tiny little lawn,' or the homeowner's association that might send me a nasty letter if I fail to replace my mulch—in my tiny little lawn." Hightower's slight smile acknowledged Zach's acknowledgment of the older man's mysterious lawn insight.

"Exactly. When you work, you spend your time for the benefit of others. That's not necessarily a bad thing. But, to some extent, others are using your life for their own end." A brief pause to let this sink in. "And when you are doing something pleasurable, who are you doing it for? Who benefits?"

"Me."

"Just you? Think. What do you like to do for fun?"

That was easy. "Play golf, read, watch movies..." His life didn't sound very exciting.

"And when you are doing those things, who benefits?"

"I do."

"Anyone else?"

"Whoever I'm betting against when I play."

"Funny. Think. Who encourages you to engage in those activities?"

"The companies that sell golf balls, make movies, sell books, and make those fancy golf tees made out of corn starch that biodegrade so I don't feel guilty."

"Exactly. Spending time in those activities generates power for someone else. What about when you sleep? Who benefits then?"

"I do." Zach was starting to understand where this coversation was going.

"That's right. When you sleep, you do so for yourself and your-self alone. No one else benefits. No one else gains power. You are spending your time—your life—in a way that ensures no other entity can use your life for its own end. For those who trade in the power that comes from human life, sleep is a problem. By promoting sleep, we help maintain the balance of power in the world you see—and the one you don't."

"Well, that sounds reasonable, I suppose. But I don't see how that pays the bills."

Hightower chuckled a little. "Oh, Mr. Tanner, I can assure you financial resources are not an issue. Many years ago, at the dawn of the industrial revolution, a small group of very wealthy benefactors founded our little organization with a very generous endowment. We have invested wisely, and have even been able to grow the endow-ment by virtue of some remarkably lucrative discoveries our research team has made over the years."

With a tap at the conference room door, an assistant indicated Hightower had a call holding.

"Perhaps we should take a break while I attend to this." Hightower nodded towards the phone.

"Sure. I could use a health break anyway, but you probably already knew that." Hightower offered a glimmer of a smile. Zach was encouraged that his overshare might have mined a bit of personality from the older man.

Making his way down the hall into the men's room, Zach approached the urinal and prepared to release his morning coffee. A man a couple of decades his senior stood at the next urinal. The older man was rumpled to the very frontier of being unkempt. He bristled with stacks of papers and folders tucked under both arms. One fidgety hand held a cup of coffee while the other contemplated a phone screen through smudgy round glasses that had slid too far down his nose. Zach could only assume the appendage for which this room was designed had been left to its own devices.

The man gave Zach a quick glance and a grunt that might have been "hello." Zach was a devout minimalist when it came to interaction at the urinal, so the simple grunt was not objectionable. Zach finished the task at hand and, with a safety shake and a zip, turned to the sink. Despite the head start, his urinal neighbor was finishing up just as Zach was about to leave.

The older man turned towards the sink and mumbled. "You kids with your thick hair and your fully functioning prostates."

"Excuse me, have we met?" Zach extended a hand, half-heartedly, since the other man had not yet visited the sink.

"John Ragsdale, head of R&D." Ragsdale shifted his papers under one arm and extended his hand without hesitation, apparently unencumbered by concerns about hygiene.

"I'm Zach Tanner, and I just started today."

"Oh yes, I worked a bit with your predecessor, wherever the hell he is now."

"Excuse me?"

Ragsdale opened his mouth to speak again, but at that moment, his cell phone rang. With the universal "gotta take this call" nod, the rumpled man hustled out the door.

Zach did a second precautionary hand wash. There is an average of 150 kinds of bacteria on each human hand, and Zach figured Ragsdale had just added several more to the mix.

As Zach exited the bathroom and entered the hallway, Hightower's assistant appeared beside Zach. "Mr. Hightower will be on his call for a while longer. Perhaps you would like to see your office?"

At the end of hallway, she turned the handle of a wood paneled door and they stepped inside. It was a large room, dramatically different from what Zach had seen in the rest of the building. The room was sleek, modern, minimally decorated, all black leather, graphite, and bright white halogen. One wall was a glass window from ceiling to floor. To the right was a large desk adorned with a shockingly thin Apple laptop and a generous flat screen monitor. The wall on his left, opposite the desk, was tiled with a dozen large screens that extended from ceiling to floor.

Zach picked up a large touchscreen remote from the corner of the desk and the wall sprang to life: A living, breathing, 900-square-foot wall of data. The screens streamed with charts, graphs, tickers, video feeds. Zach dove in with his eyes, looking for patterns. There was something familiar about this data. Dots of different colors displayed on a map, time series charts showing both a positive and negative outcome, pie charts showing the same. He recognized the pattern from something he had seen before. Zach sighed. He had seen everything before.

At that moment, Zach heard a firm knock on the door. He turned and said, "Come in," but by that time Dr. Ragsdale had already taken several strides inside.

The doctor extended his hand towards Zach. "Let me welcome you again to Sopros." They shook hands. "And don't worry, I washed them this time. But good for you not letting that stand in the way of first impressions earlier." Ragsdale slumped down in the chair opposite Zach's desk.

"I assumed you didn't dribble," Zach said as he made his way into his own chair.

"Whatever helps you cope."

Zach smiled and contemplated Purell. "So, what do you do for Sopros, Mr. Ragsdale?"

"I lead research and development. The geek stuff. I have teams that focus on things like pharmaceuticals, electronic devices, medical issues."

"You sound like a bit of an R&D Renaissance Man."

"Some might say so. I am an accomplished dabbler. So, do you understand yet what you will be doing for Sopros, Mr. Tanner?"

"I am here to fix things," Zach said without a hint of emotion.

"Well, thank the Good Lord, our deliverer has come!" Ragsdale raised his hands in faux celebration. "So, you think you are pretty smart, then?"

"You know, I find the really smart people, the top one percent, are often the most collaborative and open to new ideas. They are confident enough in their abilities so as not to be insecure in the presence of someone brilliant. It is the folks just below that level, the top fifteen percent, if you will, who cause the problems. They have all the hubris of the gifted but are burdened with the insecurity and paranoia that comes from knowing they are not quite as smart as the world thinks they are."

"So, are you in the one percent or the fifteen?"

"I guess we'll find out."

"What have you figured out so far?" Rasdale gestured towards the wall of monitors. "I imagine this all still looks a bit like gibberish."

"Well, at first glance this reminds me of a former client who had a product adoption problem. But there were two things going on. In some areas, sales were down because of general strategic issues, changes in consumer needs, etc. But there was an isolated area where usage dropped sharply and dramatically, indicating a new external factor, probably an aggressive competitor testing a new product. So, right now, my guess is you have a systemic decline due to a certain set of factors, and then an aggressive new competitor who is really disrupting things in an isolated area. I think we should tackle the second problem first, before it spreads."

Ragsdale was silent for a moment. "You got all that from a few minutes of studying that wall of data?"

"It was at least nine minutes, and the charts are very intuitive."

Ragsdale smiled. "Alright, hotshot, it sounds like you are starting to get a handle on things." Then his voice took on a more serious tone. "But you realize this isn't the sort of job that will ever make you famous, there is nothing here you can take credit for."

"Why would I possibly want that?" Zach replied without irony.

"Right answer."

Zach spent the rest of the day poring over analysis and making repeated trips to see Ragsdale and Hightower to ask questions. By the time Zach's head found his pillow that night, he still had a lot to learn about the details of Sopros' operations. But he was certain of one thing: Something very bad was going on in his hometown of Oakdale, TN. As he drifted off to slumber, he noted that he had lay awake in bed for eight whole minutes, a new personal record.

The next morning found Zach at his desk early. He was adding to a list of discovery questions compiled the day before when his door swung open and Ragsdale sauntered in. Zach looked up from his laptop.

"Oh yeah, I don't really knock. Yesterday was just a first day courtesy."

"Like washing your hands in the bathroom?"

"Exactly." Ragsdale dropped a small package on Zach's desk and took a seat. "I thought maybe we could open this together, seeing as someone took the time to put both our names on it."

Zach looked at the plain brown box and saw the label was addressed to "Zach Tanner and/or Ragsdale." The package had been sent via UPS.

"So, apparently you told someone you were working here, and told them my name after we met yesterday, and whoever that was managed to prepare a package and ship it to us by this morning." Ragsdale made a statement with the voice of a question.

"I didn't speak to anyone outside this office yesterday."

They both stared at the package.

Ragsdale broke the silence. "Well, aren't you going to open it?"

"Do you think it is safe?"

"Why do you think I brought it to you to open?"

Zach grabbed a letter opener from his desk and gingerly ripped through the packing tape. As he opened the flaps of the box, both men realized they had been holding their breath. Both exhaled as they looked inside.

On top was a handwritten note. Zach read it aloud. "Jeff said to contact you both. I think something might have happened to him, and I think I might be in danger. Zach, call me ASAP." Zach looked at Ragsdale. "Jeff?" Ragsdale shrugged.

Under the note was a one-page handwritten note:

"30.1254, 28.1324. Volunteer"

Under that note was a second sheet of paper on which was sketched a handwritten table with numbers in several columns labeled "Dosage, Urine, Blood, Sleep Hours, Sleep Quality, and Dream." Numbers filled in several of the cells on the grid.

Under the papers were two vials of liquid. One was clear, the other looked a lot like pee. Zach tried not to think about that. There was also a small Listerine bottle filled with what looked a lot like blood. Zach chose not to contemplate that, either. Finally, at the bottom of the box was a cell phone—the cheap, disposable kind drug dealers use.

"Is this sort of thing typical around here?" Zach asked.

"Only since you showed up."

Zach turned on the cell phone. There was one number in the memory. He dialed it, put the phone on speaker, and placed it in the middle of the desk. Both men leaned towards it.

A woman's voice answered, "Who is this?"

"You first."

There was a momentary pause.

"Zach?" the woman's voice said apprehensively.

"Yes. Who's asking?"

"Zach! I'm so glad I found you." A note of enthusiasm joined the paranoia in her voice. "Did you get the box? Is it safe?"

"Yes. It's safe enough. Was that blood?"

The woman laughed a little. "Yes, it's blood." She had the vestiges of a Southern accent, but it had been softened, probably by effort or years away from home.

"In a Listerine bottle?"

She laughed again. Louder this time. "I had to improvise." Something about the lilt of her voice sounded familiar.

"Who are you? Is this your blood? Did you kill someone?"

"Do you still fall asleep in strange places?" she asked.

Zach scanned his mental archives to recall the voice. But he didn't have to scan very far.

"Jill?"

"Yes." His mind raced. He had spoken with Jill just about every day for the first twenty years of his life, but that was a decade or more ago.

"Where are you? Are you in some kind of trouble?"

"I am afraid so, although I don't really know any details. I have been spending time with Jeff, and I got very sick, and he sent me this strange text and then disappeared."

"We need to meet. Where are you?"

"That's not really a good idea. I'm pretty sure I'm being watched. It wouldn't be safe for either of us. Jeff said I could trust a guy named Ragsdale to help. Do you know anyone with that name?"

Zach looked across the desk. "Yes, we've met. He's a researcher. We took a pee together. He has prostate problems from the sound of things." Zach wasn't sure why he offered that detail. Ragsdale huffed silently in feigned outrage.

"Gross, and not tremendously relevant. How do you know him? Were you working with Jeff?"

"No, but I might be now. I mean, I just started a new job."

"Well, shit. Maybe you can find him. But in the meantime, see if this Ragsdale person can take a look at the samples I sent."

"Ok."

"Be careful, Zach."

"One more thing," Zach interrupted.

"Yes?"

"Was that pee?"

"Bye, Zach."

Click.

Zach pressed the End Call button and looked across the table at Ragsdale. "So, Jeff is not on leave?"

"It would appear not."

They stared at the box in silence for a few seconds, contemplating grief but not engaging it. "Any idea what this is?" Zach asked, holding up the first sheet of paper.

"Looks like GPS coordinates maybe."

"That's what I thought. I'll go check it out," Zach said as he folded the sheet of paper and placed it in his sportscoat pocket.

"And I'll go see what I can figure out from these samples." Ragsdale reached for the box, but Zach grabbed the box and pulled it towards himself.

The two men stared at each other for a moment. Ragsdale broke the silence. "So you do not trust me?"

"It's nothing personal, it's just that I don't know you."

"Jeff trusted me, Jill said so."

"And now Jeff is probably dead." Zach's stomach churned as he said the words, but he pushed those feelings away for the moment.

"Yeah, and Jeff also trusted you. Told Hightower you would be a great addition to the team someday. How do I know this is really all a surprise to you?"

"You guys did your homework on me. Hightower even knows how big the azaleas are by my front door."

Ragsdale stared at Zach for a moment and smiled. "Do you recall the cable company doing some work on your street last month?"

"I do. Grey van."

"Of course, you do. Well, I'm your cable guy. Hightower trusted me, so I came to check out your azaleas. And you know what else I saw? I saw a guy with no life, with no one. No friends, no chatting with the neighbors, no women coming over. From the looks of your internet traffic, not even any late-night porn. Just an occasional call to your grandparents and asleep by ten. A guy with your brains could be anything, but you choose to be alone and silent. You crave nothing other than to be given interesting things to think about, and to be left alone."

Zach was not crazy about the picture Ragsdale painted, but he could not dispute the veracity.

"So, you stalked me. Is that supposed to make me trust you?"

"The point is that I know you. I know that you are crazy smart, and above all you value solving complicated problems and getting to the bottom of things with little concern for ego strokes and personal feelings. Believe me, if I had something to hide, you would be the last son of a bitch I would recommend to Hightower."

Zach slid the box across the table. Ragsdale picked it up and spoke a little more softly. "I'm really sorry about your friend. He may have been a little misguided, but he wasn't a bad guy. Besides, a friend is a friend."

"Thanks." Zach nodded and turned to look out the window as Ragsdale walked out. Zach had very few human connections in his life, which was generally ok with him. Connection caused feelings, and feelings were complicated, ill-behaved bits of data that defied analysis. Zach liked his connections safely ensconced in the amber of memory, providing proof of his humanity without the messy matter of having to actually feel human. But what Zach felt now broke the amber.

"You ok?" Zach heard Ragsdale ask from behind him.

"I honestly do not know."

FOUR

ZACH LEFT THE OFFICE FOR A short walk around the block and a little fresh air. When he returned to his office, he saw a woman seated facing his desk, her back to the door. Dark brown hair, shiny and straight, just a little past her shoulders. As he walked in, she looked over her shoulder and started to stand.

"Oh, please, don't get up," Zach said as he walked past and took a seat at this desk.

She extended a hand across the desk. "It's great to meet you. My name is Annabeth James, SVP of Analysis for Sopros. I am responsible for compiling all the data we use to run our organization and making sure our leadership team has the information they need. I've prepared a few notes to help you get up to speed." Her handshake was firm, but her skin remarkably soft. Zach strongly suspected the scent of whatever perfume and/or skin care product she bore had transferred to his palm, but a whiff to verify seemed unseemly.

A binder lay open on the desk between them, beside it a pair of designer glasses. Fit. Ivory skin, brown eyes, silky brown hair pulled back using some kind of apparatus that was obscured from his view.

Her smile was quick and perfect, her white teeth a striking contrast to her red lipstick. He thought the red may be a little too red for the office, but it perfectly matched her fingernail polish and the thin red stripe on the white blouse she wore under her black suit jacket. The top button was open, which was normal. The second button was also open, which, while not inappropriate, was something that bore notice.

The real story was in the third button, which restrained the ample contents of the blouse with a slight but visible strain. The blouse held his attention for perhaps one second longer than was appropriate, a fact he involuntarily acknowledged with a brief flush in his cheeks. He looked up quickly to find her eyes already locked on his. An awkward second passed before her lips parted into a broad smile.

Zach's analysis complete, he admitted to himself she was gorgeous, and in all likelihood very smart. But he also admitted to himself she was exactly the type of woman who would have no interest in him. Zach was smart and successful and not bad looking, but he was self-aware enough to know he was also a little odd. Odd played well with hipster girls and artists and all manner of desperate women with a clock ticking loudly in their ears. But women like Ms. James had lots of options. Women with choices would not choose odd, and Zach would not choose to settle, so fate chose for him to be alone.

Ms. James slid the binder towards him, her hand briefly touching his as she made the exchange.

Ms. James motioned to the binder she had just handed Zach. He flipped it open to the first page. "Why don't we get started?"

The next half hour was filled with a steady stream of statistics, dutifully following the order of the charts in the binder.

"The average adult in the U.S. gets 6.8 hours of sleep each night. At this level, brain function is sub-optimized by approximately 4 percent, while physical impairment is minimal. However..."

Zach interrupted. "How do you gather this information? Do people volunteer to be monitored?"

"I'm afraid it isn't quite as simple as that."

Zach raised an eyebrow, and Ms. James continued. "So much of tracking sleep is really about tracking motion. It is pretty simple, really. When you are still for a long time, you are probably asleep. And when you are lying flat in the middle of the night and moving around a lot, you are either sleeping poorly or..."

Zach blushed a little. She did not.

"So you track movement using what?"

"Satellites," she said matter-of-factly. "We don't monitor everyone, of course. But we try to get a good sample—a few folks from each community, from each demographic."

Ms. James reminded Zach of someone, and it only took a moment to figure it out. Jill. Jill had the same hair color, same skin, same perfect smile, but far more personality. His friendship with Jill began on the monkey bars in first grade, continued through first cars, and had come to an abrupt end when she failed to appear for her wedding to a mutual friend.

"Did that answer your question, Mr. Tanner?"

"Please, call me Zach."

"Then you should call me Beth," another smile.

He stood and walked towards the mini fridge on the other side of his office. "Well, Beth, would you like a bottle of water? Maybe a Coke?"

"A Diet Coke would be great."

"Beth, how long have you been with Sopros?" He pulled two Diet Cokes from the fridge and turned to find Beth was standing by the couch near the fridge.

"Eight months this week." He handed her the soda.

"You've learned a lot about this place in eight months." She acknowledged the compliment with a smile that was a bit more natural. Zach responded with a smile that was slightly more awkward.

They were at a bit of an impasse, standing by the couch facing each other. "Uh, I guess let's have a seat here," Zach motioned towards the couch. "What did you do before you came here?"

"Most recently I was with a consumer packaged-goods company based in Beijing. You wouldn't have heard of them. But it was a big operation. Before that it was grad school in London, undergrad in North Carolina."

"A Tarheel? I thought I detected a bit of a Southern accent." Zach was now seated but she was still standing, his eyes level with the captivating third button.

Beth stood there for a moment, looking at the couch, then back to Zach. "I—I have to get home. It is late, and I have to pick up my dry cleaning." It was obviously a very poor lie, and an even worse excuse. "Can we finish this up tomorrow?"

"Sure." Zach shrugged. Ms. James turned and walked out. Zach was at a loss to understand her sudden agita, but he had become somewhat accustomed to not understanding emotional reactions. He scanned the couch to check for stains, glanced at his reflection to check for dangling boogers or spinach teeth. For lack of a better explanation, he chalked it up to random gastrointestinal discomfort on her part.

The sinking sun was bathing Zach's office in orange, so Zach made his way to the front desk.

"Is Hightower still in?"

"No, I am afraid Mr. Hightower has left for the evening." The receptionist's digging through her handbag made it clear her evening was drawing to a close as well.

Zach grabbed his keys and made his way to his car.

Just outside the parking deck, a homeless man held out his hand, "Spare a dollar, sir?"

"Not tonight." Zach had other things on his mind.

"Jill said you would help me out!" the homeless man called out as Zach walked away.

Zach stopped and went back. He bent down to get a closer look at the man seated on the sidewalk.

"Did you say Jill?"

"You think a homeless man can't get a name right? I know what I heard. Right now, I need to hear the sound of foldin' money."

Zach pulled a twenty from his wallet and handed it to him. "Jill also told me you were kind of cheap." The homeless man's hand stayed out, palm upward. Zach pulled two more twenties from his wallet.

The homeless man pulled a cell phone from his pocket and handed it to Zach. "I wouldn't have kept this one anyway. Just an old flip phone. I'm not some kind of savage."

Zach was home a few minutes later. He strode up his walkway past his tiny azaleas and up his front steps. Sitting at his kitchen table, Zach attacked a carton of Chinese food he had picked up on the way home. He wasn't exactly sure what it was. He had neither the patience nor the culinary acumen to sort through a Chinese food menu. The average Chinese restaurant menu had 122 items. This seems like a lot, until you consider there are approximately 1.2 billion people in China. About one distinct dish for every ten million people. Not a ton of variety actually. Zach ordered Chinese by color, meat, and level of spiciness. The nice folks at his favorite rice dive understood this. Tonight's meal was "Chicken, Brown, Spicy." Lord knows what was in it. He didn't really care.

Ordinarily he would eat Chicken Brown Spicy in front of the TV, but tonight the TV was off. Zach stared at the cell phone the homeless guy had given him. Staring at a cell phone with a blank screen doesn't seem like great diversion, but it was more than enough to keep Zach occupied. He focused on it as he thought through the events of the day. He replayed every conversation, every step, but found himself playing solitaire with a deck of, at most, forty-three cards.

The ring of the mystery cell phone startled him and broke his concentration. The vibrating phone danced across the table, but he snatched it up before it could evade him.

"Hello?"

"So, how was your first day? Did you learn where the bathroom is? Get a tour of the cafeteria? Did you have someone to sit with at lunch?"

"No, but I did get a jar of someone's pee in the mail."

"Office warming gift?"

"You tell me."

"It wasn't pee, it was water. Did you get Ragsdale to look at it?"

"Yes."

"Do you have the results yet?"

"No."

"Did you meet the girl? I heard there was a girl."

"What? There were a lot of women in the office."

"I heard she looked like me. That was the whole point."

"You mean, Ms. James? Yes, she did look like you. Even had a repressed Southern drawl."

"Poor Jeff. He just couldn't handle it."

"Couldn't handle what?"

"Men are stupid."

"What?"

"I can't get into it now. I'm sure you'll figure it out. Call me as soon as you hear something from Ragsdale. But don't use this phone. I won't answer it. If they get to you like they got to Jeff, I can't have them calling me and tracking me down."

"Ok."

"And Zach?"

"Yeah."

"Don't let them get to you."

Click.

So, the city hot Annabeth James had some kind of role in whatever was happening. Another card, but still far from a full deck. Zach tapped the cell phone on the table in a rapid, random, repeated rhythm. His thoughts kept pace with the beat as he replayed his time with Ms. James and her enigmatic exit from his office. Perhaps she and Jeff shared a few other secrets. He was sorting through this thought when the tapping of the phone on the table ceased, and Zach's chin came to rest on his chest.

An hour or so later, an alarm went off, reminding him to go to bed. Zach had put this precaution in place a couple of years ago, after one too many times waking at the sunrise to find his head resting on the table beside his dinner plate from the night before.

Bedtime was also when he typically called to check on his grandparents, something he had not done in a few days. It was a little bit late to call, but they were probably still awake—propped up in bed dozing through the final act of a primetime drama while waiting to catch the local news.

"Hello, this is the Tanner residence." His grandmother's alertness belied her age and the hour.

"Hello, Grandma, this is Zach. How are you doing?"

"Hello dear. We're doing ok. What time is it?"

"Don't you have a clock? It's 10:20."

"Well, we had a power surge a few weeks ago that fried our clocks. The EMC passed out these little alarm clocks someone donated. But the instructions are too small to read, and your grandfather can't figure out how to work it. Maybe next time you come, you can look at it?" Zach was always the one who helped fix things around the house. Whenever Zach felt bitter about being without a father, he remembered his grandparents had also lost a son. He felt a responsibility to take care of them as a son would.

"How have you and Granddad been sleeping lately?" Zach could hear his granddad snoring loudly in the background. He sounded awful, snorting and coughing.

"Not too good, son. We've just been real restless. We sleep, but we just don't feel rested when we wake up. Maybe it's the dreams. I'm afraid your grandfather is having one now." He heard her sigh as she shook his arm. "Ed, it's OK. Sleep, hon."

"Dreams? Are you having nightmares?"

"Not exactly. It's more like exercise, or work. It just feels like I'm always trying to figure out something in my dreams. Some nights it's numbers, just all kinds of numbers and math. Other nights it's shapes, like I'm trying to build something. Other times I'm surrounded by strangers, like being at a party or the first day of a new job. Meeting lots of folks, trying to get to know them, figure them out. Your grandfather has been having them too, poor thing. I guess I put the idea in his head by talking about my dreams."

"Sounds exhausting. Are you on any new medication?"

"Nope. Still swallowing the same cup of pills every night. And we've cut out spicy dinners too. Your granddad has been fussing about not having his international food nights, but I don't want to make us any more restless." Growing up, they had always tried to expand their cultural horizons by regularly eating foods with an ethnic flair. Walking through the "Ethnic Aisle" at Piggly Wiggly probably made them feel sophisticated, but Zach figured they really did it for him. He was always curious about the world outside the city limits. Enchilada Tuesdays, Lasagna Fridays, Chow Mein Mondays. This exotic ethnic cuisine was usually provided by Old El Paso, Stouffers, or La Choy. Still, he appreciated the effort.

"How long has this been going on?"

"Three, maybe four weeks now. I don't know what we're going to do."

"Have you been to the doctor?"

"No, but we tried to buy some sleeping pills at the Pig. They were sold out, though."

"Sold out?"

"Yep. So was Revco. Darnednest thing." The drugstore was actually now a Walgreens. But, years ago, before a spate of retail mergers, the local drugstore at that location was a Revco. Zach supposed his grandparents, like most folks in town, just figured it wasn't worth the effort to learn new store names every few years. Everyone knew the place.

"It's not a Revco anymore, grandma." He couldn't help it.

"I know, it's Walfords."

"Walgreens."

"Whatever. If they promise me their name won't change again, I'll learn the name. Until then, it's Revco."

"Fair enough."

"Besides, I still have that set of tumblers with 'Revco' written on them from the fair when you were little." She was right, of course. He had won a carnival game loosely based on the board game "Memory" when he was about 12. Won a sweet set of plastic tumblers with Revco logos. Zach wasn't sure if it was pride, frugality, or just habit, but those same faded tumblers were still in heavy rotation in the Tanner household. And they always had a way of coming out when company was over, as did the now well-refined story of his victory over the carnival folk.

"I'll let you go, Grandma. I can hear the news is starting."

"Yep. Let me go hear what kind of meanness people are up to tonight.

Thank you for calling us, Zach. We always love to hear from you. Makes our night." He felt both happy and a little guilty, but definitely loved. It was always that way when he called them.

"Ok. Goodnight, Grandma. I love you."

"I love you too, Zach."

Click.

Zach didn't tell her yet about his new job. Maybe the next call. She would ask questions. He would try to explain. She wouldn't understand. It was enough for her to know that he had "a big important job in the city." She could tell her friends that at choir practice, and that was enough.

If she only knew.

When he put his head on the pillow, he started to mentally recap his day. But he didn't even make it out of the morning elevator ride before he dozed off.

FIVE

THE NEXT MORNING FOUND ZACH ASSAULTING the alarm clock repeatedly in an effort to either find the snooze button or permanently disable the device. Being able to quickly fall asleep is a blessing, but the corollary curse was his almost complete inability to wake up without extraordinary assistance. He employed a small army of clocks in various places around the house to harass him into wakefulness every morning. On this morning, he was eventually successful in shutting off the incessant wail of the first clock. But then his backup alarm—his smart phone—started chirping. It was time for the day to begin.

After ingesting three times the legal limit of Diet Coke on his drive to the office, he stumbled up through the lobby to the elevator. When the elevator doors opened, Ragsdale was there waiting for him.

"We need to talk."

"Have you been just standing here waiting on me?"

"Actually, he's been pacing," the receptionist offered.

"My office or yours?"

"Yours. Mine smells like pee."

"I knew it."

After a brisk, silent walk to the end of the hall, they opened the door and entered Zach's office. Zach offered Ragsdale a seat on the leather couch, but he had already made himself comfortable at the conference table and was arraying a stack of papers in front of him. Zach took a seat in the chair opposite him.

"Can I get you something?" Zach offered as he pulled another

Diet Coke from the office fridge.

"Where did you get these samples?" Ragsdale asked.

"They were given to me."

"By who?"

"Someone who said I could trust you."

He frowned a little. "Someone from outside Sopros?"

"Maybe."

"Don't get cute. This is no time to be a smart ass."

"I'm just trying to protect my source."

"You have no idea. These samples show presence of a substance that was never supposed to leave these walls—never supposed to leave my lab, for that matter."

"It did come from an outsider."

"Dammit. It must be Jeff."

"Jeff who?" Based on his conversation with Jill, he suspected he already knew the answer.

"Jeff, Mr. L, Mr. Lyle, Mr. Jeff Lyle, Mr. Hostile Work Environment, Mr. Security Breach. Whatever you want to call him. He was a big fan of this stuff, wanted to do live human testing right away. I noticed some missing from my lab a few months ago. When I confronted Jeff, he said he took a little to test it on himself, since we didn't have clearance to do official tests. I thought the little twerp had finally grown a pair, willing to use himself as a guinea pig. But I guess he just found someone else to be his guinea pig. Nice."

"Is this something you're still working on?"

"No, Jeff made a big pitch to the board, but they shut it down. Concerned about potential for misuse. Really pissed him off. I thought he was going to go back and ask again. But then the thing with Ms. James happened, and that was that."

Zach wanted to ask about Ms. James but focused on the more urgent matter at hand. "So, what does this stuff do?"

"The chemical we found in the samples was Somnucogipam, an experimental drug we developed in our R&D lab. Somnucogipam is designed to interact with the part of the brain that guides mental activity while sleeping."

"Dreams?"

"Exactly. This drug makes the brain super sensitive to external stimuli while sleeping. Think of it like a big antenna for your brain. The idea was to give people this drug before they fell asleep, then use some kind of external stimuli to steer their dreams. For instance, take Somnucogipam before you go to bed, listen to ocean sounds while you are asleep, and have dreams about being at the beach. We designed it as a way to make sleep more desirable, make people want to sleep. Imagine how quickly you would go to bed every night if you were guaranteed wonderful dreams. We aren't really a consumer products company, but we could have licensed the tech to someone. It would have been a game changer."

"But what if you are afraid of the ocean? Or someone plays a different sound while you are asleep?"

"Exactly. This drug basically opens the mind so that it can be steered while someone is asleep. Theoretically, if you were using this drug while sleeping, someone could apply the right stimuli and give you unbelievably pleasurable dreams, or terrible nightmares."

"So, that's why it wasn't approved?"

"In case you couldn't tell, Sopros is a very conservative organization. Bringing Jeff's precious flat screen monitors into the building seemed like a huge innovation. This...well, this was never going to fly."

"It's not great that Jeff swiped a little of this stuff. But it sounds like the worst anyone could do is give folks a few bad dreams."

"That should be the case. And the urine sample showed the chemical had degraded significantly through the digestive process. The body should metabolize it within a few days. But..." Ragsdale's voice trailed off a little. He stared up at the ceiling as he chewed on the cap of his Uni-ball pen.

"But, what?"

"There is something I can't figure out. The other sample—"

"The non-pee sample?"

"Yes. In that sample the chemical was suspended in another substance—tap water."

"So?"

"The samples we had in the lab were either pure or suspended in distilled water. This sample had traces of chlorine and minerals consistent with a municipal water supply—probably somewhere in a rural area."

"Why would someone want to put this in a municipal water supply?"

"I don't know. But it wasn't Jeff alone. It would take a pretty big investment to produce the drug in quantities large enough to impact a water supply."

"Who would want to do that?"

"Someone who found another use for our little drug."

SIX

ZACH ENTERED THE GPS COORDINATES INTO the maps app on his phone. The spot was in the library of Georgia State University. Google maps told him it was 0.8 miles away, 22 minutes by foot. Zach was pretty sure he could beat that. At around 6 feet tall, his stride was about 3.5 feet. So, it would take him around twelve hundred steps to get there. Zach figured the app was calibrated for the typical adult in the U.S.—five foot, eight inches, stride about 3.0 feet, about 15 percent shorter than his. So, all else equal, he figured he should get there in around 18.9 minutes. Not really a productive line of thought, but he couldn't help himself. He crossed at the next streetlight and headed west, walking quickly.

He got to the building right at 18 minutes. He always walked fast when he was thinking. The double doors swung open and closed continuously, alternately admitting and disgorging a steady flow of traffic. A bleary-eyed guy who had tried in vain to tame his bed head clutched a grande something-or-other as if it was a bar of pure gold. A knot of fashion-conscious girls talked a little too loud in a vain attempt to gain the attention of two guys with dimples and obvious hangovers. A security guard was watching the crowd stream past, doing a very thorough job of making sure no coeds had visible weapons or contraband items between their neck and their knees.

Zach fell in with the line and pressed inside. Rows and rows of books stretched out in front of him. This building had four floors, each the size of half a football field. A quick involuntary calculation of linear shelf feet and average book width led him to conclude it housed approximately 1.2 million books. Looking at the phone GPS, it appeared he should head for the southwest corner. He selected north-south isle, Fa-Hi, and started walking. Somewhere between Faulkner and Hausner it occurred to him that the GPS couldn't tell him which floor was his destination. The aisle terminated at a wall lined with chairs and couches, and he took a right, trying not to contemplate the source of the stains on the well-worn dark orange upholstery.

The coordinates on his phone finally matched those on the sheet of paper near one particularly ratty couch. There was no apparent place to "volunteer" as Jeff's note had instructed. He checked the ceiling for a camera, the floor for a trap door. He even held his nose and dug through the couch cushions for some kind of clue, to no avail.

With no answers to be found in the vicinity of the ratty couch, Zach walked down the hall and took the elevator to the second floor. A black sign with white letters identified this as the Media Lab. He reached the spot that corresponded to the GPS coordinates and took stock of his surroundings.

In this spot was a row of decidedly more modern equipment. There were four terminals reserved for some kind of advanced mathematical analysis. Again, no cameras, no sign-in sheet, no desk, no one to ask. He had just decided to try the next floor when he noticed a flyer taped to the pillar over terminal #2.

"Wanted
VOLUNTEERS
To participate in research panel
Minimal time commitment
Earn Easy $$"

Below the sheet were little pieces of paper with a phone number. He tore one off, slipped it into his pocket, and made his escape from academia.

A couple of blocks from campus, Zach ducked into a Starbucks to make a call. The barista made eye contact and stepped to the register just as he put the phone to his ear. He made the universal thumb and pinky finger gesture to indicate "phone call" and turned away. She frowned. Slow day, he supposed.

"Alpha Clinical Research, how may I help you?" a woman's monotone nasal voice answered.

"I saw a flyer for research panel. Maybe it's a focus group?

I want to get me some of them dollars everyone is so crazy about." Sometimes people find intentionally bad grammar to be humorous. This woman was not one of those people.

"Age?"

"32," he lied, a little.

"Gender?"

"Male." The barista for some reason was still glaring at him.

"Occupation?"

"Cook." Zach did not actually cook, but always suspected he would be good at it.

Ms. Monotone continued with a few other basic demographic and background questions, and Zach amused himself by crafting an alter ego with his false responses. Then she read a disclaimer and gave him the date, time, and location details. The appointment was that night at seven o'clock. Pizza, snacks, and non-alcoholic beverages would be provided. Party.

When her description of the evening's activities was complete, the receptionist again said, "Thank you for calling Alpha Clinical Research." That had been her greeting, but the click suggested the line also served as a goodbye. Efficient.

The barista was still giving Zach a scowl, which he resented, especially given the amount of money he had spent on overpriced bean squeezings at this establishment over the years. He stared at her, and without breaking eye contact, grabbed a handful of napkins and some packets of sweetener, stuffed them into his pockets, and walked out.

Back outside, Zach resumed his brisk pace back to the office. He was almost there when he felt a phone buzzing in his pocket. It was the cheap burner phone from Jill.

"I thought it wasn't safe to use this phone?" Zach asked.

"Well, I figured if we are both using burner phones bought with cash, they couldn't track us down anyway."

"Solid logic. And will definitely save you a few bucks on telephony."

"Do you have the test results back?"

"Yes. It really was pee."

"Duh."

"You said it wasn't pee. We were very clear on that point. I don't like handling other people's pee."

"You gonna cry?"

"Shut up. Where did you get the pee, and the water? Is it—is it yours?"

"Yes."

"Gross."

"You would rather handle a stranger's pee?"

"Actually, I think I would."

Jill laughed. She always had a great laugh. Unrestrained, and lacking even a trace of self-consciousness.

"There was some pretty crazy stuff in those samples."

"I figured. Zach?"

"Yes?"

"I am not well. And I'm pretty sure whatever is in that sample is what messed me up."

"Did Jeff give you some kind of drug?"

"Not exactly."

"We need to meet and talk."

"That's probably not a good idea, not out in the open anyway. Zach, these people are serious. They came to Jeff's apartment while I was there. I think one of them saw me leave. We need to be careful."

"Maybe someplace discrete."

"Hmmm. There's an elementary school on Church Street in Cloverville."

"Monkey bars?"

"You know it."

"I have something going on tonight."

"Ok. Tomorrow night. 9:30."

"See you then."

"OK. There is something else. Not sure what it means."

"Okay?"

"I noticed something written on an envelope I got from Jeff's apartment. It said, 'Alpha Electronics.' Does that mean anything to you?"

"Nope. But I'll check into it."

"Thanks. As fast as you walk, you are probably wherever you are going by now."

Jeff smiled. He was a block away from the office.

A cheery "ding" signaled the elevator doors to open, and Zach found himself once again in the Sopros lobby. The receptionist smiled and handed him a piece of paper as he passed by her desk.

"Ms. James would like a minute with you."

"Great, I'll be in my office."

Back in his office, Zach bypassed his desk and headed straight for the leather couch. He closed his eyes for a moment and took a deep breath.

"Mr. Tanner?" Zach jumped a little as a woman's voice jarred him from what turned out to be a deep, impromptu repose. He quickly stood and assessed how ridiculous he might look. Head was tilted to one side on the couch, probably 60 percent chance of mild bed head. Was that moisture on his chin? Crap. Drool. But she was 15 feet away, and the sun at his back. Probably not visible. Should he wipe it off, or would that just draw undue attention? Depends on whether a drip is imminent. If there is enough drool to drip, then need to wipe. OK. Use a mild nose blow as cover story for drool wipe. Done.

"Good afternoon. Have a seat." Zach motioned to the chair and resumed his seat on the couch—upright this time. With the drool issue resolved, and now that they were seated facing each other, he had a moment to consider Ms. James. Something was a little different about her. A slightly different posture, maybe a different look. Her lips were a little redder, fresh lipstick maybe.

"I wanted to apologize for leaving so abruptly yesterday. I felt uncomfortable for a moment. I was reminded of something—just a really bad experience for me." She seemed hesitant, almost vulnerable.

"I'm sorry if I did anything—"

"No, it wasn't you. Just being back in this office, sitting on the couch, you commented on my accent."

"You don't want people knowing you are from the South?"

"It's not that. It's just that, the first time I met Jeff, pretty much the same thing happened."

"So?"

"Well, Jeff and I became—very close." The pause told the story. That, and a brief glance at the floor.

"You had a relationship with Jeff?"

"It started his first day on the job. When we met, there was a little spark. I came by his office to give him an overview of research results. I normally would have sat on the chair across from him, but I found myself sitting next to him on the couch as we walked through the material. He commented on my accent."

"It's not very pronounced."

"I know, I've tried to tone it down. He said it reminded him of his high school sweetheart. I guess I looked a little bit like her too. That seemed kind of sweet. We started finding excuses to meet, reviewed a lot of research. Then, we started meeting for lunch at the diner, grabbing dinner after work."

"You don't have to tell me this."

"I know. You'll hear about it through the rumor mill anyway. You might as well get the unembellished version directly from me. There really weren't any sordid details. But that couch could probably tell a few tales." She smiled awkwardly.

Eew. He really liked this couch. Now every spot on the distressed leather took on new meaning. He resisted the urge to change seats. "So, why did it end?"

"That's the strange part. One day someone from HR and Mr. Hightower came into my office. They said someone had given them an anonymous tip that Jeff had coerced me into an inappropriate relationship. And they said they had already spoken to Jeff and he had resigned."

"But he didn't coerce you?"

"No, not at all."

"But why would he admit to it?"

"I don't know. Jeff was a little odd. He seemed a little...I guess a little damaged. He would sink into a pretty deep hole sometimes, get pretty depressed. I could never piece everything together, but I guess he had a pretty rough relationship with his parents. Maybe he had trouble with women in the past. But I can't imagine why he would confess to something he didn't do—especially if it cost him his job."

"Have you talked with him?"

"No. That's the really strange part. His number has been dis-connected. I went to his apartment and no one was there. He has just disappeared."

"That's crazy."

"I just hope he is OK. But it kind of hurts, you know? On the one hand, I hope he is OK. But if he really is OK, I kind of hope he gets hurt a little."

Zach stared blankly. As many times as he had come face to face with the different flavors of crazy, he still didn't know how to react. Certainly the "woman scorned" variety of crazy was a particularly strong vintage, not to be taken lightly.

"Men are pigs," he offered. He figured he might as well get that out there. Ms. James smiled a little.

"You read my mind. But, really, I don't think Jeff was a pig. I think something happened. I don't mean something physical, not like he was hit by a bus. But maybe he went a little nuts. He always seemed to have a bit of a dark side. It wouldn't surprise me if he has been sitting in a dark room alone for the last six weeks.

Who knows what goes on inside his head. You would understand if you knew him."

"I guess I'll have to take your word for it." She clearly knew Jeff pretty well. She looked genuinely worried. Her shoulders hunched a little as if she might cry. Zach's natural reaction was to touch her arm, give her a hug, do something to show a little sympathy. But, given her history in this office, and whatever happened on this couch, he opted instead for a change in subject.

"Do you know anything about a special project Jeff may have been working on? Something maybe the board wasn't too crazy about?"

Zach thought he saw a glimpse of surprise in Ms. James' eyes, but it vanished before he could be sure.

"Jeff was always trying to come up with new things, pushing the envelope. He mentioned something about the board not liking one of his ideas. But he didn't really say much else."

"Well, maybe it was nothing." He held her gaze for a moment. She smiled, glanced at the floor.

"I really should be going. My schedule is crazy this afternoon." Ms. James stood, and so did Zach. She stepped towards him and touched his arm. "I appreciate your letting me confide in you about what happened with Jeff." She gave his arm the slightest squeeze, "and I really look forward to working with you."

Zach felt strangely touched by the vulnerability of Ms. James' disclosure. The small town chivalry of his small town childhood gave him the urge to protect her, and the hard-earned cynicism of adult-hood made him wonder if that was her intention.

Zach spent the next couple of hours digging through the files left in his desk and on his computer, but he didn't find much that would shed light on what happened to Jeff. As the sun drifted low and his office was enveloped in a cloud of orange light, Zach turned off his lights and headed for the lobby.

As Zach merged onto the highway, he called his grandmother.

"How are you, dear? Are you just now leaving work? I hate that you work so late." It was barely six o'clock, but Grandma's idea of "late" was skewed by the fact that she had awakened at 5:00 a.m. every morning for the past 81 years.

Of course, she wanted to know everything about his new job. Was his work fun? Did he have any friends? Was he eating right? Zach was pretty sure she wanted to ask about the regularity of his bowels; he was thankful she refrained. These were many of the same

questions she asked after his first day of school, and he supposed
she would keep asking so long as she was around to ask. At this
stage of her life there was really nothing she could do to help him
in any tangible way. But just knowing that there was someone out
there who cared enough to ask if he was eating right, who wanted to
know if he had someone to eat lunch with at work—knowing there
was someone out there that cared made Zach stand a little straighter.

After the normal topics were covered, he gently steered the conversation towards the alarm clock. It was probably a long shot, but
Jill had mentioned something about gadgets from Alpha Electronics.
Grandma confirmed there had been some kind of power surge. It
seemed to just impact devices with radios. The guy at the hardware
store said maybe it was sunspots or something that came over the
airwaves. He was the official town expert on all things scientific,
and the only man to have ever taught both physics and shop class at
Oakdale High. So, clearly, he would know.

"Grandma, what kind of clock did you get?"

"Just a regular old alarm clock. Digital, you know. Big numbers."

"Who made it?"

"Ed, who made that alarm clock we bought?" Her query echoed
into the other room, bouncing off walls nearly covered with pictures
and furniture overburdened with knick knacks.

"Huh?" The inevitable response bellowed from the other room.

"THE ALARM CLOCK! WHO MADE IT?" Sometimes you
wonder why people yell. They yell because it works.

"Oh. It was Alpha something. Alpha Electronics, I think."

Damn. That was quite a coincidence.

SEVEN

THE DIRECTIONS TO THE FOCUS GROUP led Zach to a nondescript two-story office building right off the highway. It was a perfectly positioned stop on the evening commute from the city to the burbs. The pitch was simple: Stop off on your way home, sit around a table with some other folks and tell us what you think about some product, eat some free snacks. Try not to nod off when the conversation lags. Then, head home to the screaming kids with $50 cash in your pocket. Just enough to take the family out to Applebees and have enough left over for a few lotto tickets or a covert bottle of cheap scotch.

Of course, his intentions were a little different. He would be listening much more than he was talking. And he would have no trouble staying awake. He just needed a little Diet Coke.

The receptionist greeted him at the front desk. She was middle-aged, tiny—probably an even five feet, wearing an outdated business suit and a forced smile. She led Zach to a room with 7 other people, mostly students, and gave him a clipboard with several forms. They asked for general demographic and lifestyle data—age, income, marital status, exercise habits, health problems, etc.

He lied, of course.

With the exception of his first name, pretty much everything else on the form was complete fabrication. Even under normal circumstances, he wouldn't surrender this kind of information. But with all this talk of ancient societies, malevolent alarm clocks, and random vials of pee, Zach was feeling especially cautious.

After forms were completed, the host placed a basket of snacks on the table. Then she returned with a large tray of bottled water.

"Can I get a Diet Coke? Something with Caffeine?"

"We don't have any soda. But we do have coffee and bottled water." She could have been nicer, but apparently chose not to.

"Is there a vending machine in the building?"

"I'm sorry, it's broken." She was not sorry.

"Fine, I'll take some coffee." She pointed a tiny finger to a table in the corner of the room where there sat a carafe, neatly flanked on each side by a tower of Styrofoam cups and a basket of creams and sweeteners. He filled his cup and took his seat just as the moderator entered.

"Thank you for coming. Our client has asked us to talk to people like yourselves and learn more about how you maintain a healthy lifestyle—how much you exercise, how you balance work and play, how much you sleep..." She continued through the rest of her introduction and called attention to the mirror on one wall, behind which were representatives from her client. They would be watching and taking notes.

"I know it's a little warm in here. We're working on getting the AC reset. In the meantime, Sally has brought in some nice cold bottles of water. Perhaps that will help." They were some kind of off brand Zach had never heard of with a meaningless name—Glacier Springs or something. The "spring" could be someone's garden hose for all he knew, but the water was cold, and the room was hot. Everyone reached for a bottle, including him.

"First, let's talk about exercise. How you decide when to exercise..." The moderator led them through a "lively and honest" discussion about habits and opinions regarding exercise, diet, sleep and a "generally healthy lifestyle."

As the discussion closed, the receptionist came in again and gave everyone a large manila envelope.

"Take a look inside your envelope. You'll find three things. First is an envelope with $50 cash, in appreciation for your time tonight."

Zach noticed there were a lot of empty bottles of water around the table. The participants had really been chugging the H2O. A typical adult can sweat four liters per hour under intense exertion. He figured everyone here was doing at least a fourth of that.

"Next, you'll find our personal health tracker. We'd like you to use this little gizmo to capture some information for us over the next week."

The health tracker device was small, about half the size of a box of matches. On the front was an LCD screen and two buttons labeled "Start" and "Stop."

"On the side, you'll find a scroll wheel. When you turn the wheel, the LCD will display several ways you can spend your time: sleep, work, play, eat, exercise, etc..."

Zach was having a hard time focusing. Truthfully, he really had to pee. He had drunk a lot of water. Everyone had.

"What we'd like for you to do is use this gizmo to track your activities for the next week. When you start to exercise, simply turn the scroll wheel until the LCD displays 'exercise,' then select 'start.' When you are done, select 'stop.' Do the same thing when you sleep, work, play, and eat. Just push the 'start' button when you start and 'stop' when you stop."

Salty snacks, no air conditioning, large amounts of mystery brand water—something wasn't quite right. Zach entertained a suspicion.

"Does this thing, like, just send all that data to you wirelessly?" an inadequately shorn collegian in a hoodie queried.

"I'm afraid we're not that fancy. That's why you need the third item in your envelope. It is a small postage paid envelope. Just drop the device in the envelope at the end of the week and put it in the mail. Once we receive the package, we'll send you another $100 cash." That drew seven smiles, five head nods, and one half of an ill-advised high five.

Zach needed to get a sample of that water. As the meeting wrapped up, he put the gizmo and the return package in his sportscoat pocket and grabbed a bottle of water. As he walked past a row of bookcases to the door, the receptionist intercepted him.

"Did you find me a Diet Coke?"

She didn't look amused. "Excuse me, sir, but you cannot take that water with you."

"I have a long commute, I just thought I would drink one on the way. You know, since I don't have a Diet Coke or anything."

Again, no smile. "Those bottles of water are leftover from another client. It is a brand that hasn't launched yet, so we cannot let them outside the building until the product hits the market." She held out a tiny hand, palm upward, to punctuate her implicit request.

"Can I at least take one last sip?"

An exasperated sigh, "Yes."

Zach removed the lid and took a drink. He motioned as if he would hand it to her, but instead he placed the opened bottle on the top of the book case, well out of her reach.

She gave him what must have been her angry face. But it was so similar to her normal face that he wasn't sure. "Good night, sir."

He feigned mild regret. He reached up to hand the bottle to her, but instead knocked it over. The cold liquid hit his hair just over his forehead and streamed down his front. His hair, shirt, and, unfortunately, more personal areas, were thoroughly soaked and chilly.

She laughed. To his surprise, her face did not crack under the strain. He summoned his dignity and, still dripping, walked to the car.

Once inside the car, he fumbled in the glove box for the travel sized bottle of Tylenol that had been there since the previous presidential administration. He dumped its contents in the cup holder of the car. Then, he squeezed the moisture from his hair and shirt into the bottle. It wasn't much, maybe a tablespoon. But it should be more than enough to fill one of Ragsdale's little beakers.

Then he cranked the car and squealed out of the parking lot. The adrenaline from his little escapade was mildly invigorating. Also, he had a feeling a urine sample would need to be produced forthwith.

At the first red light, he pulled the tracker gizmo from his pocket and looked at the back of it. He wasn't surprised to find the inscription:

"Alpha Electronics."

Zach's house key slid into the lock and turned before the garage door had a chance to close behind him. He was exhausted, and this was no time for loitering in the garage. He fed the necessary digits into his alarm keypad so that its whining didn't become a scream. He initiated the standard bedtime protocol and, eight zombie-like minutes later, he sat on the edge of the bed, teeth brushed, face washed, cell phone recharging, bladder emptied, a glass of water on a coaster waiting for nighttime dry mouth. Not that he hadn't drunk enough water tonight, but Lord only knows what was in the stuff he drank at the focus group. Tonight, there was an addition to his routine—a voice activated handheld tape recorder placed on his night stand. He wasn't sure what would happen once his head hit the pillow, and the recorder would capture any sound that he made.

He contemplated the little gizmo he had received in the focus group. Forty-six percent of him wanted to smash it to pieces on the hardwood floor. But the other fifty-four percent knew it wouldn't tell him much broken. He used the scroll bar to select "sleep," clicked the start button, and turned off his lamp. As his head hit the pillow, he briefly contemplated trying to stay awake. But that thought was so unrealistic as to bring a smile to his tired face.

Zach's eyes closed, his breathing deepened, every muscle relaxed, and his brain scrambled for a moment to review the events of the day. But then his body took over, and all was dark and quiet.

Scientists say ninety-five percent of people dream on any given night, and those dreams last an average of forty-five minutes. With seven billion people on earth, that's over 315 billion hours of new original content created every night. That's more content in one night than every book, movie, and song created in the past 100 years. The problem, of course, is most people forget their dreams within just a few minutes of waking.

Zach's dreams began almost immediately, which was unusual. In the first dream, he was trying to read a book. He recognized the letters, but they were all jumbled. Not quite words. Maybe some were. It was tough to tell. Someone was demanding he read the newspaper. It probably would have been a stressful dream. But before Zach could begin to toss and turn, he slipped into a more normal dream. It was a recurring dream of his. He was walking through the field behind his grandparents' house. The sun was setting, the air was cool enough to cause a chill, but not cold enough to be uncomfortable. The grass was tall and brushing against his pant legs.

Then, another dream began, abruptly. He was given a simple puzzle to solve. It was a basic puzzle, it had rings and pieces that had to fit together just so. Apparently, he completed the puzzle quickly. Then there was another one, a big pile of little blocks or something, hundreds of them. There were several kinds. Apparently, it was his job to figure out how many of each kind there were. It was hard. Again, the dream started to become stressful, but then he drifted away to another, more normal dream. Still walking through the field behind his grandparents' house, this time he could see a small animal—a rabbit, probably—scurrying through the thick growth at his approach. Then, another dream started. This time a man held a gun to Zach's head, and he was yelling loudly. In front of dreaming Zach was a wall with words written in many different languages. Zach's job was to read them, explain them, maybe. But subconscious Zach had no interest in that kind of dream. So, in a moment, he was walking through the field in his grandparents' back yard again.

This pattern continued through the night. Stressful, intense dreams would begin. They typically involved some kind of problem to solve and some sense of urgency to solve it. But there was no focus or persistence to these dreams. They would end as quickly as they began, and Zach would return to his normal, deep peaceful sleep.

For the first time in a long time, maybe ever, he actually welcomed the shrill audio assault of his alarm clock. It was the bell signaling the end of a fight, or at least of this round. He grabbed the Alpha Tech tracker, pushed the button to indicate he was awake, then stumbled into the bathroom to start his day.

As he shuffled to the toilet, it occurred to him he might be about to lose some valuable evidence. There was, of course, a sense of urgency that would not permit him to go and find a suitable vessel. So he pulled open the bathroom drawer and fumbled for a container. The only option was, once again as luck would have it, a Motrin bottle. He dumped the contents on the countertop and quickly refilled the bottle with something decidedly less sanitary.

If he were to suddenly drop dead, investigators searching his house and car might conclude he was a desperate Motrin addict who lacked indoor plumbing.

EIGHT

ZACH DIDN'T TAKE THE ELEVATOR TO his floor at the office, opting instead to go directly to Ragsdale's lab. He burst into the door with more drama than he intended. Ragsdale had his back to the door, but quickly spun around in his rolling chair to face Zach. In his left hand he held a tall Starbucks coffee, a generous portion of which was splashed on the sleeve of his lab coat. In the other hand he held what appeared to be some kind of fast food breakfast in a cup. A plastic spoon protruded from an amalgamation of eggs, grits, bacon, and who-knows-what crammed into a paper container. A greasy splash of the concoction was dripping from his right sleeve.

"Decent people knock, Mr. Tanner."

"Fancy talk coming from a man who is wearing half his breakfast."

"You startled me. I spilled. I bear neither shame nor blame for the condition of my garment."

Zach pulled the two Motrin bottles from his coat pocket. "Two more samples for you to test."

"More pee, I suppose?"

"Just one of them."

"Which one?"

"It should be obvious once you open the bottles."

"Doesn't anyone have proper specimen bottles? Are these samples yours?"

"As a matter of fact, they are."

"Are you, in fact, some kind of Motrin addict? Who has empty

Motrin bottles just lying around?"

"Invention is the spawn of necessity. I grabbed what was handy."

"Why do you want to test your pee? Did you get your hands on some of our little sleep drug?" he asked jokingly.

"As a matter of fact, I did."

"No shit," Ragsdale said solemnly. He walked across the room and closed the door. "There is something you should know about this drug. How much did you take?"

"What's the big deal? You said the effects were temporary, right?"

"Zach, the drug I originally designed was temporary. But the sample from the water you gave me yesterday had been modified. It contains a genetic agent that, with the right dosage, permanently alters brain chemistry."

"Shit. How much does it take?"

"I don't know. I'm trying to figure it out. But the sample you gave me from the other subject showed very high concentrations in the urine. That tells me that her body was starting to produce the chemical on her own. I'm not sure it can be reversed at that point. You need to go drink as much water as you can and get this out of your system. Give me another urine sample at the end of the day."

"Ragsdale, we have to fix this. Just run the tests, let me know as soon as you have something. I'll be upstairs."

"And, Ragsdale—"

"Yes?"

"Try not to spill any of that on your sleeve."

"Funny man."

Zach walked into his office and tossed his briefcase on the desk. He grabbed the touchscreen remote and fired up the wall of monitors. Out of the corner of his eye he noticed a person sitting on the couch and executed a fairly significant startled flinch.

It was Ms. James. She had been sitting on the couch, her upper body turned so that she could stare out the window. She quickly stood.

"I'm...I'm sorry. I shouldn't be in here, I suppose. When the office was empty for a few weeks, I got into the habit of having my morning coffee in here. Great view. I...I didn't think you would be in this early."

Her eyes were red, it looked like she had been crying. Crap. Zach didn't know if he should acknowledge the tears and risk embarrassing her, or worse, starting a long conversation he really didn't want to hear.

"No problem. But you did scare the crap out of me." He chose the classic "ignore it and it will go away" strategy so popular with his gender.

"I'm sorry. I need to get to my office and get started anyway." She patted her nose with a small wad of tissue as she walked towards the door. She brushed past him and left a hint of her perfume suspended behind her. Just as she reached for the handle, she stopped and turned.

"Oh crap," thought Zach, "a conversation."

"Have you heard any news about Jeff? I'm just so worried about him. I thought maybe Mr. Hightower had shared something with you."

And there it was. She was pining away for her estranged boyfriend, sitting on the couch that was apparently ground zero for their trysts. The love couch, of course, unfortunately just happened to reside in Zach's office.

"No, I haven't heard anything." He lied, of course. He supposed it would have been the kind thing to relieve her concerns by telling her that her estranged lover was alive and well and leaving cryptic messages in Waffle Houses. But he refrained. He told himself it was because he didn't want to share unnecessary information until he understood more about whatever Jeff was involved in. But it was at least as likely that he just didn't want to start a long, weepy, and therefore supremely uncomfortable, conversation.

She looked for a moment like she was going to ask another question. And indeed if Zach had displayed the body language of someone who wanted to listen, she might have returned to the couch for a good cry. But he completely ignored her fragile emotions, using a tone of voice and body language consistent with talking to a stranger in the subway about the weather. He wasn't being rude. Ok, maybe he was a little. But he needed to establish some boundaries. He had worked to crack her icy shell, but now found himself scraping up the pieces and looking for super glue. With a sniffle, Ms. James took her exit.

After Ms. James left, Zach turned his attention to the wall of monitors. One screen was tuned to CNBC and one of their various anchor team combinations of old fat white guy and hot twenty-something financista. Ordinarily he would have started his day on that channel, but today he left it on mute.

Zach studied the metrics on the other screens, although he didn't fully understand them. The high-level numbers—total U.S. sleep minutes per day per capita, distribution for major demographic groups—all followed steady patterns. There were maps that tracked sleep quantity and quality by geography. Zach zoomed in on Tennessee, then again to Oakdale. It looked like grandma and granddad weren't the only ones not getting any rest. The numbers were bad for most of the community. Sleep patterns had been heavily disrupted. People were sleeping the same number of hours, even more in some cases. But the quality and depth of sleep were terrible. It's like a whole city was tossing and turning every night.

Using the dropdown menus, he ran a quick query. He pulled up every zip code that had hours of sleep constant or increasing and quality of sleep currently in the bottom two deciles. He was starting to be pretty impressed with Jeff's little number wall. There were probably a hundred zip codes in the U.S. that fit this pattern. The next question, of course, was whether this phenomenon was a recent development or a longstanding habit. A few seconds later, he had a giant chart with a time scale on the bottom and a line for each zip code. He stared at it for a moment. He squinted as if he couldn't see it clearly, but obviously he could.

"Holy shit."

Before he had a chance for the involuntary mental replay of his grandma's standard "no cursing" admonishment, Ragsdale burst into the room.

"People with good manners knock."

"People with good manners don't give other people aspirin bottles full of pee."

"Fair enough."

"What the hell is going on? Where did you get those samples?"

"They are mine. Are they similar to what you found in the others?"

"Yes, very similar. How did this stuff get into your pee?"

Zach told him he had received an anonymous tip about a focus group. For the moment, Zach omitted the fact that Jeff had made contact. Zach wasn't sure if Ragsdale knew about his relationship with Jeff, and Ragsdale's trust was important. Zach told him about all the water they were given at the focus group, about the hot room, and the receptionist's apparent willingness to resort to fisticuffs in order to prevent him from taking a bottle of water home.

When he finished, Ragsdale leaned back in his chair, ran his fingers through his already messy hair, rubbed his eyes, and let out a particularly long, deep sigh.

"What we had before was Jeff giving samples to a couple of

random people to satisfy his own individual curiosity. Hightower and I knew about that. But this—this is a much bigger deal. Someone with real resources has seen the potential in Somnucogipam and is investing a lot of money to try it out on real people. I just can't figure out what they are trying to do with it."

"Why do you say that? They want to disrupt people's sleep, right?"

"Sure. But to what end? Who benefits when people can't really sleep deeply? It doesn't make sense."

"Maybe this is some new kind of terrorism. Talk about bringing a nation to its knees—imagine having a big chunk of the U.S. population unable to sleep for weeks."

"Not really the kind of drama we normally see from terrorists, is it? Don't get me wrong, the impact on our society would be much worse than a few car bombs. But it doesn't fit with terrorist M.O."

"But the drug can impact people's dreams, right? Maybe someone is trying to brainwash people?"

"I can see why people would try, but that would not really work. Once someone wakes up, their conscious mind takes over. The drug only makes you more impressionable while you are asleep. Once you wake up, whatever you dreamed under the influence of the drug fades away like any other dream."

"So, if it isn't about influencing people, or randomly hurting people, maybe it is about using people. What would someone do if they could harness human brainpower on a large scale?"

They both paused for a moment. Ragsdale spoke, "Honestly, you could do just about anything. Anything a computer can do, a human mind can do better. Companies, government, law enforcement, criminals—over the past decade, all of them have been in an arms race to build computers that are faster, more powerful. But even with the billions of dollars invested, nothing man has built can match the computing power of the human mind."

"So, if this drug enables people's minds to be influenced while they sleep, that is only half the device, right?"

"Right. The drug only works if there is some kind of stimulus. You have to send messages to people taking this drug while they are asleep in order to impact their dreams. I just don't know how you would do that on any kind of scale. Maybe if everyone fell asleep to the same TV or radio station playing in the background."

"Could it be something on a different frequency? Maybe a signal that could be received by the brain on a subconscious level, but not heard audibly?"

"That's theoretically possible. I've seen some research on sub-conscious perception. You can communicate with people in that way. But it doesn't work in a normal environment. It takes a near absence of all external stimuli, people have to shut out everything else, clear their minds."

"Like when you are asleep?"

"Exactly. The technology was never useful because it is very difficult for a person to completely block out everything, shut off their conscious mind so that the subconscious can hear. But if you are asleep... Yes, it should be possible."

"What would it take to deliver this kind of signal? A big computer? Some kind of brain scan setup?" He walked across the room towards the coat stand and started searching the pockets of his coat.

"Actually, no. It could be quite small. As long as the device was within close proximity, say, three feet from your brain, the signal could get through just fine."

At that point, as if rehearsed, Zach's hand found the device given to him at the focus group. "Something like this?"

"Maybe. Where did you get that?" Ragsdale held up his hand and motioned for Zach to toss it.

Zach complied, without regard for whether or not it would be caught. As the device floated through the air, Zach briefly contemplated how anticlimactic this conversation would be if Ragsdale turned out to be completely uncoordinated and let the device shatter on the floor.

Thankfully, that did not happen. He turned it over in his hands and studied it. "What is it supposed to do?"

"The focus group facilitator said it was a simple device for tracking how much time you spend on daily activities—sleeping, eating, working, etc. Kind of a glorified stopwatch."

"We'll see about that. Toss me a screwdriver."

"I don't have a screwdriver."

Ragsdale gave a snort of mild disgust and started using whatever he had handy to try and pry the device open—fingernails, a pen, badge clip, his teeth.

"For goodness sake, don't chip a tooth. Don't you have a screwdriver in the lab?"

Ragsdale ignored him. But Zach fished a mini multi-tool from his desk drawer and handed it to the doc. A few seconds later, they were looking at the insides of the little device.

"This is a lot of hardware for a 'glorified stopwatch.' It looks like some kind of transmitter. Not a normal radio frequency. Low power."

"Could that send the subconscious signals you were talking about?"

"Sure. But there is something else under here as well. It's blocked with a plastic cover. I can't get to it with your crappy little tool here. I need to get to the lab and take this thing apart carefully."

Zach decided to ignore the unfair criticism of his keychain. It was an 8-in-1 tool, but apparently one of those 8 uses was not the disassembly of covert dream control devices.

"Just be careful, I don't want to void my warranty."

Ragsdale didn't acknowledge Zach's joke. He was studying the device intently as he walked quickly towards his door.

"Ragsdale, be careful with that thing. It needs to keep working. Whoever is behind this, I'm not sure yet that I want them to know we know what's going on."

"That's easy, we don't know what's going on," he said.

"We know more than we did yesterday."

The doc smiled and hustled down the hallway.

Zach closed his door and turned back to contemplate his wall of data. With the drama of Ragsdale's entry and the impromptu gizmo dissection, he had forgotten for a moment about his own momentous discovery.

On the wall were around seventy lines on a chart, seventy zip codes showing the same strange sleep pattern, the same time series trend. Each was more or less normal at the beginning. Then there was some kind of disruption. The sleep quality index dropped dramatically all at once, improved slightly, then remained flat. Every area followed this same pattern. But they did so in groups. Every week, another ten or so zip codes fell into this pattern.

Zach had seen this pattern before. It was a product rollout, a conquest. Someone was systematically rolling out something, ten zip codes at a time. And apparently it was very effective.

NINE

DOWNTOWN STREETS HAD BECOME DARK HALLWAYS obscured by the extreme angle of the sun. As Zach drove out from the shadows of big downtown buildings and towards the place where he had arranged to meet Jill, it actually became a little lighter outside. The sun shone bright in his eyes, forcing him to view highway signs through a very narrow squint.

He arrived at the school before it was truly dark. Jill was probably already waiting in the tree line, but she was very clear about not wanting to be seen together in the daylight. So Zach drove a couple of streets over and treated himself to a vanilla milkshake while he waited. Nothing soothes the soul and comforts the mind quite like frozen butterfatty dairy. Today was no exception.

His straw was completing its noisy quest for the last drip of melted shake as Zach approached the monkey bars in the middle of the dark playground.

"Nice job, super spy."

Zach startled a little, and an involuntary gasp re-routed that last drop of milkshake from his throat up through his nasal passages.

"You scared the crap out of me."

"Yes, I suppose you had no reason to expect I would be here." Jill always had a gift for sarcasm. He could barely make out her features in the darkness, but he recognized the voice and the sarcasm, even after a decade had passed.

"Funny. I didn't think I had to be particularly quiet. Do you really think we are being watched?" Jill looked past him, scanning the parking lot and street, then looked over her shoulder at the trees.

"Maybe not. But I see no reason to take chances. We are dealing with some pretty serious people."

She took his hand and led him to the edge of the tree line. Zach's pulse quickened a little, his palm became just a little sweaty in hers. His almost complete isolation from family and epically bad romantic life had left him somewhat unaccustomed to physical contact. She squeezed a little tighter as they slipped into the shadow of the trees.

"Over here. I found a good spot earlier."

She led him over to the base of a large tree. Through the filtered yellow haze of the playground security light, Zach saw her motion for him to sit. He complied, and she sat down close beside him. From this vantage point they could see the playground and school in front, the road to the right. She opened a makeup mirror and placed it on the ground a few feet in front of them. The woods were pitch black behind them. If anyone with a flashlight came from that direction, they would be seen in the mirror.

It was too dark to see much detail, but in his limited view through the scarcity of light, Jill was exactly as he remembered her. Raven black hair, fair skin completely void of blemish, eyes almost the exact color blue used in Maxwell House coffee containers in the mid-nineties. Her perfect smile reflected every bit of filtered light it could absorb through the trees. It did not occur to Zach that those words might be beautiful. For him, they were only accurate. As devoid of romance as the screen on a calculator.

"So, spill. Tell me what you know. What's up with the cloak and dagger and the bottles of pee?" Zach figured he might as well cut right to the chase.

"I have a feeling you know more about this than you let on." She was right, of course. He was beginning to put things together.

"You first," he said. She hesitated for a moment, probably contemplating initiating some banter on the subject of who talks first. But apparently she thought better of it.

"You know that Jeff and I were together through junior and senior year in high school."

"Yes, I recall feeling like a third wheel during most of my glory days. Thanks for that."

"Whatever. It's not my fault you couldn't talk to a girl without trying to calculate her average bone density or life expectancy or odds of ending up on the pole or shit like that."

"Ouch. True. But, ouch. Being super analytical is a blessing and a curse."

"Yeah. I know. I heard a few stories from other girls at school who went out with you. I always tried to tell them to give you a shot. There was a good heart inside that calculator." Jill smiled. Perfect, understated smile.

Zach smiled a little too. Involuntarily, which was something he noted. "Like what stories?"

"Oh, you don't want to hear any of that. It's been years!"

"Don't worry about hurting my feelings. It's been years!" They both smiled.

"Oh, Michelle from the junior prom said you told her the total volume of helium of all the balloons in the room, the pounds of shells that were left over from making the crab dip, and—this is my favorite—that the total amount of hairspray used by all the girls in the room would be sufficient to launch a Trans Am 150 feet into the air. Then you fell asleep in the limo on the ride home. Nice."

"That is not entirely true."

"Really? I'm glad to hear it. That was pretty rough, even for you."

"It was a Mustang."

They both laughed. Jill smiled and looked down, brushing a lock of dark hair back from her eyes.

"I'm sorry if that upset you."

Moonlight caught her smile. His relationship with Jill had always been strictly platonic, initially out of respect for Jeff, later just out of habit. But, even so, a beautiful woman in the moonlight gets a certain degree of latitude.

"No problem. I can take it. I'd like to say things have gotten better, but that would probably be a lie. The other night I actually slept through an entire movie—previews to credits. I woke up, and the girl was gone. Post-it note stuck to my forehead just said 'Zero.' Still not exactly sure what that means."

Jill smiled. "I'm sure working for a secret shadow organization will do wonders for your love life. Nice move there, Romeo." She laughed a little.

"Well, it can't get any worse. But we didn't come here to talk about my pathetic love life. What happened with you and Jeff? And, more importantly, why did I wind up with a bottle of your pee?"

"So, just after you left for college—I never could figure out why you left two months early—Jeff asked me to marry him."

"Wow. I'm not surprised, I guess. He loved you since before algebra. I just wondered if he would get up the nerve to ignore his parents."

"Well, he did. Finally. I told him yes. But then I started to have second thoughts. You know I always wanted to live. I mean really live. I wanted to see things, to do things. I just wasn't ready to settle down at 18. I had been accepted to a small liberal arts university in Brussels. I was going to be an artist, a photo journalist, whatever. Something fabulous. And I was determined to do it all without my parent's money. I didn't take a dime from them. Still haven't."

"So, you told him you changed your mind?"

"That's where things took an ugly turn. Jeff and I were going camping. He wasn't a big fan of the outdoors but loved going with me. I had decided I was going to tell him then. It wasn't 'no,' just 'not now.' I wasn't going to break his heart, I just wasn't ready.

"The night before we were supposed to leave, his mother was waiting for me when I got off work. She said she wanted to grab a cup of coffee and talk. They had been so awful to me, I thought I would give it a shot. Maybe she was softening up to me, you know?

"She drove over to an empty school parking lot and turned the car off. She told me that she and Jeff's dad didn't approve of our marriage. It was nothing against me, it was just that Jeff had a lot of potential, and it would take a lot of hard work to reach that potential. They thought he would be better off with someone who was of a more serious mind."

"That's a hell of a thing to say to an 18-year-old girl."

"I know, right? She just didn't think I was good enough for her little boy. Stuck up bitch. She offered me a half million dollars cash to break off the engagement and leave town. My family had a lot of money, but I didn't. A half million bucks was quite an offer. I told her no, of course. And then I did something stupid. I told her I had already decided to break off the engagement. I told her about the school in Brussels.

The next night, sitting by our little campfire, I told Jeff about my decision to wait on marriage. I explained that I loved him, that I would like to marry him someday. But he just freaked out. He said his mother already told him everything. His mother said I didn't really love him, that I had offered to break off the engagement in exchange for cash. He didn't believe her when she told him. But then when I told him I was leaving… Stupid bitch. She broke her son's heart and used me to do it. And he hated me."

"Oh my God. What did you do?"

"Well, Jeff wouldn't speak to me after that. He thought I had allowed myself to be bought off by his parents. Unforgiveable. He wouldn't believe me. That fall, I headed off to Brussels. We didn't speak for years. I guess we both moved on. I finished college, travelled a lot. I lived, you know? I did what I always wanted to do. I worked on three different continents, I ate crazy local foods, I got some ill-advised tattoos. I learned five different languages. I guess I have a knack. Who knew? I fell in and out of love with a steady stream of losers. I got out of the small town and did my thing.

"Then, about six months ago I found myself between jobs. I moved to Atlanta to find work. One morning I was sitting in the Waffle House drinking coffee, and in walks Jeff, dressed in his dapper corporate best. We ate breakfast and talked."

"Nothing soothes 15-year-old heartbreak like hashbrowns and bacon."

"You know it. We made the normal small talk. I told him about some of the places I have lived. He told me a little about his work—some kind of government organization or something. It sounded a little odd, but he didn't give me any details. He said he was seeing someone from the office, but that it wasn't that serious."

"My couch would probably disagree."

"What?"

"Nevermind. So, then what happened?"

"After an hour of chit chat, we acknowledged the big smelly pachyderm in the room. I told him again that his mom didn't buy me off, that I really did love him. But, at the time, I just wanted to see the world a little before I settled down."

"Did he believe you?"

"I think so. But it was a little uncomfortable. I think—I think he may have still had feelings for me. He said he'd never stopped thinking about me, that he hoped we could see more of each other. But I didn't really want a relationship. I was just catching up with an old friend. High school was a long time ago."

"But you kept seeing him."

"Yes. It was fun to catch up, to meet someone from back home. We hung out a little, grabbed lunch at the Waffle House a few times. We talked about home, about our families. We both obviously had rich parent issues."

"Did he ever talk about work?"

"Not very much. I never could exactly figure out what he did, or what his company did. He did ask how things were going for daddy's little radio business. I told him I didn't know, of course. But I did help him refer a friend of his to my dad. Some kind of parts distributor or something. Then one day he stopped by my apartment to pick me up for lunch. He brought a big 24-pack of that bottled water from the focus group, he said the company had a bunch of leftovers so he was giving it to friends. A couple of days later, he gave me this—"

She pulled a small travel alarm clock from her jacket pocket. It was pretty high end, leather covered, clam shell case, fancy silver trim, worked in multiple time zones. On the inside cover was an inscription:

"For my favorite world traveler – J"

Zach turned it over, and on the back noticed the manufacturer name –

"Alpha Electronics."

"Nice little gizmo."

"I thought so. It turns out my alarm clock was broken anyway, so I started keeping this by my bed."

"Okay? So he gave you a travel alarm clock. Then what?"

"Then, the dreams started."

"What dreams?"

"Come on. You must have some idea. I'm sure the shadow men in your secret building have told you something."

"Actually, it's shadow persons. It's a very diverse organization. But I would rather hear what you have to say."

"Ok. At first, I started dreaming about weddings and romantic getaways and candlelight dinners. Every night. It was crazy. I'm not a super romantic person anymore."

"Were you with Jeff? ...In the dreams?"

"Maybe. It was tough to remember. I just recalled the situations. Dreams, vague, gauzy dreams. Every night. Every night. I thought I was going a little crazy."

"Did you talk to Jeff about the dreams?"

"Not really. I didn't want him to freak out or get the wrong idea. I wasn't really looking for a whole relationship thing. I was just catching up with an old friend. I certainly didn't have any romantic feelings for him. A couple of times Jeff steered the conversation towards dreams. It seemed a little odd, but I just thought it was coincidence.

Then one day out of the blue I get this text from him—"

Her eyes began to glisten. She dabbed at her right eye with the cuff of her sweater. She was not a girl—a woman, Zach corrected himself—who cried easily. But her voice began to tremble a little.

"The text said 'I love you. Always will. Have to go now.' And then he told me about an envelope hidden in his apartment and that I should contact you. I tried to text him back, of course, but there was no reply. He didn't call either. It was like he just disappeared. Right after that, the wedding dreams stopped."

She crossed her arms and trembled a little. He wasn't sure if she was crying or shivering. Fortunately, this was a case where either symptom indicated the same treatment. He gave her a hug. She put her head on his shoulder and sniffled a little. In another time or place he might have been concerned about snot or eye makeup on his shirt, but this was not the occasion for such eccentricities.

"I'm not some blubbering idiot woman who wipes tears and snot on a man's shirt."

"I know. And I was hoping that wasn't snot."

"It's just—I don't know if I loved him. I guess I always loved him. I'm not sure if I wanted to be with him. But I enjoyed being around him. And I liked the possibility that we could have been together, that we could have been happy. It's been a long time since he and I split up, and a lot has changed. But he and I are both still single. Maybe that means something. And we are both lonely. Especially him. My loneliness was a fairly recent phenomenon. But it seemed like he had been lonely since that night by the campfire. I just thought that maybe there was a chance we could be happy together."

"Maybe you can still be together. Maybe there is an explanation for what happened."

"Maybe. But he was into some pretty serious stuff. You are too, it sounds like. He was working with some pretty powerful people. He loved it, loved the importance of it. But when people like that turn on you...I just don't know."

"Maybe I can help. What happened next? Did your life start to go back to normal after the dreams stopped? More importantly, why did I wind up with a bottle of your pee?"

She chuckled just a little. "Again with the pee... After that, my dreams changed. Big time."

"The first night was total chaos. I dreamed of everything. Numbers flying by, colors, music, pictures, faces, and lots of people speaking in different languages. It was like that dream where you show up for school and forgot to study."

"In your underwear?"

"Actually, no underwear."

"That's your choice. I'm not going to judge."

"Funny. My clothing wasn't part of the dream. It just felt like one big scary exam. I tossed and turned all night and woke up exhausted. I figured it was just from the stress, worrying about Jeff. After that first night, the dreams were different, less intense. But I still wasn't resting. Every night, just as I would drift off to sleep, I would start to dream about having conversations in different languages. Some, I knew. Some, I didn't. It wasn't really a nightmare, it just wasn't very restful. Every night, you know? The same thing. It wasn't scary, it just felt like, like…"

"Work?"

"Exactly. It felt like work. Sleep felt like work. That's a hell of a thing, right? This went on for a week or so. The whole time, I kept this clock by my bed. Jeff told me to throw it away, but I just figured he was saying to get rid of it because it would remind me of him. I wasn't really ready to let go. But then, one night I had a few glasses of wine, and I stopped being worried about him and started being a little pissed at him. So I took the clock and tossed it off the upstairs landing. It landed on the couch. That night, I slept like a baby. It was great."

"So did you think the clock had anything to do with your sleep?"

"At first I didn't. The next night, I fell asleep on the couch watching a movie. That night, the dreams started again. Same deal. People speaking foreign languages, me trying to understand, work, work, work. When I woke up, I noticed the damned alarm clock under the couch cushion. It was then that it occurred to me that the clock might have something to do with my crazy sleep issues. So I tossed it in a box in my spare bedroom. That night, things were different. I didn't have all the languages, the questions, the work, you know?"

"So, everything was fine?"

"Not hardly. I still haven't been able to get into a deep sleep. I hover in a shallow sleep, restless. And I always dream. Every single night. But now it's about random things."

"Scary things?"

"Definitely. Getting hit by a car, running down a subway track with a train following me, terrible arguments, even giant insects. It has been going on for a while, makes me feel like I'm going crazy. And then when I got Jeff's text, I visited his apartment and found the papers I sent you."

"And the pee?"

"I figured a sample might be helpful."

"It was."

"So?"

"So, what?"

"What was in my pee?"

Zach stepped a little closer and took a quick look around. This was silly, of course, since there was no one within earshot. But it made him feel better. "It contained an experimental drug. It was originally designed to help people dream more."

"Sleep more?"

"No, dream more. The thinking was that if people dreamed more, and enjoyed those dreams, then they would be more likely to sleep. Be healthier."

"What kind of crazy ass company do you work for?"

"That's a long story." Zach gave her the high points of his conversation with Hightower and what he knew about what Jeff was working on. He avoided any details around Ms. James. Jill had a bunch of questions. He answered what he could. This was all technically in violation of his privacy agreement. But he figured since the organization had basically ruined her life, she was entitled to a little information. Even though he hadn't seen Jill in years, she was his playground friend, and the bond of the monkey bars is not to be taken lightly.

Then she asked the question he had been dreading.

"Will I—" Tears were starting to gather, taking on the color of her eyes and looking like tiny little oceans in the moonlight. "Will I get better?"

God, he wanted to say yes. He wanted to give her another big hug and tell her it would all be okay. But he couldn't say that.

"Maybe. I don't know." The pools became streams, spilling from the oceans and running down the hills. He hugged her because he didn't know what else to do. "The drug was originally designed to be temporary so that your body would metabolize it within a day or two. But this version has been modified. It incorporates a genetic agent that over time permanently alters your brain chemistry. Once that happens, the effects are permanent."

"How long? How much does it take?"

"We have someone working on that. But we just don't know. This is brand new stuff."

"So, I am patient number one?"

"Well, no, actually." Damn. As soon as he spoke, he regretted it, and the question that followed.

"How is the first patient doing?"

Zach didn't answer.

TEN

IT WAS VERY EARLY WHEN ZACH got to the office the next morning. Hightower's office was the only one with a light on. The door was ajar. Zach knocked twice and pushed it open.

"We need to talk."

The older man was sitting behind his desk, dark suit and pomaded hair, white ceramic cup of black coffee resting on a leather coaster at his fingertips. He was reading through a stack of reports and looked up without sign of startle or surprise. "Yes, I suppose we do."

"Tell me about Jeff."

"What do you want to know?"

"Why did he leave?"

"He elected to pursue other opportunities," Mr. Hightower said without hesitation, as if he were expecting the question. It was the ultimate business cliché, and Zach obviously didn't buy it.

"Due respect, sir, but I know there was more to it than that. I know about the new drug Jeff wanted to test, about the girl. Did you fire him?"

Mr. Hightower returned the report he was reading neatly to its stack, put his reading glasses on top, and sat upright. He took a deep breath and rubbed the creases on his nose where the reading glasses had been resting. "Mr. Wallace resigned. I suspected something was amiss with him. His behavior had become erratic. It was apparent he was hiding something. But he was still performing well in his job. He was a man of remarkable vision and determination. He worked with Dr. Ragsdale's team to develop a chemical compound that, while ultimately unsuitable for our use, showed remarkable potential." Hightower looked into Zach's eyes as he spoke; Zach didn't blink. "Then, a few weeks ago I found this on my desk. I haven't heard from Mr. Wallace since. He simply disappeared."

Mr. Hightower pulled a crisp manila folder from his credenza and handed its contents to Zach—a single-page typewritten letter.

> "Mr. Hightower,
>
> First, I would like for you to know how much I appreciate the opportunity to work with you at Sopros. I appreciate the trust you put in me, and I believe that together we could have done great things to further the goal of the organization.
>
> Unfortunately, however, I have made a serious mistake that has violated the trust of this great firm. Over the past few months, I have grown quite fond of Ms. James. She and I had a brief relationship, but she did not reciprocate my feelings. I then made the mistake of using my position to try and further our personal relationship. I recognize this was wrong. I have apologized to her, and now I apologize to you.
>
> Please accept this as my formal resignation from Sopros. I wish you and the organization the greatest success.
>
> Best,
> Jeffrey Wallace"

"So he quit rather than face a sexual harassment charge?"

"That is what the letter says." Hightower didn't believe it either.

"What did Ms. James say?"

"She confirmed the letter, she said that they had a brief relationship." Mr. Hightower seemed profoundly uncomfortable with this conversation.

"She mentioned something to me as well. Although it seemed like she really did have feelings for him." Zach noticed a second manila folder under Hightower's left hand. "But there is more, isn't there?"

"I suppose there is." The old gent opened the much thicker manila folder. "Around the time Jeff started working here, we began to notice severe irregularities in the sleep pattern data from several towns."

"I saw the same thing in some analysis yesterday."

Mr. Hightower raised his eyebrows. "Ah yes, those screens Jeff installed. We solicited feedback from a few test subjects in the towns that were impacted. We had them keep track of their dreams for a few nights. Not pleasant."

Hightower slid the folder across the desk to Zach. Zach flipped through a few pages. Subjects said they dreamed about questions, puzzles, riddles. The topics were all over the place—math, language, art, engineering, physics...

Hightower kept talking as Zach flipped through the pages.

"Also, there was this." He slid an 8x10 photo across the desk. It was Jeff and a woman with dark hair leaving a diner. Jeff and Jill.

"Mr. Wallace had been seeing this woman for a while."

"Is it your custom to spy on your employees?"

"Not as a matter of course. But when we think our greater mission might be at risk, we do what we must."

"Are you spying on me now?"

"Should we be?" Hightower smiled. Zach didn't.

"So maybe he was just dating two women at once. That's not particularly uncommon."

"Perhaps, but Mr. Wallace didn't seem like the type to be suiting more than one woman."

He was right, of course. In the time Zach knew Jeff, his romantic focus was always on one woman. Usually that one woman was Jill, or whoever he was dating to take his mind off Jill. But who says 'suiting'?

"There is another thing. The woman that Jeff was seeing was from one of the towns where we saw the odd disruption in sleep patterns. Oakdale, I believe."

At that moment, a vibration from Zach's breast pocket suggested his phone was ringing. When he saw the name on the caller ID, dread took just the slightest hold on his stomach. It was his grandmother. She never called during the day. And she and his grandfather were at the age when any phone call could bring bad news.

Zach gave Mr. Hightower a signal and walked quickly to the door as he pressed the green button.

"Hello, Grandma?"

"Zachary, Dear." She had been crying. Dread squeezed a little harder at Zach's throat.

"What's wrong? Is it grandpa?" He began walking quickly to his office, trying to remain calm.

"No, your grandpa is fine, or at least as fine as he gets these days. It's your friend, your old friend Jeff. I'm afraid he has passed away."

Zach had suspected as much, but hearing the reality of it brought a new wave of dread. "How did it happen?"

"Well, they are keeping it very quiet. But my friend Birtie is the receptionist at the funeral home, and she told Mr. Tanner the florist that it was a drug overdose."

Drug overdose. It wasn't enough that Jeff was murdered. Whoever did it was also besmirching his character post-mortem, creating an airtight story that would keep the police from looking closer. By now Zach was in his office. He shut the door and sat down at his desk. "How did the family find out?"

"Well, he's been working in Atlanta, you know. Some big important job. No one really understood what it was, not even his family. But he wore nice suits and drove nice cars and seemed to be doing well. But there's drugs in the city, you know. And money finds drugs just like drugs find money."

"It wasn't drugs. Jeff didn't have a problem like that."

"Well, I don't know. But that's what folks are saying. If he was mixed up with drugs, there's no telling what might have happened. Where there's drugs, there's meanness. All kinds of meanness."

The sadness in his grandmother's voice hurt Zach almost as much as the news about Jeff. It had been years since Jeff and Jill and Zach last tracked dusty red clay through her spotless living room. But in her mind they were still those little kids who ate her cookies and drank her iced tea. They were her young 'uns, and now one of them was gone. She sniffled and took a deep, trembling breath.

"Anyway, the funeral is Saturday at 1:00 at the Church of Christ. Are you going to be able to make it?"

"Yes. Yes, ma'am. I'll make sure I'm there."

"That's great, dear. Your grandfather and I would love to see you. And I'm sure it would mean a lot to Jeff's family. And, Zach?"

"Yes, ma'am?"

"You stay away from drugs, you hear?"

"Yes, ma'am. Always do."

Zach wasn't surprised, of course, that Jeff was dead. He suspected it. Jill almost knew it. But that was just doubt born in this surreal pseudo-world where he had been living. Hearing the news from someone on the outside made it real, and sickening. Zach looked down at the desk, polished to a slick shine, barely even used. The last man who sat at this desk was dead, resting in a cold room in Oakdale Funeral Home, surrounded by fresh cut flowers and teary cousins.

"Shit!" Zach soft-shouted and slapped his desk in frustration.

As he did, something fell from under the desk and hit his foot.

Zach pushed back his chair and looked under his desk. There was a cell phone lying right next to his foot. On the back of it was a piece of dried chewed gum. It must have been stuck to the underside of the desk.

The screen was blank, the battery had long since expired. He dug through his desk drawer for a charger and plugged in the phone. The screen lit up. Right beside the blinking battery icon was the owner's name:

"Jeff Wallace"

The phone prompted him for a four-digit code. Zach paused for a moment, then typed "0402." Jill's birthday. The main phone screen came up. There was a series of messages to Jill. Two made a great deal of sense."

"I love you so much. Always have."

"I am so sorry. Didn't mean to hurt you. Envelope behind TV. Find Zach my office. You are not safe."

And then a third message that was a little more cryptic.

"Listn 2 rng."

Zach thought it odd that Jill hadn't mentioned this one. But then he noticed that the message had never been sent.

Zach dialed Ragsdale's extension. "Can you meet me in Hightower's office?"

"Sure. Give me five."

Zach turned to his PC and quickly booked a flight that night to Chattanooga and a rental car for the three-hour drive to Oakdale. Ragsdale was just walking up to Hightower's office when Zach got there. The door was half open, and the older man waved them in.

"What can I do for you?" Hightower asked, looking up from the papers on his desk.

"Jeff is dead," Zach said flatly.

Hightower sat up, put his pen down and sighed deeply. Before he could speak, Ragsdale jumped in. "Well, shit. I'm not surprised, I guess. How did it happen?"

"Doctors are saying drug overdose."

"Do you buy that?" Ragsdale asked.

"Do you?" Zach replied, looking back and forth at Hightower and Ragsdale.

"Jeff was a solid young man," Hightower said softly. "Perhaps he had some lapses in judgment, but a solid young man. Most unfortunate.

I assume you will be heading home for the funeral?"

"Yes, I leave tonight."

"Please give the family our best. We will send flowers, of course, and likely someone from the organization will be at the funeral to pay our respects."

As Zach and Ragsdale made their way back into the hallway, Zach asked, "Have you ever heard of 'Alpha Electronics'?"

"Sure, the company that made the gizmo you got at the focus group?"

"Yep. But I met Jeff's test subject, the girl who called us. Jeff gave her a travel alarm clock as a gift. Guess what company makes it?"

"Could be a coincidence."

"Do you think it is?"

"Nope. I'll have one of my guys start doing some research. Do you think Jill will be at the funeral?"

"Most likely, yes."

"It would be great to meet her in person, ask her some questions about how the drug is impacting her."

"I think she would be willing to do that. Jeff sent her to you, so I think she will trust you."

"That's great. And one other thing."

"Yes?"

"It looks like the amount you ingested should be metabolized by the body eventually, but it could take a few months. Remember, the drug just makes you susceptible to communications while you are sleeping. But there still has to be a communication device. Just stay away from any electronics that were bought in the past nine months or so. Just in case."

ELEVEN

A FEW MINUTES LATER, ZACH WAS in the elevator. With a quick nod to the security desk, he passed through the doors and headed to the parking deck. He wondered if Jill was trying to contact him, so he took extra care to look for signs from her. He made conversation with two random homeless guys. That cost him ten bucks. He stopped to intently study something a kid had scribbled in sidewalk chalk. This made a nine-year-old little girl very happy, and her mother a little nervous. He even studied the flyer left on his windshield in the parking garage. But it was, unfortunately, really just a "2 for 1" pizza coupon.

He slid into the car's front seat and turned the key. He found himself holding his breath as he did so. Perhaps he had watched too many movies. But it seemed like sometimes big conspiracies often involved people getting killed in dramatic ways. What's more dramatic than a car bomb?

The key turned, and no explosion was forthcoming. So he left the parking deck and headed home. He turned the bits of fact and conjecture over in his mind, playing with a mental puzzle as he drove home on auto pilot. After 15 minutes of unconscious packing, and 30 minutes of more unconscious driving, he found himself at the airport awaiting his flight.

After enduring the normal indignities of the security line, Zach made his way to the gate. Realizing that he had not charged his phone all day, and that he was the proud owner of only one battery bar, he scouted for a seat near an electrical plug-in. He found his perch, sitting on the floor leaning against a vending machine. Somehow his phone charger found its way into the outlet that originally supported the vending machine. Zach's sudden electrical wealth, while perhaps felonious, was also fortuitous. Because at that moment his phone rang.

Zach bent low to keep the phone to his face while the impossibly short power cord remained attached.

"Hello?"

"Hey, it's Ragsdale. Can you talk?"

"Sure," he grunted a little as he shifted to the classic grade school "Indian style" position so he could lean low to his left and make sure the cord stayed connected.

"Are you taking a shit?"

"No, I'm in the airport, not the most comfortable seat in the building. But I gotta have the juice. What's up?"

"We've been doing some research on Alpha Electronics. It turns out they just came on the scene about six months ago. They make a bunch of different kinds of electronic components. Cheap stuff, mostly. Parts for ordinary things—clocks, radios, TV's, microwaves. Hard as hell to tell who owns them. They're a subsidiary of a sub-sidiary of a division of a closely held whatever. We're still trying to figure it out."

"So, how much stuff are they making? Who's using their parts?"

"It was tough to tell at first. But I had one of our guys in China get ahold of some shipping manifests."

"We have guys in China?"

"People have to sleep in China, too. Focus, Zach."

"Ok. So what did they find?"

"It seemed like a pretty eclectic list to our China guy: alarm clocks with large displays, travel alarm clocks, intravenous pumps, high end cell phones, baby monitors, heated blankets."

"But China guy doesn't know what we know. This list makes perfect sense."

"Yep. These are all things you have nearby when you sleep. Shipments started out pretty slow, just a few months ago. But people on the ground say truck and rail traffic has really shot up in the past few weeks. All four factories are running night and day."

"Is there any way to stop the shipments?"

"There are just too many, and we don't know yet where they are going. Besides, we can't just go blowing up trucks and derailing trains. Anyway, I wouldn't count on being able to stop all this stuff."

"OK. What about the other part? The transmitter chip can't cause any harm unless people take the drug, right?"

"We're on that too. There are just so many ways the drug can be distributed. But municipal water supplies are probably the best bet. We made a list of all the cities where sleep patterns look odd, and I have guys sending me samples to test. I should have something in a couple of days."

"Keep me posted. We may not have a couple of days."

"Got it. And get some sleep. You sound like shit."

When the gate agent announced that boarding was about to begin, Zach still had only two bars of battery, probably not enough for the flight. So he maintained his Indian-style seat on the carpet a bit longer while the weary line of travelers shuffled down the jet way. He tried not to think about what kind of vile bacteria might be living in the carpet where he was sitting. This airport gate had been open around fifteen years, ten flights a day, two hundred and fifty people per flight. That meant over ten million people had stood or sat in this gate area, twenty million shoes fresh from the bathroom, sticky with spilled soda, cursed with gum, or, heaven forbid, socks or bare feet that escaped their shoes for a moment of comfort on this spot. Nasty.

Fortunately, the cell phone screen flashed "Fully Charged" before Zach started estimating bacterial concentrations. He gathered his things, shuffled into line with the other good sheep, and took his seat.

As the plane climbed to cruising altitude, he donned his noise-cancelling headphones and pointed his ipod towards something soft. In just a moment, he was drifting off for a little in-flight nap.

Zach had the sensation of a free-falling leap. Partial bits of nonsensical reality drifted in and out of his mind as his brain settled into the work of doing nothing.

But just as the warm, numb darkness enveloped his consciousness, Zach stopped falling. His mind began to race. Numbers and equations streamed in rapid succession. There were puzzles to solve, things to count, computations to make. It was like the math section of the hardest standardized test he had ever taken. But he could not stop. He could not look away.

He could not wake up.

"Sir, Sir! You need to turn off your ipod. We are preparing to land. Didn't you hear the captain's announcement?"

"I'm sorry. I was sleeping." Zach had never been so happy to be awakened from a nap.

"Don't feel too bad, man. She just gave me a little smackdown too." The passenger next to Zach laughed a little and pointed to his MP3 player. It was a model he didn't recognize.

"Pretty cool looking MP3 player. Is it new?" Zach asked.

"Yeah, I won it at a tradeshow in Vegas. One of those drop your card in a fish bowl drawings."

"Really, what kind of show?"

"Cybersecurity. I'm a computer programmer. I specialize in cryptography and such. Pretty surprised to get this. I usually don't win anything. Looks like a pretty nice one, too. It's a Sony."

"At least that's the brand on it. You know how electronics are, it's pretty much all made in China, then some company just slaps their brand on it."

"True." He turned it over and looked at the back side. "Looks like this one is made in China too. Some outfit called Alpha Electronics."

TWELVE

ZACH HAD LEFT THE LAND OF trendy boutiques and nice restaurants. He left the airport via a highway peppered with red lights and WalMarts and Applebees. The highway eventually became a two lane, with stop signs and Dollar Generals and Hardees. He had always been perfectly comfortable moving through these different socioeconomic worlds, taking equal pleasure in a hundred-dollar steak or a sack of Krystals.

The route was familiar, in principle. But every time he returned, something more had changed. The suburbs had pushed a few more miles outward, starter homes had sprouted in soy bean fields. A shiny new BP station gleamed where a chicken farm once delivered plump white meat and unspeakable stink to the countryside. Tiny new trees were planted amidst the new construction, penance for the giant pines and oaks that had given way to progress.

After an hour or so, Zach made the last turn onto a gravel road that led me to the only place on earth that really felt like home. A few minutes later he made a right-hand turn onto a long dirt driveway leading to a modest white Hoover-era A-frame. There was a time when this driveway was surfaced with a thick layer of gravel, but that was when the residents still had the youth and strength to exercise more control over their domain. Now the driveway was two strips of dirt only occasionally punctuated with gravel, fighting a losing battle against the encroaching fescue and clover. The once-tidy rail fence that lined the road had been overtaken by a thick mat of honeysuckle and less benevolent weeds. The grass was high, except for a small swath nearest the house.

Their little rural empire was shrinking as they had to yield more and more territory to the relentless march of age and weakness. At one time, their empire stretched around the world, and then it shrank to church and grocery store, now to mailbox. In time, the frontier would be living room, or the kitchen. They used to joke about being exiled to the Oak Grove Center, a nursing home on the eastern edge of town. But those jokes stopped a few years ago. Soon their wayward grandson would have to make arrangements, but they would never admit that.

He reached up to knock on the front door, but it opened before the first blow landed. His grandmother had been waiting by the window, of course. A fact that immediately made Zach feel infinitely loved and exquisitely sad. Perhaps she could no longer command a lawnmower, but her capacity to hug was undiminished. It is rare that a grown man, especially one like himself with no real friends or family, is the recipient of such a deep squeeze-as-hard-as-you-can hug. It felt great.

"It's so good to see you, Zachary."

"Hey, Grandma. It's good to be home." He looked over her shoulder to his grandfather seated in his chair.

"Lord's sake, Ellen, let the boy go before you squeeze him to death."

The old man's hands fidgeted on the armrests of his chair as he tried to get up, but his health was such that the trip across the living room floor was not a maneuver he could execute quickly. So Zach quickly spanned the gap of the living room floor and brought the hug to the chair.

The older man's arms, thinner than Zach remembered, shook a little as he reached up, "I love you, Son."

"You too, Grandpa."

"Your grandmother has been in the kitchen all afternoon. You had better go see what she's up to." The kitchen was not so much a separate room as it was a place just past his chair where the carpet turned into linoleum and the walls turned from wood paneling to garish floral wallpaper. He stepped across that line and drank in the sights and smells of a southern kitchen running at full capacity. Steam came from multiple pots of vegetables boiling with bacon. The oven leaked out hints of simmering pot roast (top rack) and homemade biscuits (bottom rack), and a skillet crackled and popped with fried chicken.

Some of this, of course, was for Zach. But he knew that most of this food would find its way to Jeff's family after the funeral today. Of course, the whole event would be catered, but Zach's grandmother firmly believed that homemade food was far more comforting than "store bought."

"Now, get you a piece of chicken and a biscuit, you've got to be hungry. I need to start boxing up the rest of this stuff to take with us to the church."

Addressing grief with food was a time-honored southern tradition. And as the church sanctuary filled with mourners, the fellowship hall would fill with covered dishes. There was no way to avoid tears, but hunger is something imminently preventable.

Zach grabbed a plate from the cabinet where they had always been and began loading it with a little bit of everything. Thankfully, cooking acumen is not impacted by age. The dishes smelled every bit as delicious as they did twenty years ago. He grabbed a hot biscuit, fresh from the oven and still sitting on its pan. His grandmother gave a disapproving frown that said, "You're going to burn your fingers." But she didn't say it, because she didn't have to. It had been said many times before, with little effect. Sometimes hunger can't wait for proper utensils. Besides, it was a compliment. A biscuit good enough to burn your hand over is a pretty good biscuit. He split it open with a fork, then used the same fork to lower a thick glob of his grandmother's homemade apple jelly into the steamy fluffy center. With the chicken and the biscuits and the beans cooked in bacon, this was more fat than Zach normally consumed in an entire day. But he didn't know how many more meals like this would come out of those loving arthritic hands and the cozy little kitchen. So he dug in and savored every bite.

For a few moments he allowed himself to forget about secret organizations and murdered friends and conspiracies to enslave the un-conscious minds of millions. And he simply enjoyed his jelly biscuit.

Zach's grandfather wasn't saying much, but he never did. It was a contented silence. The TV was on, but no one was watching it. The old man was watching Zach eat. Sometimes you reach a point where interaction just takes too much strength, and you can be happy to just sit and look at someone you love.

Zach had met people at college and at work who would go home on holidays to large houses teeming with brothers and sisters and cousins and nieces and nephews. He wondered what it would be like to have a world that large, to feel that much love. But he never resented the fact that it was just him and his grandparents. Zach had his dad for a few years at least, and all those days of deep conversations and big laughs and big hugs felt much closer than they were.

In a few minutes, Zach's grandmother finished her last batch of chicken and came to sit across from him at the kitchen table. In the brighter light, for the first time, he really saw her face. She looked awful. Deep, dark circles beneath her bright eyes. Her hands trembled a little. He knew what was wrong, but he asked anyway.

"Are you feeling okay, gramma?"

"No, I'm not. Your grandfather and I haven't slept well in weeks. We fall asleep, but we have the most terrible dreams. Our minds race all through the night. We toss and turn... The doctor gave us sleeping pills, but that just seems to make it worse. I feel like I might be going a little bit crazy." She gave a half-hearted laugh, and he sensed she might think it was actually true.

"Didn't you say you got a new alarm clock recently?"

"Yes. The lightning fried our old one."

"Can I see it?"

"Zachary, why would you want to look at an alarm clock? It's just a regular old clock from WalMart."

"I'm just curious. My new company is doing some work with another company that makes alarm clocks."

"One of these days you are going to have to sit down and explain to me what you do." She flipped on a hallway light and in about six steps (two for Zach), they were in the master bedroom. It wasn't a large place, and it seemed to have shrunk over the years.

"There it is, on the table right by the side of the bed." Zach noticed the large assortment of medicine bottles on the table as well, certainly more than last time he visited. There was an oxygen tank and a bed pan as well. That was new. Zach's grandmother saw his eyes.

"Your grandfather isn't doing so well, Zach. He's been sick for a long time, and not being able to sleep is about to put him over the edge. He just can't get better."

Zach nodded and looked down. There was a conversation to be had, but that would have to wait.

He picked up the alarm clock and looked at the bottom. Alpha Electronics.

As he started to put it down, he faked a little fumble and dropped it on the floor. It bounced a couple of times. He walked over to it and stepped on the screen with the heal of his shoe. He turned around to see his grandmother standing there, mouth open, incredulous.

"You're going to need a new clock." He wrapped the cord around the cracked mess and carried it out of the room. "I'll pick up another one for you in town."

She walked out behind him, shaking her head.

A few moments later, Zach and his grandparents were making their way slowly out the front door. But as Zach headed towards the rental car, his grandfather redirected them with a quick whistle and a wave towards the garage. Zach's grandfather wanted to take their old sedan and had even gone so far as to ask his grandmother to go outside and warm it up. He was the man of the house, and he saw it as his role to provide transportation. His days behind the wheel had long since passed, but he took great pride in keeping their old ride clean and in excellent mechanical condition—even if it was now someone else's hands on the steering wheel and the wrench.

Zach's grandmother was in the back seat, impeccable posture making her visible in the rear-view mirror. His grandfather was in the passenger seat, his suit hanging loosely from his arms and legs. It had fit just right when it was purchased, but that was ten years and thirty pounds ago. The old man motioned towards the car radio with a gnarled hand. "Son, why don't you turn on The Buck?"

Zach turned the radio on, knew he didn't even have to use the tuning knob. The radio in the old sedan had been tuned to AM 670 WBCK Country—aka "The Buck"—since the day it rolled out of the dealer's lot.

The gravel crunched under the tires as they pulled down the driveway and kicked up a little cloud of dust as they made a right onto the two-lane road and headed north towards town. A few minutes later they were passing through the town square, home to a collection of clothing stores, restaurants, antique shops, and more than a few vacant storefronts. Most of these were family owned businesses, unaffiliated and unfranchised, save for the Little Caesars Pizza that had set up shop where Luke's Pharmacy had dispensed heart pills and BC Powder for 90 years or so.

The radio station was playing a song Zach didn't recognize, something slow, with twangy guitar and a mournful tenor singing a twangy lead. They passed through the town square and continued north. A half mile later, the Oak Grove Nursing Home appeared on the righthand side of the road. All three of them saw it. All three of them had the same awful thought. All three of them kept silent.

The mournful song on the radio was still playing and didn't help the mood one bit. Of course, changing the channel was out of the question. Zach pressed the gas and coaxed another ten mph out of the old sedan's engine. Fortunately, some kind of interference interrupted the radio signal for a moment, and the brief crackle of static gave everyone something else to focus on. Zach reached down quickly and turned the radio off.

"Hard to get a decent AM signal anymore, all these damn phone towers and such I guess," Zach's grandfather said as he looked to the driver side. It wasn't so much an angry outburst as it was a calm observation that happened to include an expletive.

"I'd rather listen to the engine of this old Ford purr anyway," Zach replied with a smile.

THIRTEEN

THE FIRST BAPTIST CHURCH OF OAKDALE was a smart red brick structure with white doors and a short white steeple. It was nice enough to host a middle-class wedding, but not so opulent as to make people stop contributing to the building fund. "First B," as it was known, was a kind of social Switzerland in Oakdale, where people of all backgrounds could worship and gossip as equals. A fellowship hall had been added a few decades ago; it was attached to the right side of the sanctuary right at the back of the building. The building and grounds were well maintained and manicured, right down to the fresh flowers dotting the tombstones of the cemetery out back.

Walking inside for Zach was like putting on an old pair of jeans—entirely familiar, nostalgic, if a little bit more confining than he remembered. Zach's grandmother was at his grandfather's arm as they shuffled down to their customary pew—fourth from front on the right, inside aisle. As for Zach, he was intercepted at the door by a gaggle of elderly ladies who knew him from pictures in his grandmother's living room, or a long-passed Vacation Bible School or little league game. He didn't recall many names, but the faces all looked comfortably familiar. There was a series of hugs. Old men with firm handshakes left the scent of Old Spice in his palm, and one octogenarian Zach was pretty sure had snuff squirrelled between cheek and gum.

Eventually he made it to his seat, slipped past his grandfather's folded walker and his grandmother's black skirt and sat down. She patted his knee and whispered, "I'm so glad you are here." Zach again felt both happy and a little guilty. When the greatest gift someone wants is just a bit of your time, it feels profoundly selfish to withhold it.

They were early, of course. Zach's grandparents had always been punctual, but the uneventfulness of old age had compounded this tendency. A simple trip to the post office might involve significant forethought and arrival ten minutes before opening "to avoid the lines." But for an event as momentous as a funeral, they were at a whole new level of early. They had arrived at least an hour before the service was scheduled to begin so as to capture the maximum amount of human interaction his grandfather's health would allow.

Zach took his time staring around the building. The walnut podium was the only carry over from the original 1892 building. There was a stained-glass window in the shape of a cross over the choir seat and double doors to the right of the altar that led to the fellowship hall. Ordinarily he would have dreaded sitting still and waiting for an hour, but in this case, he was glad to have a little time to process.

Just as he entered a level two reverie, he felt something brush against his neck. He assumed it was a fly and swatted accordingly. But then he felt another, this time leaving behind just a hint of moisture. Zach's mind scanned its index of sensations and came up with a hit—junior high.

He turned around and looked at the wall behind him and to the right. That wall separated the sanctuary from the fellowship hall, and over the fellowship hall was a crawl space above a suspended ceiling. On that wall was a grid covering an air intake vent. And behind that grid cover was Jill. He couldn't exactly see her, but the spit ball on the back of his neck hadn't gotten there by accident. Zach had fired a few rounds from that particular vantage point over the years as well.

Zach excused himself and slipped out the double doors into the fellowship hall. In the far left corner, Jeff's family was huddled around an open casket with a minister, saying their final goodbyes. They were a well-dressed group, women in designer dresses and men in suits cut to make them look as trim as possible. Silver and gold and pearls sparkled as they played peekaboo from beneath cuffs and necklines and curled hair. Women held damp Kleenex to their teary eyes, men stood with hands on hips, little kids pulled at their mother's hands, shirt tails partially untucked, pleading for a chance to run. The group was too preoccupied to notice Zach walking past on the other side of the room. Just as well. He really didn't want to do the whole teary sad reunion thing just yet.

The fellowship hall was a large room, full of folding tables and metal folding chairs. On the wall to his left, backing up the sanctuary, was a small stage raised maybe twelve inches off the floor. On the wall to his right was a modest commercial kitchen, large steel sinks, a refrigerator, and cooktop separated from the main room by a waist-high counter. To the right of this kitchen were three doors—women's bath, men's bath, and storage closet. The door in the middle was his destination. The door swung closed behind Zach, and he proceeded to the third stall and hung his suit jacket on the door hook.

The next maneuver was easier executed by a teenager in tennis shoes, but he figured he could still pull it off. One foot on the seat, the other on the top of the tank. He lifted a ceiling tile and moved it to the left. Then he stepped up so that one foot was on each wall of the stall. Groin muscles complained, but ultimately complied. Reaching into the darkness where the ceiling tile previously was, he grabbed a section of nylon rope with a large knot on the end. The other end (he hoped) was still attached to a roof girder high above. He pulled himself up into the void.

A normal suspended ceiling, of course, wouldn't support the weight of a teenager, much less a full-grown adult. But it just so happened that steel ceiling joists ran every 16 feet or so, one right over the men's bath, one over the women's, one over the storage closet. This formed a sort of mischief highway back in the day. Cigarettes and beers were distributed and consumed in this space during long sermons, unauthorized trysts occurred amongst the darkened rafters, and rumor had it that at least one local sheriff's deputy was conceived in the storage room during revival meetings in 1976.

Using the meager light from his phone screen, he navigated a few feet down, then stepped to a perpendicular joist and headed for the dim light peaking in around the ductwork ahead. The intake duct had been bent a little by some long ago juvenile miscreant, and there was a tiny gap—maybe an inch wide, for about four inches of the duct's edge. Just enough room to project a well-aimed spitball, and just enough light to make out the dark shape of Jill holding a straw and smiling like a mischievous 14-year-old. From a few feet away, in the dim light, she looked every bit as beautiful as she ever had. As he got closer, and the light from his cell phone screen hit her face, the impact of extreme sleep deprivation became apparent once again. Her eyes were swollen and surrounded by dark circles. He noticed her hands trembling a little as she fumbled with the straw.

"Still not sleeping?"

"No. I got rid of the alarm clock, of just about everything in my apartment that plugs into an outlet. I can't figure it out."

"Maybe they hid something in the apartment." A few days ago, he wouldn't have said that, for fear of freaking her out. But he could see she was past that now.

"That's the same thing I thought. But I'm not having the same dreams as before. No tests, no thinking. I'm just super sensitive to everything. It is as if everything in my surroundings is amplified when I am asleep. I'll have vivid dreams about flies buzzing loudly, a person's footsteps sound like thunder claps. My ice maker dumped a fresh batch and I literally woke up screaming because I thought there was an earthquake. It just can't get dark enough or quiet enough. It has been weeks since I slept. I feel like I am losing my mind..."

She looked at Zach, those beautiful tired eyes full of something halfway between resignation and terror.

"Hold on a little while longer, Jill. I have someone working on it." He thought about Ragsdale and his team in their lab trying to figure out a cure, and then he thought about the prospect of thousands, maybe millions of people going through what Jill was going through right now. "I'm working on it. We're going to figure something out."

"If anyone can, you can, Zach." He was surprised and flattered, and it must have showed in his face. "Come on. You know you were always Superman in our little group. You were always smarter, three steps ahead of everyone else. Everyone knew you were going to do great things. Jeff had a trust fund, I had a passport, and you had a gift."

Zach didn't know what to say. Some things did come easier for him. He just saw things, understood things, grasped things. But that didn't necessarily mean he was going to be able to fix this. As much for his comfort as hers, he put his arm around her shoulders and gave her a hug. She leaned her head onto his shoulder and he could feel her trembling. Ragsdale had mentioned severe sleep deprivation can cause tremors.

Then, Zach felt her rub her nose across his shoulder. "Did you just wipe your snotty nose on my fancy funeral suit?"

"Maybe. But you won't know for sure until you're in the light, and I'll have lots of time to make my getaway. "

"What? You're not coming down into the sanctuary for the service?"

"No. I can't. They're tracking me. I can tell I'm being followed.

I've noticed things out of place in my apartment. They are tracking me. I snuck in here last night. I'm afraid to come out."

Mental delusion, even paranoia could be brought on by extreme lack of sleep. But Zach suspected her fears were valid. "Do you think you are in danger?"

"Yes. Neither of us think Jeff's death was an accident, right? So Jeff was probably killed because of what he knew. And Jeff and I were very close. As far as they know, he told me everything. The only way to close the loop is to kill me."

Zach held her for a moment, hoping she had not yet realized the fact he had known for a while. Let her cry for Jeff, cry for herself. He held her as she sobbed. But after a few moments, she stopped abruptly and looked up at him.

"Zach, I'm so sorry!"

"It's ok, I can get the jacket cleaned, really."

The joke did not deter her. "I did not think. I never meant to put you in danger."

"It's ok. I can take care of myself." He paused for a moment. "I might even be able to take care of you."

He hoped it was true. She put her head on his chest again and he held her close, noting both the fear and the comfort that gesture provided.

He quickly found a problem to push those feelings from his mind. "I found Jeff's phone in the office," Zach said.

Jill released him, which brought him both relief and remorse. "Really? Anything interesting?"

"I saw his messages to you. They were the last thing he sent. The last line didn't make any sense, though. 'Listn 2 rng.'"

"Yeah. I've been thinking about that too."

They were both quiet for a moment.

"Wait!" Jill said and smacked Zach on the chest. "I know what he was talking about. He had this ring, he wore it all the time. But it had a tiny digital voice recorder built into it. It was ridiculously expensive and pretty geeky, so it was totally Jeff's style." She laughed a little as she blew her nose. "He would use it all the time to record little notes to himself. He probably thought he was impressing me."

"What did it look like?"

"Big. It was made to look like a class ring or something. It had some kind of engraving in Latin on it. He said it was very special to him."

"I wonder what happened to it?"

They both turned and looked through the metal screen towards the pulpit and thought the same horrible thing. The ring probably would not have been taken by the folks who killed him. His death was supposedly a suicide; a stolen ring wouldn't fit with the story. So it was probably sent to the morgue with the body. Which meant it was either in personal effects kept by his family, or he was going to be buried with it.

Zach looked back at Jill's face in the sliver of filtered light. "I'm going to need a pretty big diversion."

A few minutes later, he was climbing down from his ceiling hideout, desperately (and successfully) avoiding stepping into the toilet upon dismount. He put his suit jacket back on, checked the bathroom mirror to remove a few stray cobwebs from his hair, and headed out into the fellowship hall.

The family was still there, clustered around the casket. One of the funeral home workers stood back at a respectful distance. He was a young guy, a helper. Nicely dressed, good posture, looking perpetually sympathetic but probably wishing he could sit down or at least check the text messages that were making his phone buzz in his pocket. Zach slipped up beside him quietly. His name tag said "Barton," but it wasn't clear if that was a first or last name.

"This must be the worst part of the job," Zach offered.

"Not too bad. Mr. Smith handles all the hard parts. My job is to carry things, show people where to go, and pretty much keep quiet."

"And then close the casket?"

"Yes, I'm pretty much the last one to see the guy. I close the lid, lock it, and that's that."

"Do you have to stand here and watch the whole time?"

"Always. Usually there isn't a problem. But sometimes folks just have a hard time letting go, or someone wants something buried with the deceased or something."

"Well, let's hope we don't have any drama today."

"Yes, sir."

Zach gave Barton a little nod and then walked over to the family. Jeff's mother was the first to see him. She was tall and elegant and sophisticated. Her jet black hair was liberally sprinkled with gray, but her features were still sharp and just barely wrinkled. She was decked in her finest black dress and understated but unmistakably expensive pearl necklace and earrings. She looked like Senior Barbie, assuming

Ken had made a fortune in real estate.

"Oh Zach, we are so glad you came."

She hugged him with the delicateness of a woman who rarely hugged. More of a pat, really. "It would have meant so much to Jeff to know you came." Her eyes were red and swollen. She was trying to maintain the composure she was famous for, but it was clear she was taking this hard. Jeff was the pride of a very proud family, heir to the throne and her personal mission in life.

"I always thought he would come back here, run the business, we would grow old watching him become the man we always knew he could be. It wasn't supposed to be like this." She dissolved in the deep, heaving tears of a grieving mother. He stepped aside and left her to the embrace of a cousin or sister or tennis partner or something. One of the senior VP's of the family business was next to Zach, dry-eyed but sporting a sufficiently sad expression. He hadn't known Jeff well enough to be truly grieved, but he was here to support the family. Zach figured it was safe to ask him a few whispered questions.

"When is the last time you heard from Jeff?"

"A few months ago, he called to recommend a new supplier to us, a friend of a friend kind of thing. But he pretty much never came around."

"I know that was tough on his parents. They always assumed he would come back to run the family business."

"Yeah. They got all excited when he called to talk shop. But then it turned out he was just making an introduction for a friend. We wound up using the new supplier, though, so it wasn't a total loss. Saved us a lot of money."

"Well, it sounds like he had found a pretty good job. I suppose he was happy," Zach offered.

"He couldn't have been too happy, based on what happened." Barton immediately looked at the ground, realizing his comment was obviously in bad taste. He had no idea how bad.

Jeff's mother put a hand on Zach's arm and saved her employee from an awkward apology. "You only have a few minutes. You should say goodbye to Jeff." She looped her arm in Zach's and led him to the casket.

Jeff was in a very sharp black suit with a crisp white pocket square. He looked like hell. It probably wasn't the undertaker's fault. He did what he could with makeup and gel and whatever tools were available to his gruesome trade. But Zach always thought that open caskets weren't a good idea for people who died young. The rule of thumb should be, if you looked better dead than alive, open the box. Otherwise, just keep the lid closed and set a nice picture on top. White cuffs and silver cuff links were visible as his hands were folded neatly on his stomach. And there, on his right ring finger, was a large platinum ring.

After a few moments, the undertaker came and put a cold hand on Jeff's mother's shoulder and began to usher the family into the sanctuary for the service. He lingered as they walked out, occasionally touching a shoulder, nodding and whispering words that meant nothing. When the last family member exited and the door to the sanctuary closed, Barton approached the casket to seal it.

At that moment, the door in the back of the room opened. It was an exit to the outside, sunlight shown in and cast a bright light onto the casket. Jill stepped into the doorway, hair in a mess, makeup running, and, oddly enough, missing a shoe.

"Where is that sneaky bastard?" She spoke loud enough to get Barton's attention, but not so loud that she could be heard in the sanctuary. Barton turned to look at her, his face somewhere between a cringe and a grimace.

"Ma'am, can I help you?"

"Yeah, you can get the hell away from that casket and let me see my man one more time."

"Excuse me, are you part of the family?"

She started walking towards him. "If boning every Tuesday and Friday night for four years makes you family, then I suppose I am. Not that any of those proper little bitches in the other room would say so." Jill was using a little extra redneck twang, for effect.

Barton positioned himself in front of Zach, between Jill and the casket, his arms extended low by his waist, palms facing Jill. "Now, ma'am, let's try to calm down for just a minute. You knew the deceased?"

"Hell, yes, I knew him. I knew him in the seat of his old truck, and in his daddy's barn, and in his place of business. Now open up that lid and let me say goodbye to my man."

She made a bumbling, drunken rush towards the casket. Barton caught her in an awkward bear hug. She winked at Zach over the undertaker's shoulder. Zach had to look away to avoid laughing.

"Ma'am, if you'll be quiet, I will open the casket for a moment and let you pay your respects."

She reached her arm over his shoulder, towards the casket, and cried, "I can't be quiet, I just want to see my Darrell!"

"Your who?" Barton let her go and stepped over to the casket.

"My sweet baby Darrell." She pointed towards the casket again, but with just a bit of hesitation.

"Ma'am, the decedent's name is a Mr. Jeff Wallace." Barton inserted his key and opened the lid to reveal Jeff.

Jill put her hands over her face and tears burst from her eyes, "Oh God." This was the first time she had seen him. The tears were real. Even Jill was not that good of an actress. She hesitated for a moment, tears running down her face, frozen as if she had forgotten a line. But then she fell back into character. "What have you done with Darrell?" she exclaimed in a quivering whispered exclamation. And then she fainted into Barton's arms. He held her awkwardly, supporting her under her arms, and looked over his shoulder at Zach.

"You deal with that, and I'll close back up over here," Zach offered. Barton nodded. He carried Jill towards one of the folding chairs lining the tables at the back of the room.

Someone with even minimal medical training, or just common sense, would have noticed that she was sobbing gently. And since people don't cry when they are unconscious, she could not possibly have fainted. But Barton had no such training. The illusion was as complete as it needed to be.

As soon as Barton's back was turned, Zach reached into the casket and pulled the ring from Jeff's finger. He hadn't given much thought to how it might feel to touch the hands of a dead man. It was not pleasant. Zach put the ring in his pocket and closed the lid. He heard the latch click into place. Barton turned and looked in his direction; the sound of the lid closing had reminded him of his primary job. But Zach gave him a thumbs up, and Barton gave Zach the 'Thanks, man' nod. Zach slipped through the door into the sanctuary.

He took his seat next to his grandmother. His grandfather raised an eyebrow and tapped the face of his watch with a bony finger. Zach put his hand on his stomach and grimaced a little, which is the best way to say "I've got the squirts" without speaking. A moment later his grandmother was digging a roll of Tums from her purse and putting two in his hand.

The service began with a hymn, then a slideshow of pictures. The pastor delivered a sermon that seemed impossibly long. A couple of friends delivered short eulogies. Ordinarily, Zach would have paid rapt attention, grieving his friend, celebrating his life, and soaking in the life lessons that invariably flowed at events like this. But all he could think about was taking a look at the ring and figuring out what its secret was. This was taking forever.

He glanced over his shoulder at the air intake and wondered if Jill had returned to her perch. He could imagine her up there, quietly crying. It was pointless to count the ceiling tiles; he had memorized that number years ago. This was scheduled to be a one-hour service, but based on the current progress it would probably run about ten minutes late. Based on where he was sitting, once the service ended, he would probably encounter seven people on his way to the exit, and at least four would likely want to say hello. Three minutes per, plus an extra minute to get from the exit to the car. So, 73 minutes from the start of the service to when he could be alone with this ring. They were 51 minutes in, so 86% complete. He could handle that.

Twenty-six minutes later—his estimate was not perfect—Zach slid into the hot vinyl seats of his grandparents' old sedan. He put Jeff's ring in the cup holder, cranked the engine, and turned the air conditioning to high.

"I'd like to thank the Academy…" A voice came from the back seat.

"What the hell?" Zach jumped a little and turned his head toward the back seat so quickly it caused a twinge in his neck. It was Jill. "How did you get in here?"

"A girl never picks and tells." She held up some kind of metal device he could only assume was an apparatus used in picking locks.

"That was some performance back there."

"Yes, a little community theatre experience goes a long way. Eventually, I let Barton convince me it was not my Darrell in the casket. I took his handkerchief and slipped out." She held his hanky in front of her face like a trophy.

"Did you watch the service?"

"Yes." She did not expound. He did not press.

At that moment, Zach saw three people walking across the parking lot. They were moving left to right, about 20 yards in front of his car. Farthest away from him was Mr. Hightower, looking even more polished than usual in a fine black suit and wingtips that reflected the hot sun like a mirror. Walking next to him was Ms. James, her ivory skin looking a little out of place in the bright sunlight, but otherwise stunning in a tailored black dress with a hemline and neckline that were somewhere between "office" and "night on the town." The rumpled figure closest to the car was the unmistakable Dr. Ragsdale.

He had done his best to dress up for the occasion, but somehow still looked like he had slept in his suit all night.

Hightower was there to represent the company, Ragsdale was crashing the event to talk to Jill. But Zach was a little surprised to see Ms. James had made the trip, given her desire to downplay the workplace relationship.

A hand reached palm up from the back seat, over his shoulder. "Let's see what's on that ring, if you're done staring at Legs over there."

"I wasn't staring. It's just—I work with them. Jeff worked with them."

Jill looked at the three again, probably at just one in particular, and paid a little more attention this time. "That must be her, then."

"Her who?"

"The city me. Jeff's work crush. Looks like his type. Me with less personality and better nails."

Zach picked the ring up from the cup holder. But then he heard a sharp knock on the passenger side window.

"It's rude to stare at people in the parking lot," Zach heard through the glass. He could see a hand on the door handle, cheap plastic digital watch peeking out from beneath the cuffs of a wrinkled suit coat.

"Who the hell is that?" Jill said, as she quickly ducked back into the floorboard.

"Ragsdale, the research guy Jeff told you about."

"Does he know about me?"

"Yes. He and I opened your package together. He knows Jeff was seeing a woman, and that Jeff used a new technology to try and influence that woman. And he knows the exact pH level of your pee."

Her mouth was opening to raise another question, but Ragsdale opened the door and slid into the seat. He spoke over his shoulder in the general direction of the form hiding in the back seat. "Hello, Jill. I'm sorry for your loss."

Jill moved from the floorboard to the seat and leaned forward. "Well, so much for secrecy."

"Doc, we were just about to see what this ring could tell us." Zach handed it over his shoulder towards Jill. "Do you know how to make this talk?"

"What's that?" Ragsdale asked.

"Jeff's ring," he replied.

"Where did you get it?"

"From Jeff."

"He gave it to you before he died?"

"No, he sort of gave it to us afterward."

"How much afterward?"

"Afterward enough."

"Well, it's hideously ugly for a man who supposedly prided himself on style," Ragsdale observed as he held it close to his right eye and closed his left.

"You're right," Zach agreed. "It does look a bit like something a used car salesman might wear on his non-bowling hand."

Jill interrupted. "Just give me the damn ugly ring." She snatched it from his hand and held it for a moment.

She closed her eyes for a second, took a deep breath, brushed a strand of brown hair away from her baggy, tired eyes. Then, she pushed down on one of the diamonds on the side of the ring. There was a brief pause, then they heard Jeff's voice. It was low and soft, more of a whisper.

"Zach, if you are hearing this, then I am dead. And I need you to know why." He paused, cleared his throat softly, and continued.

"If my company is following the succession plan, I had on file, you should be getting a call from them very soon. If not, then call this number: 555-471-7855 and ask for Ragsdale. Tell him Jeff sent you."

Zach glanced at Ragsdale. The doc shrugged.

"I have been working for a very important, very secret organization. We developed a compound that could influence people's dreams. It is relatively harmless. But I was approached by a man from some kind of other secret organization. They developed a way to guide people's dreams and harness the power of the subconscious for computation. You have heard that humans only use 20% of their mental capacity? Well, it turns out you can get to the whole thing once the conscious mind shuts down for the night.

"This thing would have changed everything. Since the beginning of history, every effort of mankind has been subjected to the same constraint—time. There are only so many hours in the day. But with this new system, people could actually work and sleep at the same time. Imagine what mankind could accomplish with the constraint removed. People could sleep more, and work more. Everyone wins." You could hear the excitement in his voice.

"I was going to change the world," Jeff's voice trailed off, he must have heard how empty those words seemed now. There was a pause, the rustling sound of a hand wiping across a few days of stubble. Then, he continued.

"This other organization proposed a small pilot. The system requires three components. The first is a drug. It makes people extra sensitive to outside stimuli while they are asleep. So if you are asleep and a sound is in your room, that sound shows up in your dream. It was supposed to be harmless, wear off in a couple of days. Ragsdale developed it, but I'm afraid this other organization may have made some modifications.

"The second part of the system is a kind of transmitter, a means for delivering a message to people while they sleep. They had developed a very simple component that could be embedded in the power supply of virtually any electronic device.

"Jill, that is what was in the alarm clock I gave you. One of those transmitters. And the supplier I referred to your dad—that firm made the transmitters. They were supposed to be putting them into a small number of devices for the trial.

"But something went wrong. We ran the trial program in our hometown. There was a large facility, hundreds of people. It was secret but supposed to be completely safe. Then, when the results came in, I could see that people were getting sick. People weren't sleeping, not really. Accidents were going up, sickness was climbing, and our life expectancy models fell through the floor. We were literally killing people slowly because their bodies were not able to recover every night.

Jeff paused for a moment. The three could hear him clear his throat. When he began again, his voice was softer, even trembling a little.

"This part is for Jill. I love you, Jill. I always have. Always will. I never meant to hurt you. I had no idea this could happen. I just wanted you to love me. I thought that maybe, if I could send you messages in your dreams, you might start to see me differently. I thought it was safe. I really did. Please forgive me."

Then, in the background they could hear the sound of voices, and of a lock being opened. Jeff spoke again.

"Oh God, they're coming. Zach, you have to figure this out. You have to—"

There was a little rustling, and then silence.

Jill clutched the ring in one fist and fell back into the seat, her other hand covering her eyes.

Zach looked at Ragsdale. "Do you think Hightower and Ms. James can spare you for a few hours?"

"Sure. We all have rooms at the hotel in town. I told them you would drop me off later. Figured we would find some trouble to get into."

Zach put the car into gear and started to back out. "Where are we going?" Jill said.

"We need to go visit your daddy's little radio business. Can you get us into the office?" He looked out the back window at septuagenarians shuffling slowly behind the car and fought the urge to honk. Probably would be bad form at a funeral.

"Sure, assuming he hasn't changed the security code. But, Zach?"

"What?"

"Are you just going to leave your grandparents here?"

"Shit." He put the car back into drive and re-entered his parking space. "Stay here." He left the car running and walked back towards the church.

Zach's grandparents were in the back of the church; they had made it about 30 feet since the service ended. There was much catching up to do, apparently. They were talking to some friends from their seniors' Sunday school class.

Zach pulled his shirt tail out a little, attached his best understated grimace, and approached the four of them. He gave the requisite greeting and handshake (for the gentleman) and light hug (for his bride of forty years). Then, he asked his grandmother, "Do you think you could catch a ride home with these folks? My stomach is just not right. I need to head back to the house for a few minutes." Zach hated to lie to his grandmother, and he strongly suspected that, as always, she saw right through him. Her ability to notice and process small details gave her a level of insight others might see as pure sorcery. He looked in her eyes for a moment and tried to decide if she suspected anything. After an awkward few seconds, she looked away and let him off the hook.

"Yes, dear. Our house is on their way. We'll be fine." She put two Tums in his hand. "I hope your stomach feels better."

"Thanks, Grandma." He turned to walk away, and she reached out and touched his arm. She pulled the sleeve of his suit jacked to indicate he should lean towards her.

She whispered in his ear, "And tell Jill I said hello."

FOURTEEN

A MOMENT LATER, ZACH WAS SLIDING back into the car with Jill and Ragsdale, the seat now much cooler after a few minutes with the AC blasting. The radio was playing, still on 870 The Buck.

"Did you guys make friends while I was gone?"

"Considering I spent a fair amount of time looking at her pee, I think we started out with an uncommon level of familiarity."

"Let it go, Old Man," Jill replied.

Zach weaved the old sedan through the slow-moving knots of elderly folk and a few unsupervised minors running through the parking lot. The soft back tires slipped just a little as he punched the gas and pulled into the street.

They headed south and passed Ragsdale's hotel just a few minutes after leaving the church. Ms. James and Mr. Hightower were walking across the parking lot from the car towards the hotel office.

"What are they doing back at the hotel?" he asked Ragsdale. "I figured they would be heading home after the funeral."

"Maybe their flight is later. Don't know. I can't imagine they have any other business in town."

Zach was driving faster than he probably should have, but he figured it was worth the risk. There were about 10 patrol cars in the city. Half of them were working the funeral procession. There were probably two at the station. The other three were patrolling probably 200 miles of roadway, each car covering 100. This trip was 20 miles, so 20% chance of seeing a cop. And, he had his "grieving friend" excuse ready.

He had never used that one before, but he suspected it had a 55% chance of success—somewhere between "late for a flight" and "late for surgery." A one in ten chance at getting a ticket. At 80 mph in a 50, his speeding ticket would probably cost $200. On an expected value basis, this speed was costing him twenty bucks, about what it would cost to watch an action movie at the theatre. Catharsis was about the same.

The nursing home was just ahead, on the left this time, as they approached the town square. The car was moving faster than the music. Zach hit the seek button to find another station, but then the radio crackled loudly, and he just turned it off instead.

"I think the static was better than the music," Ragsdale said sarcastically.

"City folks," Zach said as he looked in the rear view. Jill nodded in agreement.

Ragsdale was pounding Jill with all sorts of questions about the electronics supplier Jeff had referred to them. Jill had no idea, of course, since she was in no way involved with the day-to-day operations of the family business.

"How many units did they ship?"

"I don't know."

"What kind of devices did they put them into?"

"I don't know."

"Did they have their own power supply, or were they supplied by the host device?"

"Seriously, I don't know."

After a few minutes of this, Jill stopped responding, lay down in the back seat, and put her arm over her face. Ragsdale kept asking questions, of course. But he was just thinking aloud, making a mental checklist of questions to answer during the visit to the plant.

They entered the town square and made a right to head west. Driving past the neighborhoods and schools and occasional strip mall, Zach could see the office complex off in the distance. It was a six-story building, small by most standards, but it towered over this little town. A few minutes later, they pulled into the parking lot. The office mini-tower was in the front of the complex, the shiny glass reflecting the afternoon sun. Behind the office building was the real substance of the operation. A row of seven rectangular warehouse buildings, each one the size of a couple of football fields. The long sides of each building were lined with roll-up doors, and about half of these had trailers backed up to the building. As they got closer, Zach could see the trucks were from most of the largest retailers.

Zach glanced over his shoulder to the back seat. Jill was still lying across the seat, arm over her eyes.

"Jill, are you asleep?"

"Are you shitting me, Zach? Of course I'm not asleep. This is as close to rest as I get these days." She spoke with an uncharacteristic edge, and as she sat up, he could see her hands trembling slightly. And she looked like hell. The late afternoon sunlight illuminated wrinkles and dark circles and spots that would have looked right for a woman ten years older. The body just isn't designed to go weeks without sleeping. She closed her eyes for a second, took a deep breath, rubbed her face with her hands, and spoke in a calmer voice, "Let's go inside and see what we can find."

The sun was getting low in the sky, but the parking lot asphalt was still mid-afternoon hot. At the front of the building was a glass entryway, double doors flanked on either side by an assortment of unhealthy looking shrubs and pea gravel. To the right of the door was a magnetic card reader; below that was a keypad.

Ragsdale got to the door first, but found it locked. Jill brushed past him and went to the keypad instead.

"Do you know the combination?"

"Let's hope so. I own the place." She entered a few digits and the magnetic lock clicked open. "If the criminals of Oakdale ever figure out my birthday, daddy is going to be in a world of hurt." She smiled a little, but then saw the reflection of her face in the glass door and quickly looked away. Ragsdale held the door open, and they walked in.

The cool rush of air conditioning was bracing after the heat outside. The lobby ceiling was three stories high, on the left a curved staircase led to a landing and the second floor. On the right was a waist-high counter, home to an empty receptionist station. A few plants and moderately comfortable chairs were stationed across the lobby. Over the receptionist's desk was a framed Certificate of Gratitude from the Oak Grove Nursing Home, complete with pictures of smiling senior citizens in hospital robes.

"My dad always tried to help them out when he could," Jill offered. "The company donated a bunch of equipment to the home just a few weeks ago."

Zach's grandparents had always been very generous as well. But their means were much more limited. His grandma had a shoebox full of thank you notes for meals delivered to sick folks, or a few dollars lent to someone in need. But nothing suitable for framing. "We need to find out more about the new supplier that Jeff referred to you. Where would those records be kept?"

"It's all computerized, so we should be able to access it from anywhere. Let's just go to my dad's office." She pointed up the little atrium to the left. Her dad's office was on the top floor, one wall of glass looked out over the lobby, the other looked out over the parking lot. They walked over to the elevator and pressed the button, but the Out of Order sign directed them to the stairs.

Jill led the way up the first flight of stairs at a normal pace, but by the second flight she was swaying noticeably. As they reached the top of the third flight, her right foot slipped and she fell to that side. She reached for the railing with her right arm to steady herself, but she didn't reach out in time.

She hit her head, just above her right temple, on the cast iron handrail, and fell limp onto the steps. Her head was bleeding profusely, too much to see if the damage was severe. Zach scooped her up in his arms and walked up the last few stairs. He could not help but try and estimate her weight in both pounds and kilograms as he did so.

Jill's father's office was still one more floor up. This level was a warren of cubicles, low walls upholstered in a sensible light gray. Zach lowered Jill gently to the floor, Ragsdale grabbed a lumbar support pillow from one of the cubicles and put it under her head. Zach grabbed a cardigan draped over a nearby chair and tried to wipe away the blood. He was relieved to find the wound wasn't that severe, an inch or so long, just above the hairline. A stitch, maybe two.

Ragsdale jogged around the corner towards a storage room and returned with a pint of sherbet and a tube of super glue.

"No ice, but they had Tropical Delight," Ragsdale bent down and held the cold carton against Jill's head.

"She'll be OK," Ragsdale said with a degree of certainty. "Extreme exhaustion can lead to degradation of motor skills, among other things."

The cold carton against her head returned Jill quickly to lucidity. "Shit! That's cold. What the hell?"

"You fell, hit your head," John said, still holding the carton against her head.

"Am I bleeding?"

"Yes, you might need a stitch or two," Ragsdale said calmly as he moved the sherbet aside to get a look at the wound.

"I swear I can hardly walk these days. It's been getting worse and worse." She held up her right arm to display a series of bruises. "I got these beauties literally falling out of a taxi yesterday. It's almost like being drunk. I just can't make my hands and feet do what I want them to do."

"And it will only get worse," Ragsdale said flatly. "Now hold still." Ragsdale squeezed a big glob of the super glue right onto the open wound. Jill screamed as the sting erupted across her scalp. She swatted his arm away, sending the super glue tube flying.

"Just a little glue. It will stop the bleeding until you can get a doctor to look at that head."

Jill sat up. "Better to die of a knock on the head than to slowly fall apart. I've been doing some research. There have been a few cases of people who developed metabolic disorders and suddenly lost the ability to sleep. Most didn't live more than a couple of years."

Ragsdale nodded confirmation. "But we're not going to let that happen to you. So, tell me again exactly what your family's business does?"

Jill sat up and slid over to lean against the nearest cubicle wall, holding the cold sherbet against her head as she spoke. "Think about any random electronic gadget you might buy—alarm clocks, radios, cheap cell phones, watches, DVD players. There are dozens of brand names, some specific to a particular retailer, some available anywhere. But there are only a handful of companies who actually make the devices. They just change the plastic casing, slap a different logo on the outside, and call it a different brand. But inside they are mostly all the same. Now, think about the inside of those electronic gadgets—circuit boards, power supplies, speakers, etc. Many of those components are also the same, shared across multiple companies. It turns out there are only a few companies who make power supplies for alarm clocks, for instance. Manufacturers publish a spec and buy the component from the lowest bidder and slap it into the device. If a supplier gets sloppy or someone cheaper comes along, the manufacturer can just start using a different supplier. The parts are relatively standardized, so switching out one for another is easy."

Listening to Jill talk so articulately about her family's business reminded Zach again just how capable she was. She had never wanted to be a part of the family business, but it wasn't because she wasn't able.

"So, where does this business fit?"

"We kind of pull everything together. Say someone—a store like Target or a brand like Panasonic—wants to sell an alarm clock that costs around twenty bucks. Their product management folks will determine the features, the design, how big the display is, how strong the speakers are. Then they send the spec to businesses like us to pull everything together. We're kind of like general contractors. We find the cheapest supplier for speakers and power supplies and circuit boards and whatever. Then, we contract someone to assemble the thing. Usually this is done somewhere that labor is cheap—Southeast Asia, Central America. The product is shipped here by the container load. We keep the inventory here, where warehouse space is cheap, and ship out to stores as they need it."

"So, this new supplier that Jeff referred to you, what did they do?" he asked.

"I don't really know. I didn't really pay attention. I think they were a component supplier, not sure what kind." Jill stood up and dropped the sherbet into the nearest trash can. "But we aren't going to figure anything out sitting here in a puddle of blood and melted sherbet."

Jill was a little wobbly as they approached the stairs, swaying like a small tree in a big breeze. Zach looped one of her arms around his shoulder.

"I'm perfectly capable of walking on my own."

"Recent events contradict that assertion." She was leaning heavily on Zach and didn't protest further. This was a kind of strictly platonic, sideways unintentional hug designed for support purposes. But even this minor human contact was a welcome interruption from the physical isolation Zach normally felt.

A few seconds later they were walking through the door into the fourth-floor reception area. Jill took her arm from around Zach's shoulder.

"Thanks, Crutch."

She walked over to her dad's office door. Motion detectors turned on the lights as they stepped inside.

The wall to the left of the doorway was all glass, overlooking the lobby below. The wall to the right of that one was all glass as well, overlooking the parking lot. The desk was directly in front of them, facing the glass wall that overlooked the lobby. The desk was exactly what you would expect in the office of a wealthy elderly man in a small town. It was big and heavy and made of dark wood with a gloss finish. Behind it was a matching credenza and a very plush high-backed leather chair. A computer was on a small, metal table just to the right of the credenza, as if it were an afterthought, a geeky new employee without a place to sit.

The whole room had a strange look about it. It was dirty. But not the cluttered dirty of a space that was seeing heavy use—no drink rings on the coaster, no paper in the trash, no crumbs on the desktop. Rather, everything was neatly in place, but with a thin layer of dust painted on every surface. It was like a museum no one visited. Jill fell into the big leather chair, rolled over to the computer, and started typing. She was staring intently at the screen with her back to the others.

"Jill, why didn't you mention that your father had passed away?" Zach asked.

Her fingers stopped typing. She leaned forward and rubbed her eyes but didn't turn around. "I guess it just didn't come up. It hasn't been long. I guess I just didn't want to talk about it."

"How long ago?"

"Just a couple of months. He had a seizure in the middle of the night, choked to death. Never made it out of the bed." She shuddered just a little. "An awful way to die."

"Did he still live alone?" Jill's mother had died many years ago.

"There was a housekeeper, but she was on the bottom floor of the house. No way she could have heard him. I was away—in South America. It took them days to find me. I just barely made it back in time for the funeral."

She said it matter-of-factly, but the reflection of her face in the computer monitor belied the pain she was feeling. She and her father were very close. He was one of the few people who fully understood and appreciated Jill's wanderlust.

"So what happened to the business? Who is in charge now?" Since Jill was an only child, everyone assumed that at some point she would come home to run the family business.

"My dad's number two took over, but it is supposed to be an interim thing. He's older than my dad was and wants to get out and play some golf or whatever before he dies at his desk. And, yes, they are waiting on me to return. When my father passed away, I inherited his controlling interest in the firm. And the succession plan stipulates I have one year to assume day-to-day control of the firm, or a new CEO will be selected by the board."

"So, when you called and suggested this new supplier—?" Ragsdale began.

"Yes, it kind of carried a lot of weight." Jill turned back to the PC screen before she continued. "And, based on what I'm seeing, they started using this supplier for pretty much everything. Private label clock radios for WalMart, high-end travel clocks, digital picture frames, even video game consoles."

"What parts did they provide?" Ragsdale was now standing over her right shoulder, squinting at the computer screen.

"It looks like power supplies—all different shapes and sizes. The warehouse is full of them, and a lot have already shipped." She clicked the print button, and the small printer sitting next to the computer hummed to life.

"That would make sense," Ragsdale said. "Let's go have a look." He walked over to the door and headed to the hallway. He was out the door before he looked over his shoulder and saw the others weren't behind him.

Zach was helping Jill out of her chair, his left arm under her shoulders.

"Perhaps we should wait for our gracious hostess," Ragsdale offered.

Jill was out of her chair and leaning heavily on Zach this time as they walked out into the hallway. "My dad could probably get you there faster than I can right now."

"Here, take this." Ragsdale commandeered the receptionist's rolling chair and wheeled it over. Jill half sat, half fell into it.

"That way," she said. She pointed down a hallway to the right. "There's a freight elevator that will take us down to the warehouse."

Office chairs are not necessarily made for straight line, long distance travel. Zach fought the squirrely path of the wheels and nearly dumped Jill when they crossed the threshold into the mail room.

Ragsdale pushed the button, and they held their breath hoping the elevator worked. Carrying Jill down four flights of stairs would be manageable, but by no means desirable.

They exhaled as the button lit and they heard the whir of the pulleys. A moment later they stepped out of the elevator onto the first floor. It was another mail room, this one much more utilitarian than the one upstairs. Vinyl-covered chairs were parked at dingy metal desks, industrial linoleum bore the scuffs of steel-toed boots and dolly wheels. Opposite the elevator doors were double doors that opened into the warehouse. Zach commandeered one of the rolling chairs and helped Jill ease into it. They passed through the double doors and turned on the lights.

The warehouse was as long as a couple of football fields, and probably fifty yards wide. Long rows of shelving ran down the length of the building. The outside walls were metered with large rolling doors every thirty feet or so. Most of the doors were opened, with the back of a large trailer pressed against each opening. Ragsdale began walking quickly down the row of trucks, looking down at the printed pages from the office and back to the numbers painted in white block letters over each doorway. Zach had to half jog to keep up with him, but fortunately for Jill, this chair handled a little better at speed than the one upstairs.

Ragsdale stopped at bay 112 and began fiddling with the heavy latch. By the time they caught up with him, he was swinging one of the heavy trailer doors open. The doc went into the trailer and emerged with a cardboard box labeled "Alarm Clock Model 94-9882A, QTY 24."

Ragsdale opened the box, grabbed one of the individually boxed alarm clocks inside, and tossed it to Zach. He handed it to Jill. Then Ragsdale looked down at his paper and started walking again. The same procedure was repeated at another trailer, then another. A half hour later, Jill's lap was piled high with a variety of low-end consumer electronics.

Ragsdale looked at his printout again, then at the stack in Jill's lap. "Let's go back to the hotel."

"I wasn't planning to stay at a hotel in town," Jill said. "Not safe. I want to be very careful showing my face right now. My dad has a bunch of furnished rental homes in town. There's an empty one a few miles from here. Three bedrooms, two baths, nineteen hundred square feet of suburban luxury."

They headed for the car, stopping only for Ragsdale to commandeer a box of tools from a utility closet. Jill slid into the back seat and lay down. Ragsdale and Zach were up front. The old V8 rumbled to life, and they pulled out of the parking lot. The sun was setting, and Zach flicked on the headlights.

Zach looked at Ragsdale. "Don't we need to make another stop?"

"Yes, but I don't think that is going to be as easy. And we don't have someone with a badge to show us around."

"I think we need to find a Kinko's."

"I like the way you're thinking."

FIFTEEN

THEY HEADED EAST. JUST BEFORE THEY reached the town square, they pulled into a shopping center. At one end of the strip mall, a Domino's Pizza sign beckoned, at the other end a lone car sat outside a Kinko's branch brightly lit with fluorescent lights. The sign over the Radio Shack was turned off, but a light was on inside as a man in a short- sleeved shirt and tie cleaned up. All the other shops were closed.

Zach parked in front of the Kinko's and shut off the engine. Jill was lying on her back on the seat, her right arm over her eyes.

"Are you asleep?" Zach asked, innocently enough.

"Funny. How about you just assume I'm not asleep from now on?"

"Sorry, maybe that was just wishful thinking."

Without opening her eyes or moving, Jill held up a cell phone in her left hand. "You guys can handle this. Just leave me here. I'll call if I need you."

"Fair enough. Ragsdale, if you don't need me in there, I'll walk down to the Domino's and grab us a pie." Only moments ago, Zach had realized he was starving. And, based on Ragsdale's raised eyebrows and vigorous nod, it appeared the doc was, too. They had forgone the post-funeral smorgasbord in favor of this expedition. Jill still had not moved but was holding one very enthusiastic thumb up.

Ragsdale walked into Kinko's and sat down at a rent-a-PC station, while Zach hung a left and walked towards pizza. The sun had fully set, taking a little edge off the heat. Zach could still feel the heat radiating from the parking lot, but it was cool enough to walk without sweating, which was really all he asked. Zach pulled open the door and was greeted by dual sensations—the smell of baking pizza and the throbby twang of southern rock cranked much louder than Domino's corporate guidelines permitted.

The two scruffy twenty-somethings behind the counter looked a little surprised at the presence of a customer. Zach ordered a couple of medium pizzas, probably more than they needed, but better safe than sorry. It could be a late night. As he took his seat on the sticky vinyl bench, he closed his eyes and focused on the lyrics of the song blaring overhead.

The nights have been so lonely since you went away
I could not get to sleep
Try as I may
But now you're back and you're here to stay
Still it looks like another sleepless night
Oh, but darling that's alright

Sometimes when Zach's mind was racing, he found it easier to re-direct it than to shut it down. A song could provide a useful diversion. Hearing the song, memorizing the words and singing it backwards.

Alright that's darling but oh
Night sleepless another like looks it still
Stay to here you're and back you're now but
May I as try sleep to get not could I
Away went you since lonely so been have nights the

Often nonsensical, but sometimes poetic. It took a lot of concentration. Just the kind of meaningless diversion Zach needed to clear his head.

When he was done, he looked at the clock on the wall. Seven minutes had passed. Their pies were taxiing slowly down the counter with the others. Pizza moved through the oven on a conveyer belt at the pace of two pizzas every four minutes. His pie was number nine awaiting takeoff. So, about a 16-minute wait.

Hopefully Jill was getting some sleep. Zach looked out the window towards the car. For some reason the car was rocking. A little light filtered through the windows and he could see what looked like arms flailing in the back seat.

Zach threw open the door and sprinted across the parking lot. When he was about ten yards away, he could see Jill twisting and flailing around in the back seat. She looked unconscious, like she was having a seizure. He yanked the car door handle.

Locked.

Zach dug in his pockets for the keys. He dropped them on the pavement. Shit. Picked them up again. It seemed like eternity before the key turned and the doors unlocked. He jumped into the back seat and pulled Jill upright. She was definitely seizing. He pried her mouth open and saw her tongue was curled up and starting to slip down her throat. He grabbed it with his finger and held it against the bottom of her mouth. She gagged a little, then her eyes popped open.

"What the hell?" she screamed, "Oh, God, Zach!" She threw her arms around his neck and sobbed. He held her close and could feel the sobs rippling through her. "Thank you, Zach," she said, more softly.

"What happened?"

"I fell asleep—finally. But just as I started to drift into a deep sleep, the dreams started again. At first it was just like before. Words, languages, text streaming in front of me. I had to read it all, explain it all. My work was being measured. But then the pace increased dramatically. Words and phrases streamed by crazy fast, some were backwards, some were transposed on top of each other, lights were flashing, loud electronic tones alternated in the background. I couldn't handle it, but I couldn't look away. I couldn't disengage. Couldn't wake up. And then my body began convulsing. I could feel myself choking. Thank God you saw me."

Ragsdale had seen the commotion a few moments later and was now standing outside the car behind Zach. "Are you okay?"

"Okay-ish," Jill replied, "But I certainly don't want to go to sleep anytime soon."

"This wasn't some random health issue, was it?" he asked Ragsdale. But they all knew the answer.

"Was the car on?" Ragsdale asked.

"No, I had the keys with me."

"They must have had a way to send the signal." The doc reached under the seats, checked the glove box, the trunk. "I need some equipment." He turned and started walking briskly towards the Radio Shack.

"Ragsdale, they're closed," Zach said.

"No problem. I speak geek," he said without turning around.

Ragsdale walked over and knocked. The manager opened the door, looking annoyed. But a minute or so later he was smiling, then laughing, then inviting Ragsdale inside. A few minutes later the doc left the shop with a bag under his arm and a wave from the proprietor.

Ragsdale dumped the bag on the hood of the car. It only took him a moment to put batteries into a handheld frequency scanner and dive into the car. He waved the device around the front seat first, fiddled with the controls a little, and frowned as he didn't find anything. He waved it through the back seat as well. Jill made no effort to move. She still lay on the back seat, forearm over her eyes.

Ragsdale frowned as he swept the meter across the front seat. No reading. But then he placed the device on the seat right next to where Jill's head was laying. The LCD display on the meter flashed to life.

"There's something here." Jill sat up quickly, as if she'd just found herself with a snake for a pillow. Ragsdale reached under the seats, dug into the crease where the seat bottom and seat back met. Nothing. But then he grabbed the utility knife from the toolbox. He made a quick X-shaped slice through the rear passenger seat.

"Ragsdale, my granddad is going to kick your ass," Zach said, hand rubbing his forehead.

"Just tell them doped up teenagers did it. Old people blame everything on doped up teenagers," Jill offered.

"You know I can't lie to my granddad."

"An odd crime, ritual defacement of auto upholstery. Kids these days..." Ragsdale offered from the back seat.

"Maybe he can knock out a window too, just to make it look convincing." Jill would have made an excellent criminal.

Ragsdale was up to his forearms digging through the foam and springs inside the seat. "Nothing here."

"Maybe it's under the seat," Jill offered.

"You can't get much more under than I am right now," Ragsdale said as he probed the dusty nether regions of the old car seat's insides.

"Shit." He pulled his arm out of the seat and slid onto the pavement beside the car. "Found it."

A small metal box was attached to the underside of the car, a strong magnet keeping it securely attached to the frame. He pried it free and carried it around to the front of the car by the toolbox.

"Well, at least you didn't rip up the seat for nothing," Jill said. Zach frowned. Ragsdale ignored them.

The box was wide and thin, about the size of two decks of cards side by side. Ragsdale held the scanner against the box. "This thing is definitely receiving a signal, in about the same frequency range as the alarm clock I tested back at the lab."

"So this box was sending out the dream commands as well?" Zach asked.

"Yes, and it sounds like whoever is doing this has found a way to induce seizures using intense stimulation during dreams."

"Those assholes murdered my dad," Jill said as she slumped into the car seat.

Ragsdale sat down on the torn upholstery, next to Jill. "And it looks like they are after you too. But the signal can't get through as long as your conscious mind is in control."

"So, I have to stay awake?"

"Yes. Don't even doze. Not until we figure this out. When we get to the house, we'll do a sweep for any devices with a signal, clear out a safe place for you to rest."

"So I'll be able to actually sleep?" she said hesitantly, hopefully.

"Probably. But you need to understand that you have ingested a great deal of this drug. It makes you extremely sensitive to outside stimuli while you sleep. That's what makes the signals have such a powerful impact on your dreams. But any external stimulus can impact your sleep. A creaking house, a flashing light, even a buzzing fly. Any small disruption in your surroundings will be amplified dramatically in your sleep. We'll do our best to shut everything out, but I'm not sure we'll be able to completely eliminate outside stimuli."

"It's funny, when I first fell asleep, before the flashing lights and the text started, I heard this unbelievable loud rolling thunder. It was deafening, like the ground was shaking."

"Are you pretty hungry?" Ragsdale said.

"Holy shit. Was that my stomach growling?"

"Probably," Ragsdale offered. "Remember, all your senses will be amplified when you are asleep."

"Well, by all means, let's go get that pizza," Zach said as he slid into the front seat and cranked the car. Ragsdale came around and got into the passenger side.

Jill was lying in the back seat again, right arm over her eyes. "And see if they have some Red Bull," she said without looking up.

They ate the pizza as they drove. It wasn't delicious, but it wasn't bad. Hunger has a way of lowering culinary standards. Jill was guzzling Red Bull in the back seat. The radio was on again. Jill had selected a classic rock station to help her stay awake.

They turned left into the town square and headed north. Passed the hotel again. Ms. James' rental car was still in the parking lot. Something by AC/DC was keeping a good rhythm with the spinning wheels. The nursing home was on the right again, its lights now dimmed save for a few windows lit by those who were flaunting curfew or under some kind of medical duress.

Brian Johnson's wail was interrupted by a loud crackle from the radio as they continued north passing the nursing home, passing the now-dark church where the funeral had been held.

"Did you finish things up in Kinko's?" Zach asked Ragsdale.

Ragsdale handed him a laminated badge. "Absolutely, Inspector Peters." On the badge was an official looking seal and the words "Inspector Zach P. Peters, U.S. Occupational Safety and Health Administration."

"Zach P. P. Really?" He heard Jill laugh out loud from the back seat.

"Seemed appropriate," Ragsdale replied. "Now, let's go get a look at that plastic."

SIXTEEN

IT WAS WELL AFTER DARK WHEN they approached the plastics plant. But there was no mistaking the facility. Sodium lights lit up the grounds like daylight. A four-story office building, darkened for the weekend, was in the front left corner of the property. At the center of the complex was a wide two-story building, steel walls painted generic tan. The lights were all on, which wasn't a surprise since the place ran at least two shifts per day.

Zach pulled right up to the front of the building and parked in one of the spaces marked "Reserved." He clipped his badge to the outer pocket of his sportscoat. Ragsdale did the same.

Zach leaned into the back seat. "Are you going to be okay in here?"

"I'll be fine," Jill said. "Four Red Bulls in thirty minutes. I'm probably at higher risk for cardiac arrest than falling asleep."

She was sitting up now, leaning into the corner where the door met the back seat, one leg up on the seat beside her. She was furiously tapping the top of an empty Red Bull can with a fingernail. Taptaptaptaptaptap. Her eye twitched with every third or fourth tap.

"OK. Call if you need us."

Jill held up her cell phone and nodded as she took another drink from the can.

Ragsdale and Zach got out and started walking towards the front door.

"So, what's the plan?" Zach asked.

"Standard random inspection. We are passing through on our

way from Mobile to Atlanta. Just want to do a walk-through of the manufacturing floor."

"And take some samples of the product?"

"Of course."

"Standard procedure?"

"Yep." Jeff mentioned this kind of thing a few times. OSHA stops in unannounced a few times a year. A couple of times it was a shakedown, crooked bureaucrat skimming a few bucks to buy a new boat or his wife a new set of boobs or something. But generally, it's a non-event."

"Non-event. Let's do that kind."

Through the double glass doors, they could see a security guard behind a waist-high counter, flanked by security monitors, a TV, and a really sickly looking ficus.

When they opened the door, the security guard startled a bit and looked up from the newspaper he was reading. Not many visitors this time of night.

"Can I help you?" the guard asked. But by then Zach and Ragsdale were close enough that their badges were visible. The guard glanced at the OSHA logos dangling from each man's lapel. "If you gentlemen will have a seat, I'll call our foreman."

Ragsdale and Zach had a seat in the two vinyl chairs that served as the waiting area, a faux wood laminated table between them held a stack of what must be the world's most boring magazines. A copy of *Plastic Dynamics Monthly*, a whole stack of *Bottling Insider*, a copy of a white paper from one of the plant engineers entitled "Screw Top March: Applying Military Cadence to Bottle Plant Operations."

Zach had barely made it through the table of contents in his copy of *Plastic Dynamics* when the double doors beside the security guard swung open and the plant foreman emerged. He was tucking an errant shirttail into the narrow space between a moderately-sized belly and the faded black leather belt that held up his khaki Carhart pants. His sleeves were rolled up to mid-forearm, revealing lots of hair to go with meaty calloused hands. A white hard hat with the company logo protected his bald head and round red face.

"Good evening, gentlemen. My name is Bo Gentry, second shift foreman. What can I do for you?"

"We are here for a random inspection. Just need to do a walk-through and check a few samples. You know the drill."

"The drill, I know," said Bo the Foreman.

They walked over to the double doors, grabbed loaner hardhats from the hooks by the door, and walked out onto the factory floor.

Only about half of the workers even acknowledged their entrance with a glance. Standard drill. Nothin' unusual. Besides, getting distracted around heavy machinery is a great way to lose a digit. Bad form when OSHA is on the floor.

Ragsdale and Zach showed enough interest to maintain their cover, stopping at several of the control stations, scribbling notes, asking questions about lubricants and alignment and throughput and such.

Bo pointed a meaty finger to the left. An opening large enough to drive a truck through was draped with thick, clear plastic blinds. "Resins we use for input are stored back there. They are pumped through those pipes," he pointed to two large pipes running overhead towards the start of the assembly line.

"Finished product is shipped out through the docks out back."

"Well, let's take a look."

"Sure thing."

Bo led them through the back of plant, past another set of double doors. "This is the shipping office," he said. It was a room with a few metal desks and concrete floor painted grey. Computers were at each desk, their keyboards grimy with the inexplicable black dirt unique to warehouses. It was a little brighter than the office at the electronics factory. A couple of sickly houseplants and framed motivational prints added a measure of, if not beauty, at least diversion from the stark surroundings. A water cooler stood guard by another set of doors at the opposite end of the room, little cone paper cups at the ready.

They passed through those second doors and into the warehouse. Long rows of big industrial shelves to the left, long rows of rolling doors on the right. Three forklifts were parked in a row in between the shelves and the doors. Zach caught Ragsdale's eye and gave him a nod.

"Oh, this is not good. What shit is this?" Ragsdale said and started walking quickly towards the forklifts. Bo looked a little panicked and hustled along after Ragsdale as fast as his much shorter and much fatter legs would carry him.

"The dust in here is killing me, I'm going to get some water." Zach pointed over his shoulder towards the office with his thumb. But Bo was much too worried about his new forklift problem to notice.

Zach walked back through the double doors, right past the water cooler, and sat down at the closest computer. There was a password, of course. But approximately 46% of people use the word "password" as their password, another 23% have the password written on a piece of paper near the computer. So his odds were pretty good. In this case, his good fortune took the form of a Post-it note stuck to the underside of the keyboard. It bore the word "zucchini," which he thought would probably be easy enough to remember. But perhaps the user suffered from gourd confusion.

Zach typed in the characters, and a few seconds later, he was trolling through the shipping database looking for companies that had recently ordered plastic used for water bottles.

There was a pretty long list: "Ohio Springs," "Mountain Crest," "Meadow Mist," and the inexplicably simply named "FreshWater." He could hear Ragsdale talking loudly in the warehouse and imagined Bo nodding in acquiescence. Zach probably had a few minutes. He ran a report of all the locations that had received this plastic in the past six months and hit print. The printer started warming up. And then he heard footsteps, not from the warehouse behind him, but from the double doors in front of him. Shit. The printer was humming like an airplane about to take off. He was pretty sure OSHA didn't normally print out shipping reports, and whoever was on the other side of that door probably knew that. He reached to the back of the printer and unplugged the power cord. The door swung open.

It was what appeared to be a night manager. Short-sleeved shirt, cheap tie, khaki pants, leather shoes with thick rubber soles. Nervous eyes darted out from behind dirty glasses, a thinning swatch of blonde grey hair hit a furrowed brow. "Sir, can I help you with something in here?" His plastic laminate name tag said "Brown," which seemed about right.

Zach's heart beat a little faster, and he broke into a mild sweat. Classic fight or flight response. But he wasn't trying to escape a mountain lion on the Cro-Magnon plain. He was facing off in a battle of wits with an assistant night manager at a plastics plant.

Zach reached down with his right hand and hit the height adjustment on the chair. It dropped dramatically so that his arms had to reach up to touch the keyboard. "This work station is completely out of compliance. Just a total disaster. No wrist rest. No lumbar support. No anti-glare screen on the monitor. And this chair is a carpal tunnel death trap. How many hours a day is this workstation occupied?"

"Uh, well, we uhm..."

"Who is the manager of this department? I need to cite this in my report."

Brown hesitated for a moment, then said, "Bo Gentry."

Well played by the night manager. "Mr. Brown, is it?"

"Yes, sir."

"Mr. Brown, I need you to please find Mr. Gentry and ask him to come here, please."

"Uhm, yes, sir. Right away." Brown hustled away.

As Brown passed out the swinging doors into the warehouse, Zach pulled out his phone and quickly took pictures of the report on the computer screen. If he was going to steal data, he might as well be environmentally friendly and let that dinosaur of a printer rest in its geriatric electronic bliss.

A few seconds later, Bo came back into the room, followed closely by Brown and Ragsdale. Zach tapped his watch and yawned. Making up fake OSHA regulations can be tiring. He asked Bo a few more questions and made a show of writing notes on a legal pad. Bo and Brown looked a little stressed, maybe even sick. It seemed only humane to let them off the hook. "Just a few violations, but overall not too bad. Look for our report in a couple of weeks. A caseworker will follow up to make sure you have implemented our recommendations."

Ragsdale and Zach thanked Bo the Foreman for his hospitality, hung their hard hats on the hook for the next visitor, and walked towards the front door.

Jill was still in the car, wide-eyed and fidgety. It had been almost an hour.

"How are you holding up?" Zach asked as he and Ragsdale slid into their seats.

"OK, all things considered. No sleep, no seizures. A little bored."

"They had some great magazines inside," Ragsdale offered.

"I'm not sure a six-month-old issue of *People* is going to hold my attention right now. Did you guys get what you were looking for?"

"Almost. We just need to shop for a little refreshment on the way to the house." He forwarded the camera phone pics to Ragsdale's phone.

The doc looked at the screen and nodded. "Quite a little shopping list."

The first stop was a Food Lion a few blocks from the plastic factory.

"Get me a Zagnut," Jill said.

It was 9:55, and the store closed at 10:00. The cashier gave Zach and Ragsdale an unpleasant look, a stockman looked up from his broom long enough to frown and glance at the clock.

"Bottled water?" Zach asked as Ragsdale grabbed a buggy. Broom man pointed towards aisle four.

Zach looked at the picture on his cell phone. "You get the Mountain Mist and the Fresh Water. I'll get the others."

"Be sure and get a couple of different bottles, different lot numbers if you can."

A few moments later, the buggy was filled with an assortment of bottled water. Different brands and sizes, new bottles from the front of the shelf and dusty old ones from the very back. Zach grabbed a 12-pack of Red Bull from the end cap as they passed. Ragsdale grabbed another.

They pushed their load quickly to the front of the store to raised eyebrows from the cashier.

"We're really thirsty," Zach offered.

Ragsdale put the Red Bull on the belt. "And really sleepy."

The cashier dutifully scanned the merchandise. "Will there be anything else?"

"I would like a Zagnut bar, please," he said.

"Make that two," Ragsdale offered as he raised two fingers.

Cashier lady nodded towards the candy rack behind them. Ragsdale grabbed a couple of Zagnuts, Zach grabbed a Snickers, and they were on their way.

Zach popped the trunk and loaded up the hydration. The old car's suspension creaked a little under the load. Sliding into the front seat, Ragsdale handed a Red Bull and a Zagnut over his shoulder to Jill.

She sat upright and freed the candy bar from its wrapper. "Did you get everything you need?" She said this between her first and second bite.

"Yes, we did," Zach answered. "Ragsdale, how long will it take for you to analyze these once you get back to the lab?"

"Lab, Hell! I brought the lab with me. Just stop by my hotel on the way to Jill's house."

"It's not technically on the way." The observation came from the back seat.

"What's your rush? It's not like you are going to go home and go to sleep."

Zach glared at Ragsdale.

"What, too soon?" In the rear-view mirror he could see a smile break across Jill's face.

They pulled back onto the main road and headed south

towards the motel.

The Quality Inn Oakdale was a tidy and functional, if not particularly glamorous, establishment. A small lobby was home to a sleepy night manager in a poorly fitting green blazer, a coffee pot, and some donuts of questionable vintage beneath a glass dome. Ragsdale got out and walked into the lobby, gave a little nod to the manager and took the elevator upstairs.

Jill and Zach stayed in the car with the engine running and the A/C on medium. Zach stole a glance in the rear-view mirror towards Jill. She was lying down again in the back seat, eyes closed, chest gently rising and falling as deep breaths metered her fight against sleep. Zach lingered a little longer on the sight than perhaps he intended, then redirected his gaze out the back window.

He saw Ms. James' rental car was still in the parking lot.

He looked back at Jill. "Will you be OK by yourself for a few minutes?"

Jill gave the thumbs up with her left hand, her right arm still covering her eyes.

"I'll lock the doors behind me."

When Zach walked into the lobby, he was met with a rush of cold from an air conditioner that, while it probably struggled to fight off the heat at midday, was now chasing the last traces of warmth in a rout. He shivered a little as he walked to the front desk and thought for a moment that the night manager's hideous green blazer might be pretty warm.

"An old friend of mine was in town for the funeral."

"Jeff Wallace's?" *Maybe make a quick assessment of green blazer guy here.* "Hard to imagine someone with so much money would want to kill himself. Money can't buy happiness, but with his kind of dough, I think I could give it a hell of a try, right?"

A little crass, since Green Blazer didn't know if Zach was friends with Jeff. But it was getting late, and maybe the cold was getting to him.

"We were shocked. He always seemed so happy," Zach replied sternly.

Green Blazer's mouth opened, and he flushed a little red. "Oh—so you knew Mr. Wallace?"

"Only for about twenty years." Zach let the silence hang there for a minute as the discomfort built. Green Blazer deserved to feel uncomfortable, of course. But Zach also needed a favor from him. After a nice long awkward pause, even a slightly questionable request is a welcome change of pace.

"So, a friend of mine is in town for the funeral, staying here. I told her I would stop by, but it's getting a little late. Do you know if she will still be here tomorrow?"

He paused for a moment, as if considering the Official Corporate Policy he'd been forced to read before he got his Green Blazer. Then he stepped over to his PC and hit a couple of keys. "What is her name, sir?"

"Annabeth James, probably checked in yesterday."

"Yes, I see her. She has a late checkout tomorrow, looks like she'll be leaving her room around 4. Perhaps the two of you can catch up over lunch in our Applebees." Green Blazer pointed through the doors to the restaurant that shared the parking lot. "Hotel guests receive 10% off an entrée, or a free dessert."

"Thanks. Perhaps we will." They definitely would not.

Zach grabbed a piece of hard candy from the bowl on the counter and unwrapped it as he turned and walked towards the car. He tapped on the window, and Jill unlocked the door.

"Did you know there is an Applebees over there?" he asked as he settled behind the wheel.

"I did," she said. "But that fact is only relevant if I find myself the victim of a strange disease that can only be cured by cheese fries."

"Jill, why do you suppose Ms. James from Sopros is staying overnight? Mr. Hightower's car is gone. She doesn't know anyone here. She never met Jeff's family. I'm not sure they even knew about her."

"Maybe the little bitch is just taking in the sights here in Oakdale. Tourism is our 13th largest industry, you know. Just behind orthodontia, but curiously ahead of candle making."

"Why would you call her a bitch? What do you have against her?"

She cocked her head a little to one side and raised her eyebrows as if to say, "think about it."

"Because she dated Jeff?"

"Perhaps. But mostly because she looks fabulous and tight skinned and perky, while I look like I'm coming off a 22-day bender. Any woman who looks younger or skinnier than me is, by default, a bitch. If you dated the same guy, double bitch." She leaned back into the seat and took a deep breath, then spoke in a much calmer, quieter voice. "But I'm pretty sure I know why she is staying another day."

"Why, then? I assume you guys aren't getting mani pedis together tomorrow?"

"The executor of Jeff's estate has a meeting tomorrow at 4:30 p.m., to read Jeff's will. Maybe she thinks Jeff left her a little something."

"Maybe he did?"

"If she thinks that, she is not just a bitch. She's a dumb bitch."

"Beth is many things, but I do not think she is at all dumb."

"So, it's 'Beth' now, is it?"

A knock on the trunk of the car interrupted them. Zach turned to see Ragsdale standing at the back of the car, a large metal case in one hand and another on the ground beside him. In a moment they had the cases loaded and were easing the old sedan out of the parking lot.

SEVENTEEN

"WHERE TO NOW, JILL?"

"One of my dad's rental houses. Just past the nursing home. I'll tell you when to turn."

Zach did as she said, but probably drove faster than she expected. They were riding in sleepy silence when the radio inexplicably crackled. Startled into alertness, Zach noticed a large complex on the right, about a mile off the main road. A long two-lane ran directly to it. Well-manicured, well lit, and completely quiet. It was Oak Grove Nursing Home. It was one of the largest retirement homes in the region. Contracts with government agencies and a few large insurers pulled in patients from all over the state. One whole floor was dedicated to caring for patients in comas, or who were otherwise unable to move or interact. The world needs these kinds of places, and it looked happy enough from the outside. Zach shuddered at the thought of his grandfather, or one day his grandmother, living out their final days suspended between industrial linoleum and fluorescent lights.

In about seven minutes they were turning into a standard middle-class subdivision. Streetlights glowed orange between every three or four houses, sidewalks lined the streets. It was late, and the denizens of the burbs were tucked away neatly in their beds, resting on the eight hundred thread count sheets they bought as a splurge from Linens & Things. At Jill's instruction, Zach took the first right, then the second left, and ended up in a cul de sac—a dead end in the maze of streets that made up this little development.

The house was nice by suburban standards: too much for the waitress to afford, but not quite as nice as where the orthodontist might live.

"That's the one," Jill said and pointed to a two-story house on the left. Brick front, vinyl siding on the sides and back. Probably a half acre lot, the front yard dotted with a few trees that were not quite mature, probably planted when the house was built five or six years ago.

Zach parked, and they made their way to the front door. Jill pulled a key from her pocket and tried the lock with trembling hands. After a couple of failed attempts, she finally managed to guide the key to the keyhole. But then the lock wouldn't turn.

"Let me try." Zach moved her hand from the lock. Her skin was soft, but moist and clammy. She was not well. It took just a little bit of force and the dead bolt turned. "Just an old lock," Zach said as he pushed the door open.

The entryway was an eight-foot square of synthetic wood flooring. A large opening to the left led to a living room, and beyond that a kitchen. To the right was a set of French doors that led to a small office. Straight ahead, the hallway divided into two halves. The right side became a staircase that led to bedrooms upstairs. To the left was a hallway that led to the back side of the first floor. At the end of the hallway on the left was the other side of the kitchen, on the right was a small dining room. The carpets were worn, but freshly cleaned. You could still see the path of the steamer that had tried to fluff the high traffic areas.

Ragsdale opened the French doors and dropped his cases onto the faux mahogany laminate desk. "Jill, I guess you get first choice of bedrooms." He looked to his left to get Jill's reaction, but she was not there. He formed the first letter of her name, "J", but then he saw her waving hand just visible over the back of the couch in the living room to their left.

"I think I'll be sleeping here tonight, guys."

"You won't be sleeping anywhere yet." Ragsdale hustled into the room with his new Radio Shack toy. "Let me sweep this room for electronics."

He moved slowly around the room, carefully watching the display on his gizmo. The first victim was a DVD player, which he unceremoniously yanked off the shelf beside the TV, causing more mess than was really necessary. He tossed it to Zach, which was also a little unnecessary, but managed to elicit a chuckle from the patient on the couch. Zach put the DVD player on the office desk, along with the electronics they had commandeered from Jill's distribution center. In a few minutes they added a digital clock, a small electric fan, and a universal TV remote to the stack.

That last item caught Jill's attention. "Seizures are one thing, but getting up to change the channels is just barbaric."

Ragsdale switched off the scanner. "You should be safe from transmissions here. It will still be difficult to sleep. The drug has made you extremely sensitive to outside stimuli. But I'll be as quiet as I can." She put a throw pillow over her closed eyes, gave a slight smile and nod, and waved him away.

Ragsdale was already disassembling an alarm clock. He was using a screwdriver, not to actually remove screws, but to pry apart two halves of the device's plastic case and break it open. Zach was about to comment on his decidedly low-tech approach to disassembly when his cell phone rang. His grandmother.

Zach turned on the speakerphone so he could work while he talked. But when he heard his grandmother's voice, he knew this wasn't just a check-in call. "It's your grandfather. You need to come home right now."

She spoke in measured, careful tones, but her voice was weak and her breathing shallow.

"Is...is he OK, Grandma?"

"I'm afraid not, Zach. He's had a seizure. It happened so quickly, so violently, while he was asleep. I tried to help, but there was nothing..." Her voice dissolved into deep sobs. She was the strongest person Zach knew, but her heart had just been cut out.

"Oh God, Grandma. I'm on my way." His voice sounded distant. It was like he was floating outside his body. A hundred thoughts raced into his mind, but a kind of mental tunnel vision saw through the clutter. He had to get home right now.

"Zach, you need to have someone drive you. You won't be in any condition to drive safely," his grandmother said with as much sternness as she could muster. Amazing, at the most painful moment in her life, she was still thinking about Zach. Everything he knew about love, he learned from her.

He hit the "end" button on the phone and turned around. Jill was standing there. She put her arms around him. He wanted to just stand there and sob in her embrace, but he couldn't. Emotion was a wild animal he feared, stronger than him and beyond his control. Zach smiled, nodded, and pulled away. Work, thinking and solving, was the antidote for any emotion. Zach looked towards the door.

Ragsdale held up the car keys. "I'll drive you."

"The hell you will. You have to stay here. With her." Zach needed to be alone. Being with people required emotional reserves he did not have. And the thought of something happening to Jill filled him with a new dread, yet another feeling he did not have the will to process.

Jill put her hand on his arm. "I'll be fine, Zach. Ragsdale already swept the room."

"Look, I'm pretty sure none of us think my grandfather's death was an accident."

Somber nods confirmed his assertion.

"Ragsdale has to stay here and figure out who did this. Whatever is going on, it is worth killing for. And if they tried to kill you with a seizure a few hours ago, there's nothing to say they won't try some less elegant means again. Stay here, lock the doors, figure this shit out. I'll be back in by the morning." He grabbed the keys from Ragsdale's hand before there could be any objection and took two steps towards the door. Then, he turned back and grabbed the scanner from the desk. Ragsdale nodded in approval as Zach turned again and rushed to the car.

Zach's mind was racing and his head pounding as he slid behind the wheel. He backed out of the driveway, and the rear tires chirped as he floored it out of the cul de sac. A couple of sleepy suburbanites probably turned over in their cool sheets and blamed the disruption on someone else's teenager.

Zach didn't remember how he got back to the main highway. His subconscious handled the driving. A torrent of tears was held back by just a thin wall of composure. But he couldn't let himself dissolve into sobs and grief just yet. He had to focus.

If the seizure that killed his grandfather was related to the seizure that Jill experienced, then it was intentionally caused. Why would someone want to intentionally kill his grandfather?

He wasn't rich or powerful or outspoken. Just a tired old man. His health was such that he could do little more than watch TV and shuffle the short distance from the kitchen table to the bedroom. He was a threat to no one.

"It was because of me."

Zach spoke aloud into the silence.

Someone was trying to scare him. Maybe they heard about today's little fact-finding mission.

Zach's mind stayed busy with the problem at hand, avoiding the thought of being responsible for his grandfather's death, and his grandmother's grief. Digesting that horror would have to wait.

A few minutes later, the tires of the old sedan crunched up the long driveway towards his grandparents' house. The Olson's car was there. Old friends from church. Probably his grandmother's third phone call after the 911 and Zach.

An ambulance and a fire truck were in the driveway as well. Zach felt bile bubbling up in his stomach. He left his bag in the car, opened the door and wretched on the gravel, the flashing red lights making the moment even more nauseating.

Two paramedics looked up at his car, then continued packing up their gear. Old people die all the time. It is what happens. They probably thought this wasn't as bad as some.

They had no idea how wrong they were.

The screen door creaked open, normally a happy, familiar sound. Zach stepped into the living room. His grandmother was sitting on the couch, sobbing, dabbing tattered Kleenex to eyes that were already red and puffy with tears. Mrs. Olson was beside her, hand on her back, looking up and whispering what he hoped was a prayer.

"Oh, Zach—" His grandmother cried out when she saw him and started sobbing even more deeply. He sat down beside her and embraced her. She put her face onto his shoulder and cried. The curls of her white hair were in his eyes and soaking up the tears he couldn't hold back any longer.

They sat that way for a few minutes. The paramedics made a couple of trips back to the bedroom, followed by a middle-aged man in a black suit. The undertaker. Grandma saw him and pulled away.

Zach's grandmother looked him in the eyes, held him with her gaze, and asked softly, "Zach, would you like to see him before they take him away? He looked very peaceful right at the end."

Zach nodded. His grandmother always knew how to help him manage his feelings. She took his hand and led him down the hall.

"It was awful," she said. "We had just dozed off, and then he started flailing and rolling around. He was just shaking all over. I tried to wake him up, but I couldn't. I could hear him choking, I tried to get his mouth open…"

She held up her hands and Zach could see two badly broken

fingernails and several deep scratches.

"But he wouldn't wake. And then, then he just got still, just stopped."

By now they were at the bedroom door. She pointed to his grandfather still lying there in the bed. The undertaker saw them and stepped back from him, respectfully standing beside a gurney that waited a few feet from the bed.

"He knew where he was going. He was at peace," she said as she grabbed Zach's hand again.

Zach squeezed her hand. "Yes, Grandma, he is in a better place now."

She bent over and kissed the old man's cool forehead, stroked his thin gray hair with her arthritic hands.

Zach kissed his cheek and whispered in his ear, "I'm sorry, Grandpa."

He started to walk away. Then turned back to whisper one more thing.

"They won't get away with this."

A few minutes later they loaded Zach's grandfather into a hearse and drove him down the driveway, away from the home where he'd spent 54 years. His bride was sitting in a little high-backed chair in the corner of the bedroom, staring at the bed and the rumpled sheets.

Zach stayed outside for a while, rinsing his mind with the memories that sprouted from every fence post and tree trunk in the yard. He wandered around back, out of sight of any window, and slumped down to the ground, his back leaning against the dark side of the house.

Zach did not want to. He did not have to. But he needed to. He could not think clearly until he let it out. He ripped off the bandage, lanced the boil. Zach let himself cry. He was not prepared for the depth of it, his chest heaving deep silent sobs and a river of tears and snot. It was an odd thing, how the human body dealt with psychological distress by secreting fluids. Zach pondered the point of his grief even while it swept over him. After a few moments, the tears slowed and then stopped. Emotional healing would take time, but at least the wound had been field dressed. Zach stood and brushed the grass from his pants, then dried his eyes and nose with a tissue from his pocket.

Making his way back inside and to his grandparents' bedroom, Zach found his grandmother still sitting and staring at the bed. She glanced towards him and gave a half smile, then turned her gaze back to the sheets. Zach picked up the scanner, flicked it on, and walked towards the bed.

The needle immediately jumped as he stood next to the nightstand. He picked up the TV remote control that sat by the lamp. It was brand new, the buttons barely worn. He picked it up and threw it against the wall. His grandmother startled as the plastic cracked against the old plaster wall.

"Zach, what is going on?"

He thought about making up an excuse but lacked the energy or the justification to concoct a lie.

"Grandma, the company I work for isn't an ordinary company. It is a secret enterprise, a very old organization doing very, very serious work. I didn't realize how serious at first."

She nodded, not so much to say, "I understand" as "keep going."

"It turns out Jeff worked there too. A few months ago, he had the same job I have now. He helped put together a new system, a new invention. It was supposed to change everything, in a good way. Jeff figured out a way to transmit messages to people when they were asleep, influence their dreams. There were two parts to it. First, a drug makes people extra sensitive to their surroundings when they are asleep. We are not sure how the drug is delivered, but we've found it in bottled water and sodas. Second, a transmitter embedded in ordinary electronic devices broadcasts signals that can be picked up by your mind when you are asleep. Normally these signals are tasks to perform, problems to solve. You give the brain a job just like you would a computer. Then, the same sensors detect brain activity and transmit the answers the sleeping people come up with. This whole thing was supposed to allow people to accomplish things, figure things out, even when they were asleep. But something went wrong. Some very powerful people, I don't know who, were just using Jeff as part of a bigger plan. They started using the technology to make people work while they were asleep, like computers churning out computations all night. Apparently, they have figured out a way to make this signal also impact physical processes, like seizures. Jeff discovered what they were up to…"

"And, now he's dead." His grandmother spoke very calmly, deliberately. "Zach, you have to go to the police. You are in danger." Zach's safety and well-being had been the foremost objective in his grandmother's life since the day his father died. That responsibility trumped even the grief of losing her husband of 57 years.

"I can't, Grandma. They would never believe me. These organizations operate outside normal laws. Besides, I don't know who I could trust."

She was quiet for a moment, as if trying to decide whether this explanation was valid. Then she spoke again.

"Then you have to figure this out yourself. And you have to stop them."

"I know, Grandma. I know."

"Can Jill help you?"

"What makes you think—"

She gave a quick negative nod that indicated there was no point in maintaining a ruse.

"She is in very bad shape. I'm afraid Jeff tested out the new technology on her. He wasn't trying to hurt her. He was actually trying to make her fall in love with him, feed her thoughts about marriage in her sleep. But it went wrong. She hasn't slept in weeks. Her body is falling apart. They tried to kill her as well. Seizures, just like Grandpa." Zach looked over at the bed again and imagined his grandfather's tired, frail old body convulsing like Jill's had.

"Well, to be rich and smart, Jeff doesn't have the sense the Good Lord gave a frog. You can't make a woman love you. Even if it worked, it wouldn't be right."

Zach had not really taken the time to contemplate that, although he was now pretty sure Jill had.

"And that poor girl. I can't even imagine." Grandma had only seen Jill a few times in the past decade. But to Grandma, she was still that rambunctious little girl with the skinned knees eating cookies at the kitchen table after school.

"Is there anyone who can help you?"

"Dr. Ragsdale. He's a scientist from my company. He's working on it now, hiding out with Jill. Somewhere safe."

Zach picked up the scanner. "I need to check the house. If they came after Grandpa, there's no reason to think they won't come after you as well."

"Zach, don't worry about me. I'll be fine. You need to go help this Dr. Ragsdale and look after Jill." She objected, but he was already walking slowly around the room, watching the needle on the scanner.

He picked up the TV remote and tossed it on the bed. A minute later it was joined by a digital wall clock from the hallway and a DVD player from the guest room. "Grandma, I need you to look for anything you have bought in the past year that takes a battery or plugs in. Bring it in and put it on the bed."

Several minutes of unplugging and carrying later, a pile of a half dozen devices were piled on the sheet where his grandfather spent his last painful minutes. Grandma stood beside him as he held the scanner over the bed. The needle maxed out.

"How is that possible, Zach? Everything is unplugged."

"The transmitter has its own rechargeable battery supply. I'm not sure how long it holds a charge. But you can probably assume days. If you have the drug in your system and fall asleep within range of one of these, these folks can influence your dreams."

He pulled the four corners of the sheet together to make a bundle, slung it over his shoulder, and carried it outside. Ragsdale already had plenty of samples, but he tossed these into the trunk anyway. He wanted them as far away from his grandmother as possible.

Zach went back inside to find his grandmother sitting on the couch, staring blankly at his grandfather's chair.

"You go ahead, Zach. Mrs. Olson ran home to get a few things. She will be right back. She'll sit with me tonight."

Zach bent to one knee and gave her a big hug. He could feel her trembling.

"I love you, Grandma. We are going to find these guys."

"I know, Zach. You can do this. You can do anything."

He squeezed her tight and felt the scanner from his jacket pocket stabbing into his ribs. He pulled it out. The needle was moving.

"Grandma, are there any other electronics in this room?"

"No, dear, I moved everything out."

She stood up and he frantically dug through the cushions and looked under the couch. Nothing. He stood up and turned to her. She had her hand over her heart, fresh tears in her eyes.

"Zach, I had a pacemaker put in a few months ago. Outpatient procedure at the hospital here in town. I didn't tell you because I didn't want you to worry."

Zach pointed the scanner towards her. The needle maxed out.

"Oh, God. Grandma." He hugged her again.

At that moment, his cell phone buzzed in his pocket. He grabbed it instinctively. A new text message was on the screen.

"If you love your grandmother, just walk away." Zach stared at the screen for a moment. It did not surprise him, of course. He was convinced he had uncovered a conspiracy, he was convinced he was in danger, and it only stood to reason the danger would escalate. The direct threat was not a surprise, but what he felt was. Zach felt rage. Pure, hot, indignant rage. His grandmother had never harmed anyone, had treated everyone with kindness.

Zach had only been close to a few people in his life—his grand-parents, Jill, Jeff. And now two of them were dead, one was very ill, the other had just been threatened. Zach wanted to squeeze the phone until it crumbled. Zach wanted to hurt these people, whoever they were. In that moment, he was willing to do anything. Zach did not release that emotion, fearing it might blind his mind. But he tucked it away for later, a dagger to use if needed.

"Grandma, you cannot sleep tonight. Under no circumstances can you let yourself fall asleep. Tell Mrs. Olson that you accidentally took the wrong medication and the doctor told you to stay awake for 24 hours until it clears your system."

"Zach, the love of my life was taken from me tonight, and the person I love the most in this world is in serious danger. I don't think I was going to get much sleep tonight anyway. I'll make coffee just in case. Don't worry about me."

She kissed him on his cheek and stood up straight to walk to the door. God, she looked strong all of a sudden. Zach headed for the car and drove towards Jill and Ragsdale, the constraints of the speed limit suddenly irrelevant.

EIGHTEEN

ZACH KNOCKED TWICE ON THE DOOR of the rental house. Twenty seconds passed, so he knocked again. A full minute later, he knocked a third time.

Ragsdale opened the door in full fluster. The doc was back in the office hunched over his laptop screen before Zach crossed the threshold. "Getting pretty close," Ragsdale said over his shoulder.

"How's Jill?" Zach said softly.

Zach heard a throaty voice from behind him, "I was asleep, until I had a dream about someone hitting me in the head with a baseball bat."

"That would be this guy's 'pound on the door' routine," Ragsdale offered without turning around.

"No shit, Einstein," Jill said, voice slightly muffled by her hands as she rubbed them over her face.

She sat up and patted the seat beside her. "Have a seat. How was your grandmother?"

"Terrible. It was just awful. Granddad started having seizures while he was asleep."

"Just like me?" Jill said.

"Yes, only he was on heavy sleeping pills. Grandma couldn't wake him up. He just never woke up."

"Did you figure out what device they used?" Ragsdale asked. He had taken a break from his work and sat down in a chair across from the sofa.

"A TV remote, I think. There's a whole pile of stuff in the trunk.

But that's not all." He tossed his cell phone across the table towards Ragsdale, who looked at the screen and frowned. Ragsdale tossed it back and Zach handed it to Jill.

"Oh God, Zach." She looked at the screen as if it was a snake about to bite, then looked back at Zach with tears in her eyes. She loved his grandmother. Everyone did.

"Did you sweep the house with the scanner?" Ragsdale asked.
"Yes."

"She should be safe, then."

"I'm afraid it's not that simple."

Ragsdale raised an eyebrow.

"She has a brand new pacemaker."

No one said anything. Jill squeezed Zach's hand.

"Come over and look at this." Ragsdale stood and walked back to the office. Zach followed quickly. Jill stumbled into the room, leaned against the wall and slumped down to sit on the floor. She pulled her knees into her arms and laid her face on them.

Ragsdale had dragged a small kitchen table into the office, and on it was lined up an assortment of about 30 water bottles. Each one was labeled with a Post-it note and a number.

"The number indicates the presence of the drug, in parts per million." He pointed to a spreadsheet displayed on his laptop. There were columns for brand, stock number, and parts per million. "It doesn't appear there is any real pattern to the numbers. Pretty random amounts. But all of these samples had a high enough concentration to induce the heightened dream sensitivity."

Zach thought he saw a pattern in the numbers—he was usually the first to see patterns in things. But sometimes the existence of a pattern doesn't really mean anything.

"So how did they get the drug into the water?" Jill asked.

"I'm not sure. We would have to visit all the bottling plants. I'm sure there are plenty of ways to pollute the system, if you really want to."

"There are at least five brands there, from maybe eight or ten different bottling plants." Zach spoke as he read the labels on a few of the bottles. "This stuff is everywhere. Shutting this down is not going to be easy."

"There's more," Ragsdale said as he pointed to the other corner of the room.

On the floor by the desk was a pile of broken consumer

electronics, plastic cases cracked open, broken wires sticking out from odd places, buttons and springs and screws scattered around the floor. Ragsdale's fingers were covered with a host of cuts of varying degrees of severity, scars from his battle to tear asunder what Chinese factory workers had put together.

On the desk was a neat line of about fifteen small square electronic components. They all looked the same. Small, about the size of two matchboxes, covered in metal, with two wires protruding from one end.

"This is a pretty impressive device, from an engineering perspective. It is a completely self-contained little parasite. It contains a modified cellular antenna, a very tiny sub-frequency speaker, a very sensitive receiver, a basic silicon board, and a battery. The two wires connect to the device's power supply, charge the backup battery. I found one of these in every one of those devices. These are all too big to fit into a pacemaker, so there may also be a more advanced version. But this could be embedded in pretty much anything."

Jill picked one up. "So, how do they work?"

"I was able to download some of the basic code from the chips." Ragsdale picked up a sheet of plain white copy paper covered with notes and some basic diagrams. "When you first plug in the host device, this little thing boots up and starts to transmit a low-level probing signal. The person has to have taken the drug to be sensitive enough for this thing to impact their dreams. If someone who has been taking the Somnucogipam falls asleep near the device, the device sends out a kind of diagnostic test to the sleeper. The diagnostic appears to administer some basic tests—languages, math, spatial reasoning. After that, the device starts to get instructions from the master signal it is receiving. "

"But, why?" Jill tossed the device unceremoniously back onto the table. "Why would someone go through all this trouble to make people dream about working and solving problems? Who could possibly benefit?"

Zach looked at Ragsdale and began to suspect the answer. "Ragsdale, you said these things have some kind of receiver built in?"

"Yes." He picked one up and pointed to a tiny circular component covered with gold mesh. "This is it right here."

"What kind of signals does it pick up? Are we talking about a microphone?"

"Sort of. But it is pretty specialized. It only picks up signals on a very specific frequency, and then only short variations."

"So, it's picking up some kind of biological feedback?"

"Maybe. I can't be sure."

The three of them stood in silence for a moment, looking at each other.

"Fine, hook me up. I'll try it," Jill offered.

"The hell you will." Ragsdale and Zach said, strangely in unison.

"It's too dangerous, Jill," Zach said. "Last time you went to sleep near one of these things you almost died."

"But you guys can wake me up quickly if something happens. Besides, there's no way that thing knows who I am, right?"

She looked at Zach, then at Ragsdale. "Right?"

"Well, actually, biofeedback can be very individualized," Ragsdale said. "It is theoretically possible that things like breathing patterns, heartbeats and brain activities are unique enough that they can be used to create a unique key, a signature that is uniquely yours. If someone has figured out which patterns are unique across individuals, then even a simple device like this could access a remote database to determine who you are."

Jill shuddered. Zach grabbed her hand. Partly to comfort her, partly to comfort himself.

"I'll do it. I already have the drug in my system," Zach offered. "And it doesn't seem to have as much effect on me as it does on others. The dreams just aren't as intense."

"OK," Ragsdale said.

"And we'll be right here to wake you up if it looks like things are getting dangerous," Jill said. She squeezed his hand a little. It was nice that she didn't go immediately. He hadn't had 30 seconds of continuous physical contact from another person in about eighteen months. It would be a shame for him to die in his sleep tonight.

"Well, let's get to it. I am getting pretty sleepy, anyway." Zach walked over to the couch, took off his shoes, and began arranging the pillows.

Jill sat down in the love seat across from him, pulled her legs up into the chair, and stared through dark-circled eyes. At first, she was staring at him, but in a moment she was staring through him, with the glassy eyes of someone who was losing a two-front war against both falling asleep and staying awake. Unable to do either effectively, she hovered blankly in between.

Ragsdale set up one of the transmitters on the coffee table by

Zach's head. He had soldered wires to several places on the device. The other end of the wires fed into some kind of meter that plugged into his laptop via USB port. Ragsdale sat down in a high-backed chair to the right of the couch, just beside Zach. He put the laptop on the coffee table, Zach could just see it out of the corner of his right eye. The screen was divided into two halves, one window labeled "Incoming," the other labeled "Outgoing."

"Zach, I've tapped into the receiver and the transmitter. I'll be able to see everything the device is transmitting to you, and whatever signals it is picking up. I adapted a basic reader application to scan the signals and convert to text." Zach found himself staring across the dark living room at Jill. He couldn't tell if she was staring back at him or just staring. Such was the state of their mutual fatigue and inadequate lighting.

Ragsdale took a black plastic watch from his wrist, pushed a few buttons, and tossed it so that it landed on Zach's chest. "Put this on. Runner's watch. Will help us monitor your heart rate."

"You don't run."

"You don't know that."

"Pretty sure."

Zach saw Jill's face break into a smile. He smiled back. And with that as his muse, closed his eyes. Eight deep breaths later, he was asleep.

As he drifted to the edge of REM, the screen on Ragsdale's laptop sprang to life. On the "Incoming" screen, basic words from a variety of languages streamed. Hundreds of languages appeared. Then, the stream narrowed to three specific languages: English, Spanish, Latin, and the words became progressively more complex.

Zach's head went from side to side just a little, his lips moving silently as if reading a book. But then the questions became harder, moved faster. Zach showed just a moment of stress, but then he re-laxed and drifted into more normal sleep. The "Output" screen flashed the words "Error. Unit Not Responsive."

The same process repeated two more times—relatively innocuous signals were sent and received. But when the intensity increased, Zach would just drift away, disengage from the signal.

After forty-five minutes, Ragsdale shook Zach's shoulder. He woke up.

"We could see they were sending you some kind of test. Words in different languages. But every time the questions would get more intense, you would stop interacting—just disconnect from the signal."

"Yeah," Zach said, willing himself to wake up. "That's what my dream felt like. I was sitting in a classroom. People were talking in different languages, someone was writing on the board. I understood a lot of it, just casual conversation.

"But then a man was in the dream, the school principal, I think. He told me to answer harder questions, and answer quicker. He started yelling about how I was going to fail. After just a couple of moments of that, the dream changed, and I was sitting in a diner eating a bowl of cheese grits. They were delicious."

"Well, at least the dream had a happy ending," Jill said as she smiled. It was a beautiful smile. It turns out that fatigue has almost no effect on one's teeth, their whiteness or symmetry. Zach was thankful for that.

Ragsdale was not smiling. His brow was furrowed in thought, and his mouth was bent downward into a frown. "For some reason, you don't seem to be as receptive to external stimuli while you are asleep."

"I've always been a sound sleeper."

"Yes, but this isn't just about the soundness of your sleep. This is about your ability to block out the outside world while you are asleep. Most people, even while in a deep sleep, still have the outside world creep in. Someone turns on the light in the room, and the sleeper dreams about the sun shining. Someone turns on the fan and the sleeper dreams about the wind blowing. When people sleep, the physical body is still sensing the outside world, and those senses impact dreams. The people behind this are using a drug to make people abnormally sensitive to outside stimuli. And they're using these little transmitters to create very focused messages. Because you are so resistant to the outside world while asleep, you are also resistant to this system."

"So, great. They won't be able to kill him." Jill seemed a little flustered as she looked at Ragsdale, "Why is that a problem?"

"Because we can't stop this until we figure out how it works, and we can't figure out how it works unless we monitor the whole thing in action," Zach answered for him.

Ragsdale nodded.

"Well, then we have about 68 bottles left that I can drink." Zach walked over to one of the cases lying on the floor and grabbed a bottle. "If I drink enough of this, it will work eventually, right?

It's like local anesthetic. Some people just need more than others."

"Zach, we don't know how much it would take, given your resistance level. Besides, the more you drink, the greater the risk will be that the condition becomes permanent."

Ragsdale looked at Jill, but didn't say what he was thinking. *Like her.*

Jill spoke up again, "Then let me do the test. I can't possibly get any more screwed up than I am right now."

"No!" Ragsdale looked at her and spoke more loudly than either Zach or Jill expected.

"I'll do it," Ragsdale said. "Zach, you monitor the machines."

"That's ridiculous," Zach said. "You're the only one here who hasn't taken any of this drug. I'm not going to let you screw yourself up. Besides, you are older than Jill and I put together. I'm afraid you might wet yourself. And I'm sure as hell not cleaning that up." They shared a tired smile.

"What if you boosted the signal? It's not that I am completely unresponsive to the outside world when I'm asleep. It just takes a lot to get through to me."

Ragsdale raised his eyebrows and scratched the thickening stubble on his chin.

"I suppose I could amplify the signal 5, 10 times if I increased the power supply. We could also put it very close to your head, to minimize loss of clarity."

He grabbed the transmitter and walked back over to the table in the office. He produced a small portable soldering iron from one of his boxes and started to work.

"This will just take a couple of minutes. Why don't you go pee or something, so you don't wet the bed? And give me a sample while you're at it. I need to establish a baseline drug concentration level for this test."

"You just want to play with some more pee," Zach said as he walked into the foyer between the living room and office. Ragsdale raised a middle finger off the soldering iron but didn't look up from his work.

A few minutes later, Zach was back on the couch, a fresh cup of warm urine on Ragsdale's desk. Jill was on the loveseat, looking at him from across the room, just as before. Zach was lying on his side, right ear on the pillow, facing Jill. Now the transmitter was sitting on the pillow just in front of his forehead. He could see it in his peripheral vision, its long cord snaking back to Ragsdale's laptop.

It occurred to Zach he must be the world's most boring daredevil. Normally folks mock death by climbing a mountain or base jumping from a cliff or jumping a motorcycle over a dozen cars. Zach was merely lying comfortably on a couch, but he was keenly aware that he was no less at risk. They did not know how this process worked, they could not be sure this nap would not be his last. Still, Zach willed his eyes to close and tried not to think about the unknown but undeniably deadly gadget literally pointed directly at his brain. It took twelve deep breaths this time, and Zach was asleep.

The Incoming screen flashed just as before—a long series of words in several different languages. They became more difficult, faster.

Zach's eyelids squeezed together. His head nodded back and forth a little. He was clearly agitated, but he remained asleep.

This continued for a few seconds. Then, the Outgoing screen displayed a message:

LANUGAGE PROFICIENCY: English 9/10, Spanish 6/10, Latin 4/10.

Ragsdale felt a brush against his arm. He noticed Jill had pulled a footstool up beside him. She was staring intently at the screen, hand over her mouth.

"What the hell?" He asked the question they both were asking.

Then they noticed a new stream in the Outbound screen. This time, it was a stream of numbers, equations. It started out with basic multiplication and division. It moved to algebra and calculus. Then things became even more complex. Proofs from graduate-level mathematics classes streamed across the screen. Zach's pulse had increased significantly, and he was fidgeting noticeably with his hands. Jill reached across the laptop in front of Ragsdale to grab Zach's hand, but Ragsdale stopped her. "We can't wake him yet. We need a little more."

Then, the outbound screen flashed another message.

BASIC MATHEMATICS PROFICIENCY: 10/10

ADVANCED MATHEMATICS PROFICIENCY: 10/10

THEORETICAL MATHEMATICS PROFICIENCY: 10/10

Ragsdale whistled just a little.

"What's wrong? Is he smarter than you?" Jill smiled as she looked at Ragsdale. Zach had always been the smartest person she knew. For some reason, it made her proud to watch someone else appreciating his intelligence.

This pattern continued for several more minutes. Additional streams of questions streamed across the Incoming screen. They covered problem solving skills, chemistry, and computer codes. In each case, the questions started out basic, then became progressively more complex. At the end of this string of questions, a rating was transmitted on the Outbound screen. Zach was restless the entire time, his pulse much higher than normal for a sleeping state. But he didn't seem to be in any true physical distress.

Then, another stream started. The Incoming screen displayed: "Job A2873D265Q."

It was soon followed by lines of what looked like computer code. Almost immediately, a stream of code started streaming through the Outbound screen. At first the outbound text flowed much more quickly than the inbound, but after a few moments the inbound flow increased to keep pace. Zach was noticeably agitated now, tossing restlessly from side to side. He was beginning to sweat a little, his eyes squinting as his lips moved to the sound of invisible words.

"What's going on?" Jill asked, her voice shaking just a little.

"He is thinking, figuring things out. But it looks like someone else is at the controls."

"They are telling him what to think?"

"More specifically, it looks like they are giving him problems to solve."

"Like a computer?"

"The human brain is the most advanced, powerful computer on earth. Especially if that brain is owned by someone like Zach."

"But they don't know it is him, right?"

"They may not care. It looks like they ran some diagnostics first to find out what his aptitudes were. I think whoever is transmitting just knows they have a really smart guy who is good at math."

"Then, he should be safe?"

Ragsdale opened his mouth to speak, but the data stream was interrupted by new text that silenced them both:

IDENTIFIED; zachTanner034g

There was a pause, and the incoming stream went blank. Ragsdale and Jill both leaned back from the screen, as if it were about to attack.

The Incoming screen sprang to life again. This time it was a massive stream of text and numbers, moving so quickly the screen was blurry with characters. Zach's heart rate jumped, then he began to thrash around, arms and legs beating against the couch cushions. He began to choke.

Jill practically leaped over the coffee table, knocking the laptop to the floor in the process, and started shaking Zach's shoulders. Ragsdale ripped the device from its cords and threw it across the foyer into the office on the other side of the house.

Zach awoke with Jill's hands on each side of his head, her lips a few inches from his. She was screaming for him to wake up. But when his eyes opened, her lips broke into a smile, and a different kind of tears fell out of her beautiful, tired eyes. They paused there for a moment, hearts racing from the terror of the past few minutes, and perhaps also due to the proximity of their lips. But then she fell into a hug. He could feel her hair against his face. Some kind of perfume, understated under normal circumstances, only a whisper now after a long day. But she still smelled intoxicating. He felt the moisture of her tears soaking through his shirt. After a moment, she sat up and she wiped her eyes.

Ragsdale was the first one to speak. "That was a hell of something." It was a little nonsensical, but pretty much captured the moment.

Jill looked at Zach, "What happened to you?"

"Well, I dozed off, just like any other time. But right as I started to reach a really deep sleep, my mind started racing. It was like I was taking tests, trying to figure things out. It's very fuzzy, I can't recall any specific questions. But I think there were different topics—math, languages, other stuff. I just felt like I was working the whole time, like my mind couldn't completely shut down."

Again, a beat missing in conversation. Let him recover. Show some action. Etc.

"So, Ragsdale, what did we learn?"

"Well, this is definitely a two-way communication. They figure out what you are good at. And then they give you tasks to do in your sleep, and they capture the output. It's almost like—"

"Outsourced computing?" Jill offered.

"Exactly."

"What kind of computing? Are we talking about data processing?" Zach asked.

"It is tough to tell. We could only see bits of code. But, theoretically, it could be anything. The applications are endless—medical research, cryptography, data mining, simulations, anything. Depending on how sophisticated their platform is, they could use this system to do just about anything a computer does, with one big difference." Ragsdale was getting pretty animated, pretty excited. He was standing as he spoke, arms waving around in over-animated gesticulation.

"You might consider dialing back the giddiness just a bit, Doctor Science, in light of recent events." Jill had retreated to the loveseat to recoup.

Ragsdale looked a little embarrassed. Zach jumped in. "What's the big difference?"

Ragsdale's eyes got big, and his arms extended as if to make a grand statement, but then he checked his excitement and assumed a more sedate posture. "The sheer power. That's the difference. A typical computer can only handle a few hundred billion bytes of information. But the human mind is the most advanced processing engine in the world. The human brain can process something like three quadrillion bytes. If they can string together enough people, they could have access to computing power the world can only dream of—things we didn't think we would see for a generation."

"So, this could be worth a lot of money?" Jill asked.

"Absolutely, this would be worth a fortune. But it's not just money. It's power. With this kind of computing engine, just about any code could be broken, any encryption penetrated."

"It's worth enough that someone would kill to protect it," Zach said. Some faceless bastard had killed his grandfather, threatened his grandmother, tried to kill him. He glanced at his cell phone but didn't read the message again.

The room was silent for a minute. Zach was coping with a fresh wave of grief and a torrent of rage. Ragsdale was trying to put a few missing pieces together. Jill was framing a question.

"So, why me? Why Zach? Why would they want to kill us? Why are we a threat? It's not like anyone would believe us if we went public. And it's not like we can stop this by ourselves."

Zach stood up and began to pace a little. Pacing had always helped him think, mostly because it was one of the few sure-fire ways to ensure he didn't fall asleep. "Since your dad passed away, you are the sole heir of his electronics business, right?"

"Yes."

"And it looks now like that business is a pretty key part of the system. It must have taken a long time to set up all these distribution relationships, get these parts into so many devices. And if whoever is behind this thinks that Jeff may have told you what was going on, there would be a risk you would use your control of the company to put a stop to it."

"Hell yeah, I would. But it would pretty much have to be me.

These contracts are about 50% of company revenue this year, and the management team is making a lot of money because of these deals. They are not going to shut it down on a tip. They would need hard proof."

"Or the majority shareholder overruling them," Zach said.

"So, what happens to your company stock if you die? I mean, it's not like you are married or anything." Ragsdale did not mean it the way it sounded.

Jill frowned. "But, what about the water? We still don't know how the drug is getting in the water, or how we can stop it."

Zach stared across the room at Jill. Then his eyes moved to the coffee table beside the couch. On it lay three stacks of magazines. Sophisticated magazines for educated folks, suitable for a house that was being frequented by potential buyers. *National Geographic*, *Southern Living*, *The Economist*. A buyer may read *National Enquirer*, but they probably would rather buy a home from someone who read *National Geographic*. Each magazine was in a separate stack, bound side facing towards the front door, the past four months of each title stacked in chronological order.

"Holy shit," Zach exclaimed. He ran to the computer in the home office. It had gone into sleep mode and prompted him for a password.

He hit control-alt-delete to bring up the login screen and yelled over his shoulder, "Ragsdale, what's your pa—" But Ragsdale was already there, and he reached over and typed in his password. Zach took back control of the keyboard and alt-tabbed back to the spreadsheet with the water bottle stats.

"Look at this. The numbers look pretty random. But lot numbers are probably roughly chronological, right? And if you sort the list by brand name, then by lot number." He did so, as he was speaking. "It's like magazines. The lot numbers are sequential within each brand, just like magazine dates are sequential within each title."

"Holy hell," Ragsdale said, much more softly than Zach had. He gazed at the updated chart on the screen. The vertical axis was drug concentration. The bottom axis was time, with oldest on the left and newest on the right. And on the chart, the previously random dots were now in five distinct lines. Each line corresponded to a brand. And each line sloped consistently downward from left to right. Drug concentrations were lower in newer bottles of water for each brand.

"That is definitely not random," Jill said, looking over Zach's shoulder. It had taken her a few seconds longer to make the trip across the room. "But why would the concentrations go down over time?"

"Maybe they figured out they needed less of the drug and just ramped down the dosage," Ragsdale offered, in a very unconvinced tone.

"Or maybe," said Zach, "Maybe it's not the water that is delivering the drug." He turned to ask something of Ragsdale, but the scientist had already grabbed an empty water bottle and began attempting to cut out a piece of the plastic with a pair of desk scissors unsuited for that purpose. He added a few additional cuts to his finger, courtesy of the sharp shards of plastic, but didn't look up.

"Zach, grab me some cups of water. Tap water. And make the cups all the same if you can."

"On it!" Zach yelled from the kitchen, where he was already filling up cups for the experiment. Jill had resumed her position on the floor, knees pulled up to her chin, face resting on her knees.

A moment later, Zach returned with three cups on a tray, each one identical, each half filled with tap water.

Ragsdale placed a drop from each on a slide and slid them under the microscope. "No presence of the drug."

Zach put Post-it notes on three of the cups. They read, "Test," "Control," and "Rinse." Ragsdale rinsed a piece of plastic water bottle in the "Rinse" cup, then dropped it in the "Test" cup. The "Control" cup sat empty.

He pressed a button to start the stopwatch on his wristwatch.

Jill returned to the couch, lying on her side with her eyes closed. She raised her head as if to ask a question, but thought better of it. She really didn't want to hear Ragsdale speculating for the next few minutes. Better to get a little rest and hear the real facts when they were available. She took slow, deep breaths, and tried to sleep.

Zach looked at Ragsdale, "How long?"

"We probably should give it a couple of hours. You figure it takes several days for a bottle to get to market, so it's okay if it takes a while. And it couldn't happen too quickly and still be stable."

"Maybe we should try to get some sleep."

Ragsdale chuckled at the irony, but it was a good suggestion.

"I scouted out the place while you were gone. Master bedroom upstairs has a king-sized bed. I call dibs on that, since sleepy beauty there has the couch. Two other bedrooms upstairs, one has a twin bed and the other is set up like a home gym."

"I guess I'll take the twin, then."

"Alright. It's 1:15 a.m. I set my watch alarm for five. Get some sleep."

Ragsdale dragged himself upstairs. Jill was at least superficially asleep on the couch. But Zach was not going to sleep. It wasn't that he couldn't sleep. He could always sleep. But he didn't want to. He wanted to think.

The last day had been a march to the drumbeat of chaos, taxing on the mind and the soul and the body. He needed to think.

But it would be nice to also have something to drink. He walked into the kitchen. Faux oak cabinets surrounded black appliances. A built-in wine rack to the right of the sink held an assortment of fake wine bottles. It probably wasn't a good idea to leave actual alcohol in an untended rental house. The cabinet just to the right of the sink yielded a tall glass. It was cheap, thin and light. But it was fully waterproof, which was the point.

The refrigerator held a case of bottled water. "And this is the lovely gourmet kitchen, can I get you a bottle of water? The appliances are natural gas and Energy Star compliant..." Zach mumbled to himself in his best cheery realtor voice.

He grabbed a couple of ice cubes but decided to forgo the bottled water in favor of tap. He was turning on the brushed nickel water faucet when he noticed one of the wine bottles didn't look like the others. He retrieved it from its perch and noticed the bottle was actually bourbon in a round bottle, wine cork stuffed in the top to make it look like the others.

Apparently, realtors need to kick back sometimes too.

Zach pulled the cork and poured. After a sip, he realized he was hungry. Few things complement late nights and fatigue quite like cold pizza.

Ragsdale had deposited the leftovers on the counter. The refrigerator would have been better, of course, but rancidity didn't seem like a significant risk after just a few hours. He grabbed the box in one hand, his bourbon in the other, and shuffled into the living room.

He fell into the first chair he saw, which just happened to be facing the couch where Jill was sleeping. He propped his feet on the coffee table, the pizza box in his lap, and alternated bites of room temperature pizza with bourbon.

He found himself staring at Jill. First, because she was right in front of him, but also, he wanted to. She was beautiful, of course. She had always been that. And, even though lack of sleep was taking its toll, she was still stunning.

She was lying on her side with her head on her arms, facing him, a few locks of raven black hair drifting across her closed eyes.

Zach had never really thought of Jill as anything more than someone he grew up with, and the girl Jeff loved. But now he was realizing she was one of the few people in the world he was actually connected to. In a strange way, this childhood friend he hadn't seen in a decade was the closest thing he had to family other than his grandmother.

And, she was beautiful. He closed his eyes.

Once Zach drifted off to sleep, and the sound of his breath was slow and peaceful, Jill opened her eyes and headed upstairs to sleep. But a few hours later she was awake again. Ragsdale had swept the room for transmitters, so she hadn't had any "working" dreams. But the lingering effects of the drug had made her sensitive to any outside sound while she slept. An hour or so after she went to sleep, she began to dream about a massive tornado blowing through her home, rattling shutters and blowing furniture around the room. She awoke to find it was the sound of Ragsdale snoring, asleep in the master bedroom. She put on a robe and slipped out into the hallway, the cheap carpet rough on her bare feet, and headed down to the kitchen for a shot of the bourbon still stashed there. But when she reached the fourth step, it creaked terribly loud, and it startled her. She froze for a moment, then sat down on the step right above the creaky one. She was just about to get up and continue when she saw Zach straight ahead, four stairs down and across the room, sleeping in a chair with his chin on his chest.

A half-eaten slice of pizza lay on his shirt, and a hand with greasy fingers hung limp off the side of the chair. The other hand held a half-empty glass of bourbon, perched precariously on his thigh. She smiled and laughed to herself. Typical Zach. The only man alive who could actually sleep in that position. If you could sleep on the top of the monkey bars, a living room chair is nothing. He had accomplished a lot since those days on the playground and was a successful, good looking, responsible man. But in the few days she had seen that, behind the nice suits and impressive resume, he was still the lonely little boy just barely getting by on the small ration of love life had afforded him.

Jill had always found Zach a little fascinating. They had shared so many of the same childhood experiences, but his story was so much different from hers. She had never really depended on her parents' money, but she had the luxury of knowing it was there. And everywhere she went she was something of a mini celebrity. In this town, it was because of her family. Abroad it was because of her personality. She had a natural charm and easy way of making people love her. But Zach was blessed with no such magnetism. If anything, he had quite the opposite condition. In this town, he was pretty much invisible, being without any family and having just a couple of friends. There was a distance about him that made his politeness and kindness seem like a thin curtain pulled closed over a dark, lonely pit.

But he was a remarkable boy—a remarkable man. The most brilliant person she had ever known, and probably the kindest. But altogether invisible to most of the world. She found herself standing over him, removing the greasy pizza from his chest and depositing it on the coffee table. A lock of dark brown hair had fallen across his temple and was causing a mild twitch every few breaths. She brushed it back gently and put a very soft kiss in its place. She didn't really know why. But she wasn't a person who spent much time thinking about why. She smiled, turned, and padded softly back upstairs, skipping the creaky fourth step on her way.

NINETEEN

"SON OF A BITCH!"

The exclamation startled Zach. It was Ragsdale. He was in the office. The first few rays of daylight were creeping in around the closed curtains. Jill was standing in front of him, looking at him with the kind of understated smile someone has when they are actually happy, not just trying to look happy. And she was also holding a cup of coffee, which she handed to him.

"Geez, Zach. I thought I looked like hell. Where's your dignity, man?"

He looked down and saw that a half-eaten slice of sausage pizza was napping on his chest. The bourbon was more or less intact, except for a large splash of it that had spilled onto his pants.

"I see you found the booze."

"You knew about this? Holding out on us?"

"I've stayed in this place a few times. But realtors are still showing it. Have to keep the bottle stashed so I don't find some realtor passed out on the sofa."

"I'm going to need a clean shirt."

"Why don't you go nuts and put on clean pants too?"

Ragsdale came barging into the living room. "Are you coming in here, or not?"

"Coming!" Zach tried to stand. But propping one's feet on a coffee table all night isn't exactly great for circulation. He fell forward. Jill caught him. Coffee splashed onto Jill's shirt.

"Don't start that shit. You have to carry me, remember?

I'm the sick one."

"Sorry."

"At least now we match." She pointed to the coffee stain on her shirt that was roughly the same size as the pizza stain on Zach's shirt.

"Check this out." Ragsdale was holding the two Post-it notes Zach had placed on the cups earlier. He stuck them to the wall. Under the word "Control" on the first cup, Ragsdale had written "0 PPM." On the second, under "Test," he had written "20 PPM."

"Twenty parts per million after six hours," Ragsdale said.

"Six?"

"Yeah, Van Winkle. You overslept. But at this rate, the concentration would be strong enough to affect sleep after just a couple of days."

"So, it wasn't the water?" Jill asked.

"Nope." Ragsdale and Zach spoke at the same time.

Ragsdale continued. "It's the plastic. They weren't contaminating the water supply. The drug is built into the plastic of the bottle. It leaches into the water slowly. That's why the concentrations went up over time in each bottle. Bottles that had been on the shelf for weeks had higher concentrations because the drug had more time to leach from the plastic bottle into the water. The FDA doesn't test for this drug. They don't even know it exists. So, there's no way they could stop it."

"But, we can," Jill said as she looked directly at Zach, and then at Ragsdale.

"Jill, you and Ms. James look very much alike, you know that?" Zach dropped a seeming non sequitor.

"Yes, she is a younger, hotter version of me. Thank you for bringing that up."

Ordinarily, Zach would have felt the need to dispute and reassure. But there were pieces to be put together. "This plastic is really important, absolutely vital to whoever is behind this, right?"

"Of course," Jill answered.

"And the plastics manufacturer owned by Jeff's family is the supplier. So, the bad guys need control of that company."

Ragsdale and Jill both nodded. Jill took a seat on the couch, Ragsdale on the chair to the left of the couch. Zach remained standing. He thought better when he was free to pace.

"So there are two ways to control the company. You can get Jeff on your side, since he will be the controlling shareholder one day. Or, you can get control of the company directly. Primary plan, and backup plan."

Zach was pacing back and forth. He had picked up a ceramic cherub from the coffee table and was tossing it lightly between his hands as he paced. "Jeff said people had approached him with this idea. They were trying to get them on their side, trying to get him to buy into what they were doing. They sold him a story about how they were going to solve the world's problems make the world better."

"And it worked," Jill said sadly.

"Yes, but it didn't work forever. Once he saw the side effects, he had second thoughts. Once he saw what it was doing to you..."

"They needed a backup plan," Ragsdale interrupted.

"Exactly. This is too big to risk on one person having a change of heart. And Jeff is sole heir to the company; no siblings, no kids, no wife." He looked at Jill, not intentionally. She looked uncomfortable; he looked away.

"But what if he got married? At first, I thought it was a coincidence that Ms. James looked so much like you, that she started working at Sopros shortly after Jeff did, and that they had an affair. But now it feels a little bit like a setup. They put her there to seduce Jeff. She was their hot little brunette insurance policy." He tossed the ceramic cherub from his left hand to right with authority. It was a hideous thing, perhaps the decorator was trying to be ironic.

"So, maybe that's why Ms. James decided to stay in town an extra day? She is in his will," Ragsdale said.

"Or, maybe she has a marriage certificate," Zach replied.

"That's crazy." Jill was visibly agitated. "He wouldn't fall in love and get married that quickly. He only knew her a few months." Zach could see a unique combination of hurt and outrage behind Jill's suddenly very alert blue eyes.

"Jill, just because she is in the will, or even married to Jeff, it doesn't mean he actually married her. These folks have tried to kill both of us in the past twelve hours. Forging a document or two wouldn't give them pause, especially if it meant they got complete control over the plastics company they needed."

"Well, the bitch and whoever she is working for are in for a pretty big surprise." Jill's face showed a little bit of smugness that had mixed with the rage.

Zach and Ragsdale looked at each other, shrugged, and raised their eyebrows. They weren't sure if Jill was contemplating a pipe bomb or a garden variety bitch slap.

Zach asked the question, softly. "What are you going to do, Jill?"

"I don't have to do anything. I've already done it. Actually we—Jeff and I—have already done it." She paused, took a deep breath, and continued.

"Five years ago, Jeff and I ran into each other here in town. We were both back meeting our families. And it turns out we were both flying out to Europe on a Monday, with a layover in London. We wound up sitting next to each other on the flight and talked a lot. It was so easy, so comfortable. We were both pretty lonely, in our own different ways. I was planning to stay in London until Thursday. Jeff said he had some unexpected change to his work schedule and would be in town as well. I'm pretty sure he just made that up. But, either way, he stayed. We spent a lot of time together, spent a couple of nights together.

"Maybe it was the nostalgia, I don't know. But we were both scheduled to fly out to different cities Thursday morning. So Wednesday afternoon, we took a drive in the countryside to Haslemere, just outside of London. We were so far away from everything. Far away from our families, from this town. It was just us. I had been running around the world for years. Jeff was just lonely in the way that only Jeff could be.

"Anyway, after a lot of talking, and a lot of wine, and watching the sunset sitting on the hood of his convertible, we found ourselves knocking on the door of the vicar at the Anglican Church of Haslemere. We were married right there in the living room of the parsonage, with his wife and a gardener bearing witness. In the twilight in the middle of nowhere. It made perfect sense.

"But the next morning, I panicked. I couldn't believe what I had done. It wasn't that I didn't love Jeff. I'd always loved him. But I always felt like he loved me more, you know? It was like, if we were married, I would be his whole world. But he would be just a part of mine. It didn't seem fair to him. It didn't seem fair to me. So, I panicked. I couldn't bear to see the disappointment on his face when I told him.

"So, I was stupid. I left him a note on my pillow. And I ran. I ran until I was on another continent, in another world, with other people. I always assumed he had the marriage annulled. I sure would have. But when we started seeing each other again a few months ago, he told me we were technically still married. I was shocked, but I suppose I shouldn't have been."

Ragsdale spoke first. "So, if you are still married to Jeff, then you would be the beneficiary of his estate?"

"Right. And it doesn't matter if Ms. James falsified a will or a marriage certificate, neither one would trump the fact that we were husband and wife."

"Do you have proof?" Ragsdale asked.

"Yes. I saved the marriage certificate. She pointed to a backpack leaning against the living room wall. I carried it with me. It reminded me of Jeff, of being happy." She paused for a moment. "Maybe I also thought of it as an insurance policy against dying alone." She forced an awkward smile. "I really am a terrible person."

"Does anyone else know?" Zach asked. "Because if they do, you could be in even more danger than we thought."

"No, I never told anyone. Jeff said he didn't, either. His family would freak out. I think he enjoyed having it as our little private secret. Maybe it was his insurance policy too."

"Well, Mrs. Peters, it sounds like you have a meeting at a law-yer's office this afternoon," Zach said.

"I wouldn't miss it for the world."

Ragsdale peered at them over the top of his glasses. "You had better get moving. The meeting is in a couple of hours. And both of you look like hell."

"A little courtesy, please, Science Boy."

"Pardon me, ma'am. You'll look fine after a shower and a change of clothes. I'm not sure there's anything we can do for Pizza Shirt over there." Ragsdale nodded his head towards Zach.

"You are no vision yourself," Zach offered.

"Yes, but I am a sloppy, paunchy, middle-aged scientist. Looking ragged is an eccentricity that is permitted me, if not expected of me. The world expects much more of you, however."

"I'm going to take a shower. I'll be back down for you to inspect my appearance in thirty minutes." Zach walked toward the stairs.

Jill had tired of the exchange and was already on the second step, walking upstairs. Zach followed her. Walking up stairs behind a woman creates its own set of challenges. Walk too close, and you look like a glute-addled pervert. Walk too far away, and it looks like you are intentionally trying to avoid looking like a glute-addled pervert, which suggests you are acutely aware of your closet pervish thoughts. Zach, of course, desired to avoid both direct and implied pervishness. So, he paced himself about four stairs behind Jill. As he did so, he wondered if he would have felt self-conscious about this a few months ago.

Jill reached the top of the steps and turned to open the first door on the right. She glanced over her right shoulder with a quick smile, "Are you looking at my ass, you little perv?"

Zach should have expected that, of course. But he blushed. Mostly because it was true.

"You wish," he said as he brushed past her. It wasn't much of a comeback, but it avoided an awkward silence. He turned to the second door on the right. She was still at the first door, hand on the knob, door opened just a few inches, looking at him. There was a brief silence. Not awkward, but definitely a little different.

"See you downstairs," she said. "And take a minute to press your shirt or something. I am going to look funeral hot, so you need to at least try and keep up."

Jeff stood in the shower and let the hot water pound on his face. It felt good to get out of those nasty clothes. Sleeping in clothes is bad enough. But when you wear a suit to a funeral, climb around in a dusty church attic, walk through a plastics factory, break into countless sweats from fear or exertion, take two restless naps, then top it all off by spilling food on them and sleeping in them all night... Well, those clothes would probably never be the same. He wondered if they were worth cleaning. The socks and t-shirt and underwear should be fine, given enough hot water and bleach. The pants, maybe with an extra shot of DEET from the dry cleaner, could be salvaged. The shirt would probably have to be burned.

Fortunately, he had packed shampoo and conditioner. Ordinarily he would have left it at home and used whatever the hotel provided. But he had planned to stay with his grandparents rather than a hotel. And his grandparents had used Pert exclusively since its introduction in 1983. They had been captured by the advanced technology of shampoo and conditioner in one. Zach was no fop, but Pert made his hair feel like a fistful of twine. So he had tossed into his bag some travel-sized toiletries he commandeered from a Marriott at some point in the preceding months.

A few minutes later, Zach was in the living room. His white dress shirt was beyond repair, so he was wearing a more casual striped shirt and a pair of nice khakis. It was more casual than he would have liked for a reading of a will, but there were no other options. He added his blue suit jacket from the day before to dress things up a bit.

He was sitting in a living room chair that more or less faced the stairs. Ragsdale was to his right, in the office, fussing with the carcasses of what looked like a couple of dismembered clock radios. Ragsdale turned and stepped into the foyer between the living room and office. He had made no pretense of improving his appearance. "I suppose I should head up and change clothes, or at least comb my hair."

"Actually, I think there is something you need to look into while Jill and I visit the lawyer. Besides, you weren't technically invited to the reading of the will."

"Is it bad form to crash a reading of a will? I wasn't aware there was a protocol. So, where am I going?"

Zach was about to explain to Ragsdale what he had in mind, but he heard a door open at the top of the stairs. For some reason, Zach stood up and faced the stairs.

He found himself sucking his stomach in just a little. Ragsdale glanced at him with an eyebrow raised. But then Jill appeared at the top of the stairs. She was taking the steps slowly, to accommodate her three-inch heels and crippling fatigue. A black dress started just above her knees and broke into an elegant 'V' across her chest before it finished in abbreviated sleeves that only partially covered her shoulders. The dress fit her snugly enough that you couldn't help but stare a little, but not so snugly that decent folk would feel compelled to look away. She had applied more makeup than usual, and it hid the effects of the sleep deprivation. Her skin was ivory and a perfect contrast to the deep black dress.

"Funeral hot," she said as she descended the last step into the foyer.

"I should say so," Ragsdale said, and a slow up and down stare delivered for dramatic effect. "Oh, to be young again."

Zach's mouth was strangely dry, so he just nodded in agreement. He stole another long glance and a brief moment of eye contact.

"Zach was just explaining that he has a little errand for me to run while you two are at the lawyer's office."

"Oh yeah? Well let's hear the plan." Jill passed between them and took a seat in the living room, knees together to the side, as one would expect. There are any number of products in the typical woman's beauty regimen that contribute to her overall scent—soap and lotion and makeup and perfume and hair products and such. Zach didn't know the components of Jill's particular apothecary, but the combined effect was compelling to the point of distraction.

It lingered for a moment as she brushed past. Men that are married or otherwise spend a lot of time in the company of women may find they take the wonder of this phenomena for granted. But Zach's state of general social and romantic isolation was such that he took nothing for granted. He gave himself a moment, took a breath, then continued his conversation with Ragsdale.

"Jeff's message mentioned something about test subjects here in town—a pilot program. At first, I assumed he was talking about the town in general, just a bunch of individuals. But when you are in the early phases of testing a complicated technology, what kind of environment do you want?"

He looked at Ragsdale, who played along. "Well, you want to be able to closely control the treatment—the dosage of the drug, the type of signals you are sending. But you also want to be able to monitor the results."

"And would the ideal situation be to have test subjects scattered all across town, in their separate houses?"

Ragsdale saw where this was going. "No, definitely not. There would be too many variables to control—the dosage of the drug, distance from the transmitter and receiver, other stimuli in the room that might also be impacting the dream."

"You would want a controlled environment, with a lot of test subjects, where you could control all those variables very carefully. And if you had such a test facility setup, what would you need?"

Ragsdale was getting excited now. He was speaking more loudly, faster. "A large population of test subjects whom you could control. Preferably ones already being monitored by medical devices and consistently taking medication. And, assuming you were doing the type of advanced computation we think they are doing, you would need a shit-load of bandwidth, probably wireless."

"So, in the past day the stupid car radio crackled with loud static three times. And guess where I was all three times?"

Jill motioned with her hand for Zach to keep going. She was growing a little tired of the Socratic approach, eager to hear where this was going.

Ragsdale picked up the explanation, "You were probably near a facility with a large number of people under medical care, with regimented schedules, standardized diets, being monitored for various medical conditions."

Jill's eyes opened wide. "The nursing home!"

"I'm afraid so. It is the perfect test site for this kind of system. It's just a theory, of course, but we need to snoop around a little and find out more," Zach said.

Ragsdale was already packing a few instruments into his weathered leather briefcase. "We need to get food and water samples, scan patient rooms for transmitters and receivers, look for some evidence of a high bandwidth wireless antennae."

"Absolutely. And Jill and I can't go there. Too big a risk someone there would recognize us, ask us what we are doing. You can go there and play the grumpy, rumpled old doctor bit and wander around unmolested."

A few moments later they were in the car and backing out of the short suburban driveway. Zach drove, Ragsdale sitting in the passenger seat. His leather briefcase was on the seat behind him, stuffed with devices whose function was not immediately apparent. He hadn't shaved this morning, or likely yesterday, for that matter. And his hair had once again triumphed in its battle with the comb. He was dressed well enough to give the appearance of moderate wealth, but still looked like he could have slept the night in his clothes. In short, he looked exactly like a physician two decades into his career who was finishing up a double shift. He stared out the window, left hand stroking his stubble, right hand strumming on his leg. His lips moved slightly as he refined his cover story and rehearsed his lines to himself.

Jill was in the back seat, sitting upright this time. All the better to not rumple her dress or hair. She wanted nothing more than to lay down and steal a few moments of rest in the back seat. But, much more than that, she wanted to look amazing when she strode into the lawyer's office. She didn't want to give that little bitch the satisfaction of seeing her look as bad as she felt. She was funeral hot and wasn't going to sacrifice that for a few moments of rest.

TWENTY

IT WAS ONLY A FEW MINUTES before the radio skipped again, and a few seconds later, Zach slowed the car and made an easy left turn into the long driveway of the nursing home. The road had been smooth blacktop, but the driveway was concrete, poured in sections with a seam every twenty feet. The driveway was long, and the car was moving slowly, "ka-thump," pause, "ka-thump…"

Ragsdale found his heart racing fast, in stark contrast to the plodding pace of the sedan. He was not a bit intimidated by the technical aspects of what he was trying to do. Quite the opposite. The last few weeks had energized him in a way he hadn't felt in years.

"Let me out here, don't get too close to the building." Ragsdale pointed towards the entrance to the employee parking lot. A second lot, separated from this one by a narrow band of grass and landscaped shrubs, was designated for guests.

"We should be done at the lawyer's office in a couple of hours. Will that be enough time?" Zach asked as he put the car into park.

"Should be, as long as they don't mistake me for a patient and put me in bed."

"Well, you do look pretty damn old," Jill chimed in from the back seat. "Don't worry, though. I hear they serve this pudding that tastes great and helps you shit regularly."

"Well, I'll definitely bring you back some of that." Ragsdale turned to Jill and smiled as he spoke. Staring out from beneath his bushy gray eyebrows, he made direct eye contact with Jill.

"Take care of our boy, okay? Don't let him doze off in the lawyer's office and embarrass himself."

"Don't you have somewhere to be, old man?" Zach asked.

Ragsdale grabbed his briefcase, slid out of the car, and started up the short path connecting the two parking lots to the building.

"So, are you going to get into the front seat, or just sit back there and let me play chauffeur?"

"Well, I was enjoying the opulence of this luxurious Chevy Impala back seat, but I suppose I could move up front and ride like common folk." Jill slipped out of the back seat, opened the passenger side door, and slid into the front seat. Her skirt came to rest about six inches above her knees, and Zach allowed himself to steal a glance in their direction.

"Seat's still warm from Ragsdale," she said.

"Old man butt warm."

"Lovely. Thanks for that."

They made a left and headed back towards town on State Route 12. The lawyer's office was on the town square, just about a mile away. A long, straight road—Dodden Ave—intersected the highway just before the town square. A Dollar General store occupied the right corner of the intersection.

Zach glanced in the rear-view mirror and saw a black sedan coming up quickly behind him, a town car maybe. The driver was steady, despite the high speed, keeping the big sedan dead straight. Zach's glances in the rear-view became more and more frequent. It appeared the driver might actually collide with them from behind. The last cross street before the square was a scant hundred yards ahead when Zach looked in the rear-view once again and nearly choked. The black sedan had pulled out into the opposite lane and was attempting to pass.

"What the hell?" He slammed the brakes hard. Jill's head slung forward and almost hit the windshield before the seat belt caught.

The sedan whipped in front of Zach just ahead of the intersection. But then, to Zach's surprise, the driver continued to the right, crossing into the Dollar General parking lot. He was going full speed towards Dodden Ave, clipped a shopping cart and sent it reeling. He was cutting the corner through the parking lot, still at full speed.

For a second, Zach assumed the driver was just in a hurry, cutting through the parking lot instead of taking a right at the intersection. But then a sharp chill swept over him.

He saw a tractor trailer barreling right to left down Dodden Avenue towards the intersection. By this time, Zach had come to a full stop. The big truck veered ever so slightly to the left, headed almost right at Zach and Jill's now stationary vehicle.

Then the town car came bouncing over the curb from the Dollar General onto the street. The driver took a hard left and struck the truck with the length of the car, passenger side doors crashing against the driver side of the tractor's cab. The rig jumped violently to the left as the passenger side of the town car exploded into a shower of glass. But the momentum of the truck was such that it did not stop. It veered right for a moment after the impact, but then continued straight, blowing through the intersection right in front of Zach and picking up speed as it headed out of town to the left. For a moment as it passed, the driver turned to look at Zach, and their eyes met for a split second.

To the right, the good citizens from the Dollar General were streaming out towards the town car.

"You OK?" Zach said to Jill.

"Fine. Or close enough. Do you think we should stop?"

But at that moment, the town car made a big turn back onto the street and sped off in the opposite direction of the truck, sprinkling bits of glass down the road as it went.

"I guess they are ok, then."

"Good thing. Whoever that was might have just saved our lives."

"Jill, are you sure no one knew about yours and Jeff's marriage?"

"Well, you can never be one hundred percent sure. But I certainly didn't tell anyone, and I doubt Jeff did either. Why?"

"If you had just survived a high-speed hit-and-run accident, and were trying to keep a 20-ton big rig on the road, do you think you would turn to look at some random bystander?"

"I suppose not. Why?"

"When the driver passed, he was looking right at me."

"Are you sure?"

"We made eye contact. He was passing through the intersection at 50 mph. But he was looking back at us."

"Could have just been a coincidence," Jill suggested.

"Maybe. But there's something else."

"What?"

"I didn't see any skid marks. And he would have hit us had that Town Car not hit him first."

Jill swallowed hard. Zach didn't say anything else. He took a right at the town square and followed it around, keeping the old courthouse on his left. Two left turns took him to the back side of the courthouse. The lawyer's office was there on the left. It was a classic old home from the 1870's, converted into the law offices of Latimer and Reed. A three-story building with tall white columns punctuated a front porch that ran the length of the front of the home. It was set back maybe 200 feet from the road; a narrow driveway expanded into a small parking lot on the left-hand side of the house. A second, more narrow, driveway ran from the parking lot away from the back of the house and connected to a street that ran perpendicular to the one Zach was on.

As they pulled into the driveway, they caught a glimpse of the taillights of a nondescript blue sedan pulling out of the second driveway and into the other street. "Did that look like Ms. James's rental car to you?" Jill asked.

"Maybe," Zach replied as he eased into a parking space and turned off the car. There were two other cars there, a Cadillac and a Lincoln; big, domestic luxury sedans well suited to the employ of a small-town lawyer. Jill made a brief check of her makeup, and apparently deemed it acceptable. She pushed a few wayward locks of black hair behind her ears, reached over and put her hand on Zach's. "You ready?"

Her hand was cool and soft on his. "Let's go."

They proceeded down the walkway and climbed the four stone steps to the front porch. Jill stumbled a little on the second step; supreme fatigue, uneven surfaces, and high heels conspiring to make her unstable. She put her arm in Zach's to steady herself and left it there until they reached the front door.

Zach reached for the door knob, but the door swung open before he reached it. It was Judge Latimer, wearing his hat with his car keys in hand.

"Oh Zach. My assistant was just about to call you. It appears we'll have to reschedule the reading of Mr. Wallace's will."

"What happened?"

"There were some complications. I can't really go into details. You understand."

"Of course." Zach looked over Latimer's shoulder and into the house cum office. The ceilings where 12 feet high, framed by elaborate crown molding painted white. The floors were original, hundred-plus year-old oak stained dark. To the left was Latimer's office; Zach could see a heavy antique desk through French doors that stood open. An older man in a brown tweed suit was sitting in a chair with his back to the front door. He was staring down through round black-rimmed spectacles at a document he held in his lap.

"Hello, Ms. Anders, I didn't expect to see you today." Latimer turned to Jill and smiled.

"I thought I would come along and provide a little moral support for Zach. This is a difficult time for all of us." Jill dabbed her nose with a tissue that appeared from her tiny purse.

"Well, it is a delight to see you. I just wish the circumstances were a little better."

There was a brief pause. The niceties had been exchanged, and there wasn't much left to say. Zach extended his hand to Latimer, making eye contact briefly before his gaze drifted to the man in brown tweed in the office. Tweed had picked up his briefcase and was making his way to the back door. Zach glanced back into Latimer's office and noticed a wood tray on the credenza behind the desk. It held an assortment of personal items—a watch, a wallet, a couple of nice pens—sitting on top of a stack of photos and documents. Zach had definitely seen that watch before. He heard the sound of a car cranking, but neither of the big sedans appeared in the driveway. Tweed must have gone out the back exit.

Zach put his hand on Jill's back. "Didn't you say you needed to step inside for a moment and use the powder room?" She hesitated for only a moment, then recovered.

"Yes, Mr. Latimer, may I step inside for a moment?"

Latimer hesitated for a moment. He opened his mouth to make an objection, but then thought the better of it. "Of course. Just go straight down the hall. On the right." He stepped back and to the side, motioning Jill to come inside. Zach started to follow her in, but Latimer moved back in front of the doorway. "Perhaps we can just sit here on the porch?" He pointed towards a row of rocking chairs lining the front porch, gently rocking the mild afternoon breeze.

"That sounds good. I never get enough rocking chair time in the city. But I left my cell phone in the car, and I'm expecting a call. Let me run and grab it. I'll be right back."

Zach went down the three broad porch steps and onto the sidewalk. The path curved to the right side of the house and out of sight of where Latimer was rocking on the porch. The big Cadillac was gone. Zach walked right past his car and around to the back of the house. The back door was closed, but the door wasn't locked. Zach eased it open, betting the old floorboards wouldn't creak as he stepped inside. He came up the hallway, past the bathroom where Jill was killing time behind a closed door, and came to Latimer's office on his right. He stepped in through the open French doors. A window from the office looked onto the front porch, where Latimer rocked slowly with his back turned to the window.

Zach moved quickly to the tray on the credenza behind Latimer's desk. He moved Jeff's watch to the side and picked up what he assumed was Jeff's wallet. He opened it up and found a fairly typical mix of credit cards and business cards and the like. But Zach went straight to the inside pocket. He was looking for something that would be kept deep in the wallet and not used very often.

He didn't find exactly what he was looking for, but found the next best thing: a small laminated copy of Jeff's university diploma. He looked at the back side of the document, where it was pressed against a photo. And there it was. Barely visible, but he could make out the silhouette of a man and woman in front of a vicar, holding hands and smiling for the camera. Over years of being stored close together in the inner sanctum of a wallet, the ink of the photo had partially transferred to the laminated card. Apparently, Jeff did keep a copy of his and Jill's wedding picture. But a quick check through the stack revealed the photo was no longer in the wallet.

Jeff stole a glance at Latimer on the front porch and wondered if there was time to look through the stack of documents. At that moment, Jill came up the hallway, an auditory assault of heels and hardwood. Latimer stood and started walking towards the front door. Zach dropped to the floor and pressed against the short wall just below the window that faced the front porch. He took his cell phone from his pocket and slid it across the wood floor so that it came to rest in the foyer.

At that moment, Jill came into the foyer, saw the phone on the floor, and then saw Zach. Zach put his finger over his lips and pointed out to the porch. Jill smiled and nodded, picked up the phone and put it in her purse. She opened the front door and practically bumped into Latimer, who was coming back inside. It opened to the left, so while Zach could see Jill, Latimer was screened by the big front door.

"Oh my, I'm sorry," she said with a laugh that was about thirty percent too ditzy for her, but Latimer bought it. He tried to take another step forward, but she stepped in the same direction. They bumped into each other, and she laughed again. He blushed. She put her hand on his arm and squeezed it just a little. "I am such a klutz."

This was probably more contact than Latimer had had with an attractive woman since the Nixon administration, and he lost all focus for a moment. Zach held his thumb to his ear as if it was a phone. Jill caught the cue from the corner of her eye and didn't miss a beat.

She pulled Zach's phone from her purse. "For some reason, I have Zach's phone. I must have picked it up by mistake. Do you know where he is? He's expecting a call."

"Oh, yes." Latimer returned to his senses with a shake of his head. "He just went to the car to look for it." He stepped back and let Jill exit, then followed her as she led the way down the front steps. Zach jumped up and headed for the back door. He wasn't nearly as concerned about noise this time and managed to knock over a few papers on his sprint for the back door. He half slid, half ran across the wood floors in his leather soled shoes, pushed the back door open and stumbled down the steps into the back yard. His first step slipped, and he thought for a moment his little foray might end with a face-down fall in the back yard grass. But his next step found traction in the pea gravel and he sprinted around the corner of the house into the small parking lot. He was standing by the driver side door when Jill and Latimer came around the corner, his hand on the car door. He was breathing heavy and the car was still locked, but he suspected Latimer would not notice either condition.

Jill held his cell phone in the air. "Zach, I have your phone! I must have picked it up by mistake."

"Great. We should get going, then. Mr. Latimer, thanks for your hospitality. I assume you'll call us when the reading of the will is rescheduled?"

Latimer took a deep breath and looked a little relieved. "Absolutely. Ya'll have a great afternoon. I'll call you as soon as I know."

A moment later, Zach and Jill were back in the rental car, backing out of the driveway. Latimer was pulling out of the driveway frontwards, so he was facing them as they both exited.

"I think you need to do a little more cardio if you want to play super spy," Jill said with a smile, turning her head so that Latimer couldn't see the motion of her lips.

"Maybe. But you have the flirting with old men thing down pat.

I thought poor old Latimer was going to need a heart pill."

"Don't sell me short, Zach. The man would need a defibrillator." She smiled broadly and waved at Latimer as Zach put the sedan in drive and pulled onto the street.

Zach drove at normal speed, but carefully, his gaze constantly shifting from side to side to the rear-view mirror.

"Looking for speeding tractor trailers?" Jill asked.

"That was no accident, what happened earlier. Did you notice how quickly Ms. James's car was leaving the lawyer's office?"

"Maybe she was late for something."

"What could she be late for? The reading of the will was supposed to take at least an hour. Surely she wouldn't have planned anything else during that time. And did you see the other guy leave as well? He was sitting in Latimer's office. Why was he there?"

"Maybe he had another appointment."

"No. Latimer was the only attorney in the office. And he wouldn't have scheduled two meetings at the same time. Besides, the man left right as we arrived. Whatever business he had, it was the same time as the reading of the will, and it was cancelled. Did you recognize him?"

"No. I definitely don't remember seeing him at the funeral. And I had plenty of time to study the crowd from my little perch. Probably not someone from Jeff's family or his business, or he would have been at the church."

"So we have a stranger and a woman who maybe thought Jeff had left her a bunch of money cancelling a reading of a will on very short notice. And a very jumpy small-town lawyer, who seemed very uncomfortable around us."

"He seemed almost surprised," Jill offered.

"That's right. Exactly. Surprised. Surprise is when something happens that you aren't expecting." Zach was thinking aloud more than drawing any firm conclusions.

"Or when something you expect to happen doesn't," Jill replied.

"You were right," Zach said as he pounded the steering wheel with the side of his fist. "You were right when we met at night by the school playground. We aren't safe. These people are willing to do anything." He took a series of short turns and headed out of the crowded town streets towards the wide, open road they used to enter the city. They passed the intersection where the wreck had occurred, and Jill craned her neck as they passed and saw for herself the absence of tire marks on the pavement.

"They wanted to keep us from the meeting," Jill said.

"No, they wanted to keep you from the meeting."

"But why?"

"Because of this." Zach pulled Jeff's laminated diploma card from his shirt pocket and handed it to Jill. She flipped it over and immediately went pale.

"They know."

"Oh yes, they know. And whatever they have planned depended on someone else taking control of Jeff's family business. They had to get you out of the way."

"Zach, we have to split up. It's not safe for you to be with me."

"It's a little late for that, Jill. We've been together enough, they'll assume I know. Or, at least, they won't be willing to take any chances. We're equally screwed now. And they'll want to make another move quickly, before we have a chance to tell anyone else."

"Ragsdale!" They both spoke at the same time, realizing that he too might be in danger. Jill pulled a prepaid cell phone from her purse and quickly dialed his number.

"So, were you just going to leave me at that place all day?" Ragsdale said with feigned disgust. The whole damned place reeks of Lysol and cheap tapioca pudding.

"We can't come get you right now. We think someone tried to kill us."

"Kid, that's not something you think. You usually know."

"Well, we know, then. You can't be seen with us right now. It's not safe. You need to find another way to get out of there."

"Way ahead of you. I borrowed a rental car from an out-of-town doc who was napping in the on call room."

"You stole a car?"

"I prefer borrowed. All rental cars look the same. I'm old, I get confused."

"Ragsdale, you badass car thief, you."

"Let's not get carried away. It was just a Chevy Malibu. Not even sure that qualifies as grand theft. Also, I'm pretty sure I stole a cat."

"A what?"

"A cat. There was a cat asleep in the back seat. I guess the guy didn't like travelling alone. The little bastard must be shedding or something because my eyes are watering like crazy." Ragsdale inhaled deeply and released a sneeze whose force and moisture Jill could hear even over the phone. "Do you think I can just throw him out the window?"

"No! Don't you dare."

"OK. I'm headed back to the house now to pick up my things. I guess we need to find a new place to roost tonight. Tell Zach I think his hunch was right about the nursing home. I need to run a few tests, but if I found what I think I found, we are dealing with some pretty sick people. Pulling into the house now. I'll call back in a few."

Zach and Jill were heading in the general direction of the rental house and could just barely see the rooftops of a few of the more elevated homes in the subdivision. They didn't dare get any closer. Zach checked the fuel gauge—still almost a whole tank. They would just circle around this wide, open stretch of road until they identified a good hiding place. They had good sight lines in every direction, and the road had wide shoulders that flowed gently into pastureland, so avoiding any wayward tractor trailers would be easy.

TWENTY-ONE

RAGSDALE PULLED INTO THE DRIVEWAY OF the rental house and put the car in park. The cat weaved in and out of his legs as he walked up the sidewalk. "Damn cat. Bad enough he's got me sneezing out brain tissue, now he's trying to knock me on my ass."

Once on the front porch, he retrieved the key from under the flower pot where Jill left it and unlocked the front door. "Damn, left my bag in the car," he muttered to himself and turned to head back towards the rental. The cat, however, continued inside the house, assuming he owned the place, as cats will do.

Once inside, the cat did pause for a moment at a thin red ribbon of light that ran from one side of the foyer to the other, just a few feet inside the door. He first noticed the reflector on his left, stuck to the wall with a bit of tape, the red light dancing on its surface. His feline eyes followed the stream to the right, finding its origin to be a small penlight-sized device affixed to the other wall.

The cat, of course, did not notice the wireless transmitter attached to the laser. Not that he would have known what that meant. His head tilted to one side and his ear twitched. His tail moved slowly as he contemplated taking a swipe at the dazzling red light.

The cat also didn't know about the small amount of explosives attached to the gas line in the basement, or the large crystal meth lab that had been hastily assembled in that same basement as a cover story. The cat just saw a pretty light, and his tailed twitched slowly as he raised a paw and prepared to strike.

Ragsdale felt the searing heat on the back of his neck first, even before the sound. Next came the force, a shock wave like a hot hand of an angry God striking him on the back. He fell forward, his knees hitting the hard concrete sidewalk and his face landing in the cool soft grass. Next came the sound, thunderous at first, followed by the crackle of fire. Right on the heels of the sound was the pelting of debris, sleet pellets of glass and wood and shingle stinging the back of his neck and gathering on his clothes. Then the adrenaline hit his bloodstream like an explosion, and he jumped to his feet and ran.

Taking cover behind the car, he turned and looked back at the house. The bigger pieces of debris had settled, but the house was fully engulfed in flame. The cat—well, there really was no longer any cat to speak of. Ragsdale thought of the cat briefly and sneezed as the smoke burned his nose. "Little bastard saved my life."

The doc got into the car and squealed out of the driveway. There was no point in waiting around for the fire department. They would ask questions that he simply did not have time to answer.

Jill saw the smoke first, a thick black finger that appeared from nowhere and quickly reached several hundred feet into the air. Tears filled her eyes before the words formed on her lips. Zach saw it too. But for him, the instinctive response was to grip the steering wheel tighter and pin the accelerator to the floor. Jill was still holding her cell phone in her hand, and she immediately began to dial Ragsdale's number. Her fingers were clumsy with panic, and she misdialed once, then again. "Dammit!" she yelled as she tried a third time. She screamed in half surprise, half relief as an incoming call caused the phone to ring in her hands. She hit the speaker phone button, and Ragsdale's voice filled the car. It was noticeably calm, in stark contrast to the screaming of the car engine and Jill's panicky cocktail of curses and sobs.

"Guys, we need to find another house."

Zach exhaled, suddenly realizing he had been holding his breath. "You think so?"

"That stupid cat saved my life. There must have been some kind of trigger inside the house. The cat went inside and, well, you know. Most of my gear was in the house, I'm afraid."

"We need to find a new place. Someplace folks wouldn't associate with any of us."

"Hopefully someplace with fast internet and a good microscope," Ragsdale requested.

Zach looked at Jill. "I think we know a place. There are a bunch of temporary classroom trailers behind the high school. Cheap locks and not visible from the road. We have just enough time."

"That should work," Ragsdale said. "Let me go figure out some new transportation, and I'll meet you there."

"Hey Rags, I'm really glad you are not blown up," Jill said.

"Me too, kid," Ragsdale said as he hung up.

Zach glanced in the rear-view mirror. "I am pretty sure we are being followed."

"So, we need a new ride and a way to lose the loser who is following us."

A few minutes later they pulled into the hotel parking lot and approached Green Jacket at the front desk.

"We'd like a room, please," Zach said as he handed over his credit card.

"Yes, sir. No problem. We have a lovely honeymoon suite available, if you would like."

Zach started to respond that they would need separate rooms but found his throat a little tight. Jill jumped in to save him. She put her hand on Zach's arm and gave the desk attendant her best two-dimpled smile. "No thanks, a standard room will be just fine." She looked at Zach's uncharacteristic blush and couldn't help herself, "Won't it, dear?" She gave his arm a little squeeze. She smiled as she noted how his bicep instinctively flexed when she did so.

The attendant swiped the credit card, gave his monologue on room rates and hotel amenities that neither Zach nor Jill really heard. They both had noticed the nondescript sedan that had pulled into the parking lot shortly after them and parked facing the hotel.

"Can we have a room facing the front parking lot, please?"

"Of course."

A few moments later they were walking down the hallway towards their room. Zach paused by the supply closet that was, as is usually the case, just by the ice machine. He grabbed a mop, and they made their way to room 214. The carpet was a garish pattern of yellow and red and brown, a pattern that looked like a giant woven basket. Immediately inside the door, on the right, was the bathroom. A king-sized bed was on the right, facing a large TV on the wall to the left. There was a big double window at the far end of the room, curtains closed against the afternoon sun. A very uncomfortable looking brown chair was parked with its back to the window.

"Charming," Jill said.

"It's all about the view," Zach said as he peered through the curtains and noted the sedan that was following them was still parked below.

"I assume your mop head will need a body," Jill said as she handed him a pillow.

Zach broke the mop handle in half and stuck the jagged end through the end of a pillow. A spare bed sheet was wrapped around the pillow to add some shape to the torso.

"She doesn't look a thing like me. I'm way hotter," Jill said.

"And she clearly lacks your wit." Zach walked over to the window and opened the curtains so that just the sheers were closed, rendering him and Jill as silhouettes to the parking lot below.

"Ok, let's sell this." Jill walked quickly across the floor, put Zach's arms around her and pressed herself close. Her arms found their way around his shoulders, and she stood on her tip toes until her lips almost touched his. Zach's heart raced. He was simultaneously incredibly uncomfortable and remarkably happy. The gauzy outline of their silhouette through the window sheers would convey the story to the onlookers outside.

"You're going to have to kiss me if you want to sell this." Her breath was warm on his lips. He breathed in her words and followed their path to lips.

It was easier than he thought, more passionate than he expected, and didn't feel at all like they were pretending. His fingers found their way to her hair, threading into her dark locks just by her temples, and holding her close. Her hands moved from his shoulders around to his chest and felt for shirt buttons. One button gave way, and she nudged him back a little with her hips. He took the cue and fell backwards onto the hideous floral print bed comforter, and she fell on top of him. They stayed that way for a few seconds longer than was necessary, her lips on his, her hand slipped inside the opened button onto his chest.

Jill crawled forward just a little so that she could reach the lamp on the table by the bed. With the flick of the switch, they were all alone in the darkness, hearts racing for more than one reason. Jill slid off of Zach and sat upright on the edge of the bed. Zach continued to lay flat, or at least most of him did. A minute passed, then another. The LED numbers on the nightstand clock marched through the 4:30's, all the way to 4:36 before one of them spoke.

"Do you think that's enough?" Jill asked first.

"Six minutes? Give me some credit."

"Ok. We'll give it another four, but let's not overdo it. This has to be believable. Besides, our ride is probably leaving in a few minutes."

The next four minutes passed in relative silence, then Zach stumbled over to the chair and sat the dummy upright. He shuffled the chair just a little so that its back was fully to the window. Then he rotated the TV on the dresser so that it faced the chair. Jill stepped into the hallway and used the other end of the broom handle to bust the light bulb in the hallway. With the hallway dark, you couldn't see that the door was open. Jill crouched just by the open door. Zach pulled open the heavy drapes so that only the sheers covered the window. Then, crouching low on the floor by the ugly chair, he used the remote to turn on the TV and flip through the channels until he found a movie that was just starting on HBO. From the outside, the sheers provided just enough clarity to make out a silhouette, but they hoped not transparent enough to differentiate a person from a mop-headed robe dummy.

Zach crawled across the floor to join Jill. They slipped into the hallway and closed the door behind them. The exit sign by the stairwell was a reliable beacon, and there wasn't anything to trip over.

They made their way to a freight elevator, then to the loading dock in the back of the hotel. Zach cracked the door an inch to see if anyone was monitoring this rear exit. No one was. And why would they, when they had such a good view into his hotel room from the front?

They stepped out the service door and onto the loading dock. Zach hopped down the four foot drop onto the concrete below. He twisted his ankle a little, but was pretty sure he suppressed any display of his discomfort. He turned to offer Jill a hand with the jump, but she was already coming down the stairs right beside the dock.

She was moving noticeably slower than she had been earlier.

"You OK?"

"Fine, I suppose. I just don't want to twist my ankle by jumping."

They crossed through the small deserted parking lot in back of the hotel, it wasn't more than a hundred feet of weathered asphalt. At the edge of the parking lot was a narrow median that had been planted with a neat row of trees when the hotel was last remodeled a decade ago. Some of the trees were actually still alive.

And on the other side of the median was the Waffle House

parking lot. They were at the back of the restaurant, the only side with no windows. In front of them were four buses from the city high school, neatly lined up side by side. No one really knows why all the bus drivers gathered at the Waffle House after making their afternoon run, but that had been the custom since the busses ran on leaded gasoline.

Zach and Jill slipped in between the second and third bus, walking from back to front until they reached the front door. It was open. Locking up a bus is kind of a pain, and the risk of theft was minimal. No kid wants to take a joy ride in a Bluebird.

They stepped inside and made their way down the center aisle of the bus to the back row, crouching low so their heads couldn't be seen through the windows. When they reached the back of the bus, Zach slipped into the last row on the right and sat down, making himself as comfortable as he could in the narrow space and hard floor. Jill did the same to the left, facing him from across the aisle.

"Just like old times," Jill said.

Zach looked at the back of the seat that was just a few inches in front of his face. A variety of initials, a couple of hearts, and a couple of crudely crafted depictions of male genitalia graced the back of the seat. "News over here is that Sarah hearts Casey, Mr. Wilkerson is a homosexual, and someone named Jason has a strangely deformed penis. What's the news over there?"

Jill laughed and turned to her seat. "Well, let's see. Cindy is apparently a bitch. Casey apparently performs fellatio, so Sarah might be barking up the wrong tree. And, no news of Mr. Wilkerson's sexual orientation."

"Some things never change, I suppose."

"I suppose. I'm not sure if I feel worse for Cindy or Sarah."

They felt a little shudder from the front of the bus. The driver was making his way up the steps. He was, by any measure, a very large man. Eating bacon and waffles five times a week will do that to you after a few decades. And his beleaguered knees were straining to convey his heft up the stairs to his perch behind the steering wheel.

Once in his seat, he brought the clunky diesel motor to life and slid the bus into gear. Zach and Jill could feel the vibration on the floor as the engine's torque hit the axle beneath them, and the big bus pulled out of the parking lot into the street. Even at a nice private school, buses are still utilitarian and unrefined. Society has still not degenerated to the point that teenagers are concerned with a smooth ride.

Zach and Jill jostled around in their floorboard perches until the bus finally came to a stop in the parking lot of Oakdale Preparatory School. The driver engaged the parking brake, killed the engine, and struggled down the steps, leaning heavily on the hand rail. He pushed the door closed behind him, but didn't lock it. The school parking lot was surrounded by a high fence and was well lit at night.

They gave the driver a few minutes to lumber across the parking lot and listened as he cranked his car and pulled away. The other buses arrived, and their drivers did the same. Within a few minutes, the parking lot was silent. They were alone.

At this point, it was approaching seven p.m., but there was still another hour before dark.

"We should probably wait until it is dark," Zach said, "just in case someone in a passing car glances in this direction, or someone's hanging around the campus."

"I have heard that sometimes young hooligans will drink alcohol and fornicate behind the gym after school."

"Exactly the kind of malfeasance we are trying to avoid."

Jill smiled. It was probably his use of "malfeasance." It was great making someone smile. Zach never really thought of himself as funny. He was clever, but you could be clever by yourself. Being funny required interaction.

"Zach, you never really dated anyone in high school, did you?"

"Not really. I was not really a part of the social scene. Didn't play sports, couldn't afford to take the trips and do a lot of extracurricular stuff." He said this without much emotion, just a simple statement of fact.

"But you were such a clever guy. Brilliant, really. Wasn't there an Asian chick or someone that caught your eye?"

"First, SO racist. Second, being smart doesn't really do much for your social standing. But, it's OK. I never really expected to be popular, so I guess I didn't miss it."

Jill looked again at the graffiti on the back of the seat, then back at Zach. She wondered how high school had really been for Zach and wondered if she missed a chance to make it easier.

"Don't shed any tears for me. If these anatomical drawings are accurate, this Jason guy is the one you really should be worried about."

TWENTY–TWO

FORTY-FIVE MINUTES OF REMINISCING AND A shared pack of gum later, they decided it was dark enough to make their exit. They made their way to the front of the bus, walking upright this time, and proceeded down the steps. Even Jill, in her frail physical condition, descended the steps with less strain than the bus driver.

Oakdale Preparatory School was housed in three one-story brick buildings, arrayed as points in a triangle. Covered pathways extended from each building into the center of the triangle and converged in a large covered gazebo. The rest of the space between the buildings was covered in thick green grass, occasionally highlighted by small trees and benches. It looked like, and actually was, a great place to be mocked by your peers while trying to play Frisbee, eat lunch, or talk to a girl.

But the courtyard and the buildings were not of interest to Jill and Zach. Just to the side of Building 2, beyond the glare of the parking lot lights, and only dimly illuminated by temporary floodlights, were four temporary classrooms arranged in a neat square. These particular buildings were home to the science labs, and despite the ostensibly temporary nature of the structures, they had been home to the labs for several years. Zach checked the first two buildings, then found what he was looking for on the door of the third. "Computer Lab."

They walked up two wooden steps and tried the knob. Of course, it was locked. Zach was contemplating options for breaking and entering when he heard the crunch of footsteps on the walkway between the two buildings. A flashlight swung towards them as the person turned in their direction. There was really no viable exit path; if they moved, they were sure to be spotted. They pressed against the door to reduce their profile, and Jill squeezed Zach's arm as the footsteps grew closer. The light danced across the walkway, up the side of the building, and finally settled right on their faces.

Zach was trying to formulate a compelling explanation for their presence and had pretty much settled on "We're lost," when a familiar voice came from the other side of the flashlight.

"You kids lost?" It was Ragsdale.

"If you are going to get inside, you are going to need a key." He held up a tire tool. "I took the liberty of disabling the alarm system."

"You scared the shit out of us," Jill said as she let out a long, slow breath.

"You think that's scary, try having a house blow up right in front of you. I'm still digging bits of sheetrock and shingle and furry dead kitty out of my hair. Speaking of which, are you guys sure you weren't followed?"

"No." Zach grabbed the tire tool. "We ditched the rental and hitched a ride on the short bus." The edge of the tire tool was flat and thin, like a giant flathead screwdriver. Zach wedged it into the door frame and popped the door open.

Zach flipped on the lights and illuminated the room. They were standing right at the midpoint of the building, a single room a hundred feet long, thirty feet wide. Tables lined each wall, leaving the center of the room open. To the left, the tables were home to probably twenty workstations, computers neatly standing at attention waiting for their next command. To the right was a table with all types of computer and electronic components stacked amongst an assortment of tools. The humming of all those hard drives and fans fought against the hissing of the air conditioner for auditory and temperate supremacy.

Jill settled into one of the rolling chairs and laid her head on a table. She let out a deep sigh, then something like a groan. Fatigue had become a continuous sensation; she felt its lead weight on her with every yawning breath or blink of her stinging eyes. The panic and stress of the day had added a new layer of psychic fatigue as well. She felt as if she could doze off leaning on the table and not wake up for a month. But just as she started to doze, Zach shook her shoulder gently.

"Not now. Not in here. It's probably safe to assume this room isn't clean." Zach was feeling the same fatigue, but a cocktail of grief and adrenaline was a more than sufficient antidote.

"There's also a chance they could track us down," Ragsdale said as he took visual stock of the room. "Part of the boot up sequence identifies the sleeper. And if the device can transmit a signal, it can also transmit a location. I suspect that's how they found the house this morning."

They were right, of course. For a brief moment Jill wondered if being caught would be all that bad. At least it would be over. But that was ridiculous. Jill sat up straight and rubbed her eyes. "So, what do we do now?"

Zach looked at Ragsdale. "Well, as far as we know there are three components to the system—the drug that makes people sensitive to outside stimuli while they sleep, the devices that transmit the messages, and whatever centralized brain is running the system. We only need to knock out one of the three to stop this."

Ragsdale sat down on one of the tables and rubbed his eyes. "Well, eliminating all the devices is nearly impossible. We would have to sweep every building in this city, and anywhere else this system is being tested. The most elegant solution would be eliminating the command center. But we have no idea where it is, or even if it is centralized. They could be managing this via a decentralized structure, each node gathering bits of instructions and passing it along to its peers."

"So, what about the drug?" Jill asked.

Ragsdale continued, "We know how the drug is being delivered— it is being embedded in plastic drink containers that leach it into beverages. It would have been easier to just put it in the water supply. But there is a good chance someone would have noticed. Public water supplies are tested regularly, but no one checks bottled water once it leaves the factory."

"I own the plastics factory now. I could order a recall, pull everything from the market."

"That wouldn't quite do it," Ragsdale said. "People have ingested a great deal of this stuff. It could take months for it to work its way out of their systems, and for many the effects may even be permanent." He looked away from Jill when he said this last part. He was afraid to see the look on her face. But his concern was wasted. She already knew her condition, and she was far too tired for dramatic emotion.

"What we need is penicillin," Zach said. Ragsdale and Jill looked at him blankly. "Not actual antibiotics. But that kind of approach. This thing is already out there, it's too late to prevent it. We need to help people fight it off, help them recover."

"Good idea. But where would we start? Developing new treatments can take even the largest pharmaceutical companies years, decades."

"And why does it take so long?"

"Well, you have the regulation and the bureaucracy, of course. But the real issue is grappling with so many unknowns, so many options. There are an almost infinite number of chemical compounds that could be tried, as well as an enormous number of possible genetic therapies. Working through all these approaches takes testing, trial and error. And that takes time. A lot of time."

"But what if you had a head start? What if you had a drug therapy that worked, but you didn't know why?" Zach said.

"That would shorten the process, of course. But—"

Ragsdale cut himself off and smiled. He got it.

Jill looked from Ragsdale to Zach. "So?"

"I have ingested a great deal of the drug," Zach said. "And we know they have targeted me with the system. But for some reason I am highly resistant. It doesn't seem to have the same effect. There is something about my body chemistry, my genetic makeup, that makes me resistant to this compound."

Ragsdale picked up the thread, "So, we would start with samples of your blood, your DNA, and compare it to samples of everyone else, people we know are impacted."

"Right. And that should tell us what makes me resistant to the drug."

"Well, yes," Jill said with a little bit of frustration. "But that kind of research could still take years and requires massive infrastructure. We have at most a couple of days and a few dozen PC's in a trailer."

"Oh, I think we can do better than that," said Ragsdale. "We have the largest, most powerful computer the world has ever seen, in the form of a few hundred sleeping seniors over at Oakdale. They may be surviving on Ensure and hard candy, and barely able to walk, but they are still alive. Even the weakest human brain has more computational power than a supercomputer.

"When I was in the nursing home, I found my way into the basement, where all those huge power cables led and the wireless signal originated. It was kind of a hub, sending instructions and pulling back data from each node—each sleeping patient in the building.

I was able to tap into the control panel. You would not believe the processing power, the kind of computations they were doing. It was unbelievable."

"I can't believe you got in there. Wasn't there any security?" Jill asked.

"That's the thing about having something no one knows exists— you can hide it in plain sight and no one would know the difference. It looked like an ordinary data center, a big one for a nursing home, but nothing dramatic. A guard by the door would have just drawn suspicion. All I had to do was get through the electronic lock on the door."

"So, how can we use it?" Jill asked.

"When I was there, I installed a small device on the network. I intended to use it for monitoring and testing the system, using basically the same software we used to monitor Zach when he was asleep. With some modifications to the code, I think I could use that software to send and receive instructions."

"Can you access it from here?"

"I can access it from any internet connection. But I don't have the equipment here to analyze biological samples. That kind of equipment is only at hospitals, or testing labs, or research facilities."

"There's a hospital in town, about twenty minutes away."

"Yes, but I don't think they'll let me have access to the equipment. I would need more than a fake ID. But Tennessee Tech is just an hour or so drive from here. I know a couple of folks. They'll let me use the equipment to analyze our samples. Then I'll come back here and upload the data. Let's see if the bedpan can find the answer."

"Bedpan set? Really big talk for someone who is only a decade away from incontinence himself," Jill said.

"Kid, I eat bacon five times a week. My heart will give out long before my bladder," Ragsdale replied. "Now let's get some samples."

"What's it going to be?" Zach said, "Blood or pee?"

"I've had quite enough of handling urine—from the both of you." He looked over his glasses at Jill. "For this, we'll need a blood sample, and a couple of swabs from the inside of your cheek. They probably have what we need in the biology lab. But first," Ragsdale looked at Jill, once again with her head down on the counter, "First, let's see if we can find a way for you to get some rest."

Over the next half hour, Ragsdale and Zach swept the building for transmitters. He pulled a trashcan from under one of tables and filled it with an assortment of computer mice and other electronics that had offended his scanner.

"Is it safe yet?" Jill said with a deep yawn.

"Probably, but give me another half hour, just to be sure."

Ragsdale turned his focus to the pile of components and tools piled at the far end of the trailer. He began fussing with a couple of wireless transmitters and other odds and ends.

"I'll go check the other buildings, see if I can find something to collect a blood and DNA sample," Zach offered. Ragsdale nodded. Jill nodded as well, slower, though, and with less eye contact.

A half hour later, Zach returned with a cardboard box. In it were a handful of vials, syringes, and swabs sealed in sterile packages. "Found the biology lab. Everything we need. Even a little something to keep you perky during your drive over to the university." Zach produced a six-pack of Red Bull that he had scavenged from the biology lab refrigerator. "They were right there next to the sheep heads for next week's dissection lab." He had a few coats hanging over his arm. He tossed those on the floor. "Raided the lost and found. Maybe that will make your nap a little more comfy."

Jill slid from the chair onto the pile of jackets.

Ragsdale looked up from a pile of disemboweled electronics. "I've modified a few of these transmitters to be a jammer of sorts. Basically, they will oscillate across the frequency range the sleep devices have been using, and randomly transmit signals. It won't block incoming messages, but it will disrupt them every few seconds. To someone trying to transmit, it will basically just look like a bunch of random static. Any wireless signal within a few dozen feet of here will be interrupted every few seconds. Just a little insurance."

"Thanks, Ragsdale," Jill said as she rolled one of the jackets into a pillow.

"No problem. Now roll up your sleeve."

A few minutes later, Ragsdale had collected blood and DNA samples from both Zach and Jill. "Zach, I know this may be difficult. But, do you have anything with you that might have your grandfather's DNA? He was susceptible to the drug, and you were highly resistant to it. But yours and his DNA are obviously very similar. So it could be much easier to find the variant by comparing your sample to him."

Zach opened his overnight bag and pulled out the hairbrush he had borrowed from his grandparents' bathroom. "Great. I'll have a look. You kids get some sleep. I'll be back around sunrise."

Ragsdale grabbed his bag and the six-pack of Red Bull, turned off the lights, and made his exit.

TWENTY–THREE

THE ROOM WAS DARK, SAVE FOR the surprisingly bright light of screensavers from twenty computer monitors, bouncing Microsoft logos illuminating the room as they dance within their sixteen-inch cages.

"Come get some rest, Zach. I saved you a spot." Zach could see the outline of Jill on the floor, lying on her side, facing the door. Her head on the rolled-up jacket and her knees pulled almost to her waist.

"I was pretty sure we ordered two doubles, but all we have is one king." It was a pretty bad joke, but Zach was nervous. Jill had rolled up another jacket and placed it next to her—even with her head, but just behind her. Zach lowered himself onto the floor, exuding the normal involuntary sighs and groans one makes when lowering an exhausted body onto a hard floor.

He lay on his back with his head on the jacket pillow, Jill just to his right—lying on her side facing away from him. "These jackets reek," she said just as he got settled.

She was right, of course. He had found them in a box marked "Lost and Found" in the biology lab, probably left there a couple of months ago when the weather was cooler. They stank of teenage hoodlum, a nasty cocktail of cheap cologne, body odor, and two different kinds of smoke.

"There wasn't much of a selection, I'm afraid," Zach replied.

"That's okay," Jill said. Then she turned over and put her head on Zach's shoulder, her hand on his chest. "This is better anyway."

It was better for Zach as well.

"Your heart is beating pretty fast," Jill observed. There was no point in denying his quickened pulse, as her soft hand was resting directly over his heart.

"I suppose it is." The smell of her hair, the warmth of her face on his shoulder, the proximity of her body. For a man who went weeks without physical contact, this was sensory overload. He couldn't think of anything to say. For a full minute they lay in silence, until the words formed in his mind. Zach spoke softly, "Jill, I just—"

But then he heard the softest hint of a snore from Jill's suddenly expressionless face. He felt the depth of her breathing. She was asleep. Zach allowed himself to run his fingers briefly through her hair, touch her cheek. She didn't wake.

Zach had never been great at interpreting the softer side of human interaction. He didn't know if Jill wanted affection, consolation, or just somewhere to lay her head that didn't smell like smoke. He pondered these questions for a moment, his mind going fast, outpacing his racing heart, which far outpaced his deeply tired body. But in the space of a few minutes, his breathing slowed, his mind slipped into the warm fog of unconsciousness, and he joined Jill in a deep sleep—the rise and fall of their breathing falling in and out of sync under the dancing eyes of Microsoft screensavers.

TWENTY–FOUR

AT FIRST, HE WAS SHOOTING A machine gun, inexplicably holding the stock close to his chest. He could feel the sharp vibrations against his sternum. Then it was electric shock. Brief jolts of energy coursing through his chest as the doctors recharged the defibrillator paddles for another try.

But as he emerged from the murky depths of sleep, he realized it was just his cell phone. A text message had arrived, announced by silent vibration in his shirt pocket.

Jill was still asleep on his shoulder, her face incredibly warm on his skin. He couldn't move his right arm without disturbing her, so he fished out his cell phone using his left. With a push of a button, the screen came to life and a message appeared.

"Lucky day today. You must be very proud of yourself. We may not know where you are, but we know where your grandmother is. And she is probably not going to sleep well tonight."

Zach sat upright. Jill's head slipped off and fell into the rolled-up jacket Zach's head had been resting on. She made some mildly agitated sleepy sounds and uttered what might have been words, but never woke up.

He had to get there. He had to go. He knew they were just trying to flush him out. But he had to go anyway. Maybe there was a chance he could save her. She wouldn't approve, of course, him risking his life to save hers. She would say it should be the other way around. But there was one person on the earth that Zach was certain truly loved him. And, if she died, then what would be the point of saving himself?

Zach considered waking up Jill, but thought better of it. If she woke up, she would insist on going with him. And it was better that she just stay here. It was pretty clear that they wanted her dead, and she was safe here; or as safe as she could be.

He wrote a quick note on the back of someone's discarded homework assignment and left it on the floor right beside Jill's jacket pillow. Then he slipped outside and closed the door behind him. He reached into his pocket and pulled out his car keys.

Then he remembered. He had no car.

He briefly considered stealing one of the school busses, but that wouldn't work. He was sure to draw a lot of attention in a school bus. And once they saw it, they would know where he had come from—and know where to find Jill. No, he needed something a little less conspicuous. He walked quickly away from the modular buildings and towards building two. When he reached it, he took a right and walked along the length of the building, not stopping until he was behind it, the point farthest away from the front entrance.

Here was another building, made of steel and probably a hundred feet on all sides. The mechanic shop. Oakdale Prep wasn't the type of school where a lot of kids wanted to be auto mechanics. But there were a lot of aspiring mechanical engineers. And this building was focused on all things mechanical. Behind the building was a small parking lot, just big enough for five or six cars, surrounded by a tall chain link fence. Zach scaled the fence quickly. He had awakened from a deep sleep just three minutes earlier, but adrenaline had pounded his body into alertness. He looked at the assortment of cars in the lot. He had no idea what kind of experimental atrocities were being performed on each of these cars, or if they would even start. But these were the only vehicles nearby that weren't thirty feet long and yellow.

He slid into the first car, a mid-sized domestic sedan. To his surprise, the keys were in it. He hastily shoved the key into the ignition and turned it on. No response. He popped the hood to find there was no engine.

The next vehicle was a full-sized truck, probably ten years old. He kneeled on the concrete and looked up under the grill. There was an engine. All four tires were inflated. Zach slid inside. No keys. No ignition switch, for that manner. The cover was off the steering column and a mass of wires hung halfway to the floorboard. He remembered this lesson from his semester of shop class more than a decade ago.

A few minutes later he touched two bare wires together and the truck's big engine growled to life. He put it in gear and eased forward, scraping the side of the car to his left before gently nudging the front fender of a car that was perpendicular to him on his right. The car slid sideways under the force of the truck and he passed right by. The next step did not require finesse. The gate was locked, and there was no other exit. Zach floored the accelerator and sent the truck careening towards the fence, accelerating as fast as he could in the small parking lot. The fence gave way easily, just adding a few scratches to the already banged up front hood of the truck.

Zach cut the wheel hard to the left and headed for the street. He craned his neck to see the computer lab building on his way out. The lights were still off. He imagined Jill still there asleep, her chest rising and falling in the long breaths of deep sleep. He tapped the brakes to slow the truck as he reached the end of the parking lot, but they had very little effect, slowing him just enough to make the hard left out of the driveway while keeping all four wheels on the ground. He floored it and went flying south towards his grandmother's house. It was late at night. The streets would be empty. He wouldn't need brakes for a few minutes anyway.

His instinct was to keep the big V8 wide open right into his grandmother's driveway, maybe use one of the pecan trees in the back yard as a brake. The truck had airbags, assuming they had not been extracted for someone's senior project. He probably wouldn't be hurt, much.

But a quarter mile short of the house he thought better of this plan, took his foot off the gas, and began pumping the sleepy brakes furiously. The truck had slowed to about 30 mph when he took the hard left into his grandmother's driveway. The truck felt for a moment like it would tip over, but then it righted itself and coasted up the driveway. He was only going about 20 mph now, and a few donuts in the front yard slowed his momentum further. He picked out a nice big pecan tree and coasted gently into its base. A shower of still-green pecans rained down the roof. The metal hood crinkled a little, but the airbags didn't deploy. Zach slammed the shifter into park and killed the engine.

He was almost to the back door before the engine stopped

knocking and pinging. The spare house key was under the flower-pot on the patio, just like when he was a teenager. He slipped the key into the lock and called out as he turned the knob, "Grandma! It's me, Zach!" Calling attention to himself would be dangerous if someone was waiting. But Grandma had kept a four shot .22 caliber revolver in her nightstand for decades. It was not prudent to sneak up on Grandma at night.

He stumbled as he entered through the back door into the kitchen. He had taken this path in the dark a thousand times, but there was a bag of trash by the door tonight. Grandma of a few years ago would have never let trash sit in the floor overnight, but this was yet another concession to the march of age.

He regained his footing and continued calling out her name as he flipped on the lights and headed down the hall. She still wasn't answering. God, why didn't she answer?

Zach slowed a step just before he reached her door, an extra split second to compose himself for whatever was on the other side of that door. He took a hard left through the door to find his grandmother lying perfectly still on her bed. The TV was playing low, some kind of late-night talk show projecting random light on her silver hair. Her face looked so peaceful, so completely at rest.

He was too late.

He felt a tightness in his stomach, and hot tears rushing to his eyes as he walked over to the bed and looked at her.

Apparently, they didn't share the same genetic resistance to the drug.

A simple lie told to make an abandoned child feel at home. Maybe that little lie had held him close until her love could make him stay. Looking down at her now, he could see again what the kids at school always said—he and his grandmother really didn't look anything alike.

She was the only person on the planet who loved him uncondi-tionally, the only person who looked at him with pride, who made his successes and failures her own. And now...

Zach felt more alone in that moment than he had ever felt. And that was quite a statement for a man for whom loneliness was as much a part of life as sleep or hunger.

He sat on the side of the bed and picked up her left hand as the tears broke out and ran freely.

But then the left hand jerked back like a rope being snatched from his hand.

"Who are you? How did you get in here?"

From the corner of his eye he saw the right hand reaching for the nightstand drawer. He caught it just before it grabbed the little pistol.

"Grandma, it's me. It's Zach!"

"Zach! What are you doing here?" Her right hand gave up its search for the pistol and instead groped for her glasses. Zach handed them to her.

"I—I got a message. It said they were coming for you—like they did for Grandpa."

"Well, honey, I'm still here. I'm fine." She was sitting up now, saw the tears running down his cheeks and spontaneously produced a few of her own. A good grandmother never lets a child cry alone. She put her arm around his shoulders; it was light as a feather, but he felt it like it was gold.

It seemed strange. Maybe they didn't try to kill her after all? But the message... "Did you—you have any strange dreams?"

She looked up and furrowed her brow for a moment. "I suppose I had some faint dreams just as I was drifting off. Something crazy. Like a bunch of numbers and lights flashing and whatnot. It was pretty unpleasant. But it faded away pretty quickly. We Tanners are sound sleepers, you know. Or at least we used to be."

He leaned his head on her shoulder and sobbed. She thought the days had passed when she could be of comfort to Zach. At some point the parent/child—or grandparent/child—relationship crosses a point where the deeper needs are on the side of the elder. The need for time, the need for attention, the need for physical assistance, the need for emotional support. But in this moment, she had been given a rare and unexpected gift—the gift of being able to meet a need of one she loved so much. She held him tight and let him cry.

The moment was short, however. Zach sat up straight again and wiped his sleeve across his eyes. "Grandma, I've got to go. I think we may have a way to stop this. And there's a lot we have to do. But I'm afraid to leave you here alone."

"You go, honey, I'll be fine." She patted his back with her frail, bony hand. Then she reached into the nightstand drawer and pulled out her little pistol.

Zach smiled. "Grandma, you need someone else here."

"Well, I'm not calling poor Mrs. Olsen again. She sat up with me all night last night. The poor thing is exhausted."

Zach paused for a second. "Grandma, call the police. Tell them someone was driving crazy, drove a truck right up in your yard and hit a tree. You didn't see who it was, but they got out of the truck and ran out in the woods behind the house."

"And why would I tell them that?"

"Well, for one thing, it will make sure you have a couple of cops around here for the next few hours." Zach smiled and nodded in the direction of the back yard. "And also because it's kind of true."

"You were never this much trouble when you were in high school, Zachary." Grandma shook her head and reached for her housecoat. "I'd better go make some coffee."

"And maybe warm up some of those leftover biscuits. The cops will stay here all day if you keep feeding them your biscuits."

"Well, I don't know about that. But it does seem the polite thing to do."

They were in the hallway now, Zach walking quickly, Grandma shuffling behind him in her housecoat and slippers.

"Are you sure you won't stay for a quick bite to eat? I can fry up some ham to go with those biscuits."

That sounded unbelievably delicious, but he couldn't wait. A thick nest of leftover biscuits was wrapped in aluminum foil on top of the stove. He grabbed two of them and headed for the door. "I can't stay, Grandma. And I need to borrow the truck." Zach grabbed the keychain from the hook beside the door. "Now call the police right now, while I am watching, ok?"

"Ok, Zach." She pulled a cell phone from her housecoat pocket and dialed 911. As the phone rang, she looked at Zach again. "What kind of boy goes around eating cold biscuits?"

Zach smiled around the half biscuit he was holding between his teeth. He waved as he opened the door. "Love you, Grandma."

He walked quickly across the gravel driveway, now much more grass than rock, and let himself into the detached garage. His grandparents' old truck was parked inside, sleeping quietly beside the empty space where the old Impala normally resided. This old truck was a full decade older than the car and had not been afforded the pampering the car had enjoyed. "Trucks are for workin', not lookin'" Zach's grandfather liked to say. And this truck had worked a lot. Its rusting hulk sat in the midst of all manner of tools and relics stacked neatly on shelves or hanging on rafters. He pushed the button to raise the garage door, slipped into the old truck and cranked it up. The sleepy engine took a little coaxing, but eventually growled to life.

As he backed out, he could see grandma on the back porch, holding a cordless phone in one hand and pointing toward the wrecked mechanic shop pick-up truck with the other.

TWENTY-FIVE

ZACH HAD A LITTLE REUNION WITH the familiar sounds and smells of his grandfather's old truck as he made his way back to the school, but he lacked both the time and the emotional reserve for full-on nostalgia. Soon he saw the school coming up on his right, well lit and quiet, all tucked in for the night. He hoped Jill was still asleep. If she was awake, she would be pissed that he left her. She would say he didn't need to go by himself. He didn't mind a little argument, but it would just be simpler if she was still asleep.

He checked the rear-view mirror to see if he was being followed. He didn't see anyone, but he passed by the school anyway. It was about a half mile to the next cross street, a state route that followed a straight line to Caldwell County. Long and dark and deserted, if he saw taillights behind him there, something was certainly up. But after a mile or two on this new road, he still saw no evidence that anyone was watching him. He doubled back towards the school, this time making a left into the driveway, reasonably confident that everything was OK.

Everything was not OK.

He pulled into the parking lot and turned off the headlights. There was plenty of light in the parking lot. No sense in calling the attention of anyone who might be passing by. He parked behind the busses, where the truck couldn't be seen from the road. Then he got out and walked towards the temporary buildings.

As he came around the corner, he stopped cold, then jumped

back behind the building. The light in the computer lab trailer was on. A thick man in a black coat was leaning against the trailer. Red cigarette fire and puffs of grey smoke marked his location, so clearly Thick Man was confident enough to not be concerned with stealth.

Zach had never been in a real, honest-to-goodness fist fight. There were the normal incidents of wrestling around or occasional pushing and shoving in high school. But nothing had ever come to blows. Zach had certainly never been in any kind of real danger. Much of this was due to not putting himself in bad situations, staying away from the kind of people who start fights, and being terrified of being expelled from a school where he really didn't belong anyway. Of course, being smart didn't hurt. He had always had a kind of calm in very stressful situations, could think clearly when tempers obscured everyone else's judgment. His brain might give him a fighting chance tonight. He could only hope so. He had a feeling his streak of non-violence might be about to come to an end.

Zach retreated back into the darkness, feeling his way along the dark brick wall until he came to a trash can he had smelled earlier. It was overflowing with bottles, cans, paper bags, and other detritus left behind by a week of teenagers at lunch. He groped through an assortment of sticky, squishy, and even pointy objects before finding what he wanted. He took two brown paper bags and put a glass bottle in each. He couldn't see what kind of bottles in the dark, but they were heavy and smelled like piss.

He stood up, pulled out half his shirttail, and messed up his hair a little. He stepped from the security of the shadows and headed into the light towards the trailers. He walked confidently, with just a bit of stumble and sway. No overselling. Zach had only been drunk a few times in his life and couldn't recall the details enough to accurately reproduce the drunk's gait. But watching other people walk while intoxicated was much more helpful anyway. He took an occasional faux sip from one of the glass bottles for effect.

He timed his approach so that he was out of sight of the guard for as long as possible. The first guard finally noticed him when Zach was only about ten feet from the trailer. "Hey, stop right there. Who are you?" The guard flipped his cigarette onto the ground and quickly closed the distance between the two. He was a thick, muscular man, but actually a little shorter than Zach.

"Well, who the hell are you, Mr. Sir?" Zach said in what he hoped was a convincing facsimile of intoxication.

"School security. You can't be here. You need to go on home."

"Do you know who I am? Do you know who the HELL I AM?" Zach asked. Then he didn't wait for an answer. "I freaking ran this school. All state my junior year. Threw my breaking shit right past gorillas like you all season. Then, I blew out my shoulder..." Zach used his right hand to put the bottle to his lips again, gripped a little more tightly this time, and grimaced from the stench as he put it to his lips for the last time. The guard took another step closer and reached out to grab Zach's arm. When he did, Zach swung the bottle from his lips right on top of the guard's head with a force that caused the bottle inside the bag to disintegrate. The big guy staggered once, drew in a breath that might have become a scream, but then Zach swung the other bottle hard against the guard's right temple. He was unconscious before he hit the ground. Zach allowed himself a little smile. Not bad for a man having his first fight in his mid-thirties.

Zach reached inside the big guy's jacket and fished out a semi-automatic pistol. Zach checked to make sure it was loaded, racked one round, applied the safety, and tucked it into the back waistband of his pants. He hadn't touched a gun in a decade. But, growing up in the South, firearms held no mystique. They were just one more object in your grandmother's nightstand.

He approached the trailer quickly, but quietly. The shades were drawn, so he could not see who was inside. But he could see two shadows. One was a man, average height and a little overweight, standing facing the door. It looked like he was wearing a hat, maybe a bowler. That suggested someone with either an appreciation for classic functionality or a profound sense of irony. The second silhouette was familiar. It was Jill, seated in one of the rolling chairs in the middle of the room. It looked like she was facing the man. Zach didn't see anyone else.

There weren't a lot of options here. He had a limited amount of time before the guard woke up. He was unconscious, not dead. The journey from non-violence to assault by bottle had been a rapid one, but killing was a much steeper hill to climb. So the guard would be re-joining the party in a while. There was only one move. Zach grabbed the door handle, turned it, and stepped inside.

The situation was a little more dire than Zach had suspected.

Directly opposite him, facing the door from the other side of the room, was a man in a brown tweed suit. He was indeed wearing a bowler hat, a curious affectation Zach marveled at even under these circumstances. He was probably 60, but could have been 70. A little overweight. Black wire-rimmed glasses framing small grey eyes. He looked vaguely familiar, but Zach's mind was too occupied with other things to cull through his memory of faces. It was Bowler Hat's hand that drew Zach's attention. Or, more accurately, the small revolver Bowler Hat's hand was holding. Firm grip, no sign of uneasiness or hesitation.

The gun was pointed directly at Jill.

Jill was in a chair in the middle of the room, her hands tied behind her with cable ties probably appropriated from the supply cabinet. She had her back to Zach, but looked over her shoulder as he walked in. She raised her eyebrows and managed a pained half smile. "We have a guest."

Zach suddenly regretted the fact that the pistol was tucked into his waistband and not in his hand. Stupid mistake.

"Ah, you must be Zachary," said Bowler Hat. "I trust you found your grandmother doing well." He spoke as if he was poking a wound to see if it was fresh.

"Why did you have to kill her? She has never hurt anyone. What kind of sick freak kills old women?"

"A sick freak with a really good view of the big picture. You have no idea how much trouble you are causing. I'm sorry about your grandma. Not a lot sorry, but a little bit. You have created a great deal of extra, unproductive work. And I hate unproductive work."

Every syllable was articulated with the cadence of a typewriter. Hard consonants were sharp points deployed at the end of each word. "We had very big plans for Mr. Wallace and Ms. Bates. But that's all off now. I really needed you to stay out of this, or at least walk away until we had a chance to deal with you in a more convenient manner."

"You can let us go now. I've had enough of this. I'd be glad to just return to a more normal job and pretend like this never happened." Zach spoke as convincingly as he could.

"Mr. Tanner, I think we all know that isn't true. You are a man with a very strong sense of conscience, literally no one to live for, and probably a growing sense of vengeance. I'm afraid that kind of loose end isn't something we can tolerate."

"At least let her go," Zach pointed to Jill. "She can't do anything to stop you. Her company is run by a bunch of guys you already have in your pocket. She can disappear back to South America, or wherever she has been waiting tables and breaking hearts for the past decade." Zach couldn't see Jill's face, but imagined her smiling at this little flourish. He tried to sell it.

Bowler Hat wasn't buying.

His thin lips broke into a half smile. "I think we both know that isn't going to happen. It could take me years to recreate the infrastructure I've built using her firm. I can't take a chance on her causing any new inconveniences. It's sad, really. Her and Mr. Wallace's combined assets would have put them at the top of one of the world's most powerful enterprises. But now I'm afraid she is going to be just another bereaved suicide victim." He paused and smiled. "I am confident Ms. James will do a fine job of carrying on the great work of Ms. Bates and Mr. Wallace."

Bowler Hat put a clipboard in Jill's lap. On it was a neatly typed letter and a very nice fountain pen resting on top. Zach looked over her shoulder to see the first few lines of text. Basically, it suggested she was distraught over Jeff's death and filled with regret over spurning his love for so many years. "I'm going to need you to sign that in a few moments, my dear."

"Fuck you," Jill said calmly.

"Well, I'm afraid that won't be possible. We have neither the time nor the venue. Besides, age is much more than a number."

Had Zach been a classically trained action hero, he might have contemplated trying to quickly pull the gun from behind his back. But he knew that wasn't possible. Even if he could reach it, he couldn't extract it quickly, and there was the matter of the safety. He knew where it was but doubted his finger would find it in the limited time it would take Bowler Hat to squeeze off a round from his little pistol. A miss was a distinct possibility, but Zach knew he couldn't count on it at this close range.

"What about me? I'm not really planning to shoot myself," Zach said.

"You do complicate things a bit. You really should not have wandered into this. I'm thinking our garden variety suicide might turn into a murder-suicide. A little more dramatic, maybe it will hold the lead on the evening news for a few days. It's probably just as well that there is no one left to grieve you. I'm going to need a new note, of course. Why don't you just come over here and sign the bottom of this blank page, and I'll sort out the details later." Bowler Hat pulled a sheet of white paper from the tray of a desktop printer and placed it on the table behind him. He placed a pen on the blank page.

He motioned with the gun. "Now, we are going to trade places. You are going to walk slowly to your left, past Ms. Bates, and sign this paper. I am going to go around the other way and close the door so we are not disturbed. Don't try to be clever, or we'll have a much bigger mess than is necessary."

Zach had no choice but to play along, but he did so slowly. The only play now was to draw things out, hope for a break, hope Bowler Hat stumbled or got too relaxed, or maybe had a very convenient heart attack. Zach made his way around to the table, Bowler Hat made his way to the door. Jill watched the odd slow motion dance in silence. She had given up on creating some kind of clever escape plan. Zach reached for the pen, then turned back to face Bowler Hat.

As he turned, he saw the old man facing him, back to the door that still stood open. In his left hand he still held the little pistol. But in his right was a syringe. "It's about time for both of you to take a little nap. Don't worry, I'll take everything from here. Now stop dawdling and sign the paper." The snub nose of the revolver motioned towards the page on the table.

Zach was about to speak when he saw another snub-nosed re-volver appear from the darkness outside, into the light behind Bowler Hat. The gun was followed by a hand, soft and well-manicured, but with a firm grip and steady aim. The arm came into the light next, an inch of crisp white cuff followed by a classic dark blue suit jacket. Then, the face came into the light.

Zach took a deep breath, just as the new visitor spoke.

"Drop your weapon, Reginald."

Bowler Hat was startled and instinctively turned to face the new visitor. Zach seized the opportunity, leaping past Jill and striking Bowler Hat with a well-executed shoulder-to-sternum tackle.

The blow slammed the older man against the door frame, Zach heard the air pushed out of his lungs in one deep gasp. The new visitor grabbed the pistol from Bowler Hat's hand, but the hand hold-ing the syringe came arcing down quickly towards Zach. Zach caught Bowler Hat's forearm with both hands. The older man was strong, but Zach had the advantage of thirty years and leverage. He forced the syringe to the side, and as Bowler Hat tried to wrench his body free, the needle pierced through his brown tweed coat and into the soft flesh of the old man's right pectoral. Zach's right hand swung quickly to push in the plunger on the syringe. Bowler Hat crumpled almost immediately, landing in a pile at Zach's feet.

"Oh God!" Zach said, and stepped backwards. "Is he dead?"

"He's still breathing," Jill said. She could see his chest rising and falling. "But I'd be OK if he wasn't."

The new visitor had stepped inside and closed the door. He retrieved the syringe from Bowler Hat's chest and checked the pulse to confirm Jill's diagnosis. Then he turned and extended his hand to her. "It is lovely to meet you, Ms. Bates. My name is Andrew Hightower."

Jill nodded towards her bound hands, and Zach stepped to the desk to retrieve a pair of scissors.

"I can assure you the pleasure is all mine."

Zach snipped the cable ties from her wrists, and she stood up and stretched her arms in front of her.

Mr. Hightower was impeccably dressed in a dark blue suit. Silver hair combed back with the ample assistance of pomade. A fresh white bandage was on his forehead, only partially covering a large bruised area. Despite the struggle and brief gun play, his tie was still perfectly symmetrical and tight against his neck. The fluorescent lights on the ceiling reflected brightly in his shoes. He smiled broadly, and his grey eyes went first to Jill, then to Zach. It was then that Zach realized why Bowler Hat looked so familiar.

"Oh yes, you probably are noticing the little bump on my head." That wasn't what Zach was noticing, but it was a start.

Zach started securing Bowler Hat's hands and feet with cable ties.

"It looks painful," Jill said.

"Oh, it's not very bad at all. I was in a bit of an automobile accident yesterday. I had been following some friends of mine secretly to make sure they were ok. Then there was some nasty business with a large truck." He smiled. "But it was very much worth it."

Jill looked at Zach. "Really?" Zach nodded in the affirmative.

"Well, sir, I am certainly glad you decided to make the trip to Oakdale," Jill said as she shook his hand. "But next time, just tell us if we need to be watched."

"Fair enough."

TWENTY–SIX

ZACH STARTED SECURING BOWLER HAT'S HANDS and feet with cable ties. "Mr. Hightower, I can't help but notice a bit of a resemblance between you and Bowler Hat man over there."

"Reginald."

"What?"

"His name is Reginald. And we are half-brothers, sharing the same mother. Also, you two have a little bit in common as well."

Zach was almost afraid to ask. "How is that?"

"Reginald once held the same job that you currently hold, although I'm afraid that was many, many years ago. Back then the large wall in your office was covered with fine mahogany paneling that was not obscured by a sea of liquid crystal display television monitors.

"Reginald and I both went to work for Sopros right out of college. He started out in product development; I accepted a position in operations. We were low-level managers but rose in the organization fairly quickly—Reginald more quickly than me. He was my better in both intelligence and ambition, and it showed in his rank. After just a few years he was head of product development, a very important role in our firm. He was fascinated by new technology, much like yourself and Mr. Wallace. He spent several months systematically studying major scientific disciplines—computers, genetics, pharmaceuticals, wireless, robotics, anatomy, even botany. He was looking for technologies we could use to advance our unique charter. It was shortly after this grand tour of the sciences that he hatched a dramatic plan." Hightower paused. "Perhaps we should all have a seat."

"This does not seem like the best time to take a break," Zach offered.

"Reginald there is secured, I also bound and gagged the guard I found unconscious outside the building, and it will be many hours before anyone shows up at school."

"Good points." Zach settled into a chair and let at least a little of the tension slip from his limbs.

Hightower continued. "Have you ever had a dream so amazing that you didn't want to wake up? Have you ever woken up with the sense that you had just experienced something wonderful? Have you ever dreamed about a loved one, and it was so real you could almost touch them?" Hightower looked to Jill and Zach, their faces were all the answer he needed. He continued.

"Reginald thought that, if people could have dreams like this every night, then they would be eager to go to sleep every night. Who would put off going to bed to watch a TV show when they could dream of things more vivid or wonderful than anything the National Broadcasting Company could offer? Of course, we did not have the ability to implant thoughts into someone's mind. No one does. But, one night, Reginald had a vivid dream about riding in an ambulance, bouncing down the street with the sirens blaring. The next morning, he found out that his neighbor had been taken to the hospital in the middle of the night. An ambulance had come charging down his street with the siren blaring. This was his epiphany. There was already a biological ability for dreams to be impacted by external stimuli. He just needed to amplify those phenomena. And control it.

"To do this, he needed two components. First, he needed to be able to put someone into a sleep that was deep enough to dream, but also make them extremely sensitive to their surroundings. Second, he needed an instrument for delivering stimulus. He did several basic tests. Like giving someone a mild sleeping aid, playing the sound of birds and crashing waves, blowing a fan across their faces—then asking later if they dreamed about being at the beach. The instruments were crude, and the results were uneven. But the board thought the technique had promise and gave him permission to continue the tests. This was his pet project for several years. He steadily refined the drugs and the method for manipulating the environment, but there were still many gaps.

Then, late one evening, he woke me up with a call to my home. He was breathless with excitement, speaking fast and soft. He had been using a brain scanner to monitor the mental activity of a test subject that was asleep. He was doing the standard test protocol— sounds, scents, sensations. But then he looked at his watch and realized it was late, and he had an early meeting the next day. He thought to himself, speaking aloud in the empty room, 'It's 9:30, so if I am asleep in 90 minutes, and my meeting starts at 6:15, how much sleep will I get?' As soon as he said this, on the brain scan monitor connected to the test subject he noticed a spike in activity in the part of the brain that performs computation. He tested a few more questions and saw the same phenomena. It was faint, but undeniable. When he read a mathematical problem aloud near someone in this suspended dream state, the dreamer's brain attempted to do the computation. A brilliant, well-studied, and incredibly ambitious man like Reginald was quick to see the potential.

"My brother was eager to share the news with me. 'Do you realize how powerful this could be?' he asked me. 'Sleep has always been a place where nothing happens, no work is performed, nothing is accomplished. But now sleeping hours can be productive hours. Imagine if we can find a way to interpret the brain activity. Imagine a nation of people resting quietly, while their minds tackle the world's biggest problems. They could map the human genome in seconds, develop cures for diseases, map the cosmos. Anything scientists use computers to accomplish could be done on an almost infinitely larger scale. It could change the world.'

"The technology was far from proven, however. The tools to analyze brain activity on that level just didn't exist. Not to mention the drugs would require a great deal of refinement; there wasn't a good system for transmitting questions. I dismissed his idea as a bit of a fool's errand, but it became his passion—his obsession. He tasked different people in different development groups with separate components of the system. He was the only one who understood how everything worked together. He would occasionally share a tidbit of information with me, news that some part of the project was going well or poorly. But again, I dismissed it. It seemed a pipe dream.

"Then, two years after that late-night phone call, he scheduled a demonstration for the board. They crowded into one of the patient rooms in the company clinic and watched as he injected a test subject with an experimental drug and connected him to a brain scanning machine. He placed a speaker right next to the subject's ear. The speaker was connected by a long black cord to a computer that stood in the corner of the room.

"He asked the board to suggest a basic mathematical problem. Someone said, "three plus two." Reginald typed some instructions into the computer's keyboard. He instructed everyone to look at one particular area of the brain scan and take careful count of any movements. Then, he pressed a key to submit the instruction. The speaker emitted a series of beeps, there was a brief pause, then the area on the brain scan pulsed five times. Three plus two equals five. It was a crude, basic experiment, but the board was impressed. And shocked.

"They saw the potential, but they didn't see it the way Reginald did. They were concerned about the side effects, about who would control the system. But, most of all, they felt the system directly violated the charter of the Sopros organization. We were in the business of ensuring that mankind slept. We were not in the business of causing people to work while they slept. I felt the same way, of course. I was ashamed for having not taken his project more seriously sooner. They ordered him to immediately discontinue the experiments and destroy any components he had created.

"He was enraged and profoundly disappointed, but he agreed to discontinue his work. They took him at his word, but I did not. My half-brother would not walk away from an obsession so great, something so potentially transformational. A few weeks later, I went to see him in his lab. He had a subject under anesthesia and connected to a brain scanner.

"He insisted that I keep his secret, but I could not. The next morning, I told our CEO what I had found. They found the evidence in Reginald's lab, and he was terminated on the spot. He was enraged. He cursed me and the father we did not share. He said that I had betrayed him, that I was missing out on one of the most powerful innovations mankind had ever known. Then he stormed out of the building.

"And he disappeared.

"Our mother had passed away while we were still in college, and we had no other family. So, there was no occasion for Reginald and me to see each other. I assumed that, wherever he was, he was still pursuing this project. But I hoped that he lacked the resources to bring it to fruition.

"Then one day he gave me a call. It was quite unexpected. He said he wanted to reconcile, that we were the only family each of us had and that we should support each other. He said his experiments were proceeding well, and that he planned to use his new technology for the betterment of mankind. Apparently, he had found a way to make sending and receiving instructions more sophisticated. And he had ideas about how to discretely deliver medication to help the system perform more efficiently. He even said he had identified a couple of private businesses that would be perfect for bringing his system online without alerting the public. Although launch was still years away, he seemed positively giddy. And he was very conciliatory towards me, encouraging me to join him.

"But I knew my brother well, and I was waiting for the next part. After a brief lull in the conversation, it came. He needed my help to access something he had left behind at Sopros. It was an experimental drug that would help people hover in a stage of sleep ideal for dreaming and make their senses extremely sensitive to the outside world. Our research and development team had continued to refine the medication, assuming it could be put to productive use. I, of course, refused to help him. He seemed genuinely surprised, which suggests he did not know me as well as I knew him. After that, I never heard from him again."

"And you haven't heard from him since?" Zach asked.

"No, I never spoke with him again. I did try to keep tabs on his activities as best I could. Had some folks monitor him from time to time. If he ever became truly dangerous, I wanted to know first. That way I could thwart him. For our mother's sake." Hightower looked at his half-brother in a heap on the floor and shook his head. "It would have killed her to know what he was doing."

"What he said about having found two businesses caught my attention. He said he had identified two firms that would be critical parts of bringing his plan to fruition. I reasoned that, if I could identify those two firms, I could monitor him. Then, when the time came, I could stop him. Based on what I knew of his system, I assumed one had to be some kind of electronics concern. He would need a way to distribute his devices widely. And I assumed he would want to keep his system a secret, so that suggested it would be embedded in ordinary electronics.

"The second firm was much more difficult to identify. I reasoned it had something to do with the medication. I spent a great deal of time researching pharmaceutical firms. This was my private project, the way I would spend my evenings, occasionally my weekends.

"After months of following this thread, it occurred to me that making the drug was probably the easy part. Any one of dozens of overseas labs could mass produce the chemical to his specifications. The real challenge was one of distribution—how to get masses of people to ingest the drug without their knowledge.

"Of course, my first thought was to randomly check municipal water supplies. But that was a dead end. Water supplies turn out to be a very ineffective way of distributing toxins. The sheer volume of the water makes it very difficult to reach a high enough concentration of the drug. Most public water goes to bathing or washing or even watering lawns. Only a tiny percent is actually ingested as drinking water. Producing enough chemical to contaminate everything is logistically challenging. And, knowing my brother, he likely found the inefficiency of this approach to be distasteful. So it came down to pre-packaged foods and beverages, very common ones at that. That was the most efficient way to impact many people with minimum effort.

"So, my search was narrowed down to an electronics distributor and some kind of food or beverage producer. Still a pretty big list. But it would also have to be a private company, preferably with a very small group of owners. Less oversight. And probably a mid-sized organization. Too small, and it wouldn't have the scale to reach broad distribution. Too big, and there would be too many people involved.

"Then, of course, there was the matter of stability. Reginald would be looking for companies he could depend on for years, decades. That meant clear lines of succession, stable management. Another big factor would be geographic isolation. It wasn't a requirement, but it would certainly make things easier. Reginald might need law enforcement to look the other way from time to time, at the very least he needed as few people as possible interacting with his operation.

"So, I compiled my list of potential firms. Electronics distributors and consumer food packaging. Mid-sized firms. Private ownership, family owned with clear lines of succession. Located in geographic isolation. There were about 20 electronics firms that fit the bill, around 35 food packagers. But when I compiled my list I noticed that in only one case were both firms in one city." He looked up at Jill. "You and Mr. Wallace are both only children, sole heirs to your family business. I knew my brother could not resist so elegant a solution."

A half dozen questions were roiling in Zach's mind, but remained unspoken, because at that moment his cell phone rang.

"Hello?"

"It's Ragsdale. A friend of mine set me up with access to some lab equipment. We ran scans on the DNA and blood samples. Generated a hell of a lot of data. We have no idea what it means yet, but the old folks are going to help us with that. I uploaded a ton of instructions into the nursing home system from here. We'll be feeding the data to them in little bite-sized chunks, they'll crunch away until they find out what's so special about you."

There was silence for a moment on both ends of the line. Zach thought about how it felt to have the questions bombard his mind while he slept. Ragsdale was feeling the same twinge of remorse on his end of the line and said, "I sure as hell hate to do this to those folks. But there really is no other way. Hopefully it will only take a few nights. Then we'll be all done with this."

"Let's hope so," Zach responded.

"Alright. I'm heading back. About to leave now. Things ok there?"

"We have a new guest I think you'll want to meet. At least once he wakes up."

"Are you in trouble?"

"No, no. We could have been, but Mr. Hightower showed up at just the right time. Glad to hear you made some progress."

"Well, let's not get too excited. Even if we come up with a treatment for the drug, we'll still need to find a way to stop the transmissions."

"I think we may have some options. I'll explain later. Just hurry."

TWENTY–SEVEN

ZACH ENDED THE CALL AND RETURNED the phone to his pants pocket. "Ragsdale is making progress on an antidote. Hopefully we'll have good news soon."

Zach wanted a Diet Coke, and he needed a little fresh air and a moment to regroup. "I'll go check and make sure the guard is still out." He slipped outside and let the muggy night air fill his lungs. He looked at the grass where the felled guard had lay unconscious and could not help but notice. The guard was gone.

At that moment, Zach heard a faint sound behind him, a crunch of gravel followed by the acceleration of his heartbeat. He started to turn, but then the blow landed on the side of his head, somewhere between the temple and the ear. He was fairly certain it was not a bullet, since he hadn't heard a sound. As Zach crumpled to the ground, he began to develop hypotheses as to the object that had hit him, estimate the force, wonder if had a concussion—or worse. But then his body was on the ground, and with two giant breaths—two giant throbs from the welt already rising on the side of his head—he was unconscious.

He awoke a few minutes later. He was somehow standing upright, really just leaning backward on the chest of the guard. The large arm was looped around under Zach's arms to hold him upright. The pistol that Zach had in his belt was now in the other man's hand, and the cool steel was pressed against Zach's left temple.

"Let's go. Slowly." The guard's warm, unpleasant breath was right in Zach's ear. There really was no option but to comply. So Zach began to inch ahead, his mind racing to develop a plan.

"Where's the Chairman?" Hot breath again in his ear.

"The who?"

"You know who I'm talking about. Brown suit."

"Last time I saw him, he helped me tie up a couple of prisoners, then he drove away."

This was clearly not the response the guard was expecting. Zach could almost hear the man's brain clicking away to process this information.

Zach continued, "He brought the woman with the dark hair. Then I brought another prisoner, an old guy, and took over guarding them while Reginald went off to wherever the hell he goes."

"So you expect me to believe that you are working for the Chairman too?" Zach could infer from the man's persistent use of the anonymous honorific "Chairman" and his general state of confusion that this was just a bit of hired muscle, not someone who was involved with Reginald in the leadership of the organization.

"Of course. Why else would I be out here in the middle of the night, in this shithole of a town? Reginald asked me to help with a couple of things, made it worth my while."

"I think you are full of shit. If you are working for the Chairman, then why the hell did you knock me in the head?"

The guard loosened his grip, and Zach turned to face him. The gun was still pointed at Zach's chest, so he held his hands up—casually, just below chest level. "Look, Sparky. I have no idea who you are. But Reginald didn't say anything about there being someone outside the building. I didn't know who the hell you were and couldn't take a chance. So, I hit you over the head. Just be thankful I didn't follow my first instinct and use my knife. When I got inside, Reginald told me you worked for him. We had a hell of a laugh over it."

The gun was a little lower now. Still pointed in his direction, but without the menace that had been there earlier. Zach played his final cards.

"That's why I came out here to check on you. I figured you would wake up, you'd either laugh it off or try to kick my ass, then we'd get to work. Right? Now, come inside. We have some prisoners to attend to."

The big guy looked towards the trailer window. He could see shadows from a couple of figures milling around behind the shades.

He looked back at Zach, but Zach anticipated the question.

"I tied them up but did it really loose. Just screwing with them. I figured they would untie themselves. Give them something to do. Just an old man and a sick woman. No weapons in the room and the door is locked. They're probably getting all excited thinking they've done something while the bad guy went to get a smoke."

The guard didn't say anything but motioned with his pistol towards the door. Zach let his hands fall to his side. The big guy didn't object, and he approached the door. He pulled his car keys from his pocket and rustled one of them against the door handle as if he was unlocking the door.

Zach turned the handle and the door opened inside and to the left. He stepped into the doorway and stood to the left as well, effectively screening Reginald's unconscious body from view. Hightower and Jill were to the right of the door, just where he hoped they would be.

"Now, you two didn't think you were getting away, did you?" Zach said with his best imitation of sinister sarcasm. Jill opened her mouth to speak, but then the guard stepped in right behind Zach, holding the pistol firmly in front. Zach gave her a little nod.

The guard stepped in and turned to point his gun at the two prisoners. "Sit down." He pointed with his pistol at the chairs that were closest to Jill and Hightower.

"Close the door," he said over his shoulder to Zach. Zach closed it, but now there was nothing to block the guard's view of his boss, bound and unconscious on the floor behind him.

The big guy stepped close to Jill and put the gun right against her forehead. "I heard you were supposed to commit suicide."

Hightower made a step towards him. "Stop. Don't hurt her." And he started to reach behind his back.

Big guy quickly redirected the muzzle of the gun towards Hightower. "Settle down. I don't know what I am supposed to do with you, but the plan for this lady was pretty clear." He glanced off to the side towards Zach but didn't actually turn around. "How about you help me out with gramps over here while I take care of the bitch."

The situation had escalated much more quickly than Zach had expected. He thought they would make it inside, maybe stall for an hour or so, wait for an advantage to all jump the larger man, maybe hit him in the head again. But it was now apparent that the guard was intent on taking some very quick, very violent action. Zach could see Jill literally trembling with fear, her eyes quickly panning between the three men in the room.

Zach didn't dare hold eye contact with Jill, but quickly stepped towards Hightower. He grabbed his boss's arm and twisted it behind him, turning the older man so that he was facing the guard. While Zach's left hand pinned Hightower's arm behind him, his right hand slipped the pistol from the holster in the back of Hightower's waist band.

The big guy pushed his gun against Jill's temple so that her head turned towards Zach and Hightower. Her eyes were wide with terror as she stared directly at Zach. He couldn't imagine this being his last image of her. He couldn't imagine going the rest of his life with that picture seared into his mind. Even more surprising to him, he couldn't imagine going the rest of his life without her.

But saving her would require doing something he was wholly unqualified to do, something he would not have even considered a few days ago. But now he had no choice.

He gripped the handle of Hightower's revolver tightly. He cocked the gun with his thumb as he pulled it upward. The sound of the hammer clicking into place caused the guard to turn in Zach's direction. But the big guy's head turned well before his brain could tell his arm to point the gun in Zach's direction. By the time the guard had his pistol halfway in the arc towards Zach, Zach had Hightower's revolver pointed squarely at the big guy's head.

Even at so short a distance, just a few feet, hitting something the size of a bowling ball with a moving gun and no time to aim is a fifty-fifty prospect at best. But given the current dire situation, Zach was willing to bet his life on a coin flip. The hammer flew forward and the "crack" of the little revolver's report seemed like a high-pitched thunderclap in Zach's ears. The next few milliseconds seemed like an eternity. He just pulled the trigger again, but it was no use. The big guy was already falling. His eyes frozen in shock and terror as he crumpled to the floor. The second bullet flew through the empty air and lodged in the hard drive of a middle-aged desktop PC.

Jill ran-fell across the few steps that separated her from Zach and threw her arms around his neck. He held her close, held her up. He could feel her sobs against her chest, feel her weight as she held on to him to stay upright.

Hightower kicked the gun away from the guard's hand and checked his neck for a pulse. He looked up at Zach and nodded.

The big guy was dead.

Zach was not a violent man, certainly not a killer. But he was relentlessly logical. And his mind rightly told him that his actions had been completely justified. He could make no counterargument. So his conscience was clear as he placed the pistol on the table and checked for himself to make sure the big guy didn't have a pulse.

As he stood back upright, he saw Jill sitting in a chair, staring blankly at the dead man on the floor, a small pool of blood forming beneath him on the industrial rug.

Zach thought about the night he had met her by the school playground, how cautious she had been, how sure she had been that their lives were very much in danger. Now she just stared as Zach pulled the other side of the rug over the body.

"I think someone is still going to notice him," Jill said flatly.

"If I know my brother," Hightower replied, "this is not the kind of man that anyone will come looking for. We'll take him and the rug with us. I'll have someone pick up the car and drop him off in a suitable place." Zach just shook his head. It turned out the old guy had a contingency plan for disposing of a body. Hightower was kind of a covert Brill Creme badass.

If Zach needed fresh air a few minutes ago, he really needed it now. "I'm going to try again for that Diet Coke."

Zach paused for a moment to consider the pistol on the table beside the door, then picked it up and stuck it in the waistband of his pants. With the cool steel providing a strangely comfortable pressure in the small of his back, he stepped outside and began crossing the lighted grassy area. This time he took great care to make sure he didn't have any company out in the shadows. But as he rounded the corner of the main building to the right and crossed from light into relative darkness, he saw motion in the muted light of the soda machine a dozen yards ahead. Zach froze and considered his options. He didn't know if he had been seen, he didn't know if Reginald had another person in the area. But he did know he had almost been shot twice tonight, and he did not have any interest in making it a trifecta.

He pulled the pistol from his waistband and pulled back the hammer. The click of the metal was surprisingly loud, clearly audible over the low hum of the vending machine. The silhouette was now in view again, clearly outlined in front of the vending machine. Zach raised the gun to take aim as he stepped slowly forward.

The shadow punched one of the buttons on the machine.

"If it's all the same to you, I would rather not be shot tonight. But if you have 75 cents, that would be great. I have a serious need for a Diet Coke."

It was Ragsdale.

"You scared the hell out of me, Rags."

"What the hell? Why are you so jumpy?"

"Let's just say things got a little rough. I'll explain when I get inside."

When they stepped back inside the trailer, Jill was sitting in a rolling chair, her head resting on the cold Formica table. Hightower was standing impatiently over the lump that was the guard. He had wrapped an extension cord several times around the rug-covered lump, creating a kind of dead guy burrito. A thin sheen of perspiration glistened just below the line of Hightower's neatly parted hair. Working the cord around the heavy package must have been difficult for a man of his age. In fairness, however, Zach had no idea what kind of shape Hightower was in beneath his ever-present three-piece suit. For all he knew, the chiseled torso of Adonis could be beneath the layers of starched cotton and worsted wool.

"I brought you some help." Zach nodded towards Ragsdale.

"Is anyone going to tell me why there is a body wrapped in a rug?" Ragsdale asked a very fair question. He looked around the room and saw the form of Reginald on the floor to his left. "I guess I mean two bodies."

"Actually, it is one body, and one very sleepy old man," Zach replied. "These two guys were planning to kill Jill, and perhaps me. Fortunately, Mr. Hightower showed up and helped turn things around."

"Ok," Ragsdale said matter-of-factly. Normally the situation would have demanded a more thorough round of questions. But Ragsdale had news of his own to share. "Well, it looks like the old folks really came through."

Hightower leaned forward in his chair. Zach stood up. Before they could ask, Ragsdale continued. "It's incredible how much data they crunched in such a short amount of time. The world's fastest computers would take days, maybe weeks to get an answer. But my friends at the university called me with the results while I was on my drive here."

Jill lifted her head a few inches from the table top. "We get it. Fast. Now what the hell did they find?"

Ragsdale made a face at Jill, but she had already closed her eyes and returned her head to her folded arms on the table. He continued, "It turns out, Zach, that your body produces an extraordinarily high amount of a particular amino acid. It is a genetic abnormality—no more than one person out of a hundred thousand have this kind of physiology. You probably noticed that you always had the ability to fall asleep quickly and sleep soundly in just about any surrounding." Zach nodded. Jill nodded as well, still face down with her head rested on folded arms.

"Well, this amino acid makes that possible. So even when exposed to large quantities of Somnucogipam, you still aren't susceptible to external stimuli. Their signals just cannot penetrate your subconscious while you sleep."

Zach asked the obvious question, "That's great for me, but what about the other 99.9% of the population?"

"Now that we know what makes you resistant, it is technically pretty simple to create a medicine that helps the general population replicate your level of resistance. And I believe Sopros has the resources to quickly produce such a drug." Everyone looked at Hightower. He nodded in the affirmative.

"We can distribute the antidote the same way the original drug was distributed," Jill offered. She was sitting up now.

"How long would it take to produce enough of the antidote to treat the affected population?" Zach asked Ragsdale.

"Probably three or four months."

Zach looked at Jill. "And Jill, how much time does it typically take for you to make plastic, have the manufacturer fill and ship it, and the consumer use it?"

"It varies. Figure one week in my plant. Most manufacturers don't keep more than a month of raw materials—empty bottles—on hand. Retail turnover for beverages is typically 1 to 2 months max."

"So, 9 to 12 weeks for the drug to get into consumers' homes. Probably another couple of months for them to get the dosage they need." Zach did the math. Jill nodded. "That's a long time. A lot of damage will be done. People will die." There was a long silence.

"But that's our only play." He looked at Ragsdale. "Tell your folks to get started." Zach wasn't technically sure this was his decision, but Hightower smiled, and Ragsdale started typing a message on his blackberry.

Jill smiled. "Zach, one way or another, this thing is over in six months. You did it."

He looked at her. She was beautiful, puffy eyes and all. He held her gaze for a moment. It is a rare and wonderful thing to look into someone's eyes and see admiration, respect. Love? He thought it, but dared not believe it. Ragsdale broke this silence.

"The folks at the university are sending the specs to the lab at Sopros. My folks will start working on this tomorrow."

Hightower nodded slowly, he was staring at his brother's heavy breaths. "Yes, well, we need to get our assailant in the rug here to the trunk of our automobile. I can have some of my associates pick him up and take him to someplace secure."

"Well, let's get to it, then." Ragsdale walked over to the lump on the floor and looked for a handhold near where the shoulders would be.

"I'll take him," Hightower said, looking over at Reginald's unconscious form. "I suspect you will need to question my brother, and it is probably best if I am not here for that. But I will collect him later and get him to a place where he won't endanger anyone else."

"Ok." Ragsdale stepped back, and Zach took his place where the legs stuck out from the carpet cadaver burrito. Hightower found a grip near the shoulders, and they eased towards the door.

Ragsdale walked to the door and pulled it open. "Be careful. I'll guard the computer lab here."

Zach looked over his shoulder at Jill, "Take care of yourself." She smiled as the door closed behind him.

The big guard was a heavy and awkward load. Zach and Hightower both began to sweat almost immediately from the strain. The older man more than held his own, however, and his tie never so much as loosened. "I certainly hope I can handle this kind of exertion when I'm your age," Zach said.

"I have always been very diligent about resistance training and calisthenics," the older man replied. Zach just smiled and shook his head. They didn't say much else, the nighttime silence was broken only by the crunch of gravel and the heavy breathing of two men carrying a 250-pound package.

As they loaded the body into the trunk, Hightower spoke between grunts of exertion. "I'll see you at the bus station. You might not want to follow too closely. These roads are deserted this time of night. Two cars travelling together might draw attention."

"Ok. I'll follow in your brother's rental. No sense in having my old pickup roaming the streets at night."

Zach walked towards a black sedan parked a few feet away. It was the only other car in the lot. He assumed it must be the one that Reginald and his hefty henchman drove. "Crap, forgot to get the keys," he said after he took a few steps. Hightower was already in the car and was putting it into reverse.

"No problem," Zach thought, "I'll catch up to him."

TWENTY–EIGHT

ZACH WALKED BRISKLY TOWARDS THE TRAILER. The cool night air and the lack of a heavy load felt almost refreshing. He saw the vending machine and realized he still did not have the soda he attempted to purchase earlier. Suddenly keenly aware of his thirst, he turned towards the machine and dug into his pockets for change. He had inserted the first coin when he caught a whiff of a familiar smell. It was pleasant, but he couldn't quite place it.

The second coin was in the slot when the warning from his subconscious met the recognition from his conscious. The fight-or-flight response quickly selected the "fight" option, and adrenaline rushed into his veins as the muscles in his left leg tensed for a quick turnaround. But, before the move could be executed, he felt the cold hard pressure of a pistol in his lower back.

"I'll have a Diet Coke, if you don't mind, dear." Her lips were so close to his right ear that he could feel her breath. Her perfume was strong in his nostrils, her hand was firm on his side as she leaned over his right shoulder to speak. "I couldn't help but overhear your conversation earlier."

"It's rude to eavesdrop."

"It's also rude to shoot people and wrap them up in carpet, and tie up old men, so I don't think you have any room to talk."

"Once someone pulls a gun on you, etiquette has a way of going out the window."

"Turn around," she said as she pushed the gun barrel a little deeper into his back.

She took a couple of steps back as he turned to face her. She was wearing a tightly tailored suit jacket over a white blouse, form-fitting dark jeans, and boots with a heel high enough to look feminine but not too high that she couldn't kick some ass if needed. The security light behind her cast shadows across her face. But the dull glow from the vending machine cast muted light on her features. Her jet black hair was in sharp contrast to her ivory skin. Her hands were undeniably feminine. He could easily imagine them holding a glass of white wine, or adjusting the clasp on a necklace, or adjusting a necktie, or any of the things that seem to come so easily for feminine fingers. But tonight, her most prominent accessory was the 9mm semi automatic in her right hand, secured firmly in the grip of those long ivory fingers with the bright red nail polish.

"I'm pretty sure Hightower will frown upon you pulling a gun on a co-worker." Zach was stalling, looking for an advantage. Her grip was steady enough that he was fairly certain she wouldn't hesitate to pull the trigger if he moved too quickly.

"He's a cute old man, but by now you must know that I work for someone else."

"Bowler hat guy?"

"Well, aren't you the smart one. Yes, the chairman thought I would be the perfect person to recruit your old friend Jeff and make use of a few things from Hightower's operation."

"How did you manage to get Jeff roped into this?"

"It's amazing how a man's perspective can change when he is between a woman's legs." She said it without a blink or blush.

"I suppose the legs you speak of would be yours? Dubious."

"Wouldn't you like to find out?"

Zach had never been propositioned at gun point before, but he was pretty sure this question was purely rhetorical. He needed to stall, and he needed her to be distracted. "Jeff always did have a weakness for brunettes. It sounds like you guys were getting pretty close before his old girlfriend showed up."

She pursed her lips a little when he said that. She was surely smart enough to know what Zach was doing but conceited enough that it got to her anyway.

"Jeff certainly went slumming with that cow. But that's fine with me. I already had access to Sopros, and I'm in line to pick up his family business too." She held up her left hand to reveal a very large wedding ring that sparkled with enough diamonds to buy a house. "I'm—I'm just so sad my love is gone. So tragic. I guess I'll just have to console myself with big, giant piles of money."

At that moment, over Ms. James's left shoulder, Zach saw the door of the classroom open and a figure slip outside. It was Jill, and she was carrying the tire tool they had used to break into the classroom originally. He was at once relieved to have someone come to his aid, but afraid about how Jill would fare in a gun vs tire tool battle. He didn't dare look directly at Jill. Instead, he kept his gaze firmly focused on the woman with the gun, while Jill moved through his peripheral vision.

But for some reason Jill never looked in his direction. She left the door to the classroom open just a few inches. Then, to Zach's dismay, she walked quickly down the stairs while looking to the right—away from him.

At the bottom of the stairs, she turned her back to Zach and hurried the hundred feet or so to the temporary building closest to the school. The bathroom building. She jammed the flat end of the tire tool into the door jam and leaned hard onto the handle. The door popped open, and Jill slipped inside.

Ms. James heard the pop of the door opening and turned quickly. But her gaze focused on the sliver of light coming from the partially open classroom closest to her. "Shit!" she said under her breath as she realized her mistake. Turning her back on the classroom was a bad idea. But she hadn't yet realized that turning her back on Zach was an even worse one.

Zach's grandma had always said not to hit girls, and even now he hesitated for a millisecond. But a loaded gun has a way of making you forget the rules.

Zach lunged hard towards Ms. James. Her right hand was still pointing a gun at him, but she was looking over her left shoulder at the open classroom door. Zach's right arm came down hard on hers, pushing the gun towards the ground. Her delicate finger pulled the trigger, sending a round into the ground near Zach's foot. He saw a puff of dust where the slug landed.

His left forearm hit near her collarbone, knocking her back onto the ground as he fell on top of her. The impact knocked the breath out of him, and his deep inhale pulled in equal parts dust and perfume. Then there was a loud crack-crack sound, and another smell. Gunpowder. She was still holding the gun. There was really no time to contemplate whether or not he had been hit. He just swung his left arm over her right arm and pinned it to the ground. He grabbed her wrist and pounded it on the ground twice. The gun fell away.

Looking back towards Ms. James's face, he realized how close they were. She was staring right into his eyes. God, she was hot. He thought it was a sad commentary on his gender that a man would find a woman attractive even as she was trying to kill him. But the danger was passed now. She wasn't holding a gun. She smiled at him. That was strange.

Then all he saw was red, all he heard was ringing in his ears. He went limp. All he could think was that his testicles had exploded. Her knee had moved swiftly and hit its mark with the fury of a woman who had no remorse and three years of kickboxing classes. In a second, he was on his back, she was standing over him with the gun in her hand again. She was breathing heavily, eyes wide with adrenaline, but finger steady on the trigger.

"One way or another, going for the dick is the best way to get to a man." She smiled big, a little too big. A little crazy. A lot crazy. She took a deep breath and pointed the gun at Zach's chest.

Adrenaline is a funny thing. It enables the human body to do incredible things under extreme stress. One of the ways it does this is by diverting the body's resources away from functions that are not essential to the task at hand. Blood flow is diverted to the core of the body, which is why people's limbs are often cold right after a traumatic event. And extreme adrenaline also tends to create tunnel vision, a laser-like focus on what is immediately in front of you—at the expense of peripheral vision.

The adrenaline that helped Ms. James get the better of a man sixty pounds heavier than her was now working against her. She didn't hear the footsteps behind her, didn't see the figure approaching from behind her to the left. Her body was doing what it was biologi-cally wired to do—deal with the immediate threat on the ground in front of her.

But the real threat was just behind her, a five-pound steel tire tool descending in a steep arc towards her head. Her face still had that wild, crazy smile when she hit the ground.

Jill dropped the tire tool on the ground beside Ms. James. The nausea and shooting pains originating from his groin were enough to keep Zach from jumping up quickly. He had only managed to sit up before Jill reached him. Her embrace hit him with such force that he fell backwards into the dirt again, Jill on top of him.

He was about to speak when her lips touched his. The kiss was just the warmest point in an embrace that seemed to occupy all of him. Her legs were astride him, her chest pressed against his, her hands soft and cold on his cheeks, her hair dancing across his face and neck, her lips pressed so close that they felt like part of his own face. Her breath filling him with warmth. It was an assault of affection, a whole other outlet for adrenaline, more affection in thirty seconds than Zach had experienced in the last decade.

"You're wasting your time. After the kick he took, he's pretty much a eunuch." Zach opened his eyes to see Ragsdale standing over him. Jill's kiss continued for just a second longer before her eyes opened. She smiled at Zach and looked up at Ragsdale. "Oh, I'm pretty sure everything is working just fine."

They both stood up and brushed the dust from them. A few puffs of dust drifted slowly towards Ms. James's open eyes. She didn't blink.

The reality hit Jill as she looked down. It wasn't so much remorse as it was nausea. The adrenaline had done its work, and her body was trying to recover. She felt limp, weak all over. She grabbed Zach's arm to steady herself.

Two life-and-death moments in one night, and dawn was still hours away. Zach calculated the hours, the minutes. He couldn't help himself. It was what his brain was wired to do. He analyzed. Zach looked over Jill's shoulder at Ms. James. The blood quickly pooling beneath her head was exactly the shade of her lipstick, perhaps a shade darker than her nail polish.

Zach and Ragsdale completed the grim work of dealing with Ms. James's body in silence. There was still much to discuss, but neither man had become accustomed enough to death that it did not affect them. Jill was quiet as well, fatigue having isolated her into a kind of groggy stupor. She didn't think about much of anything as she worked from her knees, scraping a metal trash can across the stained dirt to gather up the blood. With a precision that surprised all three of them, their work was completed in just a few minutes, and their unwieldly bundle—triple bagged for safety—lay hidden in the bushes outside the trailer. Zach texted Mr. Hightower to let him know another trip to the bus station would be required.

TWENTY-NINE

WITH THEIR WORK COMPLETE, THE THREE filed back into the trailer. Jill went directly to a large pump container of Purell on one of the desks and pumped a handful large enough to sanitize her arms all the way to the elbows. The two men followed her lead until the vaguely medicinal smell of aloe vera and alcohol filled the air.

"We still need to find out where the nerve center is; we need to stop them from transmitting these signals. And we need to get out of here before kids start showing up for school," Zach drew focus back to the task at hand.

Ragsdale reached into his bag, pulled out a laptop, and began to type. Zach began to unwind the wires to the probes they had used earlier, when Ragsdale tested Zach's sensitivity to the dream signals.

"How are we going to do that? It could literally be anywhere, right?" Jill asked.

"Not technically anywhere," Zach replied, "there are probably a few criteria to keep in mind. If we can understand the criteria they used to select the location, perhaps we can narrow it down."

"So do we just guess at how they decided on a location? I mean, we don't know," Jill said.

"No, but he does." Ragsdale nodded towards Reginald's sleeping form on the floor.

"I'm sure Hightower didn't want to be here for this. Not sure what might happen," Zach said. "But this is our only play."

Jill sat down in a chair and stared blankly towards Reginald, while Zach attached Ragsdale's sensors to the old man's forehead.

"This shouldn't hurt him," Zach said reassuringly to Jill.

"I don't give a shit," Jill said without hesitation. Zach remembered Jill thrashing around in the back seat of their rental car, her body convulsing in a sleep from which she couldn't awake.

Jill thought about that too. "So, can you just ask him where his operation is located?" she continued.

"It's not quite that simple," Ragsdale said. "This system can't necessarily access specific memories or stored facts. But it uses the brain's cognitive ability, computational and problem-solving power."

Zach finished the thought. "So we can't ask him exactly what site he selected. But we can get a sense of his thought process, decision criteria."

"This is a much more complicated scenario than what we tested with Zach earlier," said Ragsdale, "but I think I have put together something that will do the trick. I was able to capture some of the code they used on Zach and make a few modifications."

Ragsdale was sitting at a desk, laptop open in front of him, Reginald on the floor to his right. Zach sat on the floor next to the sleeping man, his hand on Reginald's wrist monitoring his pulse. Ragsdale looked at Zach, and Zach nodded. Ragsdale submitted the first question:

"2+3"

There was a brief pause, an almost imperceptible twitch of the older man's eyebrows, then and Ragsdale's screen lit up with a reply: "5."

Zach squinted to see the screen, then looked at Ragsdale. It was working.

A few more diagnostic questions succeeded.

"3 x 5"

"15"

"A is to B as what is to M"

"L"

And then the questions became more complex:

"Decision criteria for selection location of a gas station."

"Traffic pattern. Surrounding population. Environmental restrictions. Crime rates."

"The last one was a nice touch," Jill whispered sarcastically. Zach shook his head but didn't speak. Ragsdale was typing the next question.

"Decision criteria for locating large centralized computing platform."

"Availability of electricity, ambient temperature, size of facility, access to telecommunications."

"Selection criteria for covert location of large computing platform."

"Clear perimeter, low traffic, inconspicuous, explainable alternate uses, proximity to leadership."

Zach read the last phrase and looked to Ragsdale. He signaled to stop the test. Ragsdale shut down the program.

"So the bastard put his facility nearby," Ragsdale said.

"I thought we were going to be scouring the whole planet, but it sounds like the facility is pretty close by. A pretty big flaw in his plan. Still a needle in a haystack, but at least it's not a needle in a hay field."

Ragsdale pulled up a map of the area on his computer. "Let's start with a 200-mile radius," Zach said, "an easy drive, doesn't require airports or helicopters."

Ragsdale was typing quickly. "I'm tagging the buildings on the map that likely have very high electrical usage." The screen was filling up with a series of red pins—factories, large office complexes, power plants.

"That's a pretty big haystack," Jill said. She had rolled her chair up next to Ragsdale.

"Ok, let's talk telecommunications," Zach said. "What kind of bandwidth would he need?"

"Well, the facility in the basement of the nursing home was handling terabytes of data every second, and that was for what, maybe 200 people?" Ragsdale offered.

"So, if he wanted to roll this out nationally, say 100 million people, then he would need 500,000 times that much capacity."

"That's a big pipe. I can't think of anyplace on this map that would have that kind of data capacity," Ragsdale said.

"What about satellite?" Jill asked. "Could they be transmitting wirelessly?"

"No way. It would require dozens of satellites and be super expensive. Someone would have noticed. For this, I think we are talking about a big fiber optic cable. I mean really big, like part of the data backbone for an AT&T or Verizon or someone."

"Way ahead of you." Ragsdale was pulling up maps of network facilities and high capacity data lines for the major telcos. Only one ran through their 200-square-mile map. Ragsdale traced it with his finger across the screen. It didn't pass near any of the places with heavy power usage.

"Shit," Zach said when he saw the data line plotted on the screen. He turned away from the computer and ran his fingers through his hair. The room was silent for a moment, maybe two.

Jill broke the silence with a question, "Couldn't they just run a line to the main cable? How noticeable would that be?"

"Pretty noticeable," Ragsdale said, "It would have to be underground, routed in such a way that it had almost no chance of being disturbed by future construction. And it would have required a shitload of digging. Even the closest heavy electric facilities are at least ten miles from the fiber optic line. It would be hard to dig a ten-mile ditch through a populated area without someone noticing."

Zack turned quickly back around.

"What if the ditch was already there?"

Ragsdale raised an eyebrow.

"What if the ditch was already there? What if they didn't have to dig at all?" He looked over Ragsdale's shoulder at the computer and pointed to a spot on the screen. "There."

"Well, that is a hell of a thing," Ragsdale said. Zach's finger was pointing at the water pipeline. It started at the McArthur Reservoir and ran about sixty miles to the south. And about halfway down its length, it crossed over a utility right-of-way that was home to a transcontinental network line. There was only one facility in the path of the water pipeline: the Adamsville textile factory. "They could have run the cable right through the water line."

"Brilliant, actually." Zach stumbled back into a chair.

"Well, let's get down there and take a look," Ragsdale said as he stood up.

Jill looked at Zach. Zach's face had flushed white. "I don't think it's a good idea for Zach to go there."

Ragsdale was about to form a question when he saw the sickened look on Zach's face. The younger man looked as if he was about to vomit.

But then Zach's face hardened. He spoke slowly, deliberately, "Launch your program again. We have a few more questions for Reginald."

"Zach, what are you going to do?" Jill asked.

Ragsdale hesitated for a moment, then sat back down at his computer. He launched the program. "Ok, what do you want to ask our sleepy friend here?"

This time Zach didn't kneel beside Reginald to keep track of his pulse.

"How to choose test subjects for potentially risky medical trial?"

Ragsdale typed out the question. There was a pause, then the screen lit up with a response: "otherwise healthy, financially needy, close proximity, limited options."

Zach nodded, then asked another question. "Risk factors for testing sleep system."

More typing, a longer pause, then a reply.

"Chronic fatigue, difficulty sleeping, erratic dreams."

Another question, "Protocol if test subject is resistant to sleep-inducing drug."

"Increase dosage."

"Likely outcome if test subject is extremely resistant, even at high dosage."

"Seizure. Potentially death."

Ragsdale looked confused. Jill put her face in her hands.

"Bastard," Zach said. He reached over and closed the lid of Ragsdale's laptop. "Let's get to that water treatment plant."

"What about him?" Ragsdale asked as he nodded towards Reginald's prostrate form.

"Hell if I care," Zach said as he opened the door and walked out into the cool night air.

When his feet made it past the bottom step and crunched into the gravel, he stopped. His head spun, and his stomach churned. His pulse raced, and he couldn't get a deep breath. His fist was clenched, but there was no one to hit. His eyes burned, but he would not let himself cry. His knees buckled, but he was determined to stand.

"Son of a bitch."

This conspiracy had defined Zach's whole life, and he didn't even know it. His father had not died of natural causes. He had been killed. A miserable frantic death like his grandfather. Zach thought of childhood nights spent staring out the window through his tears, cursing God for leaving him without a family. His life, his personality, his identity had been defined by his loneliness, by his isolation. And that smug old bastard asleep on the floor had caused it all.

His left foot just started to turn and take him back inside, but he felt her arm around his waist. She pulled his left arm around her shoulder. "Nothing you can do to him will fix this. We need to get to that water plant."

"I'm not leaving him here. I'm not risking letting that murdering bastard escape. Tell Hightower where we are going and that we are taking his asshole brother with us."

"Will do." Ragsdale brushed past while dialing his cell phone. "I'll bring the car around."

A few minutes later they were in the car, speeding to the water treatment plant. The still-sleeping Reginald was in the trunk with a particularly gory trash bag, jostling ever so slightly as the car sped along the bumpy rural roads.

———————————————

They rode in silence for a half hour, with only the hum of cheap tires on rough rural road. Ragsdale drove, although he wasn't quite sure how to get to their destination. Jill had said "south" as she slid into the back seat behind him. There hadn't been many opportunities to turn, so the information gap had not yet become an issue. He assumed one of his companions would alert him when another turn was required.

Jill sat in the back seat, on the driver's side. She stared at the silhouette of Zach's profile, dimly lit by dashboard lights. He sat upright, eyes straight ahead. He didn't doze. He barely even blinked. She could see his jaw line twitching as he ground his teeth together. She wanted to hold him, to put her head on his chest, to comfort him. He always flinched a little when she touched him, but then he held on as if it was the only embrace he would ever receive. Right now, he was a mile away in the front seat. And so she sat and stared at him staring.

Zach saw the white lines flying past, heard the hum of the tires. But for all he noticed, his eyes might as well have been closed. His mind raced through forgotten facts, experiences blurred by time, pains locked inside the stoic heart of a hurting little boy. It was all evident now. His personal pain, it turned out, was just one symptom of an evil that had touched thousands. And if he didn't stop it, would hurt millions.

His mind moved quickly, the last pieces falling into place. A thousand little insights built to a crescendo inside his head. His hand gripped tight on the pistol that was still in his pocket.

"Here. Right!" Zach shouted, shattering the silence. It would have been loud enough to startle everyone, even if they weren't hurtling down a dark road with a body in the trunk.

Ragsdale stood on the brakes and cut the wheel hard. The sedan leaned into its squishy suspension, and the tires screamed in protest as they slid onto the side street.

"Just a few miles ahead. It will be on the right." Zach pointed through the windshield into the darkness. Ragsdale and Jill exhaled, but no one spoke. Zach continued, "I always wondered how this shitty little factory stayed in business. Just about every textile operation in the Southeast closed down a decade or two ago, couldn't compete with India and the rest of Asia. Yet, this place stayed in business."

"I thought maybe it was a front for a drug operation or something," Jill offered.

"I wish it was that simple," said Zach.

"It sure as hell is in a great location for keeping secrets," Ragsdale said. "We are officially in the armpit of nowhere. I don't see another light or building for miles."

The lights of the factory were up ahead now, dimly illuminating a collection of grey concrete and steel buildings. A dozen cars huddled in the sparse light of a single bulb by the front door.

"Night shift is on duty," Ragsdale said as he slowed down the car and prepared to turn.

Zach turned around and looked at Jill in the back seat. "But I'm sure they will open the door for a sick woman who needs to call for help."

"What about the old guy in the trunk?" Jill asked.

"I assume he'll be out for a while. But even if he wakes up, he is still tied up and locked up."

Ragsdale parked the car near the front. Zach opened the rear passenger side door and helped Jill up, slinging one of her arms around his shoulders. They made their way slowly to the door, Jill leaning on Zach with a force that was half act, and half necessity.

The lobby was dark and the door was locked, but an intercom was mounted on the wall to the left. Ragsdale pushed the call button a few times urgently. There was a few moments' delay, then the speaker cracked to life and a rough voice bellowed through the static.

"Can I help you?"

"We have a woman here who is very sick. Our car is overheating, and our cell phone is dead. We need somewhere we can stop and call for help?"

"We really don't have any room for visitors," the voice replied.

Ragsdale pinched Jill's arm and she shouted. "Ooowwwwww. It hurts!"

"Please, it will only take a minute. We just need to call for help," Zach pleaded. Jill groaned again.

"Ok, ok. I'll be right there."

In a moment the fluorescent lights in the lobby flickered to life. A man walked quickly towards them. Ragsdale's hand tightened around the pistol stuck in the back waistband of his pants.

The man was tall and thin, a mess of brown hair swept haphazardly over to one side, a nose that Zach reckoned protruded about 25% farther from his face than was typical. He was probably in his early forties, a day's worth of stubble obscuring just a few wrinkles around his eyes and the corners of his mouth. The name tag on his light brown uniform shirt declared his name was "Len." He paused in front of the glass door for a just a moment, looking them carefully up and down before spinning the lock and pushing open the door. They stepped inside.

THIRTY

THE LOBBY AREA WAS SMALL. RIGHT in front of the door was a Steelcase reception desk. From the looks of it, the desk had no regular inhabitant. They could see the movement of people and machinery through a small window at eye level behind the desk. To their immediate left was a vinyl-covered couch with metal legs, flanked by large artificial plants that defied taxonomy. Just past the farthest plant was another glass door that led down a long hallway. Zach eased Jill down onto the old vinyl sofa in the lobby and turned to face their host.

"So, what's wrong with her?"

"Woman problems. I don't know," Zach said softly. Ragsdale pointed down to his loins and grimaced. Truthfully, Jill looked bad enough that Len didn't need much imagination to think she was very sick.

Len took a step backwards. "Alright. There is a phone on the desk. Dial 9 for a line. Don't let anyone in. You can stay right here until your ride comes. He pointed to the glass door and the hallway. Bathroom is first door on the left. I've got to get back to work. Pull the door closed behind you when you leave, it will lock automatically."

Len paused. "Well, ok then." He turned and disappeared through the door into the light and the noise of the factory floor.

"That was a little too easy," Ragsdale said. "I was expecting a lot more security."

"I don't think Len is privy to the inner workings of any world domination plot. These guys don't know what is going on here," Zach said.

"How can that be?" asked Jill. "The facility would be pretty hard to hide."

"Not necessarily," Zach said.

Ragsdale looked around the room. "You know something we don't know?"

"My dad worked here. He used to bring me here sometimes, when he had to work the night shift. Before he died." Ragsdale looked at Jill and she nodded.

Zach continued, "Before he died here. I was really little. I camped out on the floor in his office in a sleeping bag, watched late movies on a tiny black and white TV he would borrow from the break room."

Zach saw the look in Jill's eyes. Compassion? Pity? He tried to put a positive spin on it. "I guess it does sound kind of bad, but I thought it was pretty cool. That's the closest I ever came to going camping with my dad." He looked at her again. This time it was definitely pity. Enough of that. "Come on, down the hallway, I'll show you."

Zach walked quickly over to the front door and opened it briefly so that the security system chime went off. "That would be us leaving." Then they made their way down the hallway. Jill leaned heavily on Zach, just in case anyone was looking. There was a wall on the left, and a series of solid doors on the right. The first one was labeled "Restroom" with three-inch metal stencil letters. The next door stood open, revealing a break room. The far wall of the break room was a window looking out over the factory floor.

The next two doors were closed and unmarked. They continued past those and stopped at the last door on the right. Zach released Jill and paused as he grabbed the handle.

"This was my dad's office."

Jill put her hand on his shoulder. He turned the handle and pushed open the door.

He flipped on the light switch and the memories flooded back as the light chased the dark from the room. It was a small office, much smaller than he remembered. Concrete floors. His dad's old desk was still in use, centered in the middle of the floor. It seemed incredible until he considered the fortunes of this industry and the sturdiness of the desk. There was probably not much reason to buy a new desk in the past few decades. The desk was adorned with a decade-old computer, and there was a new calendar on the wall. Other than that, the room stood pretty much as it had when Zach had last visited it three decades ago.

This was also true for the feature Zach was most concerned with in this office: an oddly shaped bookcase, built into the exterior wall to his left. The book case was much deeper than one would expect, easily twenty-four inches, but not more than three feet wide. It was ugly, even for a Spartan office like this. Even an untrained eye could see the shelves weren't level, could see marks beneath the white paint that had been applied with haphazard brush strokes. It was curiously off center, as if no one had cared to orient its position to the axis of the room.

Zach motioned to Ragsdale. "Lock the door."

He knelt beside the cabinet. Pulling out his pocket knife, he started prying off the kickboard that covered the gap between the bottom shelf and the floor.

"Do you want to move it?" Ragsdale asked. He began looking for a good place to grip the shelf.

"Yes, but don't waste your energy. It's anchored to the wall."

The kick plate came off, and Zach reached into the dark. He began to feel around amongst the dust and dead bugs and goodness-knows-what that collects in such a space over the course of three decades. His arm was a good bit thicker than it was last time he did this, but the gap was originally made for a man anyway. After a few moments he found what he was looking for.

He gave the latch a pull, then he pulled a little harder. It finally released with a muted clang of metal on dusty metal. The bookcase shuddered ever so slightly as it released the wall mountings.

"There we are," Zach said as he stood back up.

Ragsdale put his shoulder to the bookcase and started to push as Zach continued. "Now, I'm not sure what we will find down there today. But I know what it looked like thirty years ago."

Ragsdale stopped pushing. "Down?"

"Yes. The man who owned this plant when my father worked here was a bit of an eccentric. Apparently, he wanted to build a bomb shelter under the office. He had started building it under his home, until he read somewhere that nuclear attacks were more likely to happen between the hours of 10 a.m. and 3 p.m. Eastern Time. Something about time zone differences and Breshnev's sleeping hab-its. Anyway, since he was in the office during the high-risk hours, and didn't have any family, he thought it made more sense to build it here."

"And he put the entrance in your dad's office?" Jill asked.

"Not exactly. They started digging beneath the owner's office, actually an empty room adjacent to his office. But after they dug down a few feet they got a pretty big surprise. It turns out much of this complex sits on top of a massive underground cavern. They broke through the roof of a cave the size of several football fields. The owner kept it a secret. He was afraid the government would make him shut the factory down, or at the very least have the place swarming with inspectors and researchers and such. He just kept working on his little bomb shelter."

"But your dad knew?"

"Sure. One manager on each shift knew what was going on. That way they could help the 'underground' crew get whatever access they needed, answer any questions from folks who thought they heard unusual sounds. But no one really suspected. The plant ran three shifts in those days. It was always way too loud to hear folks work-ing underground. The only real evidence is this big ugly bookcase."

"It is a bit of an eyesore," Jill pointed out as she sat down on the floor, legs crossed with her head resting on her hands.

"Well, my dad wasn't much of a carpenter, he was kind of pressed into duty. The underground crew was supposed to cut a ventilation shaft that came up in a thick stand of azaleas on the other side of this wall. But they measured wrong. One morning my dad was check-ing time cards at his desk and he heard hammering underneath the floor. A few seconds later, a chunk of his floor falls away and two workers poke their heads up through the floor. They were terrified, of course. The owner was very particular about following directions and keeping his project covert. Once he saw this hole, they would definitely be fired. And, in this town, hungry kids were more com-mon than good jobs. So, my dad took pity on them. He told them to bring up some wood and tools, and he built this big ugly bookcase to cover their mistake. He told the boss it was a class project from the local middle school."

"But he didn't really seal up the opening?" Ragsdale asked.

"My dad was a brilliant man. Inquisitive, well read. Analytical and creative. But he was stuck in this tiny town with a kindergartener he was trying to raise alone and a job that would suck the life out of someone half as intelligent as he was. So this little cavern was a godsend for him. It was like his own little private intellectual playground. He would let me go with him sometimes, sneak down to explore the cavern, look at rock formations, estimate how big it was or how old it was. But then one day he said he couldn't take me with him anymore. He said the construction was complete, and it was private property. I always suspected he still went down, though. Sometimes."

Zach's voice trailed off a little as he ran his hand across the shelf, shaking loose a little dust and a lot of memory. Zach was very young when he lost his father. He had very little to remember him by. Zach had been so focused on the task at hand that he hadn't stopped to consider how he would feel back in his father's office. He didn't have many memories of his dad, but many of the best ones happened here. And it was here that it all had ended so suddenly.

Zach felt Jill's hand softly on his shoulder. He gave his head a quick shake, rubbed his eyes with the heels of his hands. Then he put his shoulder to the bookshelf. Ragsdale stepped over to help, but Zach had already pushed the shelf a couple of feet to the side. It was big and ugly, but not particularly heavy.

With the shelf pushed to the side, they could see a rough hole in the concrete floor. It was about two feet in diameter, rough and irregularly shaped. The first six inches or so inside the hole were concrete, the gray slab of the factory floor. After that was a foot or so of dirt, smoothed and packed tight. Below that, the opening passed through a foot and a half of rock, solid granite from the look of it.

Zach pulled a flashlight from his pocket, a tiny LED borrowed from the computer lab, and shined it into the hole. They saw the top side of a suspended ceiling. A grid of metal frames supported squares of acoustic tile and the occasional idle fluorescent light fixture. All the fixtures were dark, so they assumed the room below them was empty.

"Well, let's go take a look." Zach put the tiny flashlight in his teeth and lowered himself feet first into the hole. When his feet reached the ceiling grid, his shoulders and head were still visible protruding from the office floor.

"Is that ceiling grid strong enough to support us?" Ragsdale asked.

"Right here, it is," Zach said through the flashlight gripped in his teeth. A few decades ago someone had very carefully reinforced this section of the ceiling so that it would support the full weight of a grown man and a five-year-old boy.

Zach squatted down until his head was inside the cavern—under the rock ceiling. He shuffled to his left and removed one of the suspended ceiling tiles. The room beneath was completely dark. He lay on his stomach and stuck his head down into the opening. The room was empty, only the flicker of his little flashlight bouncing around dusty walls. The last time he had taken this route, a storage shelf was strategically located right beneath this opening. But that was no longer the case. It was a ten-foot drop to the floor. Not a huge obstacle, but a big enough distance to make a man in his thirties pause and look for alternatives.

He looked up through the hole at Jill and Ragsdale, their faces peering down at him from a brightly lit industrial world. "I'm going to jump down and find something for you to climb down on."

Zach contemplated the drop for just a moment more, lowered himself through the hole, and dropped. He survived the drop with ankles intact and scanned the room.

It was much smaller than he remembered, maybe 30 feet square. Its walls were lined with a collection of metal shelves, but the middle of the floor was empty. The shelves contained an assortment of tools: Picks, shovels, long poles fitted with plates to brace the inside of tunnels, some ancient-looking hard hats and lights, even a couple boxes of what looked like could be dynamite. Rather than transport all this equipment out of the cave and have to explain to anyone above ground what underground excavation equipment was doing in the middle of nowhere, the owner had everything dumped in this room and locked up. Thirty years ago, the underground workers had used this space as a tool room, since it was at the far end of the underground facility, isolated and smaller than the other openings. This room was not part of the original giant underground cave. It had been carved out separately as part of the misplaced ventilation shaft. When the workers realized their error, they hastily widened the area into a small storeroom. Three of the walls were rough-hewn stone. The fourth wall was cinder block. The only opening was a steel door.

Zach heard Jill's urgent whisper behind him. "So, are you going to let us into your secret hideout or not?"

Zach grabbed a stepladder that was leaning against the wall and put it underneath the hole in the ceiling. The rusty metal hinges resisted his initial attempts to open the ladder, but they eventually surrendered.

Zach looked up through the opening and saw Ragsdale looking down into the hole. The fluorescent lights in the room behind him obscured his features in backlight, but highlighted his even-messier-than-usual hair as it protruded from his head in violent waves.

Over Ragsdale's shoulder, Zach could see Jill sitting on bent knees behind him, listing to one side as if she were about to collapse.

"Why don't we let Jill sit this one out? We need a lookout in case anyone wanders into the room. Besides, I'm not sure she is in any condition to be climbing around in the dark."

"Are you saying I'm too fat to use the stepladder?" Jill offered from the room above. Zach started to speak, but then thought better of it, not sure she had the strength for banter at the moment. Ragsdale eased through the hole, his foot finding the top step, and then the next as Zach steadied the ladder. As his head dipped below the edge of the opening, Ragsdale offered, "Weight is moot. Your ass would never fit through the opening."

Jill stood up and looked into the darkness. "I'm going to make myself comfortable in the corner. Zach, when the old man lets his guard down, kick him in the balls for me." Zach gave a thumbs up. He couldn't see Jill's expression with the bright light behind her. But he could clearly see her full silhouette and appreciate the lunacy of Ragsdale's assertion. Jill blew a sarcastic kiss and slid a cardboard box over the hole. The room went dark.

THIRTY-ONE

RAGSDALE PRODUCED A FLASHLIGHT OF HIS own and shined it towards the door in the middle of the cinder block wall. A brief pull on the door handle confirmed the door was locked. "Well, that is a little anticlimactic," Ragsdale muttered.

"Only if you don't have a key," Zach said as he ran his fingers across the dusty door frame, feeling in the dark as he had seen his father do so many times decades before. This old store room was clearly no longer in use, locked up and forgotten. There was no reason to think the key had been disturbed. He was just about to think perhaps he was being too optimistic when his fingertips skimmed across a flat metal something on the far right edge of the door frame.

"Got it."

Zach held the key tight in his hand for a moment. It was likely the last person to touch this key had been his father. Zach didn't have too many remaining connections to his dad. However bizarre the circumstance, this little token was a welcome reminder. Zach wiped the key clean on his pants leg. It took some force to push it into the lock. Slow and gritty, it slid past the tumblers into place. The lock turned reluctantly as Zach twisted the key counterclockwise. The lock disengaged with a metallic clang that reminded them to start breathing again.

Both men had been considering what they might find on the other side of the door. A dead end into an empty black cave, a man with a gun, a bustling computer data center. But it was all speculation, and unproductive speculation at that. The only way to find out was to pull the handle open and take their chances. Zach took a deep breath. And pulled.

They could have predicted what they saw, but neither had. Flush against the door opening were 2x4 studs that extended well below and above the door opening. On the other side of the studs was the back side of drywall sheeting. A seam ran parallel to the floor about halfway up the door opening. A little bit of chalky joint compound was stuck to the backside of the drywall just below the seam, suggesting that the other side of the wall had been finished smooth. It was very likely that whoever was on the other side of this wall, if there was anyone, had no idea the door was even here.

Zach and Ragsdale put their ears to the wall and listened. The drywall was cold to the touch. Zach mouthed the word "cold" to Ragsdale.

The other man nodded. "Data centers have to be kept cool." There wasn't much sound, just a dull, continuous hum.

"Well, I guess we better take a look," Zach said as he flicked off his flashlight. He selected the longest key on his keychain, the ignition key for the rental car, and started to twist it into the soft drywall. Once the hole was started, Ragsdale turned off his light as well. In just a few seconds, the drywall gave way and a bright spear of light shone from the hole into the dark storeroom.

Zach peered through it. Below him was a brightly lit round room, probably two hundred feet in diameter. The walls were painted a crisp gray. It looked like a much taller room than the one they were in. The floor looked to be about eight feet below them, the ceiling eight feet above. The floors were concrete, painted a light gray. Black rubber tire tracks circled the floor repeatedly.

Zach used the key to widen the hole a bit and expand his field of vision. To the left, the tire tracks ended at the base of a large roll-up door, the kind you might see at a loading dock in a warehouse, only bigger. A few spots of oil on the floor had been sprinkled with a gritty absorbent material. To the right were steel double doors, painted in a gray a few shades darker than the walls. A keypad on the wall beside the doors probably controlled an electronic lock. In front of the doors was a small table and metal detector.

Zach pulled away from the hole and motioned for Ragsdale to take a look, but the doc had already made his own hole in the wall and was studying the room intently. "No one in the room," Ragsdale said.

"Not now, anyway," Zach replied.

At that moment, the double doors opened. Zach and Ragsdale instinctively pulled away from the wall. This was silly, of course. There was virtually no chance anyone would notice an eyeball peering through a tiny hole in a large gray wall. They both smiled and returned to their viewing stations.

A line of maybe ten men were queuing up just on the other side of the open doors. They were all dressed in a style one might call "geek business casual"—khaki pants, solid color short-sleeved button-up shirts, an assortment of casual leather shoes. Not quite a uniform, but you got the sense they were all interpreting the same memo.

The most remarkable part of their attire was above the neck. Each one was wearing a black hood that completely covered their heads and draped to their shoulders. There were no eye holes, so their vision was completely obstructed. The men weren't bound, yet none of them attempted to remove their hoods. They just stood casually in line, a few with their hands in their pockets, a couple with their arms crossed. Each one had an ID badge dangling from a lanyard around his neck. The photos on the badges were hard to make out at a distance, but all appeared to have dark hair and dark skin that matched the color of the arms protruding from the short-sleeved shirts.

A security guard was standing beside the open door, at the front of the line. He was wearing a standard rent-a-cop uniform that would have looked right at home in any mall or office complex. But the guard inside the uniform was a different species. He was easily six foot three, two hundred and fifty-plus pounds, and had a tan that suggested he hadn't been spending all of his time underground. His short-sleeved button-up shirt strained to cover his chest and biceps. He was alert, and focused, his eyes carefully scanning the line of men in khakis. On a small table in front of him was a device the size of a large toolbox, painted in a dull grey metal.

The guard spoke, and the first hooded man approached. The guard removed the man's ID card, swiped it on a card reader, and dropped it into the box. He repeated the procedure with the other nine until they were all in a neat line against the wall. The guard pulled a radio from his belt and spoke into it. Then he walked over to the tunnel entrance and typed a code into the keypad beside the large roll-up door. An electric winch sprang to life, and the door rolled up with a metallic clank that echoed through the large chamber.

In a moment they heard a distant rumble coming from the tunnel. It was unfamiliar at first, as the echoes played in the tunnel and were muffled by the sheetrock wall. A few seconds later, a large passenger van pulled through the door. It drove counter-clockwise around the edge of the room, making a tight loop and stopping in front of the queued-up khakis. Painted a nondescript dark blue, the van had double doors on one side and on the back. There were no windows except for the front doors and windshield, and those were heavily tinted.

The guard opened the double doors on the side, and the line of khakis climbed into the van without saying much or lifting their hoods. Only seconds after the last man stepped onboard, the bus rumbled off into the darkness of the tunnel. The first guard watched until the bus was out of sight, then lowered the rolling door and walked quickly across the floor to the steel double doors. He punched in a five-digit code and disappeared into the hallway. The doors closed behind him.

Zach and Ragsdale pulled back from the wall and looked at each other. Ragsdale whispered, "What now?"

"Wait. A bunch of people just left, let's see if more are coming."

They didn't have to wait very long. About five minutes later, the guard reemerged from the double doors. A few minutes after that, the big steel door opened, and another bus pulled in. The same process transpired in reverse. A line of maybe a dozen brown-skinned men in khakis, their heads covered by hoods, walked off the bus, were given card keys out of the box, and disappeared behind the double doors. The van pulled out, the guard closed the big steel door, and disappeared inside the double doors. The big room below Zach and Ragsdale was empty.

"Now what?" Ragsdale said.

"We make this hole a little bigger."

Zach rummaged around the shelves by the meager light of his keychain flashlight. First, he found some twine, old and dry, but still usable. He stuffed it into his jacket pocket. A moment later he found an old pair of tin shears. They looked like giant scissors and were probably used to cut sections of duct work many years and layers of dust ago. He held them up. Ragsdale nodded and continued rummaging through the shelves while Zach walked back to the wall. He took another glance through the peak hole to confirm no one was in the room below. Then, opening up the shears, he poked one of the blades through the hole and began slicing out a section of the drywall.

It was slow going, hardly the job the sheers were designed for.

He carved out the shape of a square, angling the blade so that the side of the drywall closest to him was slightly larger. Every couple of minutes, he stole a peak through the crack, checking the empty room as the gypsum dust drifted slowly to the concrete floor below. In about twenty minutes, Zach had a slightly lopsided square about two feet on each side, its bottom resting on the floor at his feet.

Zach put down the heavy shears, but then thought better of it. He felt the weight of them in his hand, then slipped them into his back pocket. After taking a final peek through the crack, he removed the square board and set it on top of the crate. Ragsdale studied the setup for a few seconds and nodded approval.

Zach eased himself through the hole feet first. The drop was a little greater than expected, about five feet to the floor below. Still manageable. He let himself drop, bending his knees as his feet hit the ground. Zach looked around quickly to confirm he was alone in the room, then looked back to see Ragsdale peering out from the hole in the wall Zach had just exited. Zach grabbed a chair and slid it over against the wall. Ragsdale eased out until his feet were on top of the back of the chair. Zach braced the chair while Ragsdale wedged the piece of wallboard back into place.

The wallboard roughly propped into place would not fool anyone who looked directly at it. But they were more concerned about a casual glance from across the room. And, against that standard, their little opening was barely noticeable.

They walked quickly but quietly to the double steel doors on their right. The doors had no windows, which served Ragsdale and Zach well during their covert entry. But now the lack of visibility into the hallway on the other side represented a serious liability. They kept quiet, unsure of whether someone was listening on the other side. The giant guard could be just on the other side of the door for all they knew, waiting to crack their heads together as soon as the door opened.

Zach thumbed towards the door on the right, recalling that was the door that opened first when the guard entered a few minutes ago. Ragsdale pointed emphatically to the left. Without hesitating, Zach made three downward gestures with his fist. Ragsdale joined on the second and ended with a clinched fist. Zach had already extended two fingers. Ragsdale lightly tapped his rock on Zach's scissors and took his station by the door on the left.

A prolonged and convincing deception can be a powerful weapon.

But sometimes it takes a great deal less to be effective. Sometimes you only need enough misdirection to cause a moment of doubt, a second of hesitation. That is what they counted on as Ragsdale pounded on the double doors, wearing his black jacket on his head like a hood.

It was only a few moments before they heard footsteps on the other side, heavy boots moving quickly on a concrete floor. Ragsdale began to yell towards the door. "The bus, the bus! There's been an accident!" Ragsdale stepped in front of the door on the left, Zack stepped in front of the door on the right, gripping a folded-up metal folding chair as if it was the last good thing on earth. A second later, the door in front of Zach burst open about halfway, and the guard leaned into the opening and looked at Ragsdale. Logically, it made no sense that one of the employees would be back inside the room. The rolling door was locked and could only be opened from the inside. But sometimes when adrenaline is pumping, logic is not the first one to join the party. So, the guard hesitated. Just a second. Just long enough for Zach to step out from behind the door and bring the folding chair crashing down on his head.

Zach was feeling the adrenaline rush too, and as he felt the chair bend against the guard's cranium, he took a little satisfaction in how well the ruse worked.

But then something unexpected happened. The guard didn't fall.

Instead, he unleashed a right jab on Ragsdale that sent the doc sprawling onto the floor. And, in one fluid motion, he wheeled to face Zach while pulling his pistol from its holster. Zach saw the untethered aggression in the guard's eyes and felt the warmth of his breath as they came face to face. He heard the click of the safety being released on the pistol and felt the first hint of the cold metal barrel being pushed against his stomach as the guard stepped forward.

But then the guard froze. He coughed, once, staggered. Then coughed again, a splatter of dark red blood jumping from his throat and running down his chin. His hand dropped the pistol and reached to grab the metal shears that were lodged deep into his stomach. But before he could grip them, he fell backward on the floor, his head hitting the concrete with a sickening dull crack. Dark red puddles formed almost immediately beneath his head and his stomach.

Zach looked down at his hand, outstretched as if still holding the shears. He was easily as surprised as the guard was at this development. He hadn't consciously intended to deploy the shears in that fashion, but instinct had trumped conscious intent in a way Zach found both empowering and terrifying.

A groan from Ragsdale brought Zach back to reality. He rushed over to where the doc was attempting to sit up on the floor. "What the hell?" he said groggily, his hands fingering the massive bruise that was already beginning to darken around his eye. Then, he saw the guard on the ground. "What the HELL?!"

Zach helped him to his feet. "Apparently scissors beats gun."

THIRTY-TWO

THEY EACH TOOK ONE OF THE guard's massive arms and wrestled him upright into a metal chair. Even with two of them pulling, they were both winded by the time the guard was in his new perch, hunched over with his chin on his chest. Zach picked up the pistol from the floor, flicked the safety back on. He hoped it would be of more use to him than its previous owner. Zach hesitated for a moment, then pulled the tin shears from the guard's stomach. It took more effort than he thought, and the sound made his stomach churn.

He wiped the shears off on the guard's shirt, and Ragsdale pulled the guard's hat bill down to obscure his face and draped an open newspaper across his chest. There was too much blood to ignore, but nothing to mop it up with. Zach grabbed a bucket by the door that looked like it contained the same gritty material spread around the oil stains. Basically, the same as kitty litter; it could absorb moisture and turn a slippery puddle into a pile of dirt. He spread it liberally on the puddle of blood and moved it around a little with his foot. Ragsdale grabbed the industrial mat from in front of the steel doors and put it over the whole mess. Not perfect, but close enough keep a casual observer from calling for help. Maybe.

Their hasty cover-up in place, they passed through the double doors and closed them behind. The hallway was about two hundred feet long, white linoleum floors, the same industrial grey paint, and a row of florescent lights hanging from bare rock ceilings. Another set of windowless double doors was at the end of the hallway, and three doors were on the left. The first door was open to reveal an ordinary break room: a small table and a few metal folding chairs, a dirty coffee maker on a formica counter stained with cup marks, a refrigerator that was not old but definitely not new. A plastic bin full of dark hoods sat on a shelf just inside the door.

They slipped inside and almost immediately heard footsteps in the hallway. Ragsdale turned his back to the door and started busying himself with pouring a cup of coffee. Zach did the same, trying to look like a normal employee pouring a normal cup of coffee. But he only filled the cup halfway so it would not slosh out on his trembling hands.

The footsteps faded, and both men realized they had been holding their breath. They left the room, coffee in hand, and proceeded down the hallway. A bulletin board on the right held a list of standard OSHA disclosures and a couple of memos. The letterhead read, "U.S. Special Task Force on Computational Supremacy." Ragsdale raised his wayward eyebrows and thought about the implications.

"Zach, what if Reginald isn't doing this on his own? What if this is some kind of official U.S. government operation?"

Zach hesitated and thought about his grandfather, his grandmother... Jill. "So, what if it is?"

At that moment, they heard footsteps and the sound of voices coming from double doors at the far end of the hall. Confront or evade? Fight or flight? There was no telling what was approaching them; a couple of nerds in khakis or a dozen armed guards. Zach had a feeling a fight was inevitable, but not yet. Evade and learn.

He contemplated the two remaining doors in the hallway—a men's restroom and a women's restroom. Remembering the line of men by the bus, Zach grabbed Ragsdale's arm and rushed into the women's room.

It was small, a few stalls and a counter with two sinks. It was clean but didn't smell of cleaning supplies. It was more of a clean born of lack of use, a thin layer of dust covered everything. They each dashed into a stall, set their coffee mugs on the back of the tank, and strained to listen. The footsteps got louder until they were right by the door, but then they kept moving. The men's room door opened with a tired squeak, and they heard voices on the other side of the wall. The men's and women's bathrooms shared plumbing, and apparently a very thin wall.

The first stream started, strong and loud. The guy had the urethra of a racehorse. They heard his sigh loud and clear.

The second worker was apparently having a hard time getting his stuttering prostate to cooperate. All they could hear from that side of the room was a nervous tapping of rubber shoe on linoleum.

"Drank too much damn coffee. Thought I was going to piss myself before break time came," Splatter said over the sound of cascading urine. He spoke English well, but with an accent that sounded Asian, Pakistani perhaps.

"I know," said Stutter with the same heavy accent. "No way I could have made it another two hours 'til the end of the shift." Judging from lack of sound, he was lying.

"No choice. It's so busy right now, I can't lose focus. Have you seen the kind of volume we've been running? And the word is it's still the pilot phase." The firehose stopped, and Zach heard a faint sound of zipper.

"Stop complaining, it's for your country," Stutter said as a few faint sprinkles began to strike the porcelain.

"It's not my country yet. Six more months to go." Splatter's voice grew fainter as he turned and headed to the sink.

"But at least we have a deal, not like all those suckers standing in line at immigration." Stutter's voice grew fainter now as he turned.

All Zach and Ragsdale heard after that was the sound of running water and a paper towel dispenser. Then, the men's room door opened, and they heard footsteps start down the hall.

Zach moved quickly to the door. He wanted to steal a peak inside the double doors at the end of the hall when the two workers went back inside. But just as Zach slid the door open a scant inch, the footsteps stopped. Zach froze, heart beating in his throat. The door was open slightly, but he dare not close it, lest the motion draw attention. Ragsdale was right behind him.

"What's your hurry?" said Stutter, or was it Splatter? Zach didn't care, given their urological health wasn't particularly relevant to the matter at hand. The man continued. "Let's hang out in the hall for a minute. Not rush."

"What about Pythons?" said the other worker. Ragsdale looked quizzically at Zach. Zach flexed his left arm, the one that wasn't holding the door. Big arms. Big guard.

"Big guy went to check the front door. And his buddy is minding the store in the big room. If we see one of the doors open, we'll start walking like we just left the bathroom."

Ragsdale held up two fingers and a raised eyebrow. Only two guards?

It made sense, actually. An underground facility with only one entrance. And a room full of illegal immigrant computer geeks probably was not a big security threat. The greater threat was the risk this place would be discovered. And that risk grew greater with every person who knew about its existence. They just needed to lure the other guard out and figure out some way to restrain him.

Fortunately for Zach and Ragsdale, the hallway buddies had already taken care of the hard part. Right on cue, the double doors at the far end of the hallway opened. Stutter and Splatter began walking quickly as soon as the door moved. By the time the second guard was through the doorway, the two urinators-cum lollygaggers were already bustling back towards their workstations.

Ragsdale and Zach strained to see through the barely opened bathroom door. It turned out this guard was uniquely constructed to be viewed through a cracked door. He was strikingly tall—easily six-six—and, although he wasn't as thick as his compatriot, he did appear to have spent a lot of time in the gym. This one walked differently, however, and looked at the geeks a little differently. He seemed smarter, more aware, arrogant and in charge.

The guard passed by the two urinators and cast a casual glance over his shoulder as he passed—enough to catch a glimpse of the double doors closing behind them. Ragsdale listened closely to the guard's footsteps. Then, right as the steps were approaching the bathroom door, Ragsdale darted out into the hallway, coffee cup still in hand, and started walking briskly just in front of the guard.

The big guard took two great strides and overtook Ragsdale, tapping him on the shoulder. "Who are you?"

Ragsdale stopped and turned to face the guard, doing his best to look surprised and casual. "Just finishing up in the sandbox, now off to freshen this coffee." He held up the coffee mug with a smile.

The guard paused for a moment as he sized up the rumpled doctor. Ragsdale was about two decades older and four shades whiter than any of the other workers, so it only took him a moment.

But that was just enough time. Zach sprung from the bathroom door just behind the guard. By the time the guard's hand reached for his gun, Zach's hand was already there, quickly liberating the piece from its holster. The guard felt the sharp pressure of a steel barrel being pressed into his kidneys.

"Let's just be calm," Zach said softly to the guard as he pushed just a little bit harder on the barrel. "We just have a few questions.

This doesn't have to be ugly." The guard stiffened, straightening his posture, easily growing another inch. He flexed his hands, and Zach could see the muscles in the back of Thin Man's neck, high above, tense.

The guard was not going to be calm, nor was he going to answer questions. And in all likelihood it would get ugly.

Zach looked at Ragsdale, who was simultaneously coming to the same realization that this would not end peacefully. The guard swung his right elbow sharply back and down, knocking the pistol from Zach's hand. The guard's left hand clenched into a fist and his torso twisted to deliver the full force of his wiry frame to the side of Zach's head. But when he was halfway into his swing, Ragsdale flicked the coffee cup upward, sending a wave of hot coffee towards the guard's face. Of course, the height differential was such that only a portion of the contents reached the target. But it was enough to slow him down.

While the guard grabbed his burning eyes, Zach swung the pistol as hard as he could towards the side of the guard's head. Had Zach been six inches taller, the blow might have been enough. But, as it was, the heavy steel handle of the gun hit the guard just south of the temple, maybe the top of the cheekbone. It stunned him but didn't bring him down. Zach didn't want the sound of a gunshot, but was running out of options, so he took aim. But at that moment, Ragsdale kicked the back of the guard's knee, causing him to buckle a few inches. This enabled the doc to bring the coffee mug down hard on the top of the guard's head. When the tall guy turned to face the doc, Zach delivered another blow with the pistol, and the guard crumpled to the floor.

Zach slipped the pistol back into the waistband of his pants. Ragsdale made a mock toast with his empty coffee mug. Then they each grabbed one of the guard's legs and dragged him into the women's bathroom. Using a combination of the guard's belt and the cord from the coffee maker, they secured him to the pipes beneath the bathroom sink.

They checked his pockets, but didn't find any ID. Just a pack of gum, a few tablets of "No Doze," and a Leatherman multi-tool. They tossed these into the toilet and had a mini conference outside the stall.

"I think what we are looking for is on the other side of those double doors," Ragsdale said.

"If that is where the sleep processing is originating, we are going to have to find a way to take it offline—permanently," Zach replied. "Do you think that box of old dynamite in the storage room is still good?"

"Probably," Ragsdale said. "TNT has been known to retain potency for decades."

"But that could get messy."

Ragsdale spoke the question they were both thinking, "Do you think the geeks know what's going on?"

"I don't think so. The cloth hoods, the government posters, the time clock, for goodness' sake. They're just going to work."

"Sounds like they're new to the country."

"Definitely. It's brilliant, really. Reginald goes to another country where smart geeks are trying to get into the U.S.—Pakistan or Iran, maybe. Then, he gives some bogus story about working for a green card. Smuggles them in somehow. Not that hard, really. Stick them in a cargo container with a bunch of bottled water and Power Bars. Or fly them to Canada, then just drive them right across the border. And there's something else."

"What?"

"I remember seeing in the newspaper how a van full of illegal immigrants wrecked about fifty miles from here. They said the driver fell asleep at the wheel. No survivors."

"These are smart guys. Sooner or later they will start to figure out something. Or start to ask about their green cards."

"And, when they do, Reginald just goes and gets a new workforce. No, I don't think those guys have any idea what's going on," Zach said. They paused for a moment as they contemplated their challenge.

"So, we have to get the geeks out of there," Ragsdale confirmed. Zach nodded.

"Or wait until they leave. Then, we'll need to move quickly."

They left the sleepy guard in the bathroom and headed back towards the entrance. Stepping into the break room, they checked the time cards. It looked like each shift lasted about six hours. They had some time before the bus returned.

They continued up the hallway and through the double doors into the garage area. Ragsdale was careful to prop the door open with a broom handle so that the lock would not engage. As they walked through the door, the door mat crunched and slipped just a little as it floated atop the mix of drying agent and drying blood. The dead guard was still slumped in his chair, the newspaper over his face providing only the thinnest of ruses.

Zach's careful eye could see the paleness of the guard's hand as it rested on the armrest. You can disguise the face and body to hide poor health, age, even death. But hands don't lie. The hands of the dead are pale, stiff, still. They look the same, but they lack the restlessness, the subtle movements of a living human at rest. A minor detail, the difference between sleep and death.

A few moments later, Zach and Ragsdale were slipping back through the hole in the drywall, back into the storage room. Ragsdale dragged the box of dynamite over to the hole in the wall so that he could sort the contents while maintaining a lookout. Zach slipped up the ladder leading back to his dad's old office to check on Jill.

She wasn't waiting at the top of the ladder as Zach expected. The door to the office was closed. The smart move would be to sit behind the closed door so that she would be sure to wake up if it opened. But Zach knew that probably she wasn't thinking altogether clearly in her current state. He found her across the room, curled up on the floor behind the desk. Her lips were curved into something like a smile while her back rose and fell slowly beneath each breath. Zach looked around the room quickly. Of course, there were no electronics of any kind inside this bare, forgotten workspace.

He bent down to wake her but paused for a moment. He stared at the profile that was facing him, wisps of silky hair resting on delicately manicured eyebrows. Perfectly proportioned nose that resolved into just the slightest point. Her lips were thick and red, moving ever so slightly as they ushered in each new breath. He was almost breathless at the sight of her. She was beautiful, of course. But he had seen lots of beautiful women. This was different. Other beautiful women had been like distant stars to be seen and admired in the night sky. Objectively beautiful, but so inaccessible as to be easily dismissed. But, Jill... It was as if for the first time he found a star shining right in his own home, in his own hand. Could it be that she was, or at least could be, his? Her beauty made him pause, but it was the connection that took his breath away. He bent down and kissed her forehead, lingering for a moment to enjoy the warmth of her skin on his lips, the smell of her hair.

He was about to wake her when he felt an unexpected chill, a draft of cold air. He turned and looked at the hole in the floor and saw a puff of dust coming up from the room below. There was only one other opening to the outside world, only one way to create a draft through that hole.

He ran across the room and practically leaped down into the hole. Ragsdale was no longer in the storage room, and the square of sheetrock separating it from the garage below had been removed. Running to the opening, Zach saw the mini bus from earlier parked in the garage below. He could still smell the exhaust fumes from the engine that must have just been shut down. The driver was a few strides past the front of the bus, walking quickly towards the deceased guard slumped into the chair. Ragsdale was a few steps behind him, crouching down, partially screened by the right front fender of the bus.

Zach could see what was about to happen but had no way to stop it. When the driver was still a few steps away from the guard, he stopped quickly. One hand reached for a phone clipped to his belt, the other reached for his gun. At that moment, Ragsdale leaped from behind the van and grabbed the driver's left arm, knocking the radio to the floor. But the right arm was still free.

At this point, Zach had already burst through the sheetrock, widening the neat square into a jagged hole. He was sprinting across the garage floor, reaching for the pistol tucked into his waistband, when the guard's right hand swung around to point a gun at Ragsdale. Ragsdale turned quickly, but not quickly enough.

The shot echoed in the concrete room and Ragsdale slumped to the floor. Two quick reports rang out from Zach's gun, and the driver fell backward as well, landing in the lap of the rigor mortic guard and tossing them both onto the floor.

Zach rushed to Ragsdale. The older man was holding his side, blood slipping out between his fingers. Zach took off his jacket, wadded it up, and pushed it against the wound. Ragsdale held it tight.

"The phone," Ragsdale said breathlessly, nodding his head in the direction of the driver.

Zach scanned the floor and grabbed the phone. A number was on the screen, but it hadn't been dialed. "No call," Zach said.

"Good," Ragsdale said as his head slumped back against the floor. "I would hate to think I got shot for nothing."

Zach bent down to look at Ragsdale's wound when he noticed the clamor of voices from the other side of the closed doors. Men talking excitedly, some in English, some in another language.

"Go," Ragsdale said, "I'll be fine."

Zach opened the double doors, pistol in hand. He saw a line of a dozen geeks in khakis, all wearing their hoods over their heads, awaiting their ride. They stopped talking at the sound of the door opening.

"Your bus is here," Zach said. Don't worry about the noise, just an engine backfiring. Single file line, you know the drill."

Zach propped the door open, used his foot to slide the leg of the dead guard out of the walkway. Then he took badges from each worker, just as he had seen the guard do earlier. They shuffled blindly in a neat line, between two dead men and one wounded, towards the bus. Zach escorted the workers onto the bus, climbed in the driver's seat, and made a tight loop so that the bus was facing out towards the mouth of the tunnel.

At that moment, he noticed movement in the rear-view mirror and saw the steel double doors slam closed. He slammed the bus into park and yelled over his shoulder to the hooded men in the back, "Sit tight, I'll be right back."

Walking quickly back towards the double doors, he saw water streaming out from under the doors, puddling around Ragsdale. Ragsdale looked up at him and mouthed the words, "The other guard." Zach nodded. The guard they knocked unconscious earlier must have awakened and managed to wrench free the bathroom pipes to which he was tied.

Zach held his gun in one hand and tried the door with the other. It was locked from the inside. No way in.

Well, there was one way.

Zach walked back to the bus, shut off the engine, and opened the side door. "Change of plans. Everybody out. Hoods on."

The geeks' heads turned side to side, as if they were looking at each other with questions. With a few shoulder shrugs, they filed out. Zach led them across the threshold out into the tunnel. "Now, you are going to count to 100. Then you can remove your hoods and start walking." Eleven hooded heads nodded in the affirmative. One did not.

One of the geeks removed his hood and stepped forward. "Sir, I am from Iran. I know the sound of gunfire when I hear it. I do not know what you are doing, but something is not right." The others froze when they heard him speak. The hoodless man craned his neck to look around Zach at the garage behind him. "I see two men who are likely dead, and I am pretty sure you are responsible. You have no more than seven shots remaining in that gun, and there are twelve of us. I think we need to be asking you some questions." A few other geeks removed their hoods and stepped forward.

"Look," Zach said, "I don't know how much you guys know about what you are working on. But it is hurting a great many people, and will likely hurt a great many more. I suspect you are just innocent bystanders, which is why I am letting you go."

"I am serving my new country," said the geek. "This is important work that will help people and earn me my citizenship. I won't let you stop that." He took a step forward. A few of his friends shuffled forward too. The rest of the geeks removed their hoods.

"Is that worth dying for?" Zach said.

"Sir, I have died a hundred deaths to get here. What is one more?"

Zach adjusted the grip on his gun and resisted the urge to look behind him. Then he uncocked the gun and put it back into his waistband. "Look, the people you are working for are not part of the U.S. government. They deceived you. Sooner or later you will figure that out, and then they will kill you. Just like they did the others."

"The others?"

Zach took out his cell phone and pulled up a picture of the bus crash that was in the news a few weeks earlier. "Look familiar? Recognize that van? Look at the clothes the victims are wearing, their skin color. This was the last group of workers, before you started. They started to figure out what was going on, and they were all killed."

The geeks stared at the phone screen.

"Tell me, how much of America have you seen?"

No one answered.

"Have you been to a McDonalds? Read a newspaper? Been allowed to walk around the city on your own?"

He could tell by their looks that they had not.

"That's not how America operates. People here are free, even people that have just arrived. You are living like prisoners. Trapped by very bad people."

No one moved.

"Here," Zach said. "Take this." He handed the lead geek the dead driver's cell phone. Look at whatever you want. Any page on the internet you want. Call anyone you want. Say whatever you want. That's how America works."

The man handed the phone to one of his cohorts, who started pulling up web pages while his friends crowded around.

"But you have to go now, because one way or the other I'm going to stop what is happening in that room." He pulled the gun out again but did not point it at them. The lead geek motioned to his friends, and they turned and started walking out of the tunnel.

Zach let out a deep breath, stepped quickly back inside the garage and lowered the door. He walked back over to Ragsdale.

"What was that all about?" the doctor asked sharply.

"It seems the sheep learned how to ask questions," Zach replied.

"How are you going to get past those steel doors without a key?" Ragsdale asked.

"I have a key." Zach nodded his head towards the bus. Ragsdale raised his eyebrows and half smiled. "But I need to get you out of here."

Zach looked over his shoulder at the large hole in the drywall.

"You need to take care of this first," Ragsdale said. Zach looked at the doctor's hand, caked in drying blood, as he applied pressure to the wound. "I'll be ok as long I keep pressure on it."

"Well, you can't stay here." Zach started to lift Ragsdale, but the older man groaned.

"Drag, don't lift."

Zach nodded and dragged his friend over to the door leading to the tunnel. He opened the door, checked to make sure the geeks were gone, then slid Ragsdale outside.

"I'll come back and get you when we are done, get you to a hospital," Zach said. He put his hand on the doctor's shoulder. "Whatever happens, I just want you to know—"

"Bullshit," Ragsdale interrupted with a cough. "Just be careful with that dynamite. I don't want my ride to the hospital to blow his fingers off."

Zach nodded and turned to close the door.

"And Zach."

"Yeah Rags?"

"Take care of that girl."

"I'll be back in five minutes."

Zach nodded. The steel door rolled down. He glanced at the double doors. Still closed, water still streaming out from underneath. A very tall, very angry guard with a heck of a knot on his head was inside waiting for Zach to make a move. But this time Zach had a plan much bigger than a handgun and a cup of coffee.

THIRTY-THREE

ZACH PULLED THE BUNDLES OF DYNAMITE from the dusty box and finished the work Ragsdale had started. Fifteen sticks of dynamite, one long fuse. Each stick attached to the fuse at eight-foot intervals. Zach handled the explosives gingerly. He knew the stuff could be very unstable. If this chamber were built today, something more stable and powerful would have been used, like C4. But this old dynamite would have to do. And it would do just fine.

Box of dynamite under one arm, he slipped through the hole and dropped himself gingerly back down into the garage. He moved quickly over to the van, opened the passenger side door, and set the box of explosives in the floorboard.

Returning to the driver's side, he climbed in and started the engine. Moving the bus in a slow arc, he positioned it directly in front of the double steel doors. The hallway was nearly the same width as the bus.

Nearly.

It was not nearly as tall as the bus, including the extended top. But the frame of the van, just above the windows, should fit just fine. The walls were probably constructed of standard interior wall commercial steel studs. Lightweight, non-load-bearing. They should crumple easily against the mass of the bus.

Should.

Zach stole a nervous glance at the box of dynamite in the floorboard, slid the gear shift into drive, and pressed down hard on the brake. At the same time, he pushed down hard on the gas. The engine revved while the tires squealed and smoked, a bull waiting to charge. Zach released the brake and the bus lurched forward. It was no Porsche, but it was moving quickly enough. At the impact from the nose of the van, the doors exploded backward from their hinges. The steel doorframe struck the windshield, shattering the glass. Zach anticipated this just in time and shielded his face with his arms. The side-view mirrors snapped off immediately. The side of the van ripped the sheetrock from the walls and screeched against the steel studs as two kinds of steel fought in noisy friction. The bus slipped and skidded on the wet concrete floor, bouncing back and forth between the two hall walls as it hurtled forward.

With the initial impact past, Zach glanced again at the dynamite. But he knew he didn't really need to look. If he was breathing, that meant the box didn't blow. There were only a couple of seconds between the first door and the second, but Zach kept his foot hard on the accelerator. Past the break room door, past the two bathrooms. Then, the second set of double doors were ripped from their frame by the force of the van.

Zach slammed on the brakes with both his feet, and the bus skidded to a stop, striking a rack of servers and knocking them to the floor. Partially severed electrical cables dangling from the ceiling sparked as they swayed and touched the surviving metal racks. Zach opened the door and stepped out into the room, bits of broken glass and wet drywall crunching beneath his feet.

In front of him was a gigantic room, easily the size of a football field, filled with row after row of server racks. Each rack was about six feet tall, each stacked with probably twenty servers. Thousands of tiny lights blinked feverishly, and cooling fans hummed in the background, keeping the room a crisp sixty-five degrees.

His first thought was that he needed more dynamite. The second was that he had forgotten to look behind him when he stepped out of the van. Almost on cue, the window of the open door beside him shattered as a piece of broken bathroom pipe went flying through it. Zach turned to see the guard they had tied to the bathroom plumbing earlier. He was huge, bigger than Zach remembered, if that was possible. But being alone tends to make adversaries look more substantial. And, of course, he looked very, very angry.

Zach reached for the pistol in his waistband but realized it wasn't there. It must have fallen out in the bus. The guard was running towards him now, another piece of broken pipe in his hand.

Zach knew his odds were not good. He had bested this guy before using the element of surprise and a little trickery. But this time, there was no element of surprise, no gun. Just a very angry man who undeniably had both the will and the ability to kill Zach in any one of fourteen different ways.

Zach turned and grabbed one of the computer server boxes that had been knocked from its shelf. It was a thin rectangle, like a five-pound pizza box made of metal.

Most conflicts are decided by either strength or mobility. Zach had neither advantage. And, while he knew he could do nothing about the guard's strength, he thought mobility might be an area of opportunity. So, instead of hurling his metal pizza box towards the guard's face, he flung it like a discus right at the guard's shins. Skipping over a spinning box of metal on wet floor filled with debris proved too complex a maneuver for the sprinting guard blinded by rage. He stumbled and fell forward, the pipe hurtling from his grip. He tried to catch himself with his hands, but they slipped, leaving his massive chin to absorb the full force of his fall.

Zach hoped this fall would be enough to knock the guard out for good. But as soon as the behemoth hit the ground, he started scrambling to get up, slipping over water and debris until he was upright again. Blood poured from his mouth, where either teeth or tongue had taken the brunt of the fall. Wobbly and dizzy, he stumbled forward towards Zach. A big fall, slippery terrain, and whatever was going on in that gigantic bloody mouth might even the odds somewhat. But Zach knew he was still hopelessly outgunned. The sparks from the severed electrical cable crackled near his head, but Zach didn't dare turn around.

He kept his eyes on the large man holding a piece of pipe, stumbling towards him. Zach used two seconds to generate a plan, and the remaining one second to pray that it worked. When he was a step away from Zach, the guard drew back the pipe to gather momentum for a blow that would surely shatter whatever part of Zach it struck.

But at that moment, Zach stepped back and to the side, grabbing the severed electrical cables in his left hand. As the guard's heavy blow began to descend, Zach deflected the blow with his left arm, while thrusting the bare ends of the electrical cable towards the guard with his right. Zach was just hoping to contact some bare skin. But, as fortune would have it, the sparking ends of the wires went right into the guard's open mouth. The large man went taut, as if every muscle in his enormous body had suddenly flexed at once. What might have been a scream only manifested as a gurgle of blood and sparks as the guard fell face down onto the floor. As the pipe clanked weakly on the floor, the guard shuttered once, then again. Then, he was still.

Zach leaned against the van and tried to breath, as it seemed his lungs were battling against his racing heart. One deep breath. Then two. Then—

An exploding pain cleared the fog of adrenaline and reminded Zach of the tradeoff he had made a few seconds before. At the time, giving up his non-dominant arm to prevent almost certain death seemed like a reasonable bargain. But the lightning shooting up his left arm now made him reconsider. Zach's arm had caught the pipe high in its arc, before the full force of momentum could be brought to bear. If not, his arm might have been split in two. As it was, he was sure he had a deep fracture in at least one bone. He flexed his hand and felt a whole new level of pain. His arm was working, but just barely. And based on the swelling that was already at work, he might not have use of it for long.

Zach reached across the driver's seat with his good right hand and grabbed the box of dynamite and the pistol from the floorboard of the van. Surveying the vast expanse of equipment before him, he suddenly realized the futility of the original plan. There were rows upon rows of servers. Hundreds of them. He only had enough dynamite to blow up a few. Not nearly enough to shut the entire place down. But he knew enough about the way computers work to know there was another option.

The underground river was to the right, somewhere behind a large concrete wall. So what he was looking for must be somewhere along that wall. Walking quickly to that side of the room, he quickly moved along the length of the wall. After walking for a few minutes, maybe a hundred yards, he found it.

A small room jutted out from the wall, interrupting the neat rows of servers. That had to be it. A sign on the wall read "Keep Out. Secure Area." A large deadbolt reinforced the message. Zach drew the pistol from his waistband and fired two rounds into the door jam beside the deadbolt. Two swift kicks later, the door swung open.

It was just what Zach was looking for. To the right, several massive electrical cables passed through a metal conduit into the concrete wall. They almost certainly connected to the power plant powered by the underground river. Perfect.

As Zach continued to scan the room, he saw two large emergency power generators, each the size of a passenger van, against the far wall of the room. Exhaust pipes threaded through the rock ceiling to some hidden vent above ground. Massive tanks of diesel fuel stood at the ready beside each generator, ready to power the facility if the main power source failed. Even better.

Zach used spare lengths of fuse to tie two sticks of dynamite to the main electrical cable. Then he went to the diesel tanks and used his tin snips to clip the fuel lines. Hundreds of gallons of fuel began to pour onto the floor. Zach moved quickly outside the room and saw that the fuel was already running underneath the walls of the power room and onto the main floor.

Heat is the arch enemy of computers, and an ambient temperature only ninety degrees can cause a server to fail in a few minutes. Zach reckoned it was about to get much hotter than that.

He walked as quickly as he dared back towards the van, his arm throbbing with each step. He placed the remaining sticks of dynamite every few feet, all the way back to the entry. The guard was still there, face down on the floor by the van. Zach stepped over him and walked to the back of the van. Lying on his back, he slid underneath the van and ripped the fuel line that ran from the tank to the engine. Then he pulled himself into the driver's seat with his good arm. He turned the key, and the engine rumbled to life. The engine only had a few sips of gas, just what was left in the fuel line. But Zach didn't need to go far.

He slammed the gear shift into reverse and backed the bus out the same way he came in, scraping against the walls of the hallway all the way back into the garage, leaving a trail of gasoline behind him. He put the transmission in park, killed the engine, and slid out of the seat. The stench of gasoline was thick in the air.

Despite the violence and chaos of the last few minutes, it was now eerily quiet underground. Just the faint sizzle of an electrical wire shorting. The metallic squeak of a fluorescent light fixture broken from its ceiling mount and gently swinging from its cord. A broken pipe yielded a tiny gurgling stream of water, probably running under the walls back to the underground river from whence it came. Zach started walking towards the closed garage door, towards where he had rested Ragsdale a few minutes earlier. He heard only his own footsteps.

But then he heard another sound.

The distinctive metallic click of a revolver being cocked, the cylinder rotating to chamber a round as the hammer pulled back.

"You've made quite a mess down here, young man."

Zach turned to see Reginald standing between him and the entry hole they had cut into the wall. The old man had a bit of dust on his lapel, but otherwise looked surprisingly refined considering he had ridden here bound in the trunk of a car next to a corpse. Zach started to reach for the pistol tucked into his waistband.

Reginald raised his revolver. "Now then, we'll have none of that. Let's keep those hands raised."

"Fine. Shoot me if you want. But you are out of business."

"I'm afraid it's not that easy, young man. You've made a bit of a mess, but it's not as if you've blown the place up. You are smart enough to realize that. A little spackle and paint, and a new load of educated naive near easterners, and we'll be back up in no time. The really important stuff is still all right here." He tapped his temple.

"Someone else will come. You can't hope to keep this a secret forever." Zach's mind raced as he looked for options. His eyes flashed from Reginald to the entry hole in the wall just above him. Pretty nimble for an old guy, making it through that hole and handling a 5-foot drop unscathed.

"My boy, I have been keeping big secrets since you were still toddling around after that noble hard-working father of yours."

"You remember him, then?"

"Oh yes, of course. Human beings are the most amazing machines, every one different and valuable. I try to remember everyone I meet, even common workers like your father."

"So why did you kill him?" Zach said in a forced monotone, trying to hide his rage and disgust.

"That is a serious oversimplification. I never intended for your dad to die. He did a good job, never caused any trouble. I'm not a monster. Your dad asked if there was a way he could earn a little extra money. He said he had a son who was smart as a whip, and he wanted to send him to a better school. So I invited him to participate in our little study."

Zach glared. Trembled. Pain shot through his broken arm as his pulse raced.

"Actually, your father was a pretty strange case. He seemed to have a profound resistance to our medications. We, of course, assumed the dosage was too low and administered more. By the time we figured out his natural resistance, well, I'm afraid his brain just wasn't in very good shape at all. It was quite unintentional. We were just learning how to administer the drug. We actually gave the exact same dosage to another man. He died almost instantly. That's how we figured out the happy medium. So, you see, your dad didn't die alone, or in vain. There must be some consolation in that." Reginald spoke without emotion, completely confident in the logic of his explanation.

"So I assume you killed my grandfather as well? Tried to kill my grandmother?" Zach knew the answer.

"Your grandfather was old anyway. If his death helped dissuade you from wasting your life trying to stop me, then that's a pretty fair trade. He certainly would have given his life to save you. Of course, you wouldn't listen to my warning. Which, actually, is pretty disrespectful to your grandfather's memory." Reginald spoke politely and patiently, as if explaining to a child how a machine worked. It occurred to Zach that Reginald was completely unware of how sinister he sounded.

"But why Jeff? What did he do?" Zach thought he saw a flicker of movement in the opening in the wall behind Reginald.

"Jeff was not nearly as smart as you, actually. His mind was compromised by the member in his pants. Especially when your curvaceous childhood friend showed up. He became so obsessed with winning her heart that he compromised our entire operation. He tried to influence her dreams in order to woo her. It was the stupid, desperate act of a weak mind."

"So now what?" Zach looked straight in the older man's eyes, ignoring the movement in his periphery.

"Well, I'm afraid I have to kill you. I take no pleasure in it. You have proven yourself quite capable, but I suspect your feelings about your father's death would impair your ability to work with me."

At that moment, Reginald's voice was interrupted by the moist thud of a large plumber's wrench striking the back of his head, and the metallic clang of that same wrench falling to the floor. The old man staggered forward one step, his face perplexed. He was listing badly to one side but raised his gun again towards Zach as he began to fall. One bullet left the barrel of the small revolver, but it missed Zach and struck the bus behind him. But the two seconds of distraction had allowed Zach to draw his own gun and discharge three rounds in the direction of the stumbling older man. The first one missed, the second did not, the third one was irrelevant as the old man crumpled to the floor.

Zach looked back to where Reginald had been standing and saw Jill running towards him. She had dropped quietly from the hole in the wall while the old man was speaking.

"Bastard called me curvaceous," she said as she ran up to Zach.

She threw her arms around his shoulders, pulling his lips toward hers as he embraced her. Zach was still very much unused to this level of affection, but he devoured her kiss as if it were the last meal he would ever have. He wanted to speak, needed to move, but with her body pressed against his, all he could bring himself to do was hold on.

At that moment, a wave of heat blew into his back. He turned to see the bus had burst into flames. The old man's bullet must have created a spark, igniting the fumes and gas pouring from the severed gas line. Of bigger concern than the bus was the hot thread of flame racing down the hallway behind the van, following the trail of leaked gasoline to the data center—and the dynamite scattered amongst the machines.

Zach grabbed Jill's hand and ran towards the garage door that led to the roadway out of the building. He saw the drops of blood from where he had dragged Ragsdale over to this door earlier. He couldn't let himself think about whether or not the doc was ok. Zach grabbed the chain to pull the door up. But only the first millisecond of pressure had been applied when he felt a lightning bolt of pain shoot through his broken arm. He staggered backwards as the crushing pain registered in his brain. Fighting to not pass out, he staggered forward again, grabbing the chain with only his good arm. He could hear Ragsdale yelling from the other side of the door but had no idea what he was saying. At least he was alive.

The heat on Zach's back was downright painful now, with the bus fully engulfed in flames just a few yards away. The acrid smoke of burning fuel and rubber and upholstery stung his eyes and choked his lungs. He could see the chain, but only just barely.

He reached high on the chain and pulled down, using his weight against the weight of the door. It budged only a few inches. He reached for another grip when Jill came beside him and grabbed the chain a little lower down. They both pulled with all they had, and the door screeched upward about a foot. With this new source of oxygen, the fire doubled in intensity almost instantly.

Jill dropped to the floor and slid quickly under the door. Zach flopped down as well, again forgetting about his broken arm as he extended his hand to catch himself. The pain was blinding, excruciating, it knocked the breath from him. By now the smoke was so thick he could not see anything. He slid to where he thought the door was, the smoke burning his lungs, his eyes seeing nothing but burning. To all his other discomforts was added nausea as he realized he had actually moved away from the door. The smoke was too thick to even see where the door was.

His broken arm was limp by his side, and with his good arm he went through the motions of pulling himself forward. But his attempts weren't strong enough to actually move his body.

The lack of oxygen had already affected his ability to think clearly, the hyper aware mind that defined every waking moment of his life was slowing, sputtering as it was starved of the stuff of life. He began to consider his odds of survival. Just a few moments ago he would have confidently said ninety percent plus. Now, his mind dug through cobwebs to even think at all. At that moment, he heard a loud boom, then another, and another. The dynamite. The sound must have been much louder, thunderous inside an enclosed underground room of stone and concrete. But to Zach's dulled senses, they were just muffled thuds, a danger he was vaguely aware of but now powerless to avoid.

He thought of his grandma, probably the only person alive who would miss him. He felt no self-pity with this fact. That was just how it was, how it always had been. But what about Jill? That made it harder. He had never really known love, other than the love of a grandparent. He had never had anyone look at him like... Well, at least he got to kiss her. He was glad of that.

"Move! Move, you asshole! You will not die in this stupid garage cave!" Jill's screaming and the frantic tugging at his pants leg was like the sound of a TV in another room. Then there were the fingernails. Tugging frantically at his leg, Jill's nails dug into the flesh around his left calf. He could hear Ragsdale yelling, "Get him in here!" Zach tried to move but could not. He wasn't even sure he was breathing. But then he felt his body begin to slide across the floor. One big tug, then another. Feet first across the floor. Jill was screaming. He didn't know what she was saying. But he kept moving. He felt the lower half of his body slide into the tunnel. Still searing hot, but much cooler than the inferno where he was about to die.

A moment later, all of him was in the tunnel. He felt the need to cough, but he could not. He heard the loud bang of the metal door being slammed closed against the concrete floor right by his head.

"CPR! Quick!" Ragsdale was yelling.

Then her mouth was on his again. Different this time. CPR. Breathing air into his lungs. Frantic compressions on his chest. She was trying so hard. She was doing so well. He was so impressed by her. He loved her. He wished he could tell her, wished he could open his eyes and see her. Wished he could cough. Just one breath.

And then he did.

One small cough, and then another. His lungs expelled the gift from Jill and sucked in the dank air of the tunnel.

Zach opened his eyes and saw her looking down on him, tears and blood and soot and tangled hair obscured her features but showed her soul. Behind her, Ragsdale was propped against the wall where Zach had left him.

"Is this how it's going to be? I'm always going to have to save your ass?" Jill laughed as she wiped the tears from her eyes with a soot-stained sleeve.

Epilogue

Ragsdale was still awake at a time of night when all the more well-behaved patients had been asleep for a couple of hours. But though the wound in his side was keeping him in the hospital, it could not keep him from fending off boredom by disassembling an EKG machine he'd found unattended in the hallway.

A few workers at the textile mill noted a vague smell of smoke when they arrived at work for third shift, but there was no reason to investigate the lower level that no one knew existed.

Authorities picked up a group of illegal immigrants in khakis wandering down a back road. Their story of a secret underground government project sounded like the worst cover story ever.

The back page of the business section noted that the founder of a former high-flying data processing firm had disappeared. A woodcut image of a man with round glasses accompanied the article. He was presumed dead, and so was the company.

The staff at the Oakdale nursing home remarked at how the patients seemed to be resting so much better.

A family marveled at how a prodigal daughter now suddenly showed so much interest in the family business.

But these were all fragments of unrelated circumstance, points on a constellation that no one could possibly draw.

Jill's eyes had been closed for a while, conversation having long since faded into silence. But still, he stared at her. The curve of her nose, the wisp of her hair on her cheek. She was not yet well, but she was recovering. Zach leaned over and kissed her.

He turned out the light but didn't close his eyes. Instead, he slid over beside her and held her close, closer than he had ever held anyone. The thought of her was enough for his mind tonight. And for the first time in his life, Zach Taylor did not want to go to sleep.

Made in the USA
Columbia, SC
30 December 2020